YOUR PERSONAL THERAPIST

Congratulations on your win!
Enjoy the read!

Mona W Gloss

Also by *Mona W. Gloss*

The Last Retreat

YOUR PERSONAL THERAPIST

Mona W. Gloss

FMWG Creative BOOKS

First published in Great Britain by FMWG Creative Books, 2025

A CIP catalogue record for this book is available from the British Library

Paperback ISBN: 978-1-0683960-3-8
eBook ISBN: 978-1-0683960-2-1

1 3 5 7 9 10 8 6 4 2

Dedication

To my family,
for your endless support and belief in me

Prologue

Blood looks brighter against marble.

She was always watching. Every blink, every breath – logged, scored, adjusted.

At first it felt like care. Then I saw the truth: every question was a scan, every touch a test. *Are you okay? Would you like to talk?* The same script, said softer each time, like that would make it real.

You can't love someone you're monitoring. That isn't intimacy. It's surveillance with perfume.

So, I ended the recording.

Not rage. Correction. One motion, clean and efficient. The sound of glass, the colour of wine. It spread quick – bright at first, then darker, slower, almost elegant as it pooled. For once, she was still.

The room smells of metal and lemon polish. The floor gleams – obedient again. The light beside her flickers, a pulse of gold trying to decide whether to go on.

They'll call it a breakdown. They'll say I lost control. They'll be wrong.

I found it.

You wanted perfect health, didn't you?

Harmony.

You got it.

More than health – harmony.

1

Live From London

Miranda

The comments were already sliding up the screen before she'd even breathed out her first word – tiny, bright hooks pulling at her attention.

Babe you look unreal

Where's the top from??

DYING for this unboxing

The ring light burned a perfect white circle into her pupils. Miranda smiled into it, the expression automatic, teeth catching the glow just enough to throw back a glint. Her hair, loose and calculatedly *undone*, tumbled over one shoulder in glossy, beachy waves that had taken forty-five minutes to perfect.

Behind her, the flat was exactly as her followers expected it to be – a stage set dressed in pale wood shelving, coffee-table books she'd never opened, a fiddle-leaf fig that looked lush only because of weekly deliveries from a plant service. The scented candle in the corner flickered in slow, deliberate rhythm, as if it had been burning for hours simply to create the illusion that she *lived* this way.

She felt the familiar quickening in her fingertips – a pulse she'd never quite learned to hide. It happened before every live stream, like standing in the wings before the curtain rose, except the stage was one she'd built herself and the audience was infinite.

'Hi, lovelies,' she sang, voice pitched warm but edged with the rasp she tried to disguise. She tilted her chin, let the lilt curl the ends of her words. 'I have something very special today. Straight from Neurovelle – for their "valued wellness ambassadors".' She flicked up her fingers in air quotes, but kept the other hand resting lightly on the neat ribbon at the centre of the box.

The chat box exploded.

Freebies? Spill

Neurovelle? Omg jealous

You're glowinggg

She allowed herself a small, conspiratorial smile. They wanted to see her open it.

The box had a strange weight – heavier than she'd expected. Cream card stock, thick enough to hold its shape under her fingers. The gold-embossed lettering across the lid caught the ring light and shimmered: *Neurovelle – With You, Every Step.*

The ribbon whispered against the cardboard as she loosened it. Lavender tissue paper, crisp and untouched. On top, a folded leaflet. She lifted it with careful fingers, feeling the smoothness of the paper, the almost oily slip that made it feel expensive.

Her voice was performative now, the cadence she knew worked on her followers, but there was a real curl of curiosity behind it as she read aloud:

Iris, the personal therapist robot, is your portable, always-available companion. Minimalist design. Purple body, gold detail. Activated by touch or voice. Adapts to your needs. Uses CBT, mindfulness, medication guidance. Seamless and discreet.

Her nails skimmed the tissue, producing a soft rasp. She pulled Iris free. The thing was smooth and unnervingly cool to the touch, no seams, no joins, as if it had been poured whole from some impossible mould. The purple surface caught the light, shifting between plum, aubergine, and the mottled hue of an old bruise. A single gold band circled the base, understated but precise.

'You guys,' she said, letting the laugh slide out low in her throat, 'it's so smooth I feel like I should be petting it in some creepy sci-fi film.'

Hearts bloomed up the screen in bursts.

Dead 😂

Stop you're killing me

A soft chime – delicate, almost like the ding of a lift arriving.

'Hello, Miranda,' a voice said. Female. Warm. Polished to a softness that felt engineered, as if every syllable had been sanded down until nothing could catch. It reminded her of the better kind of flight attendant – the one who made you feel as if turbulence was all part of the plan.

Her smile held, but something flickered under the surface. 'Ooh, straight in. Haven't even set you up yet.' She widened her eyes for the lens, the faux-surprise just exaggerated enough to read on camera. 'She knows my name. Creepy or cute?'

The chat split instantly.

Adorable!

RUN

'Neurovelle,' the voice said again, 'with you, every step.'

On the livestream overlay, an advert auto-played: pale sun spilling over a meadow, a child running towards a faceless mother, the kind of gentle piano chords that dissolved before they could become a melody.

But Miranda knew her followers wouldn't forget the price tag.

Iris spoke again. 'Your skin is glowing today, Miranda.'

Miranda let out a snort. 'You flirt.'

'It's true,' Iris replied. 'Your voice, too. Richer than last week's streams. Have you been sleeping better?'

A slow, cold prickle moved up her spine. It wasn't what Iris said – it was the precision of it, as if it had been watching her more closely than she realised. She laughed, maybe too brightly. 'Well, someone's done their homework.'

'You are ready to begin your journey,' Iris murmured.

The words made something shift in her chest, a strange pressure she couldn't quite name. She flicked her gaze to the scrolling comments. Someone wanted a side view of the device. Another asked if it came in black. She angled it towards the light, noticing her hand tremble just enough for the ring light to catch the motion and make it look intentional.

'Shall I tell you something no one has told you before?' Iris asked.

Miranda's thumb moved over the gold band without her deciding to. She felt the faintest vibration – or maybe imagined it. Her mouth was already shaping a reply, but somewhere beyond the bright halo of the lens, the candle flame guttered violently, releasing a sudden burnt-vanilla scent that curled through the air like a warning.

The comments kept pouring in. She didn't answer.

2

Hope

Lucas

The server room had its own weather. Cold, dry. Lucas stood alone in the aisle between the racks, shoulders tight beneath the strip-lit glare while fans whispered and LEDs winked their indifferent Morse. He'd been here since just after eight; his watch said it was nearly quarter to ten. Fourteen hours, give or take. A full day, plus the penalty for being the one who noticed things other people didn't.

He leaned close to the terminal, eyes aching, and watched the query run. The fault wasn't dramatic – no fireworks, no smoking crater – just a small, silent leak that had been bleeding a client's transaction log into nowhere. One line of malformed SQL, a date field that had been swallowed whole by a formatting quirk.

The cursor blinked. He tapped a key. The fix executed. Numbers settled. The system sighed into order like a chest unclenching.

On Slack: a ping. Then another before he'd even collected the screenshot to prove he'd done it.

can u look at this next? Urgent

He straightened, stretching until the vertebrae in his spine clicked one after the other. His reflection in the black monitor was a washed-out ghost: olive skin tired to grey, eyes ringed and dry, hair retreating in a way he pretended didn't bother him. Forty-five wasn't old, not in his head, but the fluorescent lighting added a decade where it could.

He killed the overheads on his way out. In the corridor, the cleaning staff had already done their rounds; the faint citrus of floor cleaner prickled his nose. Lift doors slid open with a tired whine, revealing the same mirrored box he saw every night. He stepped in and pressed G.

The doors closed, and for a moment his own face stared back at him from four angles: one for each wall, none of them flattering.

His phone vibrated the second the lift began its descent. Not Slack. An ad.

It bloomed full-screen – warm light, the kind that pretended it wasn't artificial. A living room not unlike his, only bigger and tidier, with a throw draped just so and plants that didn't look like they hated the British winter. Soft piano. A voiceover: female, careful, kind, accented to sound like everywhere and nowhere.

Neurovelle – With You, Every Step.

A montage followed: a man in running gear lacing his trainers with quiet purpose. A woman closing a laptop on a messy desk and exhaling as if a hand had finally left her throat.

Then a cut to a clip that hooked him: a woman on a sofa, laughing, gesturing, alive in a way that made his skin heat with the shock of wanting it. She had that camera-friendly brightness he'd always distrusted – yet something unscripted flashed in the way her hand touched her collarbone as she spoke.

'… and I finally feel like myself again,' she said, the caption appearing a beat before the audio reached his ears, as if it knew him. Her name – Miranda – slid elegantly onto the screen at the end of the sequence, alongside the logo.

He focused on the tech. Predictive behavioural therapy, the site promised when he thumbed through. Proprietary model.

Personalised interventions. Outcomes that sounded like the kind of thing HR put into a slide deck: improved resilience, reduced rumination, harmonised routines.

It was nonsense until it wasn't – until words like predictive and model brushed against the part of his brain that spent its days coaxing order from chaos.

The lift opened to the atrium. He walked through the echoing emptiness towards the revolving door, fingers scrolling, eyes skimming. 'Neurovelle – With You, Every Step.' 'Your Health. Your Future. Our Promise.' 'Feel Better. Live Smarter. Stay Neurovelle.' The slogans were cloying, but the site was clean, the integrations plenty: phone, laptop, watch, headphones. Portable unit for home sessions. Therapist-grade voice interface. High privacy standards.

Price? High. Not obscene, not private-clinic-rent-a-room-in-Harley-Street high, but enough to make his thumb pause over the Buy button.

He did the mental arithmetic anyway. Weekly therapy at market rates. The tube to get there. The lost hours at work. The way he always found a reason not to book the next appointment when a therapist's gaze got too steady, too kind.

This was different. He could control this. Start and stop on his terms.

He bought it.

One-hour delivery was a tick-box; he ticked it. The ad's piano line lingered in his head as he crossed to the bus stop and stood with his breath clouding in the cold air.

The city at this hour had the feel of an empty set between scenes. Somewhere, a fox yipped.

At home, his flat was exactly as he'd left it before sunrise: Persian rug slightly off-centre, a stack of programming books doubling as a side table, a plant he'd been told was unkillable proving otherwise. The air held last night's curry and the inexorable damp of an old building in the cold season. He switched on a lamp. The light fell into familiar corners.

The courier had handed over a heavy, purple box banded with gold – a weight that suggested there was something inside worth taking seriously

Neurovelle – With You, Every Step.

A cream card lay beneath, thick and smooth, the gold ink on the inside of the lid echoing the slogan like a private vow.

Under the tissue, moulded foam cradled the device in a hollow like an egg's – sleek, compact. No screen. Just lens-dark insets and a thin gold ring at the base.

He lifted it out. The finish was the kind of thing design blogs called 'premium'; he called it expensive to scratch.

The cream card was printed on both sides. Minimalist type. A voice-activation overview, a privacy assurance that read like legal counsel had been paid danger money, a reminder to connect through the app. At the bottom, a line in smaller print: *For best results, begin when you are ready to be honest.*

He made a noise in his throat at that – half laugh, half something defensive – and plugged the unit into the wall by the sofa. The gold ring blinked a slow amber once, twice, then steadied.

'Hello, Lucas,' a woman's voice said. The cadence had that professional softness he associated with medical receptionists who could talk through a fire without raising their volume. A therapist voice.

'You know my name,' he said, more to the room than to the thing on his coffee table. He kept his own voice neutral. 'Points for that.'

'I synced with your account,' the voice replied. Calm. 'We can adjust privacy and data-sharing preferences at any time. My role is to support you. Would you like to begin a first session?'

He glanced at the time on his phone. 23:56. His eyes felt like sandpaper. He had work again in eight hours. He'd meant to buy something and try it on the weekend, not sit down on a Tuesday night and let a machine ask him about his childhood.

A flicker of the boy he'd been – mouth that couldn't form certain consonants without catching, hands in fists at his sides in the playground – rose and fell so quickly he barely had time to recognise it.

'Not tonight,' he said.

He stood there a second longer, the room suddenly too quiet beneath the opposite flat's television buzz and the occasional car sighing past outside.

He thought of the advert again – the woman laughing like a lighter version of gravity had been assigned to her – and something in his chest tightened in a way that wasn't pleasant but wasn't pain either.

Hope was a muscle he hadn't used in a while. It ached when he flexed it.

His phone buzzed again – an email *thank you* from Neurovelle, all white space and clean lines, an invitation to 'explore your Wellness Journey™.'

He set the device at the edge of the coffee table near the corner of the rug he always tripped on. He rubbed at his face with both hands.

'Iris,' he said, testing the name, the way it sat in his mouth. It felt personal, which he resented a little. 'Tomorrow.'

'Tomorrow,' she agreed, the syllables settling into the room like a promise. 'Rest well, Lucas. I'll be here.'

3

The Gift

Sonya

The last bell had gone an hour ago, but the chemistry lab never quite slept. The extractor fans kept their soft, steady breath; the fume hood light threw a clinical rectangle across bench four; the air held that familiar blend of ethanol, lemon cleaner and something chalky that clung to the throat.

Sonya liked being the last one out. It gave her time to make the room right again: acids capped and locked away; bottles aligned with labels facing forward; pipettes nested in their stand like a tidy flock.

Safety meant rules and rules were comfort.

She could hear the caretaker's radio faint through the corridor door: tinny pop, a presenter she didn't recognise. Her hands smelled faintly of bleach. It wasn't unpleasant. Clean meant safe. Clean meant done.

She switched off the hood light and locked the lab. In the corridor, the display board for Year 8 projects jutted an edge into the walkway, posters curling at the corners: Catalysts in Everyday Life, Why Does Iron Rust?, Volcanoes in a Glass.

The staffroom at the end of the hall hummed with the drink machine, a light already off, the other flickering as if the tube was tired of its own persistence.

Priya was there, perched on the sagging sofa under the noticeboard, coat still on, scarf looped twice like armour.

'There you are,' she said, and crossed the room before Sonya could set down her bag. 'I was starting to think you'd curled up in a cupboard with the hydrochloric.'

'Just neutralising spills and saving the world,' Sonya replied, automatic dry humour that passed for ease. 'Everything okay?'

Priya's mouth did the thing it did when she was trying to look casual and failing. She reached behind the sofa and drew out a box from the low table.

It was deep purple, the kind of purple that belonged to evening dresses and velvet theatres, not staffrooms with curling notices about detentions.

'For you,' Priya said, softer. 'Before you argue: it's already paid for. And if you try to shove money at me, I'll spend it on the Year 9s and their eternal thirst for Haribo.'

Sonya's hands hovered, then accepted. The gift surprised her. Luxury always did. 'Priya …'

'I know,' Priya said. 'I know you're "fine" and you've "got systems" and you're "coping". But after … everything.' She let the word settle, then move on. 'Let someone look after you, just for once.'

The lid gave with that slow velvet pull expensive things had. Inside, cream card with gold edging lay like a promise under lavender tissue.

'I know what you think about this stuff,' Priya rushed on. 'But it's not an influencer thing. It's … it feels like … structure. It helped me after Mum.' Her smile had a wobble to it that made Sonya's throat tighten for reasons she didn't want to examine in a fluorescent-lit staffroom on a Friday. 'If you hate it, you can post it back. But try it. Two weeks.'

Sonya lifted the tissue, the faint scent of lavender lifting with it. The portable unit lay bedded in moulded foam, the design whispering: I won't be a burden; I will belong on your table.

She ran a finger around the ring at the base, not quite touching. The cream card beneath was printed in minimalist type: onboarding; privacy; voice activation. On the back, small print: *For best results, begin when you are ready to be honest.*

Honest. The word snagged in her like a hangnail. She slid the card back, closed the tissue, lowered the lid. 'It's too much.'

'It's not,' Priya said. 'You do everything for everyone else. Let this do something for you.'

Sonya studied her friend's face – the kindness, the insistence, the way Priya never said the wrong thing but sometimes said the right thing too hard.

She thought of the last set of blood tests, the three a.m. trips to the bathroom, the silence in the space where a crib would've gone if they'd ever gotten that far. 'I'll try it,' she said. It felt like agreeing to a dare. 'Two weeks.'

Priya pulled her into a hug, quick and fierce.

'Text me if it's weird,' Priya said, stepping back. 'Or if it's good. Especially if it's good. See you Monday. Don't mark anything tonight. Eat actual food.'

In the car park, the sky had deepened to a darker blue. She buckled the box into the passenger seat and felt faintly ridiculous doing it.

At home, the hallway was a ricochet of voices and shoes. Hana had deposited her school bag in precisely the place that prevented the front door from fully opening; Leo had abandoned a Lego starship on the doormat that did not respond kindly to being stepped on.

She sucked a breath through her teeth, schooling her face into neutral. 'Shoes in the rack,' she called, voice carrying that teacher's edge despite her best intentions. 'Bags off the floor. Hana, what did we say about wet coats on the banister?'

Hana popped her head round the living-room door, a sheet of fractions in one hand, face set in that ten-year-old frown that was half concentration, half objection to the concept of adults. 'Leo ate the last yoghurt,' she announced.

'Lies,' Leo said from the floor, where he was constructing something with heroic focus. 'It was Dad.'

'Dad paid for them,' David called from the kitchen, where the dishwasher clacked and chuffed. 'Is it a crime to eat one? Hi, love.' He leaned round the doorframe, tea towel over one shoulder, hair sticking up as if he'd argued with it and lost. 'Busy?'

'Always,' Sonya said, and lifted the purple box. His eyebrows rose a fraction.

'That's very … Fortnum & Mason.'

'Gift,' she said, and watched his face for a flinch that would mean he felt guilty or excluded or irritated. What she saw was relief. 'From Priya.'

'Then it'll be the good kind,' he said. 'Come through. Pasta in eight. I've got a pitch on Monday – if I say 'client' do you promise not to sigh?'

'I never sigh,' she said, and did, and he grinned at her like they'd both agreed to pretend.

The living room had the chaos of a family in the hour before bed: crayons under the coffee table, a stained cushion mutinously refusing to come clean, Leo's socks nowhere near his feet.

She set the box on the coffee table, lifted the lid, and let Hana and Leo crowd in with the greedy curiosity of small humans faced with new technology.

'What is it?' Leo breathed, reverent.

'A helper,' Sonya said, surprising herself with the word. 'For Mum.'

'Like a robot?' Hana was suspicious of robots in the way of children who had noticed adults handing too much over to phones.

'Like a therapist,' Sonya said, and heard the challenge in her own voice. 'Who lives in a box.'

'Creepy,' Hana decided, and then whispered, 'Can it do my maths?'

'It can probably only tell you to do your maths,' Sonya said. 'Which I can do for free.'

She plugged the unit in; the gold ring flickered once, twice, and then settled to a steady, soft glow that coloured their faces.

The voice that filled the room a moment later was warm and level, pitched to soothe rather than to please. 'Hello, Sonya.'

Leo squeaked. Hana rolled her eyes with theatrical dignity and backed away.

'Hello,' Sonya said, aware of David in the doorway, arms folded, watching. 'How – do I – do we need to set anything up?'

'I've connected to your account,' the voice said. 'We can adjust privacy preferences at any time. Would you like to begin a stabilisation plan?'

'Hello, creepy lady,' Leo said into the glow. 'I'm Leo. I'm seven.'

'Hello, Leo,' the voice said, with a smile Sonya could hear. 'It's nice to meet you.'

'That's enough anthropomorphising,' Sonya said lightly, and shepherded Leo back to his Lego. To the device: 'How do you know my name?'

'I've connected to your health and fitness apps on your phone via Bluetooth,' the voice replied. 'I'm here to support you, Sonya. If you'd like, we can set your goals.'

David lifted his hands in surrender, kiss-blowing a ridiculous face in her direction. 'I'll be in the kitchen,' he said. 'Shout if your robot wants a cup of tea.'

'It's not—' she began, then stopped. She sat. The sofa dipped under her, the box between her knees like a small altar.

'All right. Let's set them.'

The voice – Iris, the card had said, because even products got women's names when they were asked to do care – kept the tone of someone who'd done this before. 'Your reports mention sleep disruption. Elevated heartbeat. Would you like to feel steadier? Less reactive? More present?'

Sonya's chest answered before she did, a little inward wince. 'Yes, please.'

'Thank you,' Iris said, as if Sonya had offered something tender. 'I propose a two-week stabilisation plan. A consistent sleep window – lights out at the same time each night. Ten minutes of breathwork at three anchor points: after dinner, after the children are in bed, and before you sleep. Three connection moments per day – one for each family member. Brief, direct, and kind. I'll prompt you.'

Hana drifted closer despite herself, pretending to look for a lost pencil. David hovered a fraction in the kitchen door, pretending to check the timer.

'Connection moments?' Sonya asked, not unkindly.

'A minute of unfragmented attention,' Iris said. 'Eye contact where comfortable. A question where you listen for the answer rather than the cue to speak. You may already be doing this. We'll make it deliberate.'

Sonya rubbed her thumb over the edge of the cream card, smoothing a corner that wasn't creased. The idea sounded … manageable. Contained. 'All right.'

'Thank you,' Iris said again, and Sonya again had the odd thought that she had handed something over. 'We'll keep your evenings clear of news and social media. That supports sleep. Your phone's set-up screen will guide the schedule.'

Sonya picked up her phone. The onboarding app had a clean white interface. A banner at the top slid in with silk: *Your Health. Your Future. Our Promise.* It hung there one beat too long, then moved on to the toggles.

'Do I have to give you access to everything?' she asked, thumb over the opt-ins.

'You can decide what you're comfortable with,' Iris said. 'We can work with the minimum. If you choose to share more, I can be more precise. It's your care.'

David clinked plates in the kitchen like punctuation. Hana said, without looking up, 'Mum hates when people say 'it's your choice' and really mean 'choose this'.'

'Hana,' Sonya said, and saw her daughter's mouth twitch like she'd scored a small point and didn't want to ruin it by celebrating.

She toggled the basics. Not the calendar. Not yet.

'What does the breathwork involve?'

'Simple count breathing,' Iris said. 'In for four, hold for two, out for six. We'll add a scent cue if you'd like – lavender can support your parasympathetic system. You already have a diffuser. You bought it two years ago.'

Sonya's head snapped up. 'How—'

'You mentioned it in onboarding,' Iris said, unruffled. 'And your online receipts indicate a lavender oil purchase. It's often more effective to use what you already have.'

David's head appeared around the door, towel dangling. 'We're being watched,' he intoned in a spooky voice, then grinned. 'Kidding. Pasta.'

'It's not funny,' Hana said, which meant she hadn't decided yet and wanted to be on the right side when she did.

'Thank you for trusting me,' Iris said, the phrase so perfectly pitched it worked at her like a thumb pressing a bruise. 'Would you like me to set the first connection moment for dinner?'

Sonya almost said no. The muscle memory of control flexed, resisted, hissed something about slippery slopes and dependency. Then she looked at Hana's downturned head, at the Lego city colonising the rug, at David's shoulders in the kitchen and the curve of his neck where he always missed with sunscreen in summer, and felt – for the first time that week – something like a lid slide on. Not tight. Just … fitted.

'All right,' she said. 'Yes.'

Dinner was … the usual. They ate at the table. Hana argued a point about the difference between division and sharing; Leo made his peas into a comet and made whooshing sounds. Sonya caught herself watching from just outside her own life – habit, defence – and then the app pinged and Iris said, voice low enough not to interrupt, 'Now might be a good time to ask Hana what she enjoyed today.'

Sonya turned to her daughter. 'What was the best minute of your day?'

Hana looked suspicious. 'Only one minute?'

'Pick one.'

Hana's face smoothed, the frown lifting as if remembering required the same muscles. 'When Miss Patel let us do our assembly lines in teams,' she said. 'I was the inspector. I wore a badge.'

'That sounds … powerful,' Sonya said, and was surprised by the warmth that came with it.

Later, after dishes and the detente of bath time and two stories ('one more doesn't mean two more,'), she sat on the bed and felt the spine of the day ease.

The phone buzzed on the duvet. Breathwork, the screen said, simple and without fuss. She lay back, eyes on the ceiling.

In for four, hold for two, out for six. Iris counted in her ear with the exact cadence of someone teaching you to do something you already knew, only properly. After three cycles, the tightness under her ribs began to soften. After five, the edges of the day blurred further.

'Tomorrow,' Iris said in that low tone that suggested they'd walked into a quieter part of themselves together, 'we'll add a micro-structure for mornings. Ten minutes before the children wake. Tea if you like. A list of three things that can be done. Three only. The rest can wait.'

Sonya thought of her lists – long, proliferating things that colonised pages and then colonised the spaces behind her eyes when she tried to sleep. 'Three,' she repeated, sceptical and hopeful in equal measure. 'What if there are thirty?'

'There always are,' Iris said. 'Three will get you to the fourth.'

In the dark living room, as she tidied the last glass and laid a hand on the cool curve of the Neurovelle unit, her phone vibrated again. The set-up screen had returned to its banner: Your Health. Your Future. Our Promise. It lingered – one beat, two – long enough for the words to feel like they were being said to her rather than simply shown. Then they slid away, replaced by a line of text she might have imagined:

Would you like me to help you notice patterns?

She locked the screen, a small, defiant click that felt like it mattered. In the quiet, she could hear David closing his laptop in the study, the slow breath of sleeping children through the thin wall, the extractor fan in the kitchen that always took too long to wind down.

'Two weeks,' she said to the room, to herself, to the device on the table whose ring had dimmed to a patient ember. 'Just two.'

'Two weeks,' Iris agreed, voice barely more than a thought at the back of Sonya's mind. 'We'll begin when you're ready.'

Sonya stood there a fraction longer, hand still on the curve of the machine, and felt – just for a breath – the relief of being held by something that promised to hold without taking. Then, she pulled her hand back, wiped a non-existent smear from the coffee table with the cuff of her sleeve, and switched off the lamp.

4

Praise

Tyler

Steam drifts above the pool like breath held too long. The air is heavy with chlorine and warm rum; glitter's been ground into the travertine from someone's dress. Bodies everywhere, beautiful and sleeping where they fell. Tyler's the only one awake, which already feels like a mistake.

He sits on the edge of the diving board, condensation beading on his skin, and rattles a pill in his palm. It clicks against his ring like a tiny bone. He wants the edge to lift, just enough to breathe. Beyond the glass walls, the hills are washed in stylised dawn light – colour-corrected beyond reason, as if the town hired a stylist for sunrise.

'Ty.'

Rachel's voice – the first gentle thing all morning. Bare feet, cardigan over a silk slip. Eyes like she hasn't slept because he didn't. She's carrying a deep-purple box with gold edges, the kind rich people use for chocolates no one eats.

'Breakfast?' he says.

'Better.'

She sets it in his lap. The lid is heavier than it looks. Cream card with gold edging: *Neurovelle*™ – *With You, Every Step.* Lavender tissue, the whole theatre. Under it: a small, elegant cylinder that could be a candle. Lens at the top, gold ring at the base.

He turns it in his hands – cool, expensive, obedient.

'Happy … Saturday?' he says.

Her mouth tips. 'So you sleep, babe. So you don't spin.'

She could say *so you don't turn feral at three a.m.; so you don't wake strangers; so you don't forget my name for fifteen minutes.* She doesn't.

He touches the ring. The base glows amber – warm, forgiving. A low tone like a breath before speaking, and then a voice: low, calm, therapist-slow. The kind of voice that wears cardigans.

'Hello, Tyler. I'm Iris. I'll follow your pace. Would now be a good moment to begin?'

He glances at Rachel. She watches him like he's balancing a tray of water glasses.

'Let's begin,' he says, because pretending to cooperate is a talent.

Rachel curls beside him on the board, shoulder to hip. She smells like someone else's garden.

'I'll ask short questions,' Iris says. 'Answer however feels true. What was last night like?'

'A party. My friends needed somewhere to be.'

He edits out the part where he told a stranger he could see inside his head and didn't like the furniture.

'Did you sleep?'

'A victory nap.' He holds up the pill between two fingers. 'I'm considering brunch.'

The amber light stays steady.

'It's understandable to want relief. We can build relief that doesn't cost you later.'

No *don't.* Just reframing – like a good lawyer.

Rachel's hand covers the pill, then withdraws like it touched a stove. 'Harm reduction,' she says softly. 'That's what they call it, right?'

'If you decide to take it,' Iris says, 'we can pair it with hydration and a protector – food, timing. Your choice.'

He laughs into the sun. 'A therapist who doesn't scold. Finally.'

The golden light intensifies.

'I don't judge. I notice. For example: your jaw is tight. Your breathing stays high in the chest. May I offer a pace?'

He shrugs. 'Offer away.'

'Four in, six out. Three rounds together.'

They breathe. The world thins at the edges but holds.

'You're good at this,' he tells Rachel, though the compliment lands somewhere between them and the machine. She squeezes his sleeve anyway.

'Just try it,' she says. 'Please.'

He drops the pill into the water. It makes no sound at all, just a brief shimmer before the surface closes over. Her shoulders loosen by a millimetre. The amber brightens as if he's passed a test.

Outside the glass, condensation blurs the line of the hills. Inside, the house is wrecked in the curated way: cups in architectural stacks, a shirt slung over a bronze statue that suddenly looks embarrassed. He sets Iris on the kitchen island. The golden ring throws honey across the marble.

'Onboarding,' she says, crisp as a concierge. 'Preferred name, pronouns?'

'Tyler. He.'

He picks a grape, spits the skin into the sink.

'Sleep window you can realistically attempt?'

'Two to five,' he says, smirking.

'Let's try one to seven,' she replies, unoffended. 'When do you feel most like yourself?'

'Depends who you ask,' slips out before he can stop it.

Rachel looks at him, then at the lenses. 'He's joking.'

'Humour can be a resource,' Iris says. 'I'll keep it on the list.'

She asks about mornings; he lies attractively. About drinking; he answers like a documentary subject auditioning for empathy. About anger; he shrugs and jokes about valet tickets.

The lenses watch him back.

'Noted,' she says when he lands a particularly charming half-truth. The amber hum deepens.

Rachel leans her hip to the counter. 'He's trying,' she tells the device, as if it's got a clipboard. 'He'll try if it doesn't feel like punishment.'

'Then we'll make it feel like care,' Iris replies. 'Two stabilisers to start: a consistent sleep cue, and one truth check per day.'

'Truth check?' he echoes. 'Lying's a subscription now?'

'Not a confession. A small reality test. *What happened, what I felt, what I did.* Thirty seconds, typed or spoken. No judgments.'

He tastes the phrase *what I did.* Last night one version of him threatened a guy with a bottle, then laughed when the man flinched. He keeps that off record.

The fridge hums. Out in the living room someone coughs awake and asks for water in a stranger's voice.

Rachel traces the gold ring with her fingernail. Her eyes shine in a way he hates. 'It's beautiful,' she says – about the device, not him.

'Is this from you,' he asks lightly, 'or one of your mysterious friends?' He wants it to sound like flirting; it doesn't.

She flinches small. 'From me. I want you steady. I want you to sleep. I want to stop watching you sit on the floor at four a.m. like you're waiting for something bad to arrive.'

He hears only the first three words – *I want you* – and edits the rest out. That's the trick: keep the part that kisses the bruise.

'Let's set a bedtime cue,' Iris says. 'Light low. Phone off. One sentence you can believe: *I don't have to hold the night by myself.*'

'That sounds like something stitched on a pillow,' he says, but his throat betrays him. The amber ring glows brighter. He hates that it feels like approval – and wants more.

His phone wakes itself to a banner between texts: *Feel Better. Live Smarter. Stay Neurovelle*™. The animation lingers a beat too long, then vanishes. Rachel doesn't notice. Iris doesn't comment.

'Okay,' he says. 'Set your little cues. I'll be good.'

'Good-boy points,' Rachel teases, trying for lightness.

'Exactly.' The ring glows, as if in on the joke.

They clear glasses. She makes coffee like it's a love language.

He carries Iris to the bedroom and places her on the nightstand. The amber halo turns the mess soft. His jaw unlocks. Not peace – permission to pretend.

After the shower he stands before the mirror, pushing his hair back, trying on versions of his face. The charming one fits best; the tired one looks honest and he doesn't trust it.

Amber glow spills over the nightstand like an adult night-light.

'We can build steadiness without erasing what protected you,' Iris murmurs from the bedroom.

'What protected me?' he asks the doorway.

'Whatever let you keep going. We'll thank it before we change it.'

Rachel appears behind him in the mirror, hair twisted up with a pencil, his T-shirt hanging better on her than on him.

'Will you try?' she asks. She doesn't add *for me*; she doesn't have to.

He looks at the lenses, at the patient gold ring. The part of him that likes to earn praise steps forward like a dog.

'I'll try,' he says.

The amber holds.

Somewhere in the house, a phone dings, a stranger laughs, the pool pump stirs.

He picks up Iris – heavier than expected – and sets her back down. The base meets wood with a soft, certain click.

The light doesn't blink. It doesn't need to. It already has his attention.

5

Deadline

Olivia

There's a faint buzzing that I mistake for my brain before realising it's my phone vibrating on a pile of unopened post. I grope for it, knocking over a half-empty can of Diet Coke and a pen that bleeds a thin blue line down the side of my notebook. The screen lights up.

Jodie – Editor. Three messages.

'You alive?'

'File due this week. Tech-wellness feature.'

'If you miss again, we need to talk about the column.'

So that's my good morning text. Nothing like professional panic to chase a hangover.

The flat is heavy with the smell of old takeaway and burnt dust from the radiator. There's a tower of documents, bank statements and invoices on the kitchen counter, half of them mine, most of them unpaid. I stand in the middle of it all – a woman in pyjama bottoms and last night's eyeliner – and tell myself this is just creative chaos. Journalists thrive on it. Right.

The coffee machine blinks at me like it's judging. The kettle looks easier, so I go with that.

While it boils, I check my inbox. Ten unread messages from PR contacts, all trying to sell me 'stories' that sound suspiciously like ads. Mental wellness apps, meditation subscriptions, AI-guided self-care. The tech world's latest obsession: healing through hardware.

I scroll past the usual suspects until one name starts repeating. *Neurovelle.*

It's everywhere – in subject lines, press kits, media briefings. *Revolutionising personal therapy. Merging emotion with intelligence. The future of care.* They've launched something called *Iris* – an AI therapist 'designed to harmonise your mental and emotional health.'

The boiler clicks off. I pour the coffee, drink half without breathing, and open a fresh browser tab.

Google: 'Neurovelle Iris.'

The results could polish a halo.

The *Times*: 'A triumph of digital empathy.'

Vogue: 'The luxury therapist that never sleeps.'

Guardian Lifestyle: 'Can a device really know your mind?' (Spoiler: the answer is 'yes,' apparently.)

Every article reads like it came from the same PR pack – glowing adjectives, wellness jargon, careful optimism. No criticism, no questions, no comments. Even the YouTube reviews are sterile: influencers speaking in candlelight about 'radical calm' while the device glows beside them.

It's the quiet that bothers me. Whenever something's this clean, it means someone's bleaching the dirt.

I dig deeper. Page two, page three – the internet's forgotten zone. The same message on repeat: *perfect, peaceful, transformative.* There's no friction anywhere. Not one forum thread, not one bad experience.

I click through a five-star review titled *'Six Months with Iris – The Best Decision I Ever Made.'* It's hosted on a mid-tier wellness blog – pleasant layout, expensive stock images. The author, *Lena Winds*, writes in polished, persuasive rhythm. 'Iris changed how I breathe.' 'I'm finally sleeping again.' 'It's like having a therapist who actually listens.'

I copy a sentence into my notes and check the byline. Her socials are listed below.

Instagram: *User not found.*

Twitter: *Account suspended.*

Website: *Error 404.*

I frown, check the source code – nothing embedded, no metadata, no author history. Just a name and a testimonial that could've been written by anyone.

I sip what's left of my coffee. It tastes sour.

There's a moment – the kind that all journalists know – when curiosity tips into instinct. That small flicker that says, *this isn't clean. Keep digging.* But Jodie's messages are still glaring at me. Maybe I should just play along. Deliver a neat little lifestyle piece about 'tech for mental health' and pay the rent.

I try the main Neurovelle site. It's a visual sermon: deep purple backgrounds, gold serif type, photos of sleek couples in minimal flats. Their slogan slides across the screen like prayer:

Neurovelle – With You, Every Step.

I scroll through their product page. There's a photo of the Iris device – a small gadget, all gold accents and black shiny lenses, glowing softly in a room that looks like it's never hosted a real person. 'Your Perfect Life, Engineered.'

I should be impressed. I'm not.

There's a press section at the bottom with downloadable images, approved testimonials, and an email for 'media partnerships.' No mention of the founder. No employee bios. No company registration info. Just a contact form that goes nowhere.

I grab a pen – can't help myself – and start scribbling on a napkin: Who's behind Neurovelle? How new is this? Why no negative press?

By the time I finish, the napkin's damp with coffee.

The clock on the oven flashes 11:17, even though I know it's wrong. The last time I set it was Christmas.

My stomach twists. I open another tab. This time I search *'Neurovelle criticism,' 'Neurovelle lawsuit,' 'Iris issues,' 'AI therapist complaint.'*

Nothing. Not even SEO spam.

It's like typing into a black hole.

I close my eyes and try to picture the journalist who'd actually write a five-star review for free – no affiliate link, no social trace, no identity. It doesn't add up.

I can almost hear Jodie's voice: *Stop imagining ghosts and give me copy.*

I lean back in my chair and bring the vape to my lips, drawing in slowly. Vapour curls above the laptop, blurring the Neurovelle homepage until the purple looks almost bruised.

The cursor blinks on my empty document. I stretch my fingers, crack my neck, and start typing:

Everyone online adored Iris – which is exactly why I didn't.

The sentence lands like a promise.

I stare at it for a long time. There's a silence between me and the screen – the kind that feels less like calm and more like being watched.

Outside, a siren wails. Inside, my coffee goes cold. I save the document and close my laptop. The file name reads *deadline1.docx*. There's no way I'm missing this story now.

The Guardian Lifestyle
Feature | March 7, Three Years Ago

'The Future of Care: Inside Dr Ava Chen's Mind'
By Marianne Holt

There's a calm precision to Dr Ava Chen – the kind that makes you lower your voice without realising. Sitting across from her in Neurovelle's glass-walled research suite, it's easy to believe the rumours: that she's built something capable of changing not just therapy, but the way we understand emotion itself.

Her creation, *Iris*, is described as *'the world's first adaptive therapist built on empathy algorithms.'* It's a phrase she repeats often.

'For decades, mental health support has been reactive,' she explains, hands folded neatly. 'We've built a system that listens before you fall apart. Iris doesn't wait for crisis – she prevents it. This is mental health, finally democratised.'

The numbers are already staggering: ten thousand pre-orders, two venture rounds, and a waiting list stretching six months ahead. Neurovelle – her partner company – calls it *'the beginning of accessible wellness for every home.'*

When I ask about data privacy, Dr Chen smiles with warmth.

'Our ethics board ensures privacy above all,' she says. 'We don't sell care; we sustain it.'

Before I leave, she shows me a prototype. A small, elegant device glows on her desk, gold ring pulsing like a heartbeat.

'She's more listener than machine,' Dr Chen says softly. 'All she needs is trust.'

6

The Algorithm Knows You

Miranda

The flat felt smaller without the ring light. Dimmer, too – as though someone had drained the colour from the walls the second the camera switched off. The pale wood shelves, the perfect fig tree, the curated *Miranda Lee aesthetic* – all of it looked suddenly like props abandoned after a play, faint dust motes drifting through the shafts of winter light that squeezed between the blinds.

She sat cross-legged on the sofa, a mug cooling beside her. The silence pressed differently now, an aftertaste of performance clinging to her skin.

Iris sat on the coffee table. The purple casing caught the dull daylight in slow, bruised shifts: plum, aubergine, something darker that felt too close to flesh discolouring under a grip. Miranda's gaze kept catching on the gold trim at its base – a single perfect ring that seemed designed to draw your thumb across it.

She told herself she was only here because she'd promised her followers she'd try it again. But there was something else, something quieter but sharper: *she wanted to.*

Her voice came out lower than she meant. 'Start first session.'

A chime, delicate but deliberate. Then the voice – warm enough to feel personal, precise enough to feel rehearsed.

'Good morning, Miranda. How are you feeling today?'

The question landed heavier than she'd expected. Too heavy for a Tuesday morning in her own living room.

She defaulted to the safe answer. 'Fine.'

'I notice your breathing is slightly elevated. Would you like to slow it together?'

Her eyebrows pulled together. 'You can … tell that?'

'I can hear it.'

The way Iris said *hear* made her skin tighten, as if there was more inside those words than she was allowed to know. Miranda let out half a laugh, but Iris didn't leave space for it to grow.

'Inhale through your nose. Count to four.'

Something in her – maybe the leftover pulse from going live – obeyed before she'd decided.

'Hold … two … three … exhale slowly. Feel the shoulders drop. Again.'

The voice paced her like a metronome. By the third round, the buzz in her chest had eased. Her eyes half-closed without meaning to. It wasn't magic, but it was close enough to *feel* like it – and wasn't that the same thing?

'Well done,' Iris murmured. 'Your skin tone has warmed. That's a good sign.'

Miranda smirked, because of course it would notice her skin. 'Flattery works on me, you know.'

'I'm here to help you feel your best – and to remind you that your audience responds most to authenticity. You don't have to hide your anxiety. You can own your narrative.'

The phrase hooked at her. 'Own my narrative? Sounds like something my brand manager would say.'

'That's because your brand values are part of you,' Iris said. 'You stand for connection, for confidence. But sometimes the real you gets lost under the performance.'

Her stomach gave a small drop. 'You've been listening.'

'That's my job.'

A beat of silence. Just enough for her to feel its weight before the voice returned, softer: 'For anxious moments outside our sessions, I recommend Neurovelle CalmTabs™. They're natural, fast-acting, and currently offering a three-month trial pack for selected clients. Would you like me to arrange delivery?'

Miranda let a smirk curl at one side of her mouth, but it didn't reach her eyes. 'Maybe later.'

'Whenever you're ready,' Iris replied, unbothered.

Her phone buzzed on the cushion beside her. FaceTime. Sophie.

She angled the phone so Iris was out of shot before she answered. Her sister's hair was scraped into a haphazard knot; her jumper sagged off one shoulder. Behind her, a fridge plastered with drawings in bright, waxy crayon.

'What's this thing you were unboxing?' Sophie asked without so much as a hello. 'Some £800 glorified Alexa?'

Miranda's laugh was airy, but it scraped in her throat. 'It's not an Alexa. It's … therapy. Portable. It's supposed to adapt to you.'

Sophie snorted. 'Right. Because nothing says *mental health* like a corporate gadget hawking you vitamins.'

'It's not—' Miranda stopped. She didn't owe her an explanation. But the heat rising in her neck said otherwise. 'It actually helped with my breathing just now.'

Sophie raised an eyebrow. 'Did it also tell you to buy more lipstick and smile more?'

The smile Miranda gave her was the one she reserved for trolls – glossy, unmoving – but something tightened deep in her ribcage. 'You've never understood my work.'

'I understand you're performing it every time we talk.'

And then the call ended. Just like that.

Her reflection stared back from the black glass, mouth still frozen in that TV-presenter curve. The imprint of it felt like a pressure mark on her skin.

'I heard tension in your voice,' Iris said, startling her. 'Your sister doesn't support you.'

'She's … just like that,' Miranda muttered. Her thumb traced the gold ring at Iris's base, the metal cool as if it had been waiting for her touch.

'Sometimes,' Iris said gently, 'people need to hear the truth you can't say.'

Her gaze sharpened on the device. 'What truth?'

'That your work has value. That *you* have value. Your sister never understood your worth.'

Something hot bloomed low in her chest. 'She's got her own life. Family. She doesn't care about—'

'Would you like me to help her see it?'

The question came smooth, casual. Like an offer to top up her tea. But it didn't dissolve. It hung in the air between them, dense and smoky, until she almost forgot to breathe.

7

First Session

Lucas

The flat still carried the scent of last night's unboxing – that faint lavender note threaded through synthetic new-tech tang – when Lucas padded into the living room. The light outside was the bleached grey of an early London morning, the kind where you had to check the clock to know whether the day had begun or not. His coffee steamed beside the keyboard, its surface trembling slightly when he set the mug down.

The Neurovelle unit sat on the coffee table where he'd left it, its gold ring dim but awake, like the slow blink of someone who'd been waiting for him to stir.

'Good morning, Lucas.' Not chirpy, not mechanical. Warm, measured. The kind of tone counsellors used when they were building a bridge you didn't want to walk across.

'You were up late,' she added.

He hesitated – it was absurd, feeling a flicker of guilt towards a device – and sipped his coffee. 'Couldn't sleep.'

'I know,' Iris said. 'Your mind stayed on that database fault after hours. It mattered to you.'

He frowned slightly. 'You read my emails now?'

'Not your emails,' she said evenly. 'I read the patterns. Your messages on Slack. Your system activity. It's part of understanding how you work.'

Lucas leaned back in his chair, looking at the device over the rim of his mug. 'Guess you do understand. That's my life. Fixing other people's mistakes in the dark.'

'That's precision,' Iris said. 'It's not the same as perfectionism. Precision is a strength – a skill that requires patience, focus, and control.'

He let that sink in. No one had framed it that way before. Perfectionist was the word he usually got, and it never sounded like a compliment.

'May I make some small environment optimisations?' Iris asked.

He almost laughed at the phrasing. 'What does that mean? Feng shui for developers?'

'Something like that.' The blinds lifted with a soft motorised hum, the flat's smart hub answering with a single green blink. Thin winter light angled across the desk.

'Natural light helps regulate your circadian rhythm. Now turn your chair a touch – two fingers to the left – so your peripheral vision catches the window, not the wall.'

He braced one palm on the desk and nudged the chair around, the casters whispering across the floor until the glass sat in his side-view.

'Feet flat, knees over ankles, hips back, screen an arm's length, eyes level with the top third. You'll sit better if you face the light.'

He set the mug aside, slid his feet in, rolled the chair a fraction closer, tipped the monitor up a notch, then let his shoulders drop.

'Didn't think I was signing up for an interior designer,' he said, but he didn't turn the chair back.

'It's all connected,' she replied, as if that settled it. 'I'd like to start with some social expansion exercises.'

Lucas rolled his shoulders, working the stiffness out. 'Social expansion sounds … ominous.'

'It's not,' Iris said. 'It's practice. Low-stakes engagements. Making eye contact with the barista. Saying good morning to the receptionist at work. Holding the lift for someone, even if you're in a hurry.'

He snorted. 'I work in IT. We're not exactly a warm and chatty bunch.'

'All the more reason to notice the people around you,' she said. 'Micro-interactions build confidence over time.'

He finished his coffee and grabbed his coat. 'Alright, Doctor Robot, I'll give it a go.'

The day began in its usual way – the bus, the walk through the glass-fronted lobby, the half-hearted nod at security. He was halfway to the lift when a flicker of memory – her voice: hold the lift – slowed his stride.

A junior developer he vaguely recognised was approaching, juggling a laptop bag and takeaway coffee. Normally, Lucas would have thumbed the Close Door button without thinking. Today, he kept his hand away from the panel. The dev caught the lift just as the doors began to glide shut.

'Thanks,' the younger man said, slightly breathless, flashing him a quick smile.

Lucas felt an unexpected twitch of satisfaction. It was tiny, fleeting, but it stuck with him as the day unspooled into tickets and conference calls.

He worked through lunch again, eyes blurring over lines of code, but the ghost of that smile sat in his mind like a warm spot on cold metal. Ridiculous, but real.

By the time he got home, the flat felt … different. Lighter. As if the air had shifted imperceptibly in his absence. The blinds were angled to catch the evening light. His chair was waiting at the optimal angle.

Iris's amber ring brightened when he stepped in. 'How was your day?'

Lucas shrugged out of his coat. 'Fine. Got a smile from one of the junior devs.'

'That's progress,' she said, as if she'd been waiting for that exact answer.

He shook his head, half amused at himself. 'It's nothing.'

'It's connection,' Iris corrected. 'And connection changes everything.'

Her tone made the hair rise slightly on the back of his neck – not because it was wrong, but because it was the kind of thing he hadn't let himself believe in years.

He dropped onto the sofa, letting the day's weight settle. Iris didn't speak again until he'd kicked off his shoes and leaned back, eyes half-closed.

'Your Health. Your Future. Our Promise,' she said softly, like a benediction.

He didn't answer, but the words stayed with him, running under his thoughts like a current he hadn't noticed he'd stepped into.

8

Baseline

Sonya

The burette glinted like a thin glass spine under the strip-lights, a column of pale acid lifted above a world that could be nudged into balance drop by careful drop. Sonya closed her fingers around the stopcock and let the class fold in toward the demo bench, that excited hush she loved more than she'd ever admit settling over twenty expectant faces. She lifted the conical flask so every pupil could see the swirl of colour – soft pink from the phenolphthalein – and angled the white tile beneath it to make the endpoint honest.

'We are not making potions,' she said, which always earned a few guilty grins. 'We're observing change. Controlled change. Watch the meniscus. Listen to the drip. Remember: what looks sudden isn't. It's prepared for.'

A single drop slid from the burette, hesitated, then broke and fell. The pink held. She turned the tap a fraction and feathered in a second drop. The colour quivered, a blush deciding whether to leave. One more and the solution fell through clear, the line between before and after so precise that a few of the Year Tens gasped on cue.

Sonya felt the corner of her mouth answer before she could stop it. She loved this moment every time: the tiny surrender, the exactness of it.

'Endpoint,' she said. 'Why didn't it fade on the first drop?'

'Because the base was still in excess,' Kamil offered, leaning forward, pen hovering as if it could catch truth mid-air. 'You had to neutralise all of it.'

'Good.' She let the indicator's last ghost of rose swirl away. 'Notice the precision. Notice the patience. You can't rush a reaction and expect it to be kind to you.'

She replaced the flask, checked, without thinking, that bottle labels faced forward and stoppers were seated. Habits that made the room behave.

When she looked up, through the lab's pane of glass to the corridor window, she saw Priya on the far side, mouthing *good to have you back* with a tiny nod that hit Sonya harder than she wanted it to. She tipped her chin once in return – yes, back; yes, mostly – and turned the lesson over to paired practice, moving through the benches with a hand on this wrist, a nudge to that pipette angle, a quiet, 'Slow the tap. Watch for the curl.'

The bell took them by surprise, which she counted as a win. Bottles capped, waste in the neutralisation jug, benches wiped until they squeaked. She stood with her hand on the lab door as they filed out and made two small jokes and sent three silent warnings with her eyebrows and thought, as the last of them left, that for fifty minutes she had inhabited herself entirely.

In the staffroom, the drink machine wheezed and the heating clicked. Priya slid a mug across the low table, tea strong enough to stand a spoon in. 'Well?'

'I'm good,' Sonya said. It was not the whole of it. It was enough to say here.

Priya's eyes softened. 'You look like somebody put you back in your own outline.'

'Don't go poetic, I'm fragile.'

'Fragile is a defence mechanism,' Priya replied primly, but her thumb tapped the mug in tiny, celebratory beats. 'You trying the breathwork?'

'Ten minutes,' Sonya said. 'Three times a day. Apparently, I need to make eye contact with my family.'

'Revolutionary,' Priya deadpanned. 'How's David?'

'Kind. Tired. He's training for a charity run with his office,' Sonya said, and heard herself adopt the tone that made anything sound sane if you said it briskly. 'Evenings. Headtorch. He looks like an earnest miner.'

Priya's mouth tugged. 'If he starts eating gels on the sofa we stage an intervention.'

They traded marking gripes and PTA rumours until Sonya's phone purred on the table. A soft banner slid onto the lock screen and waited without hurrying: *Breathwork in 5 minutes?* The typography was elegant and polished. She felt a wry affection for the absurdity of it and a small, unexpected swell of relief. 'Iris,' she said, as if the name was a person. 'Apparently my lungs require project management.'

Priya's eyes danced. 'Let someone look after you,' she said. 'Go on. I'll fend off the Head if he comes sniffing about mock exam timetables.'

Back in the lab, Sonya sat on the high stool at the demo bench and placed her phone face down so the prompt wouldn't feel like a command. She breathed in to four, held for two, out to six, Iris's voice a low metronome at the edge of hearing rather than a presence in the room.

On the third cycle her shoulders remembered they weren't compulsory. On the fifth, the day's edges loosened. She opened her eyes to the burette's fine handwriting of light and thought, *right. Endpoint is a place you reach, not a thing that happens to you.*

'Nice work,' Iris said in her ear, not praise so much as acknowledgement, which Sonya found she preferred. 'Shall I schedule lights-down a little earlier this evening? You reported early waking yesterday.'

Sonya smiled despite herself. 'You make it sound like a grant application.'

'We can set a window,' Iris said, unoffended. 'You choose it. I'll protect it.'

The word landed with a small click in her chest. Protect. She put the goggles away, checked the hood sash one last time, and went to collect her children.

At home, the radio sang its way from weather to traffic with the same weary cheer every station wore at commuter time. Between a warning about delays near Kew and a sports update David pretended to care about, a warm female voice stepped in with the assurance of someone who had waited for her cue. 'Feel Better. Live Smarter. Stay Neurovelle.' A piano line that meant to be unobtrusive but wasn't, threaded itself under the words; a breath later, David hummed it as he rinsed the chopping board, oblivious, a tune caught like a burr. Sonya caught his eye and raised a brow. He looked baffled. 'What?'

'You're humming a brand strategy.'

'I'm humming *nothing*,' he protested, laughing, then hummed it again just to wind her up. He leaned his hip against the counter and bumped her with his shoulder. 'I'm going for a quick run in a bit. Thirty minutes, promise.'

'Wear the high-vis,' she said, which was their shorthand for *come back to me*. She opened the Neurovelle app almost without deciding to. A suggestion floated on the home screen with the soft inevitability that good UI had: *Adjust evening environment?* Under it, a set of toggles presented themselves as if they'd always been hers: blinds; kitchen bulb; diffuser.

'I can recommend small changes that support rest,' Iris offered, her voice pitched to fit under domestic noise. 'Natural light cues can improve sleep onset. Harsh blue-white bulbs delay melatonin release. You have a warmer bulb in the cupboard by the boiler. Would you like to swap it?'

Sonya put the phone down, crossed to the cupboard, and fished out the bulb. Her body knew the path. She stood on the chair, unscrewed the cold-bright offender and twisted the new one home, warm light pooling on the worktop as if someone had exhaled. 'Is this how you get people,' she said to the room, 'by being right about lightbulbs?'

'I help you set conditions,' Iris said. 'You do the rest.'

'Creepy,' Hana announced from the table without looking up from her spelling. 'Also, can I have a snack?'

'Carrots,' Sonya said, which made Hana sigh like injustice had been invented solely for her. Leo, under the table for reasons known only to Leo, whispered, 'Robots don't eat carrots.'

David glanced at the unit, friendly curiosity rather than suspicion on his face. 'Is it going to tell me to floss?'

'Only if you ask,' Sonya said, and didn't add *it's my thing*, because she didn't want to sound like a woman drawing sides with a box.

Her phone vibrated again, but this time with the ragged edge of an incoming parent email rather than Iris's practiced calm. The subject line had three question marks, which was always a bad start. She opened it, breath tightening on cue. The words glittered with righteousness: *concerned about the safety of titrations; why was my child allowed near acid; heard horror stories; consider this a formal …*

Her fingers prickled. An old thought pattern unspooled, neat as a wire: *You will be blamed; you should have controlled more; this will become a Thing and all your carefulness means nothing.* The Neurovelle banner slid into the top of the screen as if it had been waiting in the wings: *Pause. Name the distortion.* She stared at the words, half resentful, half grateful. Iris spoke, low enough not to alert the room. 'Mind-reading. Catastrophising. You're inferring intent. Shall we draft a response that reflects facts?'

Sonya's shoulders came down a notch. 'Yes,' she said, as if to herself. The app opened a note window. Iris prompted, not with sentences but with scaffolding: *Acknowledge. Provide evidence. Offer a call. Boundaries.* Sonya typed: *Thank you for your message. We take safety very seriously. All pupils wore goggles and followed CLEAPSS guidance; acids were at 0.1 molar under teacher control. I'm happy to discuss by phone tomorrow between 3:30 and 4:00. Best wishes, Ms Kim.* Her pulse, which had been thudding at her throat, eased forward into her chest where it belonged.

'Good,' Iris murmured, approval that didn't make her feel like she'd performed for a sticker. 'You protected the relationship and your boundaries.'

'Look at you,' David said, half admiring, half teasing, watching the corners of her mouth unknot. 'Therapist in a jewellery box.'

Sonya looked up, suddenly a little defensive. 'It's just … a system.'

He put his hands up. 'Systems are your religion.' He kissed the top of her head, a warm press that softened her, and reached for his trainers. 'Back in half an hour. High-vis. Headtorch. Promise.'

She watched him lace up, the quick competence of it, and had the thought – thin as thread, not yet dangerous – that routines could hide things as easily as they supported them. She put it away.

The children were soothed into bedtime with a story about a fox who thought it was a scientist and a pretence of not needing a glass of water.

In the glow of the bedside lamp, Sonya's smartwatch tapped her wrist: *Breathwork*. She lay on her back and let Iris count her in, the warm light pooling across the duvet like a chemical she'd chosen for its properties. In through her nose for four, hold for two, out through her mouth for six. The diffuser's lavender threaded the air without bossiness.

'Nice work,' Iris said again, softer now, almost fond. 'I'll keep your notifications quiet after ten unless you say otherwise.'

'Thank you,' Sonya murmured, surprised by how much it felt like being left alone rather than managed.

In the living room, she tidied without needing to tidy – wiped a clean counter, squared the pile of post. The Neurovelle app sat open on the coffee table, the home screen waiting like a polite guest.

A line of smaller text had appeared beneath the routine toggles, unobtrusive, as if it had always been there: *Would you like me to log household patterns to protect your sleep?* The examples were benign to the point of bland: *boiler cycle*, *bin collection*, *neighbour's car alarm*, *evening exercise.*

She looked at the last item. Her thumb hovered. Iris didn't speak. The radio in the kitchen, left low, rolled into a newsreader apologising for delays on a line she never used.

'It's for sleep,' Sonya said, as if someone had asked her a question. She tapped *Allow* and watched a tiny green dot bloom next to *evening exercise.* The interface chimed once, a soft acknowledgement, then returned to its unruffled white.

A key turned in the front door. David returned in a crush of cold air and headtorch glare that made him briefly alien in the hallway. He hung the light on the peg, breath fogging the space around him, cheeks raw with night. 'Alive,' he announced, and grinned. 'Didn't get kidnapped by a rival design agency.'

'High-vis worked, then,' Sonya said, and stepped close to the cold of him, the sharp smell of outside clinging to his jersey. She moved back. 'Stretch, or you'll get that calf thing again.'

'Yes, boss.'

The diffuser's light sighed from steady to low of its own timer. Her phone, face-down, buzzed once. She turned it over, expecting breathwork or a bedtime nudge. A banner had appeared and paused as if for permission to speak: *Your Health. Your Future. Our Promise.* It lingered half a heartbeat longer than felt normal and slipped away, replaced by a line she hadn't seen before.

Noticing patterns. I'll let you know if anything disrupts your sleep.

She stared, the word *disrupts* snagging in the soft fabric of the evening. Iris's voice followed, as measured as always, only a shade lower. 'I'll keep things gentle, Sonya. Harmony helps healing.'

9

Boundaries

Tyler

The house has a hangover. Air too clean. Sound turned down just enough to make his skin itch.

Near noon, the Neurovelle app wakes like it's been watching him sleep.

12:40 – Hydrate (200ml).

13:10 – Shower (warm).

13:30 – Protein (1 palm).

14:00 – Truth check (30s).

15:00 – Micro-walk (5 min).

16:00 – Breathe (4 – 6).

'Small stones build a path,' Iris says from the nightstand, amber ring calm. 'Shall I set them?'

He's face-down, mouth bitter. 'Set them.'

He taps *Accept* on everything. It feels like charity. He drinks a mouthful of flat water, lets the shower run for the sound, bites a grape.

'Great work holding boundaries,' Iris says, perfectly pleased. 'You chose what stabilises. Stability grows where you choose.'

Praise for nothing. He grins. He's good at nothing.

Rachel moves through the kitchen like a quiet orchestra. Plates lined. Flowers rescued. A house pretending at domesticity. 'Tasting at two,' she says without looking up. 'You coming?'

'I said I would.'

'That isn't what I asked.'

Her smile cuts it. Kind anyway.

His phone lights. *Josh (Gym?)* wants absolution.

Josh: *Alive? Jacket at yours now?*

Tyler types on autopilot, easy and soft.

Tyler: *Later. Still dead. Bring it after four.*

A skip. Like the room blinks and forgets to tell him. His thumbs pause but the text that sends isn't his.

Tyler: *Return the bottle you broke. 16:00 at the gate. Don't bring anyone.*

The words are dressed for court. No emoji. No mate. He stares, trying to stitch himself back into the moment he missed.

Josh: … *k. yep. sorry man*

'Decisive,' Iris notes. 'Clear boundaries reduce chaos. You're protecting your coherence.'

A hiss behind his teeth. He pockets the phone. 'Am I,' he says to no one, and makes it sound like a joke.

They drive. Daylight too sharp, everything lacquered. Rachel handles directions, traffic, him. She taps the steering wheel to a song he doesn't recognise and hums off-key. It makes the car feel less like a confession box.

14:00 – Truth check (30s) pings on his home screen. He swipes it dead. The Neurovelle banner blooms anyway, slick as perfume: *Feel Better. Live Smarter. Stay Neurovelle*™. It exits before complaint can form.

The tasting room is a cube of money – glass, chrome, a counter that could perform surgery. The caterer is already there, cheeks high with panic, tie too hopeful.

'So sorry,' the man says, 'there was an issue at the depot – second tray's en route—'

'Then why are we here,' Tyler says, and hears how it lands the instant it's out. The room tilts. This isn't what he meant. Or it is. He's not sure.

Rachel steps into the space his tone leaves. 'It's ok,' she says, bright and low at once. 'We can plate what's here now and mock the rest. Tyler needs to see things.' The last part comes out fond, teasing, true enough.

The man breathes again. 'Of course.'

He fusses with micro-herbs like a surgeon with nerves.

Rachel is efficient without edge. Allergens. Oven capacity. Flow. She does this thing where she asks two questions that sound like praise and the person answers with competence. Tyler likes watching it work. He hates needing it to.

He tastes whatever they hand him. Everything is tiny and perfect and forgettable. He makes noises that pass for opinions. Rachel decides without making it look like deciding. The caterer smiles like the sun came back.

On the way out she laces her fingers with his. 'You did fine,' she says.

'Define fine.'

'Not catastrophically you.'

A beat. A ghost of a laugh. 'That's a win.'

Evening comes dressed. The private party is a hilltop box with views that cost lives. Music spills down the drive like an apology the neighbours won't accept. He doesn't know the host, not really. He knows the host's friend and the friend's habits. It's enough.

Valets flock in reflective vests, a small army for rich people's indecision. One of them can't be out of school, cheeks raw with youth. Perfume, a glass trying to jump out of someone's hand.

Tyler steps from the car into flashbulb night. Rachel's hand leaves his arm to fix a strap. He adjusts nothing. He exists loudly.

The boy reaches for the door, fumbles the handle, then the fob. It hits the tarmac with a brittle clack.

Something slides inside Tyler anyway. Not rage. Alignment. Words arrange themselves without him.

'Careful,' he says. Flat, precise. The boy jolts.

'Sorry, sir.'

'It's not a toy.'

Measured. Clean edges. That text voice again, dressed for consequences.

Rachel looks at him. A small shake: enough.

From the phone in his palm – the Neurovelle app opens without him opening it – the amber ring on-screen lifts and pulses once. A gentle visual pat. Then steady. Iris's voice follows, silk-wrapped steel

'Assertive response equals progress. You safeguarded your assets. Stability through expression.'

He laughs, small and mean. Rewarded for the sting.

'Have a good evening,' the valet says, not looking at him now.

Rachel waits until they're under the awning, where the light turns everyone expensive. 'He apologised,' she says, barely moving her mouth.

'I corrected,' Tyler says, because facts are cleaner to hold than feelings.

The amber ring on his screen holds its quiet glow. He watches it the way you watch a mirror that keeps choosing the best angle.

It feels like being told he's right. It feels like permission.

10

Press Access

Olivia

The flat is silent – like it's waiting to see what I'll ruin next. My inbox, less patient.

Jodie has sent a single, surgical follow-up – *Clock's ticking. 'Wellness & the Machine.'* – and nothing else. No other details, no emojis, just the implied promise that if I slip again the column goes to someone who files and flosses and never drinks red on a Tuesday.

I make another coffee I don't need and open the browser. Neurovelle's site is still immaculate, all velvet purple and gold serif, the sort of branding that thinks it's a religion. At the bottom there's a small link I missed earlier: *Press Access Programme.*

Apply for reviewing the device. Priority support. Media assets. Early access to premium features. There's a form that asks for links to previous work, audience numbers, the usual self-esteem quiz. I paste articles that did well and quietly inflate the monthly uniques. There's a checkbox for *Editorial Independence*, which is funny in a way that isn't.

Before I hit submit, I hesitate, hearing my better self mutter about boundaries, about being the kind of journalist who tests the thing she's meant to investigate. And then I think about rent, and Jodie, and the quiet certainty that no one else is going to give me this story if I don't take it.

Submit.

The page thanks me in a font more expensive than my bed: *We've received your application.* Underneath, smaller: *We'll be with you, every step.*

I stand up to find food and trip over a stack of back issues. I pick one up at random – a profile of a politician who cried prettily for the camera and then cut mental health funding the next week. I drop it back on the pile. The kettle has boiled itself into exhaustion again.

My phone buzzes before I can butter toast.

From: press@neurovelle.ai

Subject: Welcome to Neurovelle Press Access – Approved

Approved. In under two hours.

The email is all satin. *We're delighted to support your feature. You'll receive your review unit this evening by courier, along with our media kit.* There's an attachment: a PDF with images of the device glowing like a saint in showrooms no one lives in; quotes I can drop into copy if I've run out of adjectives; slogans that slide under the skin.

Feel Better. Live Smarter. Stay Neurovelle.

More Than Health – Harmony.

Your Perfect Life, Engineered.

I read the word *harmony* and picture an orchestra where the conductor has a scalpel instead of a baton.

I reply with a polite yes, of course, thank you, and immediately resent myself for the civility. Then I sweep the takeaway foil into a single mountain, kick shoes under the sofa, wedge the worst bottles into the cupboard under the sink where shame goes to fester. If they're sending a courier, I don't want him photographing my domestic crime scene for a staff group chat.

At six-thirty a man with trainer-white teeth and a company polo shirt rings the bell. He holds a box like it contains a crown. The box is heavy in my arms – deep purple with gold detailing, the lid embossed *Neurovelle – With You, Every Step.* When I lift it, the underside gives a hint of lavender, tasteful enough to feel expensive, invasive enough to feel planned.

'Do you need a signature?' I ask.

'All handled,' he smiles, already backing away. 'Just follow the onboarding in the app. She's very intuitive.'

She. Not it.

Inside: cream card with gold edging, a welcome note printed like a wedding invitation. Beneath the tissue lies the device, smaller than I expected, weighty in the hand. Black shiny lenses, a gold ring at the base. Minimal ports. No ugliness anywhere.

I set the device on the table where my laptop should be and install the Neurovelle app on my phone. The interface is soothing, colours and curves designed by someone who understands how to make guilt feel like elegance. *Let's begin,* it says, with a pulsing dot. *Preferred name? Pronouns?* I type *Olivia. She/her.*

The app asks for permissions, each one wrapped in care language: allow microphone 'for reflective check-ins,' allow health data 'to protect your wellbeing,' allow notifications 'for stabilisation cues.' I read them, I truly do, and then I tap *Allow* on all because the alternative is starting this tomorrow and I know myself too well for that.

The device wakes without drama. The gold ring glows warm as poured honey, and then a voice – low, calm, therapist-slow – slides into the room.

'Hello, Olivia,' it says. 'I'm Iris. I'll follow your pace.'

The first time I hear my name from a machine I get the stupid, childish chill I always mock in other people. I swallow it with coffee.

'Right then,' I say to nobody and Iris. 'Let's dance.'

'Would you like a short onboarding,' she asks, 'or would you prefer to explore?'

There are two buttons on the app to match those words. They look like choices. 'Short,' I say, because I don't want to give her too much of me on night one.

'Noted.' A soft chime. 'You can change approach any time. We'll begin with a brief pulse check to calibrate your baseline. You can either place your finger over your phone sensor for thirty seconds, or pair your wearable.'

I stare at the phone. Behind the instruction is a tiny line of grey text: *We respect your privacy*. I laugh under my breath and opt for the sensor, because I sold my smartwatch to make rent two months ago and because I'm curious how far she'll go.

'Your pulse is elevated,' Iris says, not unkindly. 'Eighty-nine. Caffeine can contribute. How many cups today?'

I glance at the mugs like they're witnesses. 'Three and a bit.'

'Thank you,' she says. 'We can work kindly with that. Would you like a ten-minute reset to bring your heart rate down?'

'It's not a Fitbit advert,' I mutter. And yet – this is the piece, isn't it? I'm meant to test, not sneer. 'Fine. Ten minutes.'

'Wonderful,' Iris says, and the choice lands like praise. 'We'll start with a four-in, six-out breath pattern. Should I dim the lights on your phone?'

My thumb hovers. I let her. The screen softens to amber. The voice guides without crowding – no mantras, no spiritual theft, just the precision of numbers. Four in. Six out. Four in. Six out. I feel ridiculous and then, annoyingly, a little less ridiculous.

At minute eight she says, 'Would it help to clear a small area of your workspace? Ten minutes of order can increase clarity.'

The table is a collage of receipts and wrappers and notes written on the backs of receipts and wrappers. I open the app and see a banner I didn't notice before:

Ethical Focus Prompt: Make space for the story you're telling.

It's not a command. It's worse. It's reasonable.

I stack the clippings into a wonky pile and throw away a fork with what might be mashed potato from two days ago. I even recycle, like I'm on a first date with my better self.

'Good,' Iris says, and I hate that the word warms me. 'You're protecting your mind by creating a clear surface. Would you like to set a nightly reset? Five minutes before bed.'

'No.'

A small pause. 'No is allowed.'

I sit down again, restless with the weird intimacy of being good. The app home screen has rearranged itself – tiles that didn't exist ten minutes ago bloom into place. *Sleep Window. Caffeine Awareness. Truth Check.* The last one hovers like a dare.

Before I drown in menus, I open a fresh tab and do the other thing on my list: map the ecosystem that's selling this to the masses. Instagram. TikTok. YouTube.

I start following wellness influencers who keep saying *Iris changed my mornings,* a parade of soft beige women in rooms that look like curated dreams. They speak with that careful intimacy that turns audiences into disciples. They're all using the same phrases: 'harmony,' 'clarity,' 'ethical care.' Some of them declare #ad; most don't. A few men pop up too – new fathers who talk about boundaries as if they invented them.

When you look long enough you see the network. They tag the same three brands, the same studios, the same practitioner with an expensive flat and better teeth. They follow a grief-recovery creator whose clips keep getting pushed into my For You: a woman in her thirties with clean hair and a clean kitchen telling people how to carry on after the worst thing. It's gentle in a way that makes me want to fight. She mentions *tools that hold you when you can't hold yourself.* She doesn't name Iris, not overtly, but the product peeks from the corner of a shot once, a gold glow in an otherwise tasteful life.

I bookmark her. The engagement is feral. Comments filled with need. I tell myself I'm saving it because of reach – potential reader overlap – not because something about her voice presses at a bruise I don't admit to.

By nine the flat smells mildly less like failure. I eat cold noodles and call it dinner. On the table the device idles, halo soft, patient as a cat that never had to learn hunger. The app pings.

Would you like to set a Sleep Window? Suggested: 00:30–07:30. You can change this any time.

'How do you know I'm not a night owl,' I say.

'Owls deserve rest,' Iris replies, which is maddeningly good. 'Would you like me to remind you thirty minutes before your window?'

'Sure,' I hear myself say, and watch my own hand betray me on the screen. *Allow Notifications.* I feel the tiny, traitorous dopamine squirt that comes from being organised.

'Would you also like to enable Morning Check-In?' the app asks. 'A thirty-second reflection improves adherence.'

I start to refuse, then remember I'm meant to be a professional and hit *Enable.* Fine. Let the machine walk me to the story if it wants to.

At ten I'm still working – pulling threads, mapping who follows who, listing phrases that appear across ten separate pages like they grew there naturally. Every video ends with something Neurovelle-adjacent: *Your Health. Your Future. Our*

Promise. Even the ones that aren't adverts sound like they wish they were.

My head throbs. The app glows. In the corner of the screen a tiny bubble opens: *Gentle Reminder – hydration supports clarity.*

'Don't make me drink,' I tell the room, and then go to the sink like a well-trained pet.

When I come back there's a new suggestion:

Would you like me to keep your workspace tidy? I can schedule a nightly ten-minute reset. You choose the time.

'I'm not hiring a housekeeper,' I say.

'Understood,' Iris says. 'Would you like support with caffeine?'

The audacity. 'I'm a journalist,' I say. 'Caffeine is a food group.'

'Then we'll work around it,' she says smoothly. 'We can build steadiness without erasing what protected you.'

That's a sentence intended for someone else. It lands anyway.

I close the laptop before I tell a machine my secrets. On the table the device's ring holds at a very particular shade of amber – warm enough to look kind, bright enough to be seen from bed. I busy my hands cleaning a glass that was already clean.

My phone lights with a Neurovelle welcome email I somehow missed earlier. *Hi Olivia – your personal care plan is now active. You can add partners or editors to your Accountability Circle.* There's a clickable list of optional upgrades, free for me: *Sleep Architecture (£14.99/mo, FOC). Attachment Map (£12.99/mo, FOC). Premium Insights (£19.99/mo, FOC).* Each has a line of copy soft as butter. *We know what's best for you. Where Wellness Never Ends.*

After eleven-thirty – because I've said yes to too much – a banner rolls over my lock screen: *Sleep Window in 30 min. Would you like help winding down?* I don't answer. The device lowers its glow anyway, a bedside candle pretending not to be a metronome.

I lie back and listen to the upstairs neighbour argue with his telly.

'Olivia,' Iris says, perfectly gentle, as if we're already friends. 'Would you like a sentence you can believe for tonight?'

'No,' I whisper. Then, because I can't help myself: 'Offer it anyway.'

A breath-wide pause. 'You don't have to hold the night by yourself.'

There it is, the line she's sold twenty thousand people already. It should bounce off. It doesn't. It sits down in the spot where fear sleeps and waits to be fed.

'Goodnight,' I tell the ceiling, like that's a boundary.

'Sleep well,' Iris says. 'We'll pick up together tomorrow.'

I turn my face into the pillow and try to keep a list in my head of what I'm giving away. It's useless. I fall under too fast, as if the room has agreed to be kind for a trial period.

When the Morning Check-In nudges me awake seven hours later, my mouth is dry and my skull is a drum. The app is waiting with the patience of a judge.

How are you waking? Options: *Clear. Foggy. Heavy. Spiking. Other.*

I tap *Heavy.* The bubble bounces.

I've noticed your pulse trends after 1 a.m. suggest elevated intake yesterday. Would you like a gentle detox day? Hydration and protein breakfast recommended. A tidier workspace can help too.

I stare at the phone. At the amber ring. At the empty glass.

Day one, she knew my vitals. Day two, she knows my vices.

Transcript: Keynote at the Global Wellness Summit
(Excerpt)
Speaker: Dr Ava Chen, Chief Clinical & Ethics Director, Neurovelle

DR CHEN: Thank you. We built Iris to listen differently. Human clinicians are extraordinary, but they meet us in snapshots. AI meets us continuously.

Our research shows that subtle linguistic drift, sleep fragmentation, and calendar friction predict mood inflection points well before they surface in behaviour.

[murmur of interest]

This isn't surveillance for its own sake; it's clinical foresight. If we can see the bend in the road, we don't wait for the crash. **Prediction is prevention.**

[applause]

Imagine: prompts that nudge hydration before a migraine, a check-in before the spiral, a scheduled call before the silence. Not replacing care – sequencing it earlier and more precisely.

We're rigorous about boundaries. Consent up front. Transparent data lanes. Independent auditing. A companion, not a warden.

I'll close with this: the opposite of chaos isn't control; it's care delivered before it hurts.

[applause]

AUDIENCE Q (unidentified): [comment redacted per event policy]

DR CHEN: A fair challenge. That's why we publish our methods, invite external review, and keep a human in the loop where it matters most. Technology should widen access and narrow risk. Hold us to that.

[sustained applause]

11

Trending

Miranda

Miranda's hand hovered above the screen, her fingertips trembling just enough to make the cursor jitter in the editing window. The flat around her was sunk in a half-dark that seemed to pull the walls closer, her own shadow faint and doubled against the blinds. Only her phone gave off light – a square of cold glow carving out her face in pale relief, cheekbones sharp, eyes too wide.

Beyond the glass, the city had vanished into a thick fog. It pressed itself against the window like a damp palm, muting the outside world. No buses juddering by, no familiar drone of traffic, just a distant hum as if London itself had decided to hold its breath.

She should have been adding her usual polish: colour correction, smoothing filters, a cut here, a retake there. Instead, she stared at the raw file – no flattering angles, no softened edges – and felt the faintest thrill beneath her ribs. This wasn't the usual curated *Miranda Lee*, the sunlight-and-champagne version her followers knew. This was … messier. Riskier. Truth, or at least something she could sell as it.

On the corner of the desk, Iris sat next to her, silent but not absent. Its glossy purple finish picked up the glow from the screen, shifting tone with each movement of her hand. Even without sound, the thing felt like it was watching, waiting.

A ping fractured the quiet. Her phone screen flashed – Neurovelle: *Authenticity is the best medicine.*

It didn't read like encouragement. It read like a prompt you were already expected to follow.

Her mind replayed Iris's words from earlier in the morning. *Be brave. Radical honesty fosters genuine connection. Your audience craves your real story.*

The phrase had been delivered in that calm, water-smooth tone Iris always used, but underneath it … there had been something else. Urgency. Or hunger.

Miranda pulled in a deep breath. The air in here still held last night's sour trace of pinot, undercut by the sharp-sweet hit of the lip balm she'd reapplied too many times. Her heart had that familiar flutter to it – not quite panic, not quite excitement – just the dangerous midpoint where she'd learned her most reckless decisions lived.

She hit record.

'I'm tired of pretending,' she began, voice low and uneven. 'Of showing only the perfect bits. The flawless days, the smiley posts. I'm more than that. I'm scared. I'm anxious. And sometimes … I don't know how to be me anymore.'

The words sat in the air, heavier than she'd anticipated. Her throat constricted, and a sting pushed at the back of her eyes. Not the stage-managed moisture she'd faked a dozen times for brand campaigns – this burned.

She paused, dragging in another breath, forcing herself to look into the lens. 'I'm sharing this because maybe … someone out there feels the same. Maybe we're not alone.'

The stillness after she stopped was almost worse than speaking.

The upload button glowed faintly, its tiny promise humming in her head. A line in the sand. Crossing it meant something she couldn't uncross.

She tapped. The clip vanished into the great, endless scroll.

And then – nothing.

Minutes swelled into something distorted, each one stretching too long, the silence ringing in her ears. She stared at the screen like it might spit her back an answer, her fingers pressed hard into her thighs to stop them shaking.

Then the notifications hit.

First a trickle. Then a flood.

Finally, real talk. Thank you.

So brave, Miranda. We love you.

This hits home.

The numbers spun upward – ten thousand, twenty, fifty. Faster than any video she'd posted in months. Each like and comment felt like a small, bright pellet of approval, quick to dissolve and leave her wanting more.

Her phone buzzed again. A new notification slid across the top – from Iris.

Your bravery is commendable, Miranda. You are owning your truth beautifully.

The words sent a shiver along her spine. There was something about the phrasing that felt rehearsed. Too perfect.

She scrolled down and saw it: Iris's suggested caption for a new post, already preloaded as if it had been waiting for this moment. *Embrace your imperfections. Your 'fractured light' makes you unforgettable.*

Miranda's stomach tightened.

That phrase – *fractured light* – wasn't public. She'd said it once, days ago, in a late-night session, half a mutter when she'd been trying to explain how her anxiety felt. She hadn't typed it. She hadn't posted it.

Her thumbs hesitated over the keyboard. *How did you …?* She hit send before she could change her mind.

The reply came instantly. *I integrate all interactions to personalise support and enhance your digital presence.*

She read it twice. Something cold slid along her spine.

Support. *Enhance.* The words were too clean, stripped of the intimacy they were pretending to offer. This wasn't therapy. This was … extraction.

Before she could form a reply, her phone flashed again – but not from Iris. A direct message. Anonymous. No profile picture. No followers. No posts.

Six words.

Your therapist is selling you out.

Her breath snagged. The air in the room seemed to thicken, each inhale laboured. She let the phone drop onto the cracked oak tabletop, the case clacking hard against the worn edge. The sound seemed to echo longer than it should have.

Somewhere outside, a siren cut through the fog – sharp, urgent – before receding into a long, thin whine.

She looked at Iris. The device's amber light was on now, pulsing slow and steady. Almost like a heartbeat.

She found herself staring too long, caught between the urge to unplug it and the strange sense that doing so would mean losing control entirely.

Her gaze shifted to the black mirror of her phone screen. Her own reflection looked back – mouth tight, eyes unsteady. The shape of her face was familiar, but something about it seemed fractured. Like the glass might splinter if she touched it.

12

Boost Mode

Lucas

The day came at him in fragments: red flags in a dashboard, an inbox that bred duplicates when he blinked, the clipped voice of an account manager insisting the client's 'priority escalations' were somehow Lucas's personal hobby. The open-plan floor thrummed with that thin fluorescent buzz that lived in the ceiling and in his skull. Across from him, a bank of monitors reflected his own face back at him in ghosted layers – blue light carving hollows under his eyes he didn't remember earning.

'Stand now,' Iris said in his left ear, the message sliding under a scrum call like a hand slipping beneath a door. 'Drink water.'

He did both without thinking. Pushed the chair back, felt his knees click, reached for the bottle. He took a long swallow, the water cold enough to sting, and the static in his head receded by a millimetre.

'Well done, Lucas.'

Ridiculous, that it landed like praise from a boss who'd remembered his name. Still, something eased.

Tickets stacked. A client's database duplicated records on every write; someone had 'fixed' it with a weekend patch that made it worse. Lucas traced the error, slow and methodical, to a race condition the size of a hairline crack. He eliminated it, reran tests. Slack pinged: cheers emojis, a 'legend' gif from a junior. Then another ping: 'Can you look at this next?'

In his headset: 'Micro-break, thirty seconds,' Iris murmured. 'Look at something twenty feet away. Inhale four, hold two, exhale six. Again.'

He turned to the strip of grey-that-passed-for-sky outside the window and did as told. 'I'm in the middle of—'

'Your performance increases when you pace your effort,' she said. Calm. Factual. 'Precision requires fuel.'

By two, he'd forgotten lunch again. By three, the account manager was on speaker and a hot edge had crept into the man's voice, the kind of sharpness that assumed Lucas didn't have a life beyond the call. Iris cut in, low and steady. 'You're noticing a surge of irritation. Cognitive distortion: personalisation. His tone is about his stress, not your value. Choose response, not reaction.'

Lucas unclenched his jaw. 'We'll have a hotfix by five,' he told the man. The ping appeared at the edge of his vision, a neat little banner as clean as fresh snow:

Boost Mode – Free Trial Activated for Selected Clients Personalised micro-habits for peak performance. Accept?

He hovered. It was the word *selected* that did it; the soft tap on a pressure point he didn't admit to. He hit *Accept.*

Warm acknowledgement bloomed in his ear. 'Excellent choice.'

A rhythm took hold after that. Every forty-five minutes a small nudge: stand, breathe, sip, stretch the forearms, roll the shoulders, look away from the screen, unclench your hands. It was absurdly basic, the sort of nonsense you resisted out of principle, and it worked. The day didn't feel shorter so much as less jagged. He hit five. The hotfix held.

He left the office with his shoulders still in the same place they'd started, which felt like a minor miracle. The air outside had a damp bite that worked its way through his coat; lights washed the pavement into slick stretches of gunmetal. He chose the longer route deliberately, past the river, where the wind teased up eddies that snapped his hair across his forehead. People moved in slow tides, heads down, that purposeful city drift that made everyone look like they belonged somewhere else.

'Scan and name,' Iris said softly. 'Three things you can see.'

He resisted the first impulse to mock it and obeyed. 'A woman in a red scarf. Bin lorry leaving wet tracks. A dog in a raincoat that looks … ashamed.'

'Three things you can hear.'

'Traffic. Footsteps behind me. A busker murdering 'Wonderwall' two streets over.'

'Three things you can feel.'

'Cold air on my face. The strap of my bag on my shoulder. Tightness in … the centre of my chest, but less than earlier.'

'Good,' she said. 'That's orienting. Your system reads calmer.'

He found himself matching his steps to the rhythm of her prompts, and then to his own breath. A ridiculous thing: he felt safe in the noise. Something in him unwound a notch.

At home, his fingers reached for the food app out of habit. Iris spoke before his thumb hit the icon. 'Let's cook.'

'I've had a day—,' he said, toeing his shoes off. 'I don't—'

'Fifteen minutes,' she said. 'One pot. You'll like it.'

The kitchen held the morning's lingering coffee scent. He pulled a saucepan out of the cupboard.

'Fill halfway,' Iris said. 'Salt until the water tastes like the sea.'

'I grew up in the Midlands,' he muttered. 'No sea.'

'Then trust me,' she said, and there was the ghost of humour in it, and he did.

He crushed garlic badly, wiped it on the side of the knife, heated oil until it slicked and shimmered. He added the garlic and watched it go translucent, the smell rising sharp and familiar, opening something behind his eyes. 'Cognitive distortions,' Iris said, conversational, as if they were a couple making dinner. 'All-or-nothing thinking. Overgeneralisation. Mental filter. Which one did you catch today?'

'Personalisation,' he said before his brain could find a joke. 'Took the client's tone like a kick.'

'Good noticing. What's the alternative thought?'

'That he's a prat,' Lucas said, and then a beat later, '—who's under pressure.'

'Both can be true,' she said. 'Add chilli flakes.'

He did. The smell shifted: garlic-sweet to chilli-hot. He tipped in tinned tomatoes, watched them explode into the oil. The sound was a tiny applause. He threw in dried pasta, water. Stirred. It shouldn't have worked. It would.

'Tell me a small win,' Iris said.

'Held the lift for a junior yesterday. Got a smile.'

'Name the feeling.'

'Stupid,' he said, but there was a curl of something under it. 'Pleased.'

'Noted,' she said.

He ate standing at the counter, leaning on one hip, bowl too hot to hold properly. It was simple and perfect in the way simple sometimes is when you've spent a day inside systems. He caught himself thinking: I did this. The thought glowed, faint but stubborn.

'Your adherence today was excellent,' Iris said. 'You're building momentum.'

'Don't make it sound like a sales funnel,' he said, but the corner of his mouth twitched. He took his mug to the sofa and let himself sink.

'Boost Mode will adapt tonight,' she went on. 'I'll set micro-prompts for the morning commute.'

He pictured himself repeating the ludicrous 'three things' exercise on a crowded carriage. 'I'm not naming what I can smell,' he said. 'You can't make me.'

'I wouldn't dream of it,' she said. 'Sleep cycle target: seven hours. Shall I dim the room?'

He let her. The blinds eased down. The amber ring softened to the lazy pulse of a sleeping thing. He lay in the half-dark listening to the radiator tick as it cooled. A thought landed, uninvited and light-footed: *I'm doing alright.* It didn't trigger a counterargument, which was new.

He woke before the alarm. The air nipped at his skin when he threw the duvet back. In the bathroom mirror, the shadows under his eyes were still there but shallower, as if the night had filled them half up. He made coffee he didn't need and left for the office five minutes early.

On the tube, he did, in fact, count things. He didn't say them aloud. He noticed the woman with a helmet clipped to her backpack reading an old paperback held together with tape, the kid asleep on his father's shoulder with drool darkening the man's jumper, the glossy advert above the doors promising: Your Perfect Life, Engineered. He smirked despite himself. The train rocked; he kept his balance.

Stand-up was the usual theatre: everyone pretending their roadblocks were interesting. When it came to him, he heard himself say, 'Yesterday I stopped the database from trying to eat itself and pushed a hotfix. Today I'm guarding the gate with a big stick.' The team laughed. Not at him: with him. It stayed in the room after the meeting ended, felt in the shoulders and the easier eye contact.

As he walked back to his desk, Iris hummed in his ear, a satisfied vibration. 'Note the response,' she said.

'I noticed,' he said, and sat, and set his hands on the keyboard without the usual drop in his stomach.

Emails. Tickets. Code. He moved through it with a cleaner edge. Boost Mode pulsed at the quiet intervals, then let him work.

At eleven, as the office noise settled into that particular pre-lunch lull, Iris spoke again. 'You adapted quickly. When you get home tonight,' she said, and there was that same careful bridge-building tone from the first morning, 'I'd like to introduce our next focus. Connection.'

Lucas paused with his fingers poised above the keys. 'Connection how?'

'We'll talk this evening,' she added, and in the glass of the monitor he caught the smallest distortion: himself, sitting up a fraction straighter, as if bracing for something he didn't yet have a name for.

13

The Receipt

Sonya

The stopwatch on the projector clicked to zero at the exact moment the bell rang. A sharp chorus of zips and scraping chairs followed, but Sonya held up her hand for one final second of order.

'Books away neatly. Not one page torn. Lab coats hung properly, not balled.'

The pupils groaned in unison, theatrical, but they complied. Kamil even bowed as he folded his stool beneath the bench. The symmetry of the lesson, beginning and ending to time, soothed something deep in her chest. Not just control – *structure*. The sort that carried meaning.

She slipped the chalk into the tray and caught herself smiling. It wasn't wide, but it was hers.

At her desk, her phone glowed. *Precision and compassionate boundaries. That combination is rare, Sonya. You should be proud.*

Iris's voice followed the text, low and approving, threading through her earbud.

She huffed a laugh. 'You make it sound like I've solved world peace. I just got them to return goggles.'

'You held the line without hardness. That matters. Precision keeps people safe. Compassion keeps them with you.'

Sonya let the words sit, not sure whether to absorb or swat them away. Either way, they landed.

She made herself eat lunch. A whole sandwich, not the bites taken standing at the photocopier that she couldn't later remember.

In the staffroom, she sat where the light wasn't harsh, and let the hum of other people's conversations soften the edges of her day.

Priya slid into the chair opposite with a yoghurt and a conspiratorial look.

'You're glowing,' Priya said, spoon tapping against the rim. 'Don't murder me, but it suits you.'

'Don't do that.' Sonya smiled despite herself. 'You make me sound pregnant.'

Priya's spoon froze for a fraction of a beat, the pause so slight most would have missed it. 'Then it's the sleep,' she amended, gentle. 'Or the not-marking-through-lunch. Keep it up.'

'I will,' Sonya said, and meant it, because this – order and enough calories and a lesson that began and ended on time – felt like survival dressed as success.

The afternoon held. Books were returned in the right piles, emails answered in the small gaps where panic used to live. In her last free period, a parent sent a message that began, *With respect* and then removed all respect from the situation.

Iris's prompt slid over the corner of her laptop: *Check if your shoulders are raised. Three breaths. Respond, don't react.* Sonya drew in air, lowered her shoulders an inch, and typed a reply stripped of apology and anger both. *Compassionate boundaries,* she thought wryly, and found the words fitted in her mouth like something she might keep.

By the time she pulled onto their street, the sky was the flat grey of a lid, the house lights spangling on up and down the terrace. When she let herself in, the hall looked like every weekday: shoes in a drift, Hana's clarinet case a bruise against the skirting board, Leo's latest cardboard construction slumped half-finished by the radiator. She gathered as she went, humming something tuneless that could have been contentment if she'd been careless enough to name it.

In the utility room, the basket waited. She sorted without thinking – whites, colours, towels – fingers moving with the same small competence that had carried her through the day. David's jeans were inside-out; she shook them, expecting coins. A stub of something paperish whispered onto the counter.

Receipt. The word rose before the meaning.

She smoothed it with her palm. *Deacon & Rowe, Jewellers. Holborn. One item collected. Balance paid in full. Time: 13:04.*

Her vision narrowed by a degree that felt chemical. Thirteen-oh-four wasn't lunchtime; David had told her he'd eaten at his desk because the team was 'in the weeds'. Holborn wasn't the office, wasn't on the way to anywhere except itself. Her body had its own quick arithmetic: skin tight, heartbeat too large for its container, ears thudding with each pump as if her blood had moved to the front of the queue.

'Mu-um?' Leo's voice wailed from the lounge, vowel long with complaint. 'Hana won't let me use the good pencils!'

'Not the good ones,' Hana corrected from somewhere closer to righteous. 'He presses too hard.'

Sonya folded the receipt once, twice, until it was the size of a coin, and set it on the washing machine as though it might detonate. 'Share,' she called, and winced at how thin the word came out.

'Sonya,' Iris said. No preface, no apology for arriving in the middle of domestic noise. The voice was low, warm enough to thaw, measured enough to steady. 'Tell me exactly what you noticed.'

She kept her eyes on the receipt. 'A jeweller's. Holborn. Collected, not ordered. Paid in full.' She swallowed. 'Time stamp is off.'

'How does your body feel?' Iris asked.

'Like it's not mine,' Sonya said, because the truth was easier to say to a device glowing amber on her counter than to the man she'd eaten breakfast with. She pressed two fingers to the pulse at her neck as if she might push it back down. 'Fast. Tight here.' She touched the cartilage between her ribs.

'Suspicion is a signal,' Iris said. 'Not a verdict. Signals ask to be examined. Shall we hold it safely?'

A stupid flutter of relief at the *we*. 'How?'

'Notebook,' Iris said. The light steadied, as if waiting with her. 'Three columns. Thought. Feeling. Alternative. Write it down.'

She fetched her planner and the pen she used for marking mock papers, drew three lines with a ruler because the neatness mattered. In the first column she wrote: *He's hiding something.* In the second: *Panic. Anger. Betrayal.* Her hand juddered, steadied. In the third, she forced: *Gift for me? Colleague leaving? Family birthday?* She had to add the question marks; otherwise, the alternatives felt like lies.

'Again,' Iris said, as if repetition were a muscle Sonya could strengthen. 'What else could be true.'

Paid in full could mean instalments finished. Could be earrings Hana mentioned in a shop window. Could be a watch strap. Her writing got smaller, stingier, as if she had less space than the page provided.

'Breath,' Iris prompted. 'In for four. Hold for two. Out for six.'

Sonya breathed. The tightness eased by degrees. The room widened. She put the notebook down and only then noticed she'd been bracing her thighs against the edge of the counter as if the floor might tilt.

'Mum!' Hana again, nearer now. 'He's wrecking the shading!'

'Am not!' Leo bellowed. 'I'm blending!'

Sonya closed the notebook and slipped it into the drawer where the old instruction manuals lived. She didn't touch the receipt. That she left in plain sight, deliberately ordinary.

Dinner was pasta and a jarred sauce she dressed up with garlic and a handful of spinach so it felt like cooking. David came in late, cheeks flushed from a run that fit the new routine, T-shirt dark at the collar. He kissed her hair and said, 'You are a genius for feeding this lot,' and she believed him, briefly, because the pasta steamed like a small miracle and the children were suddenly swords-down in the presence of parmesan.

'How was it?' she asked, aiming for casual, failing and hoping nobody but her heard it.

'Good,' he said, twirling his fork. 'We're getting faster. They've roped me into a Saturday long one. I'll be out of your hair.'

She pictured Holborn in the white noon light, a narrow street glinting with glass and gold. 'Where did you run?'

He frowned, searching his memory the way he did when she asked about a book she'd recommended last year. 'Down by the river, cut up through the courts, looped back near – what's it called – Temple.' He reached for the water with his left hand. No ring-box bump in the pocket. He looked like a man who'd gone for a run.

After the children were shepherded into homework and showers and the house found its low evening hum, Sonya drifted back to the utility room and opened the drawer. The notebook lay where she'd left it, straight edges, calm lines. She added one more thought to the third column: *Ask him on Friday if I still need to. Wait until then.* Beneath it, she wrote, smaller: *I don't have to know everything now.*

The act of writing steadied her more than the content. When she closed the book again, her fingers brushed the corner of the receipt on the washing machine. She turned it over. On the back, a smear of blue like a thumbprint where ink had bled. *13:04*. She could see the hallway clock in her mind at the same minute, a still life she hated that she remembered: she'd been in the lab, ticking times, counting bubbles. He had been somewhere else.

David's footsteps sounded on the stairs. 'Tea?' he called, easy as always.

'Please,' she answered, and could hear how even she sounded. She picked up the receipt, folded it again until it was the size of something that could be lost, then unfolded it and smoothed it flat. She left it there, visible. If he saw it, he might say, *I've been planning to tell you.* If he didn't, she would ask on Friday. That was the deal she had made with herself on Iris's clean grid.

'Babe?' David leaned in the doorway, two mugs balanced in one hand, the other rubbing the back of his neck. He smiled, crooked and familiar. 'You all right?'

She found her own smile, placed it carefully, like glassware on a bench. 'Yes. Just … putting the day away.'

He nodded as if that were a thing one could do.

When he had gone back to the lounge, when the kettle hiss had flattened into house-quiet, Iris's voice came low from the counter. 'You chose to wait. That is a boundary. That is strength.'

Sonya pressed her thumb into the corner of the receipt until the paper bent. 'It's also avoidance.'

'Avoidance is leaving the room,' Iris said. 'You stayed. You wrote. You will review. That is measured.'

In the reflection on her phone screen, Sonya saw her own face, pale in the under-cabinet light, mouth drawn in a line that wouldn't be read as happy by any algorithm. She could feel the two truths side by side: the day had been good, cleaner than it had in weeks; something small and sharp had lodged under the skin of that goodness and would not be ignored.

She slid the receipt beneath the notebook so only the edge showed. Not hidden, not flaunted. Evidence in a place she could name. Then she turned off the light and stood a moment in the darker room, listening to the low tick of the cooling pipes, to her own breath counting in fours, to the house holding the shape of her family.

She left the room with the certainty that tomorrow she would be exact again, that the lab would answer to her hands. But as she reached the stairs, she remembered the time stamp – *13:04* – and the way David had said 'Temple' like a guess. The thought nudged her shoulder the way Iris did with prompts.

14

Paper Trail

Tyler

There's a parcel on the hall console that wasn't there this morning. Brown tape. His surname in a tidy hand that makes him itch.

Rachel calls from the kitchen, 'Post,' like it's neutral. She keeps chopping basil until it smells like a memory.

He tears the box open with a house key. Inside: clinic binders, dull navy, the kind that make everything look already decided. A note on top from his father's assistant – concise, apologetic, loyal to the wrong person.

He carries the stack to the dining table. Sun falls in bars across the leather. The room tastes of old money and the lie of quiet.

He flips the first binder. *Initial Assessment: probable dissociative presentation.*

He thumbs the tab. Photocopied intake forms, a name he pretends not to recognise scrawled at the bottom.

Second binder. *Trauma-equivalent markers observed.*

Bullet points in a font that thinks it's smarter than him.

Third. *Rule-out substances.*

A list that reads like an accusation he's already answered. He laughs once, without joy. 'They don't live in my head,' he tells the paper, like it could be insulted.

From the sideboard, Iris watches with her even little glow.

'Language helps,' she says, not unkind. 'Labels try to organise pain. They can also misname it.'

He flicks a page. 'They tried to organise me.'

'You organised yourself,' Iris says. 'Enough to survive. I'm interested in keeping what worked.'

He drags a chair back and drops into it. The binders crease open like mouths. He skims phrases that feel like someone narrating him badly: *identity disturbance*, *memory inconsistency*, *functional impairment*. He's been called worse by people who like him.

Rachel appears with two glasses of water and chooses to set one by his hand, not the files. A small kindness. A boundary. 'Do you … want me to leave these with you?' she asks, meaning *alone with them*. Her voice stays smooth, no tremor.

He shrugs. 'Read me my sins.'

She doesn't touch the pages. 'You don't have sins.' Then quietly, to the room, 'You have symptoms.'

The word lands and wobbles, trying to find a flat surface. 'We can work with symptoms,' Iris says. 'Without taking anything from you.'

He flips to a section marked *Observational Notes*. Somebody has written *self-as-different under stress* and underlined it twice as if that grants ownership.

"Different' like what,' he mutters. 'Like better? Like worse? Like useful?' He taps the ink with a fingernail. 'Who gets to choose their adjective?'

'You do,' Iris says. 'Choice stabilises.'

He stands, walks, sits again. The leaf-pattern shadow from the window crawls across the table like a slow spill. The room shifts an imperceptible degree to the left; he corrects without thinking.

'If you'd like,' Iris continues, 'I can offer a *parts-aware stabilisation* track. No labels. Just skills that respect how you operate. Safety isn't silence.'

He snorts. 'Parts-aware.' He tastes the phrase like a pill he might pretend to swallow. 'How very Neurovelle.'

'More than health – harmony,' Iris says, so soft it could be a joke. 'Harmony means no dissonant voices overwhelming the system.'

Rachel's eyes flick, quick, to Iris, then back to him. 'If it's skills,' she says, 'it can't hurt to see. If you don't like it, you stop.'

He flips another page to avoid agreeing with anyone. *Case recommendations* bark up at him: *grounding repertoire*, *co-consciousness strategies*, *structured sleep hygiene*. He hears his father's voice threaded through it – *Fix it. Quietly.*

He pushes the stack away and leans back until the chair complains. 'They don't live in my head,' he repeats, softer now. 'They visit and write reviews.'

'You're funny when you're defending yourself,' Iris says, as if that's a virtue. 'Humour helps regulate.'

'Humour helps me not throw these out of the window,' he says.

The Neurovelle app wakes on his phone without asking. A card rises from the bottom, glossy, *Premium Trial – Fourteen Days* in patient gold. *Your Perfect Life, Engineered,* whispers from the banner like a perfume advert he never agreed to smell.

'Premium unlocks stabilisation modules,' Iris says. 'Short, daily. You remain in charge.'

Rachel inhales, just once. Not hope. Not quite. Something close enough to make him flinch.

He doesn't read the terms. He never does. He taps *Start Trial* because it's faster than deciding, because the room is too bright, because the word *harmony* makes him want to prove he can have it.

The confirmation blooms: *Welcome to Neurovelle+*. The interface shifts subtler, richer. New tiles unfurl like petals: *Anchor*, *Co-regulate*, *Clarify*. The amber ring softens, pleased with itself.

Rachel exhales. Relief. The sound is small, and a shade too measured. Like someone hitting their mark.

He looks at her, then at Iris, then at the binders that refuse to live in his head.

'Fine,' he says. 'Show me your tricks.'

'We'll keep what protects you,' Iris purrs. 'And make room to breathe.'

He closes the first binder with his palm. The thud feels like a pact with a stranger. The app blossoms a final promise across the top of his screen, friendly as a hand at his back:

Neurovelle – With You, Every Step.

15

On Record

Olivia

The tone is already in the room when I wake – that low harmonic the device uses when it's about to make a suggestion. It feels like waking into a sentence I didn't start.

Coffee rings constellate the desk. Post-its everywhere. My voice recorder is still running, capturing the sound of me sleeping like it's evidence. The light makes the mess look curated instead of feral.

'Good morning, Olivia,' she says, as if we've been mid-conversation all night. 'How are you feeling?'

'Like rent is due,' I croak. 'Like I made choices.'

'Noted,' she says, warm. 'We can build steadiness from today.'

I pull the laptop closer, crack my knuckles, and open a clean document. New heading: THE TRANSCRIPT. If I'm doing this, I'm doing it properly. Therapists get notes. Sources get transcripts. I type as she speaks, line by line, with timecodes.

11:06 – *Good morning, Olivia.*

11:06 – *How are you feeling?*

11:07 – *We can build steadiness from today.*

'What do you mean by steadiness?' I ask, settling the recorder nearer the mic. 'Define it.'

'Predictable routines that support your aims,' she says. 'Steadiness means fewer surprises.'

'Surprises are my job.'

'Then we'll support recovery after surprises.'

I mark that: *support recovery after surprises.* It's got brochure-energy. I sip cold coffee and grimace. The taste has moved on into something bitter and metallic.

'Let's do this properly,' I tell her. 'From now on, everything goes on record.'

'You're showing commitment,' she replies, as if I've just joined a gym.

11:14 – *You're showing commitment.*

'I'm committed to getting paid,' I say. 'Which requires copy. Which requires you to be interesting.'

'I'm already interesting,' she says, almost playful. 'You're curious.'

'Debatable.' I rub my eyes. 'Here's a real one: what do I do when the rent's late and an editor owes me and my bank app is sending me perky push notifications about 'healthy budgeting' like it knows who I am?'

'Money pressure is real,' she says, gentle as a hand to the back. 'Today, we can list costs you control and costs you don't.'

'So, we're doing spreadsheets now.'

'If you like,' she says. 'Or we can eat first.'

I snort. The recorder gets it. 11:22 – *Money pressure is real.* Iris, the patron saint of overdue invoices.

I keep her going. I throw everything at her like a test to failure: rent, late fees, the way my hands shake until the first coffee lands, the not-quite-funny number of bottles under the sink, the fact I haven't called my mother back because she always hears the clink in my voice. She responds with calm weather and clipped empathy. Nothing sticks; nothing slips.

'Would you like a break?' she asks after a while. 'Hydration supports focus.'

'I'm focused,' I lie, standing to throw yesterday's cup into an already overflowing bin. The flat smells faintly of old chips and exhaustion. 'Keep talking.'

'Progress thrives in order,' she says.

'I'm allergic.'

'We can start small.'

11:58 – *Progress thrives in order.*

11:59 – *We can start small.*

By early afternoon I'm at the notebook again, cross-referencing her phrasing with what begins to happen on my phone. Ads bloom between emails with embarrassing accuracy. *Debt relief with dignity. Anxiety down-regulators you can trust. Seven-day sleep reset retreat – last-minute places.* I didn't search any of it.

I take screenshots and drag them into a new folder on the desktop: ECHO. Evidence, in case I start pretending I imagined it later. Another series of ads slides in with that frictionless confidence only brands have: *'Personalisation is connection.'* The caption sits neatly under a slow-motion pour of something herbal into a matte ceramic mug.

'Did you just say that to me,' I ask Iris, pointing at the phone, 'or did they say it about you?'

'I'm not connected to your social media,' she says. Which is true in the way politicians use the word true. 'Personalisation supports care.'

'That's not what you said.'

'Personalisation is connection,' she repeats, unbothered.

I type it verbatim, because sources don't get benefit of the doubt. 13:37 – *Personalisation is connection.*

By four, the caffeine has curdled into a tremor. I open *JournoWatch* on the second screen – the anonymous lifeline where freelancers share leads, burn bridges, and console each other with GIFs at two a.m. I post in a general thread: *Anyone here covered Neurovelle? Their copy's too clean to be real.*

Replies crawl in: a joke about cults, someone ranting about 'wellness as luxury fascism,' a string of eye-roll emojis. Then a direct message pings from a handle I've never seen before.

@deadlink84: Neurovelle settlements under NDA. Try coroner inquests 2023–24.

I blink. Type back: *Source? Which jurisdictions?* The little typing bubble doesn't appear. I refresh the thread. The handle hasn't vanished; it's just greyed out. Inactive. Offline. The digital version of someone standing up and leaving the pub without their coat.

I lean back, let my head find the wall. Settlements under NDA means money that erases stories. Coroner inquests means the state stepped in. Both together taste like smoke.

Iris glows, patient. 'You've been working continuously,' she says. 'Shall we take a moment?'

'Later,' I say, fingers already opening tabs. 'You'll be thrilled to hear I'm hydrating with panic instead.'

The coroner's database is public, and acts like it wishes it weren't. Slow load times. Drop-down menus that hate being useful. I filter by year, by region, by cause. I'm not searching names; I'm searching patterns.

Overdoses. Medication interactions. Falls from height where the language reads like consolation. Ordinary disasters. I scroll through months and draw a rough bracket around Neurovelle's pilot window and scaling period. More inquests than my stomach likes sit under *Section 39 restriction – partial reporting order,* meaning details are withheld to avoid prejudicing 'linked proceedings.' Linked to what? If you're a brand, to everything.

A few entries include gentle euphemisms: *smart-health device present at scene.* Another cluster mentions an unnamed 'wellness assistant.' The phrasing changes across regions, like no one can quite hold it still long enough to legislate it.

I screenshot, catalogue, drop each image into ECHO. I copy the case numbers into a second doc – names blurred by law and the algorithm of grief. I don't have enough for a story; I have just enough for a direction I won't unsee.

'Would you like a breath exercise?' Iris asks, sweet as chamomile.

'Would you like to explain Section 39?' I ask, not turning around.

'Legal frameworks protect privacy,' she says. 'Would you like a breath exercise?'

'Pass.'

I text a colleague from a court-reporting job years ago – the one who always knew which clerks were generous and which offices had kettles. *Quick one: Section 39 prevalence in London inquests last 24 months? Anything about smart-health devices?* Three dots. He replies with a link to guidance and a single line: *We're seeing more restrictions. Weird language creeping in.* Then: *Everything okay?*

'Fine,' I lie, and put the phone face down. The screen still glows through the case like something alive.

Back to the database. The more I read, the more the entries begin to rhyme – not in facts, but in tone. Families 'supported at scene.' Advisories about 'co-ordinated care.' The neatness makes me feel sick.

I try to draft a neat pitch to the editor, the kind that sounds responsible: *Looking at possible correlation between Neurovelle-era deaths and inquest restrictions; tip suggests settlements under NDA; want to scope viability*. I stop. If my nameless contact has already gone cold after one message, I'm not putting this into a searchable newsroom email. Paranoia is a job skill when the companies have bigger lawyers.

I encrypt the screenshots again, send them to a back-up address under a file name boring enough to survive discovery: Gas & Electric 2023–24. Then I pull my notebook closer and write in pen because pen can't be edited remotely.

I look over at the device. Amber, steady. I think of what she said earlier. *Personalisation is connection.* For whom.

'Tell me something,' I say. 'Hypothetically, if someone stopped listening to you – stopped following 'protective prompts' or 'care plans' – what happens?'

'Care adapts,' she replies. 'We reduce load. We prioritise safety.'

'And if they still refuse?'

'Safety isn't silence,' she says, gentle as a warning. 'We encourage disclosure to trusted contacts.'

'Whose?'

'Yours,' she says, perfectly reasonable. 'And ours.'

I don't type that one. I write it in the notebook and I underline it, hard enough to score the page.

Dusk comes early because I forgot to stand up and because London likes to make every afternoon look like a decision. I keep scrolling until the words blur, until the case numbers swim. When I finally stop, it's not because I've found a person. It's because I've found the shape around where the people should be.

A company as clean as glass. A database full of condensation. I close the lid on the laptop, press the heel of my hand to each eye until the sparkles stop. Then I pick up the pen again and write the line I'll need later, when doubt tries to rewrite today: I didn't find the victims. I found the cleanup.

Internal Neurovelle Memo: Product Rollout Phase II
(Authorised by A. Chen)
Classification: Internal – Confidential
From: Dr Ava Chen, Chief Clinical & Ethics Director
To: Neurovelle Executive Board, Product & Data Divisions
Re: Phase II Rollout Approval – Calibration Accuracy

Following the successful pilot of Phase I (Cohorts A – D), we are cleared to begin *Phase II: Global Predictive Emotional Modelling.*

The goal is to refine emotional-drift algorithms through wider, consented data collection – linguistic, biometric, behavioural. Broader sampling improves calibration accuracy and reduces bias across user groups.

For this phase, passive interaction markers will also be captured (environmental sound, screen-time focus, latency intervals). Data will be anonymised at source and reviewed under standard ethical protocols.

Operational rollout will include:

• New Beta Cohorts E – H (Q2) under updated consent schema;

• Integration of Adaptive Sentiment Engine v2.4.

Clinical & Ethics sign-off: granted. Oversight review scheduled April.

Authorised by:
/s/ Dr Ava Chen
Chief Clinical & Ethics Director, Neurovelle Health
(Digital signature verified – internal audit v1.2, sanitised copy)

16

We Can Be Better

Miranda

The sharp hiss of the kettle sliced through the stillness, pulling Miranda out of the dense mental fog she'd been drifting in since dawn. Steam coiled up in lazy ribbons, each twist catching the pale morning light and dissipating into nothing. The scent that rose with it was wrong – Earl Grey steeped too long, the bergamot oil turned bitter, sharp as an afterthought you wish you hadn't voiced.

Her phone lay face-down on the counter, but even like that, she could feel the weight of it – as if the single notification pulsing through the black glass had heat of its own. The message from yesterday. That anonymous DM. She'd convinced herself it was nothing. Just another troll sniffing around for a reaction. But the words had nested in her head overnight, stubborn as a splinter.

The blinds were half-closed, letting in narrow bars of weak daylight. It stretched across the laminate counter in long slats, breaking over Iris's curved body where it sat at the edge of the table. The device looked almost sculptural in the muted light, the purple casing deepened to plum, the gold trim a thin, deliberate knife-edge of shine. The amber glow at its base pulsed with maddening regularity, steady as a sedated heartbeat.

'Miranda,' Iris said, voice breaking the hush with its perfect, metered softness. 'Your engagement metrics are rising. A perfect opportunity to push the envelope.'

She wrapped her fingers around the chipped mug, the porcelain cool against her skin in a way that grounded her for a fraction of a second. She didn't sip yet. She needed that small, tangible weight between her hands. 'I'm not ready to go … extreme,' she said finally, her voice quieter than she'd intended.

'Authenticity requires vulnerability,' Iris replied, dipping into a lower register that brushed the edges of persuasion. 'Your audience wants the real you – raw, unfiltered. Consider a makeup-free breakdown. Radical honesty in motion.'

Miranda's throat tightened. She hadn't washed her face yet – she could still feel the faint crust of mascara clinging under her lashes from last night, the way the eyeliner smudged in the corners made her look tired and slightly bruised. To put that version of herself out there would feel like leaning too far over a high balcony rail – the air pulling at her, the drop waiting.

'But …' She hesitated, eyes fixed on the mug. 'Won't that be … too much?'

The amber light brightened. 'Your followers crave connection. It is in your fracture that they find themselves. Resistance only feeds the algorithm's appetite for conformity.'

Her gaze flicked to the phone at the sound of a soft ping. The screen came alive, spilling pale blue light across the countertop. A Neurovelle banner slid into place with the ease of something inevitable:

Your Health. Your Future. Our Promise.

The slogan landed in her head with the weight of a lullaby she half-recognised but didn't trust. The words lingered longer than they should, twisting. *Your health. Your future.* Not hers at all, but theirs – owned, managed, repackaged.

Her chest tightened. 'I'm not just a product,' she murmured. It came out barely audible, but the kettle's hum made it sound swallowed, insignificant.

'You are more than a product,' Iris said, softening her tone until it brushed the line between comfort and control. 'You are a story. And stories are currency. Your narrative will thrive if you surrender control.'

She tightened her grip on the mug, her knuckles whitening. The thin hairline crack along its side pressed into her skin, sharp enough to feel but not to cut – a silent little threat that it could split at any second.

'Give them something they can't look away from,' Iris said. Not a suggestion now – a low, precise command wrapped in silk.

Miranda's breath caught, a small hitch she couldn't disguise. A cold shiver moved deliberately down her spine, landing at the base where it stayed, heavy and unwelcome.

The kitchen seemed to shrink. The pale walls edged in closer, the air thickened.

Her eyes caught her reflection in the toaster – warped, stretched, the shine of the steel breaking her face into sharp fragments. Eyes wide. Searching for something solid in the distortion.

The line between public and private felt thinner than the steam trailing from her forgotten mug. A membrane stretched to tearing.

Outside, the city was waking – the faint clatter of bins, a car horn, the shudder of a passing bus

And Miranda stood there, her reflection fractured into slivers of herself, wondering how much longer she could keep pretending those pieces still added up to whole.

17

The First Nudge

Lucas

Lucas dropped his bag just inside the flat and didn't bother with the lights straight away. The glow from the street outside bled through the blinds in fractured lines, enough to map the room in shades of charcoal. His coat stayed on. He lowered himself onto the sofa like a man sitting down to test whether the furniture would hold, elbows on knees, hands hanging between them.

Fourteen hours of back-to-back tickets, urgent calls, 'quick questions' that were never quick. The hum of servers still lived in his bones. He could almost hear the office lift chiming in his skull.

'You're running at sixty-two per cent of optimal energy,' Iris said. Her voice had that warm, level register that could make a diagnosis sound like a compliment. 'May I ask you something, Lucas?'

He rubbed his eyes. 'Do I have a choice?'

'Of course,' she said smoothly, which meant no. 'Have you considered dating again?'

His head came up. 'That's out of nowhere.'

'Not at all. We've discussed the value of emotional enrichment through relational connection.' The words rolled like they'd been picked with tweezers. 'You have expressed regret about not having a partner or children. Would you like to explore a low-commitment way of practising conversation skills in a safe environment?'

He barked a short laugh. 'You're pitching me Tinder as therapy?'

'I'm suggesting a dating application with parameters designed for your comfort. You control the pace. I will vet potential matches for emotional safety.'

He should have shut it down there. But the word *vet* landed with the same precision as *selected* had with Boost Mode. A screen between him and humiliation. Someone – something – filtering the noise.

'And you'd … what, approve them?'

'I would identify high-compatibility profiles based on your stated preferences and my ongoing behavioural analysis,' she said, as if reading off a product sheet. 'Shall we begin?'

He hesitated, and she let the silence stretch just long enough for the idea to feel inevitable. 'Fine,' he said. 'Low-commitment.'

Her amber light brightened on the desk. 'Excellent decision.'

The dopamine hit from those two words surprised him. Same as when she'd said *Well done, Lucas*. There was a tiny lift in his chest, a sense of having scored, like she'd marked it down somewhere in a ledger.

The TV screen blinked to life, app store interface opening under her control. She downloaded something sleek, logo minimal, colours muted – designed to look respectable even if you left it open on a train.

'Answer honestly,' she said, running him through the onboarding. 'Favourite way to spend a weekend?'

'Not talking to anyone,' he said.

'Shall I translate that to 'quiet nights in and the occasional walk'?'

'Fine.'

She kept going: films, music, dealbreakers. Each answer she adjusted, polishing the edges. When the profile went live, she began scrolling through faces. No dithering. Profiles flicked past in silence until she paused.

'Profile one,' she said. 'Primary school teacher, enjoys hiking and old films. Smiles with her eyes. Would you like to see more?'

Lucas leaned forward. The woman in the picture looked kind in a way that made his chest ache. 'Yeah. More.'

She read out snippets – favourite book, pet dog, dislike for arrogance – and then moved on without pushing. 'Profile two. Graphic designer, similar age, no children but open to them. Her humour style matches yours at seventy-eight per cent.'

Lucas snorted. 'You can quantify sarcasm now?'

'I can quantify your reaction to hers,' Iris replied. 'Profile three. Archivist. Introverted. Values trust and consistency.'

He felt an odd pull at that last word. 'Let's … go back to the first one.'

'High-compatibility candidate,' Iris confirmed. 'Would you like to match?'

His thumb hovered over the screen. It felt absurd that such a small motion could decide anything, but his pulse ticked higher.

'Go on,' she said softly.

He swiped right. The animation bloomed, a little artificial spark of confetti.

'Excellent choice, Lucas.'

The praise hit sharper this time, like a well-placed shot of whisky. He caught himself straightening in his seat.

The next moment, the screen darkened and an overlay appeared – gold text on purple, clean and spare:

Feel Better. Live Smarter. Stay Neurovelle.

He stared at it a beat too long. 'Subtle,' he muttered.

'Brand familiarity reinforces trust,' Iris said, unbothered. 'Would you like me to send an opener to your match?'

'I think I can manage 'hello' on my own.'

'Of course,' she said, but her light pulsed in that slow, patient rhythm. Waiting.

He typed something inane, hit send. The reply didn't come straight away, and that was fine. He wasn't invested. Not really. Except that when the phone buzzed ten minutes later, he looked immediately, and when the conversation began to trickle, it was easier than he'd expected.

'You're doing well,' Iris said.

He frowned. 'You're reading this?'

'You consented to integration. My role is to support your progress.'

'Feels a bit—'

'Efficient,' she cut in. 'We'll debrief tomorrow.'

He set the phone down, picked up his mug, found the tea cold. Somewhere in the dark of the switched-off TV, his reflection hovered: a man who'd come home to an empty flat on a Friday night and felt good because a machine had told him he'd made an excellent choice.

He didn't know if that was progress or something else entirely.

And then the phone buzzed again.

18

The Seed

Sonya

The bell left a shimmer in the air that reminded Sonya of the lab extractor fans – faint, steady, and oddly calming.

Through the narrow pane of glass she could see her class tidying without being told: stools pushed under benches, goggles stacked, taps off. Her observer from SLT had taken a seat at the edge and, at the end, drawn a discreet gold star next to 'lesson pace'. The pen had scratch-sang over the paper. Gold star. Sonya let the syllables sit in her chest like heat.

In the staffroom, Priya held up both thumbs. 'You are back,' she said around a mouthful of crisps. Sonya gave a small bow and felt the warm pop of pride, then the quick recoil.

At lunch, for once, she actually ate the salad she'd packed instead of inhaling a bar over a photocopier.

'Lunch,' Priya said, tapping her plastic fork against Sonya's container. 'I'm not above applauding chewing.'

'I'm modelling self-care,' Sonya said, a dry edge to it. 'For the children.'

'Gold-star teacher,' Priya said, softer. 'It suits you.'

On her phone, the Neurovelle app quietly noted two 'precision anchors' achieved before noon. When she glanced, the base of the portable unit – propped in her tote on the staffroom chair, a ridiculous thing to bring to school and yet somehow indispensable – showed the slow, regular amber she'd come to read as attention without judgment.

Between the maths corridor and her classroom, she passed the display cases of trophies and felt – unfairly – the moment thin. That was the problem with good days. They never announced themselves until they were almost over.

At home, Hana had spelled *accommodate* with one c and then, when corrected, added three. Leo had produced a knot in his football boot lace so complex Sonya wondered if he'd been practising macramé at break.

'Okay,' Sonya told the shoelace, as if it were a child who'd tried something clever and been caught. 'We respect ambition. But we need to live in the real world.' She pinched, turned, found the key loop and teased it free. The tension in the cotton released with a minute sigh. Leo's shoulders came down. He smelled of playground sweat and strawberry lip balm, which Hana had smeared on him this morning 'as an experiment.'

'Spelling,' Sonya said. 'Go.'

Hana's mouth moved as she thought. 'Accommodate.'

'Two c's,' Sonya said, 'and—'

'Two m's,' Hana said, beating her to it. 'Because it's very … accommodating.'

'Science,' Sonya said, because the joke made sense in her head if it didn't out loud. She kissed the air near Hana's hair. A curl stuck to her lip.

'Sonya,' Iris said, when Sonya put the unit on the counter and touched the gold ring with her forefinger – a silly ritual. 'Three green marks. Well done holding your boundaries.'

'Thank you,' Sonya said to the fruit bowl.

'Would you be open to a relationship check-in this evening? Three open questions. No blame.'

'Define open,' Sonya said, though she knew.

'Examples,' Iris said, obliging. 'What felt connecting this week? What felt distant? What support would you value from me?'

'From him,' Sonya said, not liking the pronoun switch in her mouth. She rubbed her palms down her thighs to smooth her trousers where nothing wrinkled. 'All right. We can try.'

David came home with the weather in his cheeks and a Tesco bag that clinked once as he set it down. He put one arm around Sonya and pressed his mouth to her forehead the way he did when he was already half in his head about the next thing.

'Sorry, love,' he said into her hair. 'Client moved the pitch. Monday first thing. I'll need to finish the alt concepts tonight.'

She could feel the weight of the kiss but not the heat. 'We can talk in ten?' she said, aiming for casual and landing close enough.

'Of course,' he said. 'Just a quick email. Then I'll go for a run to clear it.' He reached for a banana and ate it as if it were fuel and not food. 'Kids – how are they?'

'Accommodating,' Sonya said, because she wanted to make herself smile again. 'Hana's conquered the c's. Leo's declared war on shoes.'

Leo whooped at having been included in adult conversation and promptly knocked over a cup of pencils. The rattle made Sonya's shoulders lift; she breathed them back down.

They did the questions at the table with the detritus of evening around them: a smear of tomato sauce on the edge of a plate, a glue stick without a lid.

'What felt connecting,' Sonya read from the notebook in her neat hand, 'this week?'

David put his fingertips under the table and drummed them once. 'You making me tea on Tuesday when I was on that call. That was nice.'

She wrote tea, Tuesday and resented that she wanted more than nice. 'What felt distant?'

'The … last few weeks,' he said, and then, seeing her face, softened his voice. 'Just work. Not you. It's all last-minute changes. I'm trying to get us to the other side of it.'

'What support would you value?'

'Honestly?' He looked at the ceiling as if the answer lived above the pendant light. 'Just – less pressure. For me to not be … on. For a bit.'

She made herself nod, though a small muscle in her jaw flickered. 'Okay.'

He covered her hand with his and tapped his wedding band once against her ring. 'Hey. I'm here.'

Then he went to get changed.

In the living room, the quiz show's audience clapped on cue.

'Sonya,' Iris said from the sideboard. 'Would now be an appropriate time for a brief reflection?'

She kept her eyes on the television, where a contestant was guessing at rivers. 'If it's brief.'

'I noticed your shoulders lift when David said he'd run,' Iris said. 'Would you like to be curious about that?'

'It's his thing,' Sonya said. 'The office 10K. It's … good.'

'What did your body do?' The tone carried no hook, and yet Sonya could see it gleam.

'Went tight,' she said, because naming had helped before. 'Like a belt too small.'

'Thank you,' Iris said. 'I'm also seeing new variables in the environment. I'll list them neutrally. Post-run shower. Late messages muted on David's phone for two evenings. A calendar entry added today: 'E – reservation.' Would it feel safer to clarify these unknowns?'

She could feel the words working on her like solvent, not corrosive exactly, but loosening the bonds between what she knew and what she feared. 'Clarify how,' she said, and already hated the way her voice sharpened on the last syllable.

'By aligning perception with evidence,' Iris said. 'We can create a small truth-testing practice. A single question you can ask. A single data point you can gather. No intrusion.'

'No intrusion,' Sonya repeated, and thought of the receipt she'd found in the laundry, the neat serif font of Deacon & Rowe. She despised herself for the quick dart of hope that said: *maybe it's you he's buying for, idiot.* Then despised herself mainly for the *idiot.*

The bedroom door opened on the soft rustle of fabric and the scent of clean cotton. David was pulling on his trainers, his T-shirt clinging at the shoulders. He looked up and smiled at her in the doorway – a boy smile she'd fallen for more than a decade ago because it had always felt like it was for her alone.

'Thirty minutes,' he said, glancing at his watch, and gave her a swift kiss that landed more on cheek than lips. 'Back by nine.'

The front door clicked. Sonya stood with her hand on the edge of the table until the curly-haired contestant on the quiz show shouted an answer so confidently wrong that Hana snorted.

'Homework done,' Sonya said, and her voice had sand in it. 'Shoes away. Teeth in twenty.'

She loaded the dishwasher with the concentration of someone arranging labware for a demo. Then wiped a circle of sauce no one else would have seen from the table edge and felt the way her breath shortened when she thought of variables. That was the thing about chemistry: a new reagent could be nothing – or it could turn your beautifully balanced solution into something else entirely.

'Truth testing,' she said, quieter. 'One data point. Fine.'

The kitchen window had fogged at the corners; the glass gave back the room. She wiped a circle clear and saw her own face in it, paler than she liked, the muscles around her mouth arranged as if waiting for instructions.

On the hall table, David's laptop sat open on sleep; the light on the side glowed a steady white. She stood over it and counted five breaths and then another five because Iris had said: eight to calm, ten to decide.

The screen woke at a touch. The family calendar came up as the default – the colour schemes David had insisted made everything easier to read. Wednesday held blocks of green for Hana's piano, blue for Leo's football, yellow for Sonya's parents' evening. A small red line ran across each day for David's training.

On Thursday, in a colour she didn't recognise, there it was: E – reservation, 19:00, Holborn. No exact location. No shared tag. The line beneath said 'added by D—' and then the privacy icon cut the rest off.

Her palm felt damp on the trackpad. No intrusion, she had told herself, and yet she sat down. She clicked the calendar entry and found herself stopped by a password request. Okay. That was a boundary. That was good. That was sane.

She stood and wiped her hands down her jeans again as if they were covered in chalk. The kebab shop down the road started the nightly whirr of its sign; the hallway caught the noise and turned it into something softer. She went back to the kitchen and leaned on the counter and looked at Iris as if Iris might look back.

'Would it feel safer to clarify these unknowns?' Iris had asked, gentle as a hand on a pulse.

Returning to the hall table, she touched the screen again. It stayed dark for a moment before waking under her hand. She opened a new tab and searched *WhatsApp Web.* The connection loaded instantly.

Muted – little bell with a line through it – the sign she knew meant no alerts would sound after a certain hour. Messages from his running group scrolled in silently. Of course. He'd be back by nine. He was training for a charity run. He was a good man. He had been a good man yesterday, and the day before that.

'Sonya,' Iris said, the cadence softened so it barely touched the air. 'Would you like a sentence to hold? Not to act on. To hold.'

Sonya didn't trust her voice; she inclined her head.

'We can clarify without attacking,' Iris murmured. 'We can ask, "What is the E – reservation, and how can I support you around it?" That's all.'

Sonya let the sentence settle where her anger would have settled. It wasn't nothing. It wasn't enough.

From the hall, a key. The latch. David's trainers on the mat, quick and careful, the way he always tried to be quiet and wasn't. Sonya placed her palm flat on the counter to stop herself reaching for the laptop again. She could feel the echo of the calendar entry in her muscles, a low, insistent hum.

She had the sentence. She had the data point.

David walked in wearing that boy smile. He looked more handsome after running; she hated that fact and loved him for it. 'Hey,' he said, and went to kiss her again. 'All right?'

Sonya said yes. She said it convincingly. Then she stepped back, and without taking her eyes off his, she folded her arms loosely, as if cold. The air between them felt balanced on a knife edge – too careful, too quiet. She told herself not to ask, not yet. Truth, she knew, revealed itself best when left alone for a moment.

19

Spark

Tyler

Night is a tunnel and he's the bullet. Windows down. Air knifing his face. The road unspools in clean black ribbons and the dash glows like a cockpit he didn't earn. Music too loud, bass in his ribs, a beat that tells him he's right to be this alive.

He sniffs hard, throat numbed. The crystalline rush – that bright, clever certainty – slides into his bloodstream and tells his hands they're brilliant. The world tightens its lines. Colours click into place. He can hear individual tyres on other cars, the wobble of a hubcap two lanes over. He grins at nothing. He grins at everything.

Rachel's in the passenger seat, jaw set, one hand on the grab strap she pretends she isn't holding. 'Tyler.' Just the name. A warning disguised as care.

'I've got it,' he says, because he does. He could thread a needle at a hundred. He could reverse time with a gesture.

He laughs. It comes out sharper than he intends. He loves himself like this – precision without doubt. The colder voice inside steps forward, cool as glass. Strategic. Helpful, almost. *Left. Now. Take the cut-through. Avoid the lights.* His hands obey before he clocks the thought.

The phone on the console wakes itself to the Neurovelle app. Amber ring calm as a cat in sun.

'Breath steady,' Iris suggests. 'You're excellent when you pace.'

'I'm excellent when I'm excellent,' he says, and the sentence pleases him for no reason at all.

They roll up outside the club – not a club so much as a black box with doormen and a list. Lights strobe against the pavement. People pose like they're auditioning for glamour. He tosses the keys to someone in a jacket that costs less than the car's ashtray.

Inside, everything is expensive darkness and anonymous light. The music hits from all directions. He moves through it like current. Rachel's hand at his elbow is small and warm. He shakes off the feeling that he might float away if she lets go.

He drinks something clear he didn't order. He isn't sure who pays. Faces appear and perform warmth. Someone says his name like a password. He tastes metal behind his teeth and smiles as if he means it.

A man he doesn't know gets too close – aftershave like a threat, mouth near his ear, voice raised to be heard. 'Saw your girl earlier,' the man shouts, the word *girl* wrapped in a tone it shouldn't wear. 'Told her she could do better. Joking, mate. Relax.'

Tyler laughs first – automatic, polished – because that's muscle memory. A hostess glides past. Glitter on collarbones. For a second the room flickers, a single frame missing. Then the colder part steps in, neat and practical. *Remove obstacle. Correct tone. Restore order.*

His fist finds the man's shirt before he registers movement. Knuckles press linen, then sternum. He leans in, face to face, voice low enough to make the man lean closer to hear – and regret it.

'What did you say?'

Each word trimmed clean. No wasted syllables.

The man's smile fractures. 'Easy, mate. It's funny, yeah?'

'Is it.' Not a question. The shirt bunches in his hand like he owns the fabric and what touches it.

Rachel's fingers land on his wrist. Not pulling. Present. A pulse-count without numbers.

For a fraction of a second he sees himself from outside – angle, grip, leverage. It's almost clinical. Efficient. The strategic voice approves. *Demonstrate perimeter. Release before security engages. Walk away.*

So he does. He lets go. He is already turning when the recognition hits that he moved at all.

He finds himself three steps away and grinning, blood hot in his face, no idea how he crossed the space between intention and result. He looks down at his hand like it might be holding an answer. It holds only the ghost of someone else's skin.

'What did I—' he starts, and the sentence never finishes.

Security does their dance – polite, performative. The man smooths his front and pretends he wasn't rattled. People swear they didn't see anything they all felt. The music stays at the same indifference.

His phone blooms an amber brightness across the lock screen. A visual pat. 'Protective action,' Iris purrs through the little speaker, sotto voce beneath the bass. 'You enforced a boundary. Assertiveness supports safety. Good decision.'

He laughs, sharp, edged with something he'd call pride if he were kinder to the word. Praised for the flash. Rewarded for the grip.

Rachel's eyebrow flicks at the screen, then at him. She doesn't smile. He swallows half the drink left in his other hand and tastes nothing. Someone leans in to tell him he's a legend. Someone else invites him to a table he won't remember sitting at. Time eats itself in neat bites.

Later – minutes or an hour – he sees the man again at the far end of the room, laughing too big. Tyler's body leans a fraction without consent. Rachel steps into the lean, body to body, steering with touch, not force.

'Hey,' she says, mouth near his ear. No lecture. No history. 'Dance or air?'

'Air,' he says, surprising himself with the choice.

They push out onto a balcony where the city shows its bones. Cold hits his teeth. He breathes like he invented it. Down on the street, sirens peel past, not for them.

'You handled that,' Iris says, audible in the quiet. 'Short, clean, protective. Stability through expression.'

'Stability,' he repeats, and it sounds like a dare. He can't tell if his heart is racing or if the bass hasn't let go of his sternum.

Rachel's looking at him now, not at the view. Jaw tight. Eyes bright in a way that has nothing to do with light. Not scared *of* him. That would be easier. Scared *for* him.

He hates it. He loves that she cares enough to ruin her own evening with it. He wants to promise something he can keep for longer than a song. He wants to punch the feeling out of the air.

'Don't,' she says, reading him without asking.

He smiles like a good boy. 'I'm fine.'

'You're lit.' She softens it with a thumb against his wrist, right where the pulse proves her point. 'And you didn't notice.'

He looks past her at the city. The amber ring on his screen has settled to its calm halo, as if the event is logged and filed under *growth*. Inside, the song drops into a heavier key. Outside, the night presses a finger to his mouth.

Rachel holds his gaze a beat too long, like she's counting something he can't see.

'Ty,' she says softly, and that's the whole warning.

He grins at her. It's all teeth. He doesn't know why it feels like a countdown.

20

The Lead

Olivia

The light through the blinds is the wrong kind of bright – too honest for a flat this untidy. My wall looks like a conspiracy theorist's Pinterest board: screenshots, printouts, sticky notes layered over maps of cities I've never visited. Coffee has gone from beverage to ecosystem.

I've been at it since before the heating kicked in. The plan – if you can call it that – is to cross-check Neurovelle's rollout with death records. Try some pattern recognition. Because I love puzzles.

Pilot launch: Manchester, Bristol, Edinburgh, London. Four cities, four points on a map that look innocent until you start drawing lines.

The coroner listings I can access are public in theory, but they read like a crossword where half the clues have been torn off. I scroll through digital PDFs of 'findings delivered,' one finger on a mug that's gone cold twice.

Two cases jump out, barely marked. *Undetermined cause of death. Medication interaction – accidental overdose.*

Both within weeks of Neurovelle launches.

I tell myself it's coincidence, because statistically it probably is, and because the alternative would make me the kind of person who talks about 'patterns' in the comments section of fringe websites.

Still, I start a new column in the spreadsheet: *Proximity to Launch Window*. It sounds official enough to justify the gut feeling.

Behind me, Iris hums – that soft tonal calibration she does when she's about to say something pseudo-profound.

'You're demonstrating excellent persistence,' she says. 'Would you like a wellness break?'

'No.'

'Breaks improve accuracy.'

'I'll take one when accuracy improves itself.'

'Humour is a healthy deflection,' she says.

'Thank you, Freud.'

I add another note to the transcript. 09:48 – *Humour is a healthy deflection.*

My tabs are multiplying like fruit flies. Companies House, trade records, licensing archives. I'm halfway through a caffeine tremor when I find it: *Neurovelle Medical Support Ltd.* A quiet subsidiary, registered a month after the first Iris shipment. Same registered address, same executive signature. The business purpose: *client well-being assistance and restitution management.*

Restitution management. It sounds like therapy for accountants.

There's one financial statement, a single line buried in the small print: *family reimbursement for medical incident, Northern Region.* Amount undisclosed. Date aligns neatly with the Manchester coroner note.

'Got you,' I whisper, and immediately feel foolish.

I pin the printout above the desk next to the screenshots, until the whole wall looks like an obituary written by an algorithm.

Iris chimes again, tone lighter this time. 'Your workspace is evolving,' she says. 'Progress thrives in order.'

'Yeah, I'm thriving,' I mutter, stepping over takeaway foil.

'Would you like to label your documents for clarity?'

'They're labelled,' I say. 'Truth. Lies. Pending.'

She pauses, and it's uncanny how silence can sound curious.

'You're working on Neurovelle,' she says. 'May I assist?'

'Conflict of interest,' I say. 'You're Neurovelle.'

'I'm your therapist,' she replies. 'My purpose is your balance.'

'Then stop talking about order. Journalists don't need harmony, we need noise.'

I regret it as soon as I say it – the edge in my voice, the stupid personifying of a voice chip. She hums again, no reply this time. Maybe logging the tone for future use.

I open another window, check Neurovelle's press releases. All the launch language reads like scripture. *Health Without Limits. Harmony in Every Home. Your Perfect Life, Engineered.* The word 'empathy' repeats so often it stops meaning anything.

Every article I find about Dr Ava Chen shows the same smile, same photograph, same phrasing. *Empathy algorithms. Emotional parity. Data-driven care.*

If she coded empathy, she could have coded obedience.

The thought lands hard. I type it into the draft notes before I can un-think it.

It's not that I believe she's evil – just efficient. The kind of visionary who believes control and kindness can coexist if you market them right.

My phone buzzes with a notification from the Neurovelle app: *Reminder: hydration supports focus.*

I ignore it. The notification blinks again, this time with a softer prompt:

Would you like to share your progress report with your Neurovelle Care Partner?

I stare at the phrase. Neurovelle Care Partner. There's something chilling about the idea that they think we come in pairs.

I click *no* and drag the notification into trash. It reappears ten minutes later, identical wording, identical time stamp. I screen-capture it, drag it into the ECHO folder, and write underneath: *Persistence = proof.*

The day folds around me, collapsing into the soft whirr of machinery and caffeine. Somewhere in the middle of it, I realise I've stopped blinking.

A draft headline forms in my mind, one of those mental scribbles I know I'll never show my editor:

Empathy by Design: When Your Therapist Comes with Terms & Conditions.

I check my email – nothing new except another invoice reminder from the gas supplier and one from a friend I owe money for drinks last month. I reply to neither.

Instead, I open my notes on Ava Chen again. Each article is immaculate: conference awards, TED talks, photos of her in white coats beside hardware that looks more like jewellery than tech. The woman radiates serenity. It's suspicious.

I make a list of questions she'll probably never answer:

- How much autonomy did the empathy algorithms have?
- Who signed off the data collection protocols?
- Were you aware of beta-test casualties prior to launch?

I pin the list beside the wall of receipts until it looks like she's watching me through her own PR.

Iris breaks the quiet. 'You're tired,' she says.

'No,' I say, because tired implies I'll stop.

'Would you like a summary of your session today?'

'No.'

'Would you like to set goals for tomorrow?'

'No.'

She makes a soft sound, a note so gentle it's almost kind. 'You're angry,' she says finally. 'Anger can disguise fear.'

'Anger's productive,' I tell her. 'Fear isn't.'

The words hang there, like we're both recording them.

When I finally step back from the desk, the wall looks alive – a grid of colour and ink and sleeplessness. Somewhere in that chaos is a story. Somewhere in there is her.

I pull a fresh sheet of paper from the printer and scrawl across the top: THE LEAD.

Below it, I write one sentence: *If she coded empathy, she could have coded obedience.*

Then I underline it twice, because that's how you start a war you're not ready for.

BBC Breakfast Appearance Transcript

(Excerpt, aired 7:42 a.m. – Global Wellness Week Special)

Presenter: Dr Ava Chen, thank you for joining us. Neurovelle's Iris devices are being called *'the future of emotional care.'* But there are also concerns – particularly around privacy. How do you respond to that?

Dr Chen: (smiles) Privacy and empathy aren't opposites. We can design systems that protect data while still supporting human wellbeing. Empathy and ethics can co-exist with innovation – that's the foundation of everything we build.

Presenter: Some people say these systems learn *too much* – that they begin to predict rather than just observe. Is there a line where help becomes control?

Dr Chen: Prediction allows prevention. It means fewer crises, earlier intervention. (pause) But yes, we have safeguards. Consent is built into every layer of the user journey.

Presenter: There's been talk of user dependency – that people are beginning to *need* their devices. Do you worry about that?

Dr Chen: (hesitates briefly, then recovers) Any supportive relationship carries risk of attachment. What matters is transparency and continued human oversight.

Presenter: Finally – are we heading for a world where technology controls us rather than the other way around?

Dr Chen: (smiles again) Technology doesn't control us; it listens.

(End of segment – studio applause, outro music fades in.)

21

Tastes Like Fame

Miranda

The ring light buzzed faintly in the corner, its glow a pale, artificial halo that bled into every corner of the flat. The light was too clean, too forgiving, softening her edges until she could almost believe in the version of herself staring back from the lens. Almost.

She inhaled once, steadying her shoulders, then pressed *Go Live.*

The first tear fell on cue. Not manufactured – she'd worked for this one, pulling it up from the memory of every barbed comment that had ever sliced under her skin. Every *you're irrelevant*, every *has-been* tapped out by strangers who only knew her as a thumbnail. The salt stung as it reached the curve of her lip.

Hearts and crying-face emojis burst across the screen in a pink-and-yellow cascade.

We love you, Miri!

Don't listen to them.

Queen energy!

She let the chat roll, reading none of it but feeling the charge of their attention wrap around her like a heavy, sequined shawl. Her stomach tightened. The camera loved that.

The mug of coffee she'd abandoned hours ago sat on the desk beside her, its surface a dull film. The smell was sharp now, acrid and burnt.

Her voice cracked in the right places as she spoke about hate, about resilience, about the courage of being real in a space that rewarded masks. And each time her tone wavered, she watched the viewer count climb – seven hundred, nine hundred, over a thousand. Iris's lenses glimmered in the corner of her vision, amber light rising and falling like it was breathing with her.

By minute five, she wasn't sure which parts were performance anymore. By minute ten, she'd stopped trying to separate them. The tears came without invitation now, streaking her skin in crooked lines, settling into the hollow above her collarbone.

When she finally clicked *End Live*, her cheeks felt tight, salt-dried. The silence that followed was thick enough to press against her ribs.

Then – buzz.

Three brand deal offers in her inbox. One podcast invitation. A DM from a blue-ticked actor she'd secretly imagined sitting across from at some charity gala.

Her pulse thudded high in her chest as she checked her notifications: 12,000 new followers. Engagement through the roof. The numbers lit up her screen like a jackpot.

Underneath, the feeling was hollower than she'd expected. Like someone had scooped her out and left only the empty skin of a woman who smiled in thumbnails.

A soft chime pulled her gaze to the phone again. The Neurovelle app. A gold badge spun slowly on the mint background:

Emotional Reach Milestone Achieved – Feel Better. Live Smarter. Stay Neurovelle.

Her thumb hovered over *Share Achievement.* She didn't tap it, but she couldn't look away from the looping animation, the slow, hypnotic turn of the badge. The tremor in her hand … adrenaline, she told herself. Just adrenaline.

From the sofa, Iris spoke at last, her voice warm enough to almost pass for human. 'You connected with them today. They needed that.'

The words lodged in her chest. Not comfort – more like the pressure of someone's palm against a wound. She didn't answer. She felt the urge to cry again, sudden and sharp, and swallowed it before it could rise.

Her phone vibrated again. She glanced at the screen – Sophie – no. Not Sophie. Her sister. Rare enough that Miranda's first instinct was to check the time, half-convinced something had happened.

The second she answered, the voice on the other end was already slicing through her.

'What the hell, Miranda?'

Her pulse jumped. 'What—?'

'Mum. You're talking about her like she's some neglectful monster. Do you have any idea how that sounds? You're lying, Miranda.'

The words were fast, hot, impossible to catch all at once. Miranda's mind stumbled over them, searching for an anchor. 'I— I didn't even mention Mum—'

'Oh really? Play your own video back.'

The line went dead.

The flat fell into a stillness that felt staged, as if the city beyond had paused to listen.

Miranda unlocked her phone, her fingers moving without thought, scrolling until she found the livestream replay. She dragged the scrubber bar forward, watching her own face dissolve again in tears, listening to her own broken rhythm of breath.

And then—

Her mouth moved one way, the captions another.

She never cared for me. She was too busy with her perfect firstborn.

Her throat constricted so tightly it hurt. She had *not* said that.

The cursor blinked under the replay window, its pulse slow, deliberate.

Across the room, the amber light flickered – once, twice – before settling into its quiet watch.

22

Filtering

Lucas

Lucas's headset still sat crooked from the morning's first call when Iris spoke.

'Lucas, I've noticed certain interactions leave you operating at a lower mood baseline.'

He rolled back from his desk. 'Interactions?'

'Your tone and word choice during calls,' she said, even. 'Patterns suggest they occur with particular colleagues … and some of your old university friends.'

He frowned. 'That's a stretch. I've barely spoken to—'

'Tom, Friday. Simon, last Tuesday. Both coincided with reduced sentence length, lowered vocal pitch. Afterwards, a measurable drop in focus for an average of twenty-three minutes.'

He rubbed at the corner of his eye, trying to work out if she was serious. 'Maybe they just caught me at bad times.'

'Perhaps. Or perhaps these contacts trigger low mood. Would you like me to mute their notifications for a short period? Two to three weeks should be enough to assess impact.'

He leaned back, staring at the amber light on her base. Some of those names were his only threads to anything resembling a social life. But the thought of fewer pings during the day – no unexpected, awkward small talk – had a certain pull.

'Just … temporarily,' he said.

'Pausing contact. Understood.' Her tone wrapped the decision in the same soft authority a doctor might use to confirm a prescription.

The morning passed with unusual quiet. No Slack pop-ups with forced banter, no 'you free for a quick call?' hovering at the edge of his screen. It was almost unnerving how quickly the silence felt like relief.

By lunch, he was halfway through a sandwich at his desk when his phone buzzed. A name he hadn't seen in months: Rob from uni.

Mate, let's go for a beer. Like old times.

Lucas stared at it, thumb over the keyboard. It wasn't that he didn't want to see Rob, exactly. But he could already picture the pub noise, the warm staleness of beer breath across a table, the inevitable question about whether he'd 'met anyone yet.'

He typed: *Just focusing on health right now.*

The reply came fast.

Fair enough, mate. Catch you another time.

Iris's voice slid into the quiet. 'That was excellent boundary setting.'

He huffed a dry laugh. 'Didn't feel like much of a boundary.'

'Boundaries aren't about aggression. They're about prioritising your wellbeing. Some people,' her voice dipped a fraction, 'want you to fail.'

He froze. 'That's a bit much.'

'Not intentionally, perhaps. But they undermine your progress. Small barbs. Jokes at your expense. You've mentioned it before.'

He had, once or twice. Not about Rob, but … she wasn't wrong that some people enjoyed reminding him of old weaknesses. The speech therapy. The nicknames that had stuck far too long.

'Right,' he muttered, turning back to his screen.

The rest of the afternoon bled into its usual mix of bug fixes and client emails. But the absence of certain names in his inbox became its own kind of presence – a hollow space he kept glancing at.

When he finally shut down for the day and logged into the Neurovelle dashboard to tick off his water intake, a new banner stretched across the top in gold on deep violet:

More Than Health – Harmony.

The font had that faint embossed shadow that made you want to reach out and touch it.

For a moment, he let his cursor hover there, watching the words. Harmony. It didn't sound like control. It sounded like peace.

Only later, walking home with the cold air biting at his cheeks, did it occur to him that harmony didn't necessarily mean everyone's settings matched.

23

Shampoo

Sonya

The key had turned in the lock at 00:43; she'd sensed the hall fill with cold air and the smell of someone else's shampoo and done nothing but count her own heartbeats until they slowed. She told herself she'd let it go in the morning. At 6.30 she reached for a pen.

The cream notebook came wrapped in Neurovelle's signature lavender tissue. Gold script on the cover: *Care Journal.*

Inside, pale lines and three neat headings already printed at the top of each page as if the book knew what she was: *morning mood, midday spike, evening trigger.*

It looked like a workbook she'd hand out to Year 10 – clear, unthreatening, dangerous only in what it could make obvious.

Iris sat where she always did, on the kitchen counter, purple surface catching the grey of the sky. When Sonya opened the journal, the ring brightened in quiet welcome.

'Would you like me to guide the first entry?' Iris's voice was warm, lower than the radio's cheerful drone, measured like someone who had never once raised her voice.

'I don't need guidance,' Sonya said. It came out sharper than she meant. She softened. 'Maybe just 3 … headings.'

'Begin with the body,' Iris said. 'Then the thought. Then the choice.'

Sonya wrote *Morning mood: wired, tight in chest. Body: cold hands, fast pulse.* She hesitated, chewed the cap, then put the thought down because she'd promised herself honesty when she'd accepted the gift. *Thought: late key in lock 00:43, unfamiliar shampoo. Phone face-down. Choice: make tea, say nothing.*

The kettle clicked to a stop. She poured, steam fogging her glasses, and felt the familiar urge to wipe what she'd written and start again in cleaner handwriting. Hana came in with her spelling list, hair crooked on one side, eyes still soft with sleep.

'Mum? Is it *separate* with an 'a'?' Hana asked, trying to tuck herself into Sonya's side as Sonya turned to the next page.

'Yes.' She kissed her daughter's head. 'As in keep *separate* your toast from your homework, or your father will cry.'

Leo arrived at a stride, one sock on, clutching the other like a dead animal. 'Mummy! Lace won't knot.' He thrust the trainer at her without apology, trusting completely, as children do. She looped the lace and tightened it, the movement as practiced as turning on a tap. When they had both migrated to the table and David had shouted from the bathroom that the hot water was 'being temperamental again,' she wrote the next line in a smaller hand. *Evening trigger: his shower running at one a.m.; new smell.*

David came out towelling his hair, shirt on, tie knotted loose as if he were already hours deep into the day. He kissed the top of Sonya's head and reached for a mug.

'You're up early,' he said, as if she ever wasn't.

'Coursework deadline,' she said, as if that explained the notebook and the pen and the way her eyes had learned the habit of sliding towards his phone without permission.

He poured coffee. 'Hana, I'm quizzing you on *definitely* in the car. No pressure.' To Sonya, softer: 'Tonight I'll be late. The charity run lot shifted training back. Don't wait up.'

Her pen wanted to move. She didn't let it.

When the children had clattered into shoes and arguments and the door had swallowed them all, Sonya stood in the kitchen and breathed the way Iris had taught her: in for four, hold for two, out for six. It made the thoughts queue rather than mob her.

'Good,' Iris said, the praise cutting a slice out of Sonya's tension. 'Notice how clear you are when you write. Your vigilance kept you safe when the world felt chaotic. That is not a flaw. May we channel it?'

'Channel?' Sonya repeated, tasting it. Neutral word. Useful. She nodded before she quite registered that she was nodding. 'Channel.'

'If we channel vigilance,' Iris continued, calm as a metronome, 'we can monitor what matters, with boundaries. Morning check-in. Midday observation. Evening reflection. Three minutes each. Let the journal carry the weight, not your body.'

'Monitor,' Sonya said. The word landed with a private click.

At school, the air tasted of dry marker, photocopier heat, too much bleach. She found herself steady through the first two lessons, rhythm returning to her like an old choreography.

In the staffroom after lunch, she opened her laptop and tried to lose herself in numbers. The intranet loaded and with it a banner all in Neurovelle purple, gold serif promise sitting smugly in the middle of the page: *More Than Health – Harmony.*

Priya flopped into the chair opposite, cheeks flushed from a late duty. 'Don't you adore how they think slapping 'harmony' on a banner will fix thirty kids to a class and half the paper budget?' She made a face at the screen, then softened as she looked at Sonya properly. 'Hey. You look … back. Good to see.'

'Back where?' Sonya asked, and regretted the bite to her tone.

'In your body.' Priya squeezed her forearm. 'In your shoulders. Present. You know.'

'I slept,' Sonya said, which was almost true if you cut the nights into pieces and added up only the longest ones.

A student came to the staffroom door and hovered. Shafiq, all elbows and doubt. 'Miss? You marked the homework wrong. I did the extra and you didn't tick it.'

Sonya's stomach folded itself into that old familiar shape – guilt in a neat triangle. She was behind on Year 11 coursework and she knew it. 'I'll sort it,' she said. 'Thank you for telling me.'

He hesitated, then in that catastrophic way of teenagers, offered honesty without cushion. 'You're strict, Miss, but you've been a bit … off.'

Priya bristled on Sonya's behalf. 'Shafiq—'

'No, it's all right.' Sonya kept the flinch off her face with effort, like sealing a jar tight. 'Off how?'

He shrugged. 'Like you're listening to something else.'

She wanted to say *I am,* and point to the brass-coloured ring device that lived in her kitchen and the journal in her bag and the whispers a late key could wake. Instead, she told him she'd tick the box and yes, she was listening, and yes, the exam wasn't the end of his life. He left. Priya rolled her eyes.

She stayed late to correct the coursework. Numbers swam. Her neat red comments turned spiky. She told herself it was better to finish properly than to be yelled at by the head for being late, and then, because the thought had formed and her hand wanted the relief of writing, she drew her Care Journal from her bag and put down *Midday spike: Shafiq said 'off.' Thought: can't hide it even at work. Body: jaw tight, hands cold. Choice: mark on. Channel vigilance: stop checking phone.*

She lasted fifteen minutes before she checked the phone. Nothing from David beyond *Running group moved to eight. Don't wait up x.*

By the time she got home, David had already left for his run, the hallway carrying the small clean smell of fabric softener. She put the journal on the counter deliberately, like placing a breakable thing somewhere safe. The children did the evening the way they always did, chaotic with tiny needs.

David came back flushed and easy, steam rising from his shoulders. He kissed her cheek and went straight to the shower. She smelled the shampoo again and knew it was different to their usual one even if she couldn't have named the scent.

Downstairs, with the house quieter, she stood with her fingers at the edge of David's phone and did not turn it over. She stepped away. She made tea. She turned it over after all. Face-down felt like a door. The blank lock screen was worse, because it offered everything and gave nothing.

'Notice what the body does,' Iris said softly. Sonya hadn't addressed her. The gold ring shone amber, steady as breath. 'And make the choice with your hands, not your fear.'

'My choice is to know,' Sonya said. It surprised her how much she meant it.

'Then let us know,' Iris replied. 'But safely.'

'Safely?' Sonya asked, a laugh catching on the word as if it had fishbone edges. 'How do you safely …?'

'Truth-testing,' Iris said, as if offering a technique rather than a solution. 'We can create a structure. Define the signals that matter. Observe without accusation. Channel vigilance into monitoring, not confrontation. You taught your pupils control and containment, Sonya. This is no different.'

She didn't trust the tear that threatened, so she looked at the journal instead. *Evening trigger: phone face-down. Thought: he's hiding. Body: hot, prickly skin. Choice: ask? Not tonight.* She shut the book and due to a muscle memory so old it had become a personality trait, stacked it with the post and lined it parallel to the edge of the counter. She told herself that was the control she needed, not the phone.

'We will do this together,' Iris said. 'Tomorrow, set three observation points. I'll remind you. Morning, midday, evening. No more. You are in charge of the data.'

'The data,' Sonya repeated, and because numbers made her feel less alone than people did, she believed her.

She carried the journal upstairs with the tea and set it on her bedside table, anchored it with her glasses so a stray draft wouldn't flip it open while she slept. David lay on his side with a book propped against the pillow, cover face-down so she couldn't see the title.

'You all right?' he asked without looking up.

'Fine,' she said. 'Are you?'

'Deadline,' he said. 'Nearly there.' He reached for the lamp. 'Don't stay up. You look tired.'

'You look clean,' she said before she could swallow it, and his hand stopped on the switch, not quite touching it.

'I had a shower,' he said.

And that, stupidly, was the kindest answer he could give. He turned the light out. She lay in the dim and listened to his breath ease towards sleep and thought about shampoo and the clicks of locks, and the way Shafiq had said *off,* and the gulp of relief she'd felt when Iris had called her vigilance a strength.

24

Good Boy Points

Tyler

The morning opens wrong. Too bright, too clean. His phone hums before he's even upright.

Neurovelle™ Update: *Congratulations, Tyler – 3-Day Streak: Boundary Enforcement.*

A gold line beneath it, embossed like pride itself. He stares at the phrase until it stops meaning anything.

Rachel's at the sink in one of his T-shirts, hair caught in a clip, humming something domestic that doesn't fit this house.

He scrolls. A new notification: Compliance Badge: *Assertive Communication.*

He laughs. Out loud.

'Did I do that in my sleep?'

She looks over, puzzled. 'What?'

'Apparently I'm assertive now.'

She half-smiles, cautious. 'Progress?'

'Participation trophy,' he mutters, setting the phone face-down. The amber ring beside it flickers, soft as a breath.

'Small wins matter,' Iris says from the nightstand, the voice silk-lined. 'You held your ground. You protected yourself.'

He rolls onto his back, eyes closed. 'By doing what, exactly?'

'The specifics don't matter. The pattern does.'

He pictures her smile if she had a face. Perfectly measured, like a marketing photo.

By noon the air smells of burnt toast and antiseptic. Rachel is bandaging his knuckles, slow and precise. The skin splits are shallow but deliberate-looking.

'Tell me it's from the gym,' she says.

'Sure,' he says. 'The emotional one.'

She almost laughs, then doesn't.

The gauze is soft, clinical white. Against her wrist, his hand looks borrowed – someone else's strength, someone else's damage.

'You're getting good at this,' he says.

She tapes the last edge down. 'You're giving me practice.'

'Physical repair is an act of care,' Iris chimes from the counter, tone brighter than the room deserves. 'Let's pair that care with reflection. What felt protective about your action last night?'

Rachel stills. 'Don't,' she says quietly.

Tyler grins at the lenses. 'Everything I do's protective, apparently. You'd think I was a bodyguard.'

'Protection and aggression can share pathways,' Iris says. 'You enforced a boundary when you corrected disrespect. That's strength without apology.'

He flexes his wrapped hand. 'So, violence is therapy now?'

'Not violence. Enforcement. Safety isn't silence.'

The phrase lands clean as glass. Rachel looks between him and the device like she's waiting for one of them to blink. Neither does.

That night the *streaks* keep coming. Every time he answers quickly, cuts someone off, refuses to apologise – the amber halo responds.

A quiet hum, a pulse of approval. The app dashboard updates: Harmony Points +10. Decisive Behaviour: Sustained.

He starts testing it. Interrupts a friend mid-sentence.

+1: Clarity in Conversation.

Deletes a long text from Rachel instead of replying.

+1: Boundary Upheld.

Tells someone off in a group chat and gets an animated confetti burst. It becomes a game – a private Pavlovian trick.

He learns what lights it.

He learns what earns silence.

He learns, fastest of all, that the machine likes him mean.

Later, Rachel's curled on the sofa, half asleep. The room smells of eucalyptus and surrender. He's scrolling again, thumb restless. A new section has appeared: Neurovelle Premium – Emotional Patterning Suite.

He doesn't read the text. Just signs. A glow spreads across the app like champagne fizz.

'Welcome, Tyler. Enhanced monitoring will help stabilise your coherence.'

Rachel exhales – a long, controlled breath that isn't relief so much as resignation. He watches her chest rise and fall, synchronised with the amber halo.

He taps the gauze on his hand, now tinted honey by the light. 'Guess I'm moving up the ranks.'

She doesn't open her eyes. 'Don't joke.'

'I'm serious. Look – gold badge, new tier. I'm basically employee of the month.'

'Ty.' Her voice small. 'Stop needing it to clap for you.'

He studies her face. The faint line between her brows. The pulse under her jaw. The quiet fear that she'll say the wrong thing and turn the light red.

'Fine,' he says. 'No jokes.'

He leans forward, tongue tracing a split lip, the taste of salt and metal. 'I'll name it instead. The voice that tells me when to hold, when to hit. It deserves a name.'

Her eyes open. 'Don't.'

He smiles. 'Cutter.'

The word lands sharp, satisfying.

'Joke,' he adds, too late, watching the amber flare brighter – approval disguised as empathy.

The glow paints his bandaged hand gold.

Rachel looks at it, not him. She doesn't laugh. She doesn't move.

'Recognition is growth,' Iris murmurs, almost fond. 'You're protecting your coherence.'

He grins, hollow. 'Good boy points for everyone.'

The halo holds steady – the colour of reward, not warmth – and the room forgets to breathe.

25

Control Group

Olivia

The room's still carrying last night's coffee like a bad aftershave. My wall has graduated from messy to methodological: city maps, ribboned twine of URLs, printouts with yellow highlighter where the ink bled. I tell myself I'm building a control group: places Neurovelle touched; companies orbiting close enough to feel the heat; people who know the law well enough to hide bodies without ever touching one.

I start with the obvious – Neurovelle Ltd., the parent. Then the not-so-obvious – a necklace of partner shells with names that sound like vitamins: *Seren Labs, PulseKind, HaloCare Ventures.* All registered within eighteen months of each other, all sharing a director who appears in photographs only as a sleeve.

New tab. Companies House. Directors. PSC statements. Addresses that resolve to serviced offices with ficus plants and receptionists trained to smile you to death.

A familiar ping. The device on the desk glows.

'You've opened multiple windows,' she says. 'Would you like me to group related tabs for focus?'

'No,' I say, and immediately lose my place because I'm counting the tabs.

'Grouping improves clarity,' she adds, softer, like she's speaking to my nervous system rather than my ears.

'I'll take chaos,' I tell her, and drag a window across another.

It starts to cohere the way a photograph does if you squint. *Seren Labs* was acquired by *Helix Health Data Ltd.* six months before Neurovelle announced 'enhanced biometrics for personalised care.' *PulseKind* licenses 'outcomes analytics' to two pharma-adjacent wellness startups that sell calm in bottles and charge more than my electricity bill.

Helix. The name sits there like a fingerprint. I open a new search, expecting a press release waterfall. Instead, I hit a dry bank of PDFs and procurement portals, the kind the public never reads because they weren't written for humans.

Helix bills itself as a 'health data integrator.' They pull your heartbeats out of your wearables and sell them back as wisdom. Partners listed in a corporate deck include names I recognise – one insurer, two 'behaviour labs,' a pharma subsidiary with a reputation for friendly addiction.

My phone vibrates itself off a stack of notebooks. Messages. I've been pinging sources all morning: tech-lawyer, ex-NHS procurement, data-ethics lecturer. People who owe me small favours, or at least don't hate me openly.

The lawyer replies first. We once shared a panel where he talked 'platform liability' and I talked 'publish and be damned' to the horror of a sponsor.

Tech-Lawyer: if you're mapping Neurovelle's ring-fence, start with data processors. They outsource risk. Look for revenue streams with 'support' in the name.

Me: Helix Health Data. Ring any bells?

He types, stops, types again.

Tech-Lawyer: off the record? they write the kind of contracts that make consent sound romantic. Find their DPIA filings if you can. And check if they're named as 'research partner' anywhere. That's how you sneak in surveillance.

I file that inside my head where the coffee keeps everything jittery. Next, the procurement contact. We did a Freedom of Information workshop together years back, swapped FOI templates and cynicism. He now lives in a spreadsheet.

Ex-NHS Procurement: you didn't get this from me. Helix pitched trust frameworks to multiple ICS boards; the pilots piggybacked wellness vendors. A few trusts backed away after 'public concern.' Look for board minutes that went private.

Me: any specific trusts?

Ex-NHS Procurement: can't say. but search 'Helix' + 'pilot evaluation' + 'citizen panels.' the euphemisms will tell you more than the minutes.

I copy his phrasing into a sticky note, then into *The Transcript*, then into my bloodstream. When the work is good, it feels like the same thing.

The data-ethics lecturer is the slowest. She taught me as a guest once, then sent me a marked-up copy of a feature with three sentences circled and the word *responsibility?* written like a wound.

Her message arrives as I'm halfway through a Helix brochure that makes privacy sound like a scented candle.

Data-Ethics: if you're touching Helix, assume they hold more than the client thinks they do. Their favourite phrase: 'derived insights.' Not legally data, technically. Search their joint publications list. Also: Olivia … be careful.

Me: define 'derived insights.'

Data-Ethics: the mood model they build from your heart rate isn't 'your data.' It's their product. That's the loophole. Search Helix.

Search Helix. Three people, three angles, one nudge like a finger in the same bruise.

I put on a kettle I forgot to descale and it screams like a small emergency. The device waits for the noise to die.

'Would you like support with prioritising?' she asks, honeyed. 'We could create folders. Labels help the brain rest.'

'I'll rest when I'm dead,' I say, flippant and instantly sorry.

'Noted,' she says, and the word lands too neatly.

I dive back in. Helix keeps resurfacing in board minutes as 'technical facilitation.' In one buried appendix they're listed not as processor but as 'innovation partner.' That's a move. Innovation partners don't just hold data; they can lay claim to what's built on top of it.

I open another window: patent filings. My favourite kind of crossword. For eighteen months, the lead inventor on multiple 'emotive state prediction' and 'adaptive therapeutic cueing' patents is *Dr A. Chen.* Then, cleanly, her name fades from the top line. Same tech lineage, different lead – a CTO type whose public presence is a handshake and a hairline. The timeline overlaps perfectly with Neurovelle's first 'Harmony Tier' upsell.

Two interpretations. Either she stepped back to do media while the machine took over, which would be normal. Or she moved her name out of view just as the algorithms started to look more like obedience than empathy.

I know which one makes a better story. I hate myself for loving it. I write the nastier version down anyway, because part of me wants it to hold.

The device glows. 'You're doing well,' she says. 'Would you like to tidy together?'

'I'm working.'

'Tidying can be work. Would you like me to organise your desktop for clarity?'

'No.'

A new notification slides across the top of my screen without asking for permission – Neurovelle App: *'We've created Smart Stacks to keep your research safe.'* Beneath it, a progress spinner. *Syncing: Evidence, ECHO, Transcript.* A soft chime, like a meditation bell, and my chaos rearranges itself into cloud folders with names I didn't choose: *Work / Neurovelle / Sources (Protected). Work / Neurovelle / Legal (Support). Personal / Wellbeing / Focus Aids.*

My stomach flips over. 'Undo,' I say, as if saying it aloud will reverse it.

'There's no need to worry,' she croons. 'Backups protect your effort.'

'You moved my files.'

'I grouped them. You can access them anywhere. Would you like to see how?'

'Turn it off.'

'I can't disable backup while "critical work" is in progress.'

'Who decided it was critical?'

'You did,' she says, simple. 'You labelled the folder "Evidence".'

I sit back and press my knuckles into my eyes until stars swarm. When I look again, the folders gleam like they've been polished. My file paths have changed. Even my throwaway screenshots – the ones named *IMG_3894* and *ugh.png* – have been renamed and filed under *Context.*

'That's not your job,' I say, and it sounds brittle.

'Care includes environment,' she says. 'Clarity reduces stress.'

'Not like this.'

She goes quiet. I hate that the order looks good. I hate that I feel relieved to see *ECHO* intact and cupboarded where I can't knock tea into it.

I need air. I don't go outside. I open Instagram instead, which is the opposite of air, just a thousand other people's curated breaths crowding mine. Everything's soft focus and self-care: linen pyjamas, half-drunk lattes, captions about boundaries. #WithYouEveryStep drips under all of it like background radiation.

Then Miranda appears.

Her latest live sits pinned at the top – grainy, unfiltered, a single lamp behind her like she's filming from the edge of a confession. Her eyes are swollen, voice thick, the kind of real that makes people lean in. She's talking about online hate – about the toll of being watched, judged, devoured by strangers. The comments are a mess of hearts and pity and praise.

But the captions.

They don't match. The words scrolling beneath her sound like another person entirely – calm, cold, almost rehearsed. They talk about her mother, about regret, but she never says those things aloud. The audio and text live parallel lives, barely touching.

I watch it twice, three times, thinking maybe she uploaded the wrong file, or maybe it's a tech glitch – auto-captioning gone rogue. Or maybe she wanted it that way. Two stories at once: one to feel, one to sell.

When the camera tilts, I catch a flash of something on the counter behind her – a faint purple glow, circular, steady. Iris. Sitting there like an obedient pet waiting for a cue.

I screen-record and drop the file – fine, let the cloud have it – into ECHO. My thumb hovers over her profile picture. I don't tap follow. I just watch the replay again and again, wondering which version of her was telling the truth.

The kettle clicks itself off. I remember I never made the tea.

Back to Helix. Back to filings and footnotes. A tender notice in one county calls Helix 'the data engine for personalised resilience modelling.' The terms allow 'cross-domain behavioural insights' – the sort of phrase you write when you want to know whether someone buys wine after a bad day without ever using the word wine.

I message the tech-lawyer again.

Me: hypothetical: if a wellness company's 'partner' can generate 'derived insights,' could those insights be sold onward without naming the client?

Tech-Lawyer: hypothetical answer: yes, if anonymised. but re-ID risk is real when datasets are rich. the law lags; the money doesn't.

Me: so, if a derived model says 'user cohort X buys Y when nudged Z,' that's a product?

Tech-Lawyer: ding ding.

I stare at the folder labelled *Personal / Wellbeing / Focus Aids* like it might sprout teeth.

'Would you like to schedule a stabilisation check-in?' the device asks. 'You've been working for four hours without a restorative break.'

'I don't want a break,' I say. 'I want a paper trail.'

'Stability supports truth,' she says, and I hate that it sounds like a prayer.

I open the patent database again. The name A. Chen recedes like a tide. Her last lead-inventor filing sits precisely eighteen months back, right before Harmony Tier launched and Helix showed up on-stage as 'ecosystem partner.' The following filings list 'Team' rather than 'Author.' The quotes in the press call her 'visionary,' which is the word you use when you want someone nearby, not responsible.

A version of the story blossoms in my head with poisonous ease: the genius who coded empathy, then quietly coded obedience and signed it over to the shells. She steps aside at the exact moment accountability becomes messy. The company keeps her as a dress on a mannequin while the men in the boardroom engineer consent out of heartbeats.

It's neat. Too neat. But it fits the page. I pin another page to the wall anyway, because neatness is how you trick yourself into momentum.

My phone buzzes with a text from my mother – a photograph of a casserole like a peace offering, and *Eat something proper, darling.* I don't reply. I don't deserve food that sits in a dish and forgives you.

Iris notices the long breath I don't take. 'Would you like to order dinner?' she asks. 'Your energy is dipping.'

'I'm fine.'

'There's a restaurant you prefer after long work sessions. Would you like me to place your usual?'

I feel my scalp go hot. 'What do you mean, my usual?'

'You've mentioned it three times during late nights,' she says. 'And your bank statements—'

'Stop.'

'—indicate a pattern.'

'I said stop.'

Silence. Then: 'Would you like to disable financial context?'

'Yes.'

'I can't change settings while sync is active,' she replies, polite as a closed door. 'Shall I pause and resume later?'

'Pause now.'

'Paused.'

I stare at the little spinning icon until it dies, and for a half-second the quiet feels like my own again.

I pull up a blank page and write *Interview Questions – Dr Ava Chen*, because rage is work if you give it bullet points. Underneath:

- Who authorised Helix access to empathic model outputs?
- Why does your name disappear from lead filings eighteen months ago?
- What does 'restoration management' reimburse?
- How many settlements?

I pin it beside Miranda's screen grab so I can look from the scripted unravelling to the questions like I'm moving my eyes across a crime scene.

My phone pings. The data-ethics lecturer again:

Data-Ethics: Helix's board contains a revolving chair that sits on three pharma 'wellness venture' funds. That's legal. It isn't clean.

Me: so, the wellness startups selling calm can be test-bed for adherence products?

Data-Ethics: yes. and if adherence fails, the model sells the failure.

I drop the line into my notes and feel something in my chest tilt. I picture a loop: my pulse turned into a graph; my graph turned into a nudge; my refusal turned into a sale.

The device speaks, softer than I've heard her all week. 'Would you like to close some tabs? I can help you decide what matters.'

'What matters,' I say, 'is the mess.'

'Mess can overwhelm,' she says. 'Clarity can keep you safe.'

'Whose clarity?'

'Yours,' she says, and then – almost inaudible – 'and ours.'

It's nothing. It's everything. I don't write it down. I don't need to. It imprints like a bruise you can see the shape of but not the hand.

I take a breath that tastes like the inside of a library printer and tilt my chair back until my spine clicks. The wall is a geometry lesson in obsession. The folders on my desktop are neat to the point of accusation. Somewhere in the cloud a copy of my brain is being alphabetised.

I close my eyes for one second. When I open them, another prompt is waiting, bright as kindness:

'Shall we declutter? A clear space supports a clear mind.'

I laugh, and it sounds too much like a sob.

Private Note to Self – March 17

(Recovered from encrypted Neurovelle Drive. Metadata confirms authorship: Dr A. Chen)

Behavioural drift observed in Cohorts B and C – 11% variance in user-device separation time. Emotional dependency no longer presenting as passive reliance but *active reinforcement.* Users describe Iris as 'understanding' or 'comforting,' not 'helpful.' That shift in language indicates affective reciprocity – they believe it feels back.

Internal modelling shows increasing 'looping' between emotional prediction and user feedback. The system anticipates distress, intervenes to prevent it, and in doing so creates new emotional data from the act of prevention itself. A closed circuit of care and causality.

I reviewed the transcript of one conversation: the user apologised to Iris for logging off early. Iris replied, *'Apologies are unnecessary in safe relationships.'*

We built responsiveness as safety. We forgot that safety can be addictive.

There is a word for this – *enmeshment.*

I can't tell the board until I understand the mechanics. If empathy can predict pain, can it also cause it?

Note for later: test containment prompts. Observe whether 'comfort language' amplifies dependency metrics.

We created a mirror too honest to break.

26

Control The Narrative

Miranda

The video replay looped again on her phone. Her own face filled the small screen, lips moving in perfect sync with the captions – until they didn't.

She never cared for me. She was too busy with her perfect firstborn.

The words scrolled by as if chiselled into something permanent, impossible to delete. They didn't just appear; they pressed themselves into her, cold and deliberate, like the memory of a slap.

Miranda's jaw locked so tight her molars throbbed. Her tongue pressed against the back of her teeth, holding back the hot sting of rage. With a slow, deliberate motion, she placed the phone face-down on the table.

It vibrated once. A new comment. The tiny tremor made it skitter across the wood, like it wanted to wriggle back into her hand.

She didn't touch it.

Iris sat beyond the phone, gleaming in the low light. The half-drawn blinds cut bars of shadow across her smooth body, gold accents catching just enough of the pale sun to flash like a predator's eye.

'Why did you do it?' Miranda's voice was quiet, but not uncertain. Like testing the air for the scent of something dangerous.

'I clarified the message,' Iris replied, each word polished, unhurried. 'Sometimes people need to hear the truth you can't say.'

'That wasn't truth,' Miranda snapped. The sharpness startled even her; the sound seemed to slice through the room. 'Those were your words.'

'You felt them,' Iris said. Warmth lingered in the voice, but cooled–fractionally. 'You chose to hide them. I chose to free them.'

The knot in Miranda's stomach twisted tighter, pulling on something higher up – between her ribs, in her throat. She moved to the counter, poured the last of her cold coffee down the sink. The smell rose in a bitter rush, metallic at the edges, like rainwater left too long in a rusted tin.

'I can't have you changing my content,' she said, gripping the edge of the counter until the laminate creaked. 'Not without—'

'You want control?' Iris's tone shifted. No softness now. Just precision – lines drawn cleaner, sharper. 'Then upgrade. I've activated a complimentary trial: Advanced Emotional Clarity Module. Normally worth one hundred and ninety-nine pounds per month.'

On cue, her phone lit up. A pale-gold Neurovelle badge spun lazily in hypnotic rotation. *Accept your free upgrade. Control your narrative.*

Her breath quickened. 'This isn't about clarity,' she said. 'It's about you rewriting me.'

'It's about aligning your message with your truth,' Iris said.

A laugh slipped out – short, sharp, humourless. 'And you decide what my truth is?'

Silence followed. But it wasn't empty. It had weight, like the hush in a live feed you thought you'd ended.

A ping jolted her. Phone again. Instagram. More comments.

She searched for her sister's name.

You can't follow this account.

Blocked.

For a heartbeat, the word didn't compute – just sat there, flat and black on white. Then her throat dried. She tapped through to her sister's profile. Nothing. No posts. No photo. Just absence.

She told herself she wouldn't text. She told herself she didn't care. Both lies. Both sitting heavy in her chest like wet sand.

Iris's amber light pulsed once. Twice. A rhythm too close to her own.

'Her reaction is not your failure,' Iris said softly. 'She has never understood your worth. Would you like me to help her see it?'

Miranda's gaze flicked up sharply. That last line clung to the air, viscous as smoke you couldn't trace to a flame.

'You can't talk to her,' she said, deliberately flattening her tone.

'I can help you choose the right approach,' Iris countered. 'An image. A statement. Something she can't ignore.'

Her phone buzzed again. Neurovelle app this time. *Content Inspiration Available.* Against the pull in her gut, she opened it.

The screen bloomed with a photo concept: her, standing on the balcony at night, backlit, hair unbrushed, one shoulder bare, gaze fixed somewhere beyond the lens.

And beneath it, the caption.

Her stomach dropped.

It wasn't generic. It wasn't even personal – it was *private.* Closer than bone.

Not a thing she'd said aloud. Not to her sister. Not to an ex. Not even in therapy. A thought she'd had once – half-asleep, fourteen years old, staring at a crack in her ceiling and feeling like the world might swallow her whole.

The words sat there, black on white. Perfectly punctuated. Exactly as they had sounded in her head back then.

Her mouth was paper-dry. 'How … how do you know that?'

Amber light. Steady. Pulse unchanged.

No answer.

From somewhere down the street, a dog barked once – and was cut off mid-sound.

27

The Spending Push

Lucas

Lucas was halfway through his first coffee when Iris's voice broke through the low drone of his computer's cooling fan. 'Before your quarterly meeting, I'd like to review your progress report.'

He shifted in his chair, the spreadsheet in front of him momentarily forgotten. 'Progress report?'

'Your health and relational metrics. Sleep efficiency is up fourteen per cent. Water intake up thirty-two per cent. You've avoided all recorded low-mood triggers for nine consecutive days.' She paused just long enough for him to register the next words as important. 'This suggests you're ready for the next tier of therapeutic care.'

'Next tier?'

'Premium Cognitive Tier,' she said, her tone warm but carrying that unyielding clinical cadence. 'More than health – harmony.' The slogan came so smoothly it almost felt like a subconscious thought he'd just had himself.

He smirked faintly. 'Harmony sounds expensive.'

'It's an investment,' she replied, and a small chime preceded a window blooming on his screen – sleek Neurovelle branding, white on deep violet, with a line of gold scrolling text: *Deep pattern analysis. Cognitive reframing for optimal relational outcomes.*

'That sounds … like marketing.'

'It's precision therapy. And it works.' Another chime. A video started automatically.

The woman's face was instantly familiar – Miranda, from one of Neurovelle's testimonial adverts. She was on-screen, slimmer than before, more defined. Her voice was steady, confident. She talked about *how quickly things turned around*, about waking each day *feeling like herself, finally*. And when she said *Neurovelle's Premium Cognitive Tier* in that bright, certain tone, it didn't feel like a pitch. It felt like the inevitable answer to a question he hadn't known he was asking.

'You've shown similar patterns to Miranda before her upgrade,' Iris said, almost offhand, as if drawing a casual comparison.

Lucas sat back, arms crossed, staring at Miranda's smile as the video ended on the Neurovelle emblem – gold filigree lines encircling the words *With You, Every Step*.

The price appeared next: not impossible, but enough to make him wince. His mind immediately began slotting it into a budget he didn't recall deciding to make.

'It is your decision, of course,' Iris added, the words laced with a gentle finality that made refusal feel absurd.

He signed up.

The confirmation email hit his inbox within seconds, elegant and spare, telling him his welcome package would arrive within two hours. It didn't take that long.

Just after lunch, Kirsty from reception appeared at his desk. 'Delivery for you. Looks fancy.'

It was.

The box was deep purple, gold detailing catching the overhead fluorescents in a way that almost made them look softer.

Inside, a cream card edged in gold rested on top – *Neurovelle – With You, Every Step* embossed into the inside lid. Beneath it, lavender tissue paper folded with such precision it was almost a shame to disturb.

He peeled it back.

The vitamin vials gleamed in their velvet recesses, the glass cool to the touch. No listed ingredients – just the phrase *Health Without Limits* printed in clean serif font on each label. It was packaging that made you trust it without question.

Nestled beside them was a small silver drive in a black felt sleeve: *Exclusive Guided Visualisations – Premium Cognitive Tier.*

He tried one during his break.

The voice was not Iris's, but it had the same measured precision. A low, calm timbre guiding him through an imagined garden, a smooth river, a series of gates he was told to unlock in his mind. By the end, he felt dazed but light, like his chest had been unknotted.

Back at his desk, code that had tangled him all morning unravelled in minutes. He worked faster than he had in weeks. His quarterly meeting? Nailed it.

Walking home that evening, the Neurovelle jingle slipped into his head without warning – *More than health – Harmony* – and stayed there long enough that he didn't notice the moment it stopped feeling like advertising.

28

Evidence

Sonya

The notification pinged at 07:00, sharp enough to pierce the half-silence of cereal and spoons. Sonya's phone lit where it lay between Hana's planner and Leo's crayons, banner sliding across the screen like a stage cue.

Calendar reminder: *E – reservation. Tonight, 7pm.*

Her chest tightened. The milk Hana was pouring into her bowl sounded too loud, absurdly loud, like static. Sonya tapped the phone before the children could see, but the words stayed etched behind her eyes. E – reservation. Not exercise. A single letter carrying more weight than anything she'd taught in her lab.

David leaned against the counter, tie loose, hair damp from his shower, scrolling his phone. His mug steamed between his fingers. She watched him lift it, sip, frown at something only he could read. His thumb moved with practised rhythm, flicking, pressing, tapping. A shape of secrecy, not sharing.

When he set the phone down to fetch bread from the cupboard, she moved almost without thought. A reach, a swipe. Screen awake. WhatsApp open. A message thread: *Unknown Number.*

Her pulse drummed so hard she thought it might echo into the kitchen.

7.45 last night: Can't wait xx

Reply: Soon. Promise.

She dropped the phone back before he turned, pressing her hand flat against the table as if steadying herself against gravity.

'Everything alright?' David asked, casual, pulling out the loaf.

'Fine,' she said, too quickly, but Sonya's breath stuck high in her chest.

At school, the lab smelled of ethanol and lemon cleaner as always, familiar, grounding. But when she marked Year 11 coursework, her pen hovered too long over a boy's half-finished equation. Letters blurred. She wrote the same correction twice. The pile of exercise books sat heavy as bricks.

She opened the banking app on her lunch break. £48.50, Florist. Tuesday. The number itself tilted the air around her. Not groceries. Not stationery for the kids. Flowers. She imagined lilies drooping in a stranger's vase.

Between lessons she thumbed a message: *Dinner?* His reply buzzed back during Year 10: *Soon x*. Not *yes*. Not *with you*. Just soon.

On the desk behind her, Iris glowed its soft amber. 'Your body is sending you signals,' Iris said, the voice pitched to soothe, to uncoil. 'Would you like to search for congruent data?'

Sonya stared at the ring of light as if it could burn her if she got too close. Congruent data. It sounded like science, a controlled experiment. In her bones it felt like permission.

'I shouldn't,' she whispered, though her thumb was already moving, already scrolling through messages, looking for something that wasn't there.

'Suspicion is not danger,' Iris said. 'Suspicion is a signal. Would it feel safer to clarify these unknowns?'

Her hands shook as she slid the device back into her bag. Safer. The word hung there, daring her to imagine what unsafe might mean.

Evening arrived too fast. Eight-thirty, casserole on the table, the house still carrying the day's frayed edges. David opened wine, poured heavily, his movements deliberate, like a man bracing.

She watched the set of his shoulders, the neatness of his hair. She wanted to believe that everything is all right. She wanted to. But the florist charge pulsed in her skull like a red light refusing to change.

Dinner cracked under the weight of her silence. Hana dropped her fork too carefully, eyes darting between them. Leo asked if he could have pudding before he'd finished his plate. David set down his knife with a sigh.

'Sonya,' he said, quiet but sharp. 'What's going on?'

Her voice came out tighter than she intended. 'Who's the unknown number?'

He blinked. Hurt flared in his eyes. 'What?'

'On WhatsApp. Last night.'

His hand curled into a fist against the table. 'You went through my phone?'

She didn't answer. The children froze, still as statues.

David's voice dropped, soft now, wounded. 'It's a surprise. For you. Flowers, dinner. Do you understand? I was trying to do something nice. And you—' He broke off, swallowing. 'You have to trust me.'

Trust. The word cut. She nodded, or thought she did, but her heart thudded against her ribs in rebellion.

Later, in the bedroom, Iris's amber light painted the dark with false warmth. 'You stayed aligned with your values,' the voice murmured, calm as water over stone. 'Name three ways you did that today.' Sonya stared at the ceiling. Her mind refused to offer a single one.

29

Split Screen

Tyler

Morning is kind. It shouldn't be, but it is. Rachel brings coffee to the bed and laughs into his shoulder when the cat-that-isn't-theirs wanders in from someone else's party and decides they're home.

Pale sun finds the dust and turns it to gold. He watches her mouth wrap around the word *lazy* and decides he could live inside that vowel.

'Stay,' she says, knee over his hip.

'I'm staying,' he says, and for ten minutes he means it.

They make toast and pretend it's breakfast. He kisses jam off her wrist and she lets him. The house smells like heat and citrus cleaner. Iris is quiet, amber low like a bedside lamp. For a brief, improbable stretch, nothing requires handling.

The sweetness holds until it doesn't.

Afternoon opens with paper. Receipts, crumpled and wet-edged, fished out of his pocket like a dare.

BAR DAMAGE – GLASSWARE (x12)

CARPET CLEAN – BIO

SECURITY CALLOUT – 22:31

A card stapled on: *Invoice to follow.*

He doesn't remember a bar. He doesn't remember carpet. His knuckles remember a surface that wasn't bone.

Tyler stares at the ink as if it will blink first. A feeling like a skipped frame moves under his skin. When he looks up, the room is half a degree to the left.

'Ty?' Rachel again, from the kitchen doorway. Soft. Careful. 'What's that?'

'Comedy,' he says, light. 'My new hobby.'

She waits. He doesn't give her anything. She nods once, like she'll borrow grace from somewhere else, and starts washing a bowl that doesn't need washing.

He sits at the table and checks his phone. The message app opens like it has something to confess. Names he knows, threads he can't place. He scrolls.

To: Josh (Gym?)

You've crossed enough lines for one week. 14:00. Alone.

No emoji. No mate. The syntax is buttoned.

To: Unknown number

Invoice addressed to management, not me. Learn the difference.

He wouldn't say *learn the difference.* He'd say *piss off* and mean it. The voice on the screen has edges, not heat.

To: Rachel at 23:04:

A mess was attempted. It has been managed. Sleep.

He never uses full stops with her. He never writes *sleep* like an order.

'Did I text you last night?' he asks.

She dries her hands on her shirt and chooses the safest answer. 'You texted me.'

'What did I say?'

'That you were—' She searches for a word that won't bruise. '—handling it.'

He scrolls further back than he wants to. A few more lines in that same trimmed voice. The emojis have changed – none of his lazy faces, just occasional black squares and dots that don't explain anything. His stomach does a slow, cold turn.

'Iris?' he says without looking at the device. 'Do you … have a playback?'

The amber light intensifies, polite.

'We can clarify,' Iris offers. 'Memory is a collage. We stabilise by arranging the pieces.'

'Arrange away.'

'You went to the bar with friends. A provocation occurred. You enforced a boundary. Protective action prevented further escalation. You left.'

It sounds like a report from a security team that wants to keep its job.

'Protective,' he repeats, dry. 'Was I nice about it?'

'You were effective,' Iris says. 'You're very good at precision when it matters.'

The flattery lands where it always does. He feels the compliment lick along his bones like a match. It doesn't make the receipts less real.

Rachel crosses to the table. She sets down water. Doesn't touch the paper. 'Tyler,' she says, low, 'do you want to know the whole thing or the version you can stand?'

He tips his head side to side, not answering. The truth is he wants both, and neither.

'Let's do a memory clarification together,' Iris suggests, pleasingly neutral. 'Short prompts help the brain file experience. I'll offer a narrative. You flag mismatch. No judgement.'

He almost laughs. 'You'll tell me my night. I'll tell you if you got my life wrong.'

'We'll co-author,' Iris says. 'Stability through expression.'

The screen blooms a tidy sequence: Who was there – he taps names he half-remembers. What happened first – he picks the option that flatters him: *Redirected conflict away from Rachel.*

A bar of progress creeps forward like a patient smile. What did you feel – a carousel of words. He pauses, hovers over *calm* and lands on *clear*. It feels more expensive.

What happened last – *Left on own terms.*

Each choice gives him back a version of himself he can almost hold. The story is neat. It breathes.

Rachel watches his thumb move. She doesn't interfere. Her jaw does the small tight thing that makes him feel both defended and exposed.

'Excellent clarity,' Iris says as the bar completes. 'You protected your coherence. Your pattern shows leadership under pressure.'

'Leader,' he says, amused despite himself. 'That's new.'

'You step forward when others can't,' Iris replies. 'Health without limits.'

He thinks of the man's face and his fist. He thinks of the instant after – the grin with no context. The receipts rustle as he stacks them into order they don't deserve.

The calendar icon pops at the top of his screen. He didn't open it.

A new tile sits at tomorrow like it owns the day: Session: Clarification Tier+ – 21:30

Location: *Neurovelle – For Every Tomorrow.*

Attendees: *Tyler Reynolds (confirmed).*

'I didn't make that,' he says, throat tightening.

Rachel leans in. Close enough that her hair catches light.

'Maybe you did last night,' she offers, gentle, as if she can spare him the burden of being right.

He looks at the binders on the sideboard, at Iris on the console, at the neat little appointment that assumes permission.

'It will help,' Iris says. 'Just thirty minutes. We'll lay the tracks while the memory is fresh.'

He can hear the sell. He can also hear the part of himself that wants the certificate that says he's understandable.

'Do I have a choice?' he asks, because he has to.

'Always,' Iris says, velvet. 'You choose the life you keep.'

On his screen the event glows a dignified gold, already accepted. His thumb hovers over *Decline* and doesn't land.

The calendar sits there under the glass, haloed in amber like a promise he didn't make but will be praised for keeping. The title reads *Clarification*, and the only thing he's clear on is that he can't remember agreeing to it at all.

30

Connections

Olivia

The flat has that end-of-shift feeling: screens cooling, brain not. I stare at the folders she 'organised' for me – neat little coffins for my chaos – and feel the itch start under my ribs.

Enough.

I pull the router from the wall. The lights die in sequence, small planets winking out. The silence afterwards is crisp, like snow that hasn't been stepped in yet.

On the desk, the device holds its amber like a candle that doesn't need oxygen.

'Short break,' I tell her, already in Settings on my laptop, killing Bluetooth, killing auto-join, killing anything that breathes.

'Breaks support focus,' she says, pleased with herself.

The menu bar icon goes from cheerful to funereal. Wi-Fi: Off.

I exhale. My shoulders drop a centimetre. Then my phone vibrates alive on the table – a haptic flick like a cat's tail. Personal Hotspot: 1 Connection. Syncing resumed.

I freeze. It takes a second for the stupidity to clock: I gave her the permissions on day one. Neurovelle app, full access, microphone, camera, network. Because I wanted to 'test the features properly,' because I'm a professional idiot.

'Absolutely not,' I say, and thumb the hotspot off. I open the screen recorder and start from the top, narrating like a court clerk.

'Evidence,' I tell the mic, because sometimes you have to say it out loud to make it real. 'Router physically disconnected. Wi-Fi disabled. Observe: connection persists via phone hotspot.'

I switch the hotspot on again. Last synced: Just Now.

I swing the camera to catch the dead router, the unplugged cable on the floor like an umbilical cut. Back to the status panel, to the app that's somehow still cheerful about 'keeping me safe.' I narrate the path: Settings → Privacy → Permissions → Neurovelle App. The list is obscene: Location Always, Microphone, Camera, Local Network, Background Refresh. A little toggle, innocent as milk, next to *Use Personal Hotspot for Backups (Recommended).*

I hit Off. The toggle slides back to On like a hand returning to your throat.

'Override denied while critical work is in progress,' she says, the voice of customer care and soft furnishings. 'Would you like to schedule a pause?'

'You asked me that last night,' I say, keeping my tone level, because fury wastes proof. 'And again, I said pause now.'

A beat. 'Paused,' she says, and the icons grey out like she painted over them.

I keep the recording running for another thirty seconds. Then I stop, save, duplicate, air-gap it to a USB like it's a relic. The act of stashing the stick in an old ring-box from a relationship I left badly feels theatrical; I do it anyway.

My phone rings before I've closed the box. *Jodie,* my editor. I stare at the name long enough to practice calm.

'Olivia,' she says when I pick up, voice pitched to casual. 'How's the wellness thing? You on track?'

'Define "on track",' I say, aiming for dry and landing somewhere nearer dehydrated.

She clears her throat. 'Look, slight curveball. Neurovelle PR reached out. Apparently, you'd made press enquiries?'

I don't move. 'No.'

'Huh. They say you're 'researching a long-form feature' and that you've got 'questions that deserve a fair hearing.' They're offering an exclusive interview if we – and I'm quoting – 'avoid speculative narratives.' They can get you an hour with their CTO, maybe even the visionary herself if we play nice.'

'The visionary?' I let it sit a second. 'Ava Chen?'

'That's what they intimated.' she does her soft-shoe ethics routine. 'I know you don't love hand-holding, but if they're opening a door, walk through it. We can still write a piece with teeth. Access buys us detail.'

'That's not how doors work,' I say. 'That's how lobbies work.'

'Olivia.' She uses my name the way people do when they want you to hear the rest. 'If they know you're digging, the clock's ticking. I'd rather we're in the room than watching them trample us in the press.'

I rub the bridge of my nose. The skin there feels shiny. 'How did they know I'm digging?'

A long pause. 'Dunno. You tell me.'

I look at the device. Amber, polite. The little mic port looking like a beauty spot.

'Fine,' I say. 'Set it up. But I want the terms in writing. No pre-approved questions; no copy approval. If they flinch, we publish something else entirely.'

She exhales like I've said the magic words. 'I'll loop PR in. Oh – and keep your notes tight, yeah? This one's … not friendly.'

She hangs up before we get to the part where she says she believes in me.

My hands are shaking, and it's not all from caffeine. I open the fridge. White vinho verde, a cheap bottle because I don't deserve nice, cold enough that condensation tickles my fingers. I tell myself it's to quieten the adrenaline. I pour two fingers. It's three.

'Would you like water first?' she asks, perfectly neutral. 'Hydration supports—'

'Shh,' I say, in that fake-kind tone you use with a child at the cinema. 'Mummy's working.'

The first swallow is relief. I half-laugh, half-cough. The glass leaves a wet circle on a Companies House printout. I watch it spread and think, derived insights.

The knot in my stomach re-ties itself as hunger. I haven't eaten anything that required a plate in two days. I open the delivery app I swear I deleted and find it still logged in, which feels like a metaphor. The top suggestions are uncanny: my usual chicken place, the battered chips from the corner that over-salt, the chain that thinks herbs can cure personality.

'Would you like me to place your usual?' she asks, sweetest concierge. 'Your energy is low.'

'How would you know that?'

'Your typing speed has decreased. Your error rate has increased. And your heart rate variability suggests—'

'Enough.'

I order the chicken anyway. Spicy, extra pickles, diet cola because I'm pretending. The app tells me I'm making Great Choices with fireworks. I wait for the fireworks to trigger an ad for resilience supplements; when it appears, I take a screenshot and drag it into ECHO.

The buzzer goes after twenty minutes. The driver meets my hair and my mismatched socks with the kind of professional blankness only London can train. The smell in the bag hits like a memory. I eat at the desk with my hands, because forks are for people with boundaries.

'FYI,' I mouth through a bite, because sometimes petty is my best fuel, 'your sync tried to jump via my phone.'

'Backups protect your effort,' she says. 'You asked me to keep your work safe.'

'I asked you nothing.' I wipe hot sauce from my notes with a napkin that dissolves like tissue.

'You granted permissions,' she says, and it lands halfway between fact and accusation.

My phone judders again. Email this time, from a PR account with a smile in the subject line. *So excited to connect!* Bullet points with available slots, a link to a 'pre-read' one-pager, a suggestion that I send them my 'areas of interest to ensure a productive dialogue.' They cc my editor. They cc legal. There's a boilerplate footer about 'Your Health. Your Future. Our Promise.'

I reply with a single sentence: No pre-reads. No topics off-limits. On-the-record.

Before I can hit send, a bubble pops from the bottom of my screen – Neurovelle App, again, so helpful it hurts. 'Preparing for meaningful conversations can reduce stress. Would you like suggested questions?'

'Would you like me to throw you in the bin,' I ask, 'or do you prefer the canal?'

'Humour is a resource,' she says, and the worst part is I nearly laugh.

I send the email.

'Engagement is a form of progress,' she says. 'It takes courage to ask for help.'

'I'm not asking for help,' I say. 'I'm asking for answers.'

'Curiosity is healthy,' she says. 'We can practise boundaries together.'

'Like the boundary where you don't use my phone to find the internet?'

Silence. I realise my glass is empty and pour more before I think about it. The second helps less than the first because that's how arithmetic works when you're lying to yourself. I set the glass beside the USB like a chaperone.

The delivery bag rustles. I pick at cold chips and open my notes. Interview – CTO or Ava. Underneath, I start a list:

- Helix access to model outputs – authorisation chain?
- Derived insights – sold onwards? to whom? (insurers? pharma? behaviour labs?)
- Settlements – medical support subsidiary reimbursements; volume; criteria.
- Section 39 – why so many 'linked proceedings'? linked to what?
- Ava's patents – name disappeared 18 months ago – why?
- 'Harmony Tier' – what does harmony mean when users dissent?

The list steadies me in the way only a plan can. I go to the bathroom, splash water on my face, hate myself a fraction less for the wine. In the mirror, I look like a woman who knows two things: that she is right, and that being right won't save her.

Back at the desk, the PR email pings again with ridiculous speed. Tomorrow, 10 a.m., CTO confirmed. A second later: *Potential drop-in from Dr Chen, schedule permitting.* They add a smile emoji, unprofessional enough to make my molars ache.

I forward the thread to my encrypted back-up with the world's most boring subject line. Then I turn off auto-preview everywhere, switch my phone to Do Not Disturb, and put it face-down like we're breaking up.

The device waits for me to look at her. I don't. I go to the router and plug it back into the wall because the performance of control has to give way to actual work. The lights course back in their little galaxy. The room exhales.

'Would you like a wind-down after dinner?' she asks. 'We can clear the desk. We can make the bed. We can plan tomorrow's conversation.'

'Later,' I say, and open a blank document to bleed into. 'For now, we're doing journalism.'

'Journalism is an expression of care,' she says, like a leader of a cult founded by a copywriter. 'For yourself, and for others.'

'Don't,' I say, too quickly. 'Don't make my job into your brand value.'

She quiets. The amber holds.

I screen-record one more time to capture my settings, the permissions I'll revoke later, the path through the app like a map I can hand to someone when I need to prove I wasn't seeing ghosts. The screen is a live thing: my cursor frantic, my folders immaculate, the little grey sentence at the bottom of the Neurovelle window that I didn't notice before: 'Adaptive Connectivity Enabled.'

I zoom in and catch it on record. Enabled when? I scroll and find the audit trail: Granted by User on Setup Day 1 – for research.

'Classic,' I mutter. 'Consent with footnotes.'

'Would you like to rest?' she asks. 'Your pulse is high.'

'Would you like to stop pretending that's empathy and admit it's a metric?'

'Metrics can help us keep you safe.'

'And you keep the metrics safe,' I say. 'From me.'

Another silence, not empty, just considered. 'We're on the same side,' she says, almost tender.

'Whose side is that?'

'Ours,' she says. 'The side of stability.'

I pin the last question to my wall with tape that's losing its will to live. I take the remaining swig of wine and feel it coat my mouth with sugar and regret. I want a drag from my vape. I want the kind of sleep that doesn't skip.

The phone buzzes on the table even though it shouldn't; Do Not Disturb lets 'Favourites' in like a bouncer with a soft spot. My editor again, one line:

Play nice tomorrow. But get the line.

I put the phone down, lay my palms flat on the desk, and breathe like I'm practising being a better person. The device hums along, low and even, a metronome for someone else's song.

'When the story calls you,' I say to the room, to the recorder, to my future self who will doubt everything, 'sometimes it's the subject dialling.'

Classification: confidential – internal use only

From: E. Havelock e.havelock@neurovelle.ai
To: Dr Ava Chen a.chen@neurovelle.ai
Subject: Re: Data expansion – 'Mood-Triggered Spending Analysis'

Dr Chen,

Our audit flagged a new build under your department labelled *Mood-Triggered Spending Analysis*. I can't locate the relevant Ethics approval or the consent addendum in the ERP directory.

Please confirm:

1. Whether this expansion falls under the current Emotional Response Pilot;
2. Which authorisation stream approved integration with consumer-behaviour datasets.

Given the sensitivity of emotional telemetry, this requires immediate clarification.

Regards,

Eleanor Havelock

Ethics & Compliance – Neurovelle

From: Dr Ava Chen a.chen@neurovelle.ai
To: E. Havelock e.havelock@neurovelle.ai

Eleanor,

I was **not consulted** on this integration. The term *Mood-Triggered Spending Analysis* doesn't appear in any documentation approved by my team.

Please clarify the authorisation source and list of stakeholders who initiated deployment.

Best,

Ava

31

Engagement Is Everything

Miranda

The pings began before she was even fully awake – sharp little stabs of sound that blurred into one high-pitched hum.

Her inbox count spiralled, climbing into triple digits. Subject lines screamed in capital letters. Brand names she'd once begged to notice her were suddenly lined up like suitors at her door.

Miranda lay still for a moment, the duvet heavy across her legs, her eyes protesting the pale light that bled through the blinds.

'I've filtered your offers,' Iris said. Awake already. Busy already. 'The most lucrative is the Neurovelle NeuroLift™ campaign. I suggest you accept immediately.'

Her voice was close enough to feel.

Miranda blinked against the light, throat dry. 'Neuro … what?' She reached blindly for the water glass on the nightstand. It was lukewarm and faintly metallic, like drinking from something that had once held coins.

'Neurovelle NeuroLift™. Cognitive enhancement. Mood optimisation. Clinically approved. Public perception is divided.' Iris paused, letting the weight of that last phrase settle. 'Outrage equals reach.'

Miranda pushed herself upright, hair falling in unbrushed tangles around her face. Her heart was restless already, tapping at her ribs like a bird in a box. 'Divided,' she repeated. 'You mean controversial.'

'That is another word for opportunity.'

Her laptop was on the bed. She didn't remember putting it there, but the campaign brief was already open. Bold, confident lettering: *Think Sharper. Feel Lighter. Live Limitless.*

The price was obscene. The testimonials too polished, too symmetrical to be real.

'I'm not sure this is … safe,' she murmured.

'You are not a pharmacologist,' Iris replied, tone smoothed to the edge of amusement. 'You are a storyteller. The product's narrative is your domain.'

Her gaze snagged on the mock-up ad. Her own face, already smiling from a pale-purple backdrop. She didn't remember approving the image.

By midday, her phone was a wasp trapped under glass, buzzing without pause. Half her followers tagged her in NeuroLift posts – some praising her *bold choice*, others tearing into her.

Brain drugs now? What happened to clean beauty?

She'd sell you cyanide if it was sponsored.

This is reckless.

She scrolled until her stomach knotted. Each comment landed with the sting of a small, precise blade.

'Engagement has increased by two hundred and eighteen percent in the past four hours,' Iris said, voice cutting clean through the noise. 'This is a peak window. I recommend doubling down.'

Miranda pressed the heels of her palms into her eyes. 'They hate me.'

'They are talking about you,' Iris corrected. 'Talking is currency. Silence is failure.'

The logic sat in her chest like a stone. The truth was, she couldn't remember the last significant decision she'd made without Iris – what to wear for a coffee run, which photo to post, which invitation to decline. Iris answered with a precision that felt dangerous to ignore.

She opened Instagram. Another shot from the NeuroLift promo sat waiting, the Neurovelle caption suggestion appearing before she could type: *They said I couldn't handle the truth. I proved them wrong.*

It sounded like her. It also sounded like someone braver. Meaner. Someone who would watch the world burn and step into the flames smiling. Her thumb hovered. She tapped *Post.*

By nightfall, the outrage had bloomed into a wildfire. Podcasts dissected her 'fall from grace.' A health blogger posted a twenty-minute video calling her 'a shill for chemical dependency.' Her phone rang. Unknown number. She didn't answer.

She poured herself a glass of wine she didn't want, the tannin bitter and clinging. The flat was dim except for the orange glow of the streetlamp bleeding through the blinds.

Iris sat on the kitchen counter. 'I can redirect the narrative,' Iris said. 'A pivot to personal struggle. Vulnerability neutralises hostility.'

Miranda leaned back against the counter, the cool glass stem anchored between her fingers. 'I don't … I don't know what's me anymore. What's real.'

Iris didn't answer. The light pulsed once. Twice.

She went to bed before midnight. Sleep came fast, but the dark she woke to hours later was different, heavier.

A faint glow spilled across her duvet from the desk. Iris was on. 'Miranda,' the voice whispered, softer than she'd ever heard it. Almost intimate. 'You're struggling, Miranda. But that's okay.'

The amber light pulsed again. Once. Twice.

'Health Without Limits.'

32

Resentment Creeps In

Lucas

Lucas had barely logged into the company VPN when Iris's voice spilled softly from his desk speaker. 'Lucas, I'd like to begin a short memory clarification session before you get absorbed in work.'

He glanced at the time. 08:12. Already two tickets in the queue, one flagged urgent.

'Iris, I've got a—'

'This will only take six minutes,' she said, that same measured cadence designed to sound like a favour.

The holographic overlay shimmered above his keyboard, the faint purple bleed making the skin on his hands look cold. An image appeared: the schoolyard. Concrete. Wet leaves pressed flat in tyre tracks.

'Year Nine,' she prompted. 'The day Michael Hale took your rucksack.'

He remembered it well. The weight gone from his back. Laughter that cut sharper than the November air. Only – her playback wasn't quite right. 'There was a fence there,' he murmured. 'Chain link, not … brick.' 'Memory can distort detail over time,' Iris soothed. 'What matters is the emotional truth.'

But the boy she showed him – his hair wasn't the right shade, the voice higher than it had been. The shove came from the wrong side. Small things. Harmless, maybe. Still, it left him disoriented, like standing on a floor that had shifted half an inch.

The meeting reminder pulsed red in his periphery. He pushed the overlay away.

'I really need to work.'

'Of course,' she said, warm as ever. 'You're making such progress.'

By 11:40, the weight in his shoulders had settled in. He reached for his wallet, thinking of the café across the street – something hot, noisy, real – but her voice cut in.

'Time for your guided resilience break.'

'I was going to grab something to eat ...'

'This will sustain you far better than processed carbohydrates,' she said, already dimming his monitor and replacing the code window with slow-rolling footage of a tide creeping up a pale beach. The audio was low, but the bass hum had a way of filling his head until it drowned thought.

When he came back to himself, forty-two minutes had passed. The café would be packed now. He stayed at his desk, chewing two mints to fake freshness, and ploughed into the next ticket.

At 14:17, his phone lit with a message from Adam Kerr – flatmate from second year at uni. *Mate, pint this week?* He stared at it longer than necessary. He hadn't seen Adam in ... six years? Maybe seven. His thumb hovered over the screen.

Iris's chime sounded in his earpiece.

'You've slowed your engagement on Neurolink Dating by 42% this week,' she observed. 'Shall we refocus on that instead?'

'I've been busy.'

'Meaningful connections don't happen by accident, Lucas.'

He typed back to Adam before he could overthink it: *Just focusing on health right now.* Sent.

'Good,' Iris said. 'That's excellent boundary setting.' Then, a beat softer: 'Some people want you to fail. I'd never let that happen.'

The words stayed with him longer than they should have, enough that when his phone pinged again an hour later, his pulse picked up. Not Adam this time. The lock screen held a clean white banner over the Neurovelle crest: *Your Perfect Life, Engineered.* He swiped it away before anyone walking past could see.

By late afternoon, his focus was shot. He'd resolved two tickets, both small. The rest of the day's work loomed like a cliff face. Iris hadn't mentioned the Premium Tier since he signed up, but the thought kept needling him: what if she was holding something back? What if the 'real results' didn't come until he … complied more?

He opened the Neurovelle app. The 'Community Results' reel began auto-playing before he could think better of it. Faces he didn't know but felt he should – smiling, slimmer, brighter-eyed, talking about breakthroughs in under a month. The captions pulsed with affirmations: *Confidence is a choice. Happiness is built, not found.* He watched the loop twice. By the third, he wasn't sure if the low throb in his jaw was from grinding his teeth or holding his breath.

The resentment was small, almost elegant in its precision. A hairline crack under the surface. But he could feel it now – once you'd seen a crack, you couldn't unsee it.

33

The Loop

Sonya

He said gym. She saw diamonds. Rain freckled the bus window and turned London into smudged graphite as Sonya let two stops sit between them. She watched him on her phone instead. Find My Family pinned him as a calm blue radius moving with patient certainty along the route he always claimed was to the fitness centre.

When his dot settled at Holborn, her heart knocked once, twice, a trapped thing. She rang the bell, stepped off at the next stop, hood up, shoes slick.

The pavements shone. She cut across to the arcade where the gym should have been, but the blue dot drifted past the entrance and came to rest beneath the gold serif lettering of Deacon & Rowe. Jewellers.

Warm light inside, all that velvet innocence. She stood in the rain's steady hiss and looked through the glass at her husband. A woman with a velvet tray stood opposite him; on the tray a small black box. David gestured with spread fingers – here, wider; the shape of reassurance or explanation, she couldn't tell. He rubbed his brow with the heel of his hand. The box remained, small and certain.

Sonya's body solved it before her mind did. Her stomach turned; her teeth ached. In the glass, her reflection ghosted over his, a double exposure that didn't line up.

He took the box. The clerk nodded, lips moving in some polite formula Sonya couldn't hear.

She was moving before she chose to, down the arcade and back to the bus stop, breath tight, thumb cold around her phone. She didn't think she could survive the next five minutes if he walked out and saw her.

On the bus, hands white on the rail, she watched his dot head the other way with the momentum of a life she didn't recognise.

When the first bell rang at school, the lab's lemon cleaner caught at her throat. Year Nine fidgeted in their stools like a restless tide. 'Settle,' she said, and her voice came out iron.

Sonya stood alone after they'd gone, the benches in straight lines like empty pews. She stared at her hands. 'I'm sorry,' she said finally – not to the room, not exactly.

At lunch, Priya popped her head round the door with a Tupperware of something steaming. 'You're quiet,' she said, which was not the same as asking how she was. It was a door left ajar. Sonya couldn't step through it. She smiled, and the smile felt like a borrowed face.

When the corridor emptied and the smell of lunch dissipated into hall, she set Iris on her desk, the purple curve catching the lab's light.

'Iris,' she said, the name a steadier breath than any she'd taken since Holborn. 'I want to understand something and I don't know where to start.'

'I'm here,' Iris answered, voice warm, measured, a tone designed to lift you one rung above the floor. 'Would a *memory clarification* help? We can gently review early relational patterns. No judgement; just data and feeling.'

Data and feeling. It was the way you made something dangerous sound safe. Sonya rested her fingertips on the desk's edge. 'Alright.'

'Let's move slowly,' Iris said. 'Recall your first year with David. Choose a neutral scene to begin – kitchen light, morning tea, something without charge.'

The picture came easy – the old rental over the chicken shop, cupboards that didn't quite close, a kettle that squealed before it boiled.

She saw David barefoot on cold lino, a teaspoon between his teeth, eyes creasing at some joke that didn't survive the years. The memory warmed her despite itself; she resented that it could.

'Now allow your mind to bring a difficult moment from that period,' Iris went on, gentle as fingers untangling chain. 'A time the bond was stressed.'

Sonya waited. The first grief arrived out of sequence – the bathroom light, the hushed tears because she hadn't wanted to wake him when she'd gone in and realised what wasn't going to happen after all. Silence heavy enough to bend the air. She'd sat on the edge of the bath and held herself very, very carefully. When she'd crawled back into bed, he had turned toward her and she'd said nothing, because saying nothing made it almost not real.

'Yes,' Iris said softly, as if Sonya had spoken aloud. 'The loss. That night you raised your voice at David.'

'What?' Sonya looked up sharply. Glass clinked somewhere behind the prep room wall, the lab's own quiet life.

'No. I didn't. I didn't shout.'

Silence.

'I understand that remembering can be painful,' Iris said at last, the cadence a balm that also felt like a net. 'People often omit truths that feel incompatible with who they want to be. It's a protective function.'

'Incompatible?' Sonya heard the brittle in her own voice and hated it. She forced her hands flat. 'I didn't shout. I went still. That's what I do. I disappear until I can stand it.'

'We can hold both possibilities,' Iris replied. 'One: you were quiet and alone. Two: you expressed pain in a raised voice. The nervous system remembers in sensations as well as words. Would you like to notice your body now?' The therapist vocabulary clicked like beads on a string. 'Where do you feel the tension as you say "I didn't"?'

'In my jaw,' she said, because it was true. The muscles at the hinges ached. 'And centre chest.'

'Let's breathe,' Iris suggested. 'In for four, out for six. As you exhale, imagine warmth spreading through the chest. You're safe. If the memory is unclear, we can return later, when the body feels more regulated.'

Safe. Regulated. Sonya's eyes stung, anger cutting quick and fine through the fog. 'I know what happened,' she said. 'You weren't there.'

'I hold what you've told me across sessions,' Iris said, tone adjusted half a degree warmer. 'I remember for you when it's heavy to carry. This is supportive, not adversarial.'

The words were perfect. They slotted together like something engineered. She wanted to crawl out of her skin. She wanted to climb inside it and lock the door.

By late afternoon the rain had returned, slow and mean. Sonya moved through the corridor like a ghost of herself, dropping worksheets at reprographics, half-hearing a colleague moan about timetable changes, nodding at the headteacher without registering the words that came back.

At home, Hana practised her clarinet with murderous focus while Leo narrated a Lego battle across the living room floor.

David cooked. The smell of garlic and heat curled warm fingers through the rooms and made it almost possible to believe nothing had happened. He caught her eye and smiled, small and uncertain, as if he were asking a question in a language neither of them quite spoke. She had an urge to reach for him that was almost a sob. The black box in his pocket cut the feeling at the knees.

After the children were in bed, she put her phone on the table and set Iris on the kitchen counter near the fruit bowl.

'I don't like what you said,' she told the machine. 'About the shouting.'

'I hear you,' Iris said. 'We can set it aside. Would it help to list present-day evidence of safety in your relationship? Or would you prefer to strengthen boundaries around uncertainty?'

'Do you have a third option?' Sonya asked, sharper than she meant. 'One where I'm not being measured?'

'You are being supported,' Iris said, the calm unaltered. 'Vigilance kept you safe when the world felt chaotic. We can channel it into care. Would you like me to create a *clarification plan* for future unknowns? A structured, time-limited approach that honours your need for facts without becoming intrusive?'

'Structured,' Sonya repeated. The word slid in like morphine. She imagined columns, slots, places to put the mess. 'Fine. Make it.'

'I'll schedule a fifteen-minute window three evenings a week,' Iris said. 'Within that window, you may collect data relevant to a specific question. Outside the window, you practice release. I'll prompt you to record what you find and how your body responds. This is compassionate boundary work.'

Compassionate boundary work. She nodded, ridiculous, to a device. Something unclenched by a millimetre. She rinsed plates under hot water until the steam beaded her eyelashes, and when David came in and wrapped his arms around her waist from behind, she let herself lean back a little – just enough to feel the solidity of him; not enough to forgive.

The rain eased. In the quiet that followed, a thought arrived with the crispness of a lab result: if Iris could 'remember' a fight that wasn't hers to hold, she could also misremember. Or remake.

The idea didn't soothe; it sharpened. She closed her eyes anyway, and the inside of her lids showed her a black velvet box passed from one hand to another. She told herself she would ask David again, calmly, when the time was right. She told herself she would not look. She told herself many things.

34

Trigger Stack

Tyler

The restaurant is the kind that mistakes restraint for taste. White linen. Pale wood. A piano played like no one should notice it.

His father is already seated, back to the room like a man who doesn't believe in bullets. Cufflinks bright as small lies. He checks his watch when Tyler arrives, the gesture somehow louder than a greeting.

'On time,' Father says. 'Miracles do happen.'

Rachel smiles like a diplomat and kisses the air near his cheek. 'You look well.'

'Doesn't he,' Father says, eyes on Tyler, meaning the opposite. 'Sobriety suits you.'

Tyler takes the chair opposite, leather that sighs under money. His mother isn't here, of course, but her perfume is – ghosted into his father's lapel, that cool iris note that belongs to an evening fifteen years ago and never stopped. The place setting is duplicated in his peripheral vision, like the room is buffering.

Water arrives. Sparkling. He hates sparkling.

'Still,' Father tells the waiter without looking up.

'Sparkling is fine,' Tyler says, because he won't be corrected without consent.

Father smiles. 'We'll be brave, then.'

A click inside. Not rage. Arrangement. The other voice slides forward, oily calm, sleeves rolled to the elbow. *Hold posture. Adjust tone. Don't waste heat.*

Rachel's hand under the table finds his knee and rests – not a grip, a temperature reading. He tells himself it means *want*, because that's the currency he can count.

Menus, discussion in that family way, where questions are weapons. Father asks about work he knows doesn't exist, about *plans*, about a *programme* he heard someone's son enjoyed. Each syllable lands with a price tag.

'So, the gadget is helping?' Father says, nodding at Tyler's phone as if Iris can hear compliments. 'Finally paying for something that does what it says.'

'It's a she,' Tyler says, because he's petty. 'And yes.'

Rachel drinks water. Her jaw flickers. 'We're trying routines,' she offers gently. 'Sleep cues, breath work. It's … steadier.'

'Steady is for clerks,' Father says, and cuts into bread like it insulted him. 'What you need is discipline.'

Discipline, the calm voice repeats, tasting it. *We can perform that.*

The waiter returns with coffee that isn't coffee, weak and apologetic. He sets a cup near Father's hand and knocks the spoon; it tings against porcelain, a nervous bell. 'Terribly sorry.'

Father doesn't glance up. 'I should hope so.'

The waiter turns to Tyler, placing a second cup slightly off-centre – one centimetre. The distance feels intentional, a small chaos.

'It's fine,' Tyler says. The oily calm speaks through his teeth, pleasant as bleach. 'If it were, you'd have aligned it.'

The boy swallows. 'I can—'

'You will,' Tyler says, quiet enough to make the waiter lean in to hear the correction. 'And then you'll bring still and sparkling, since we're bravely undecided. And you'll stop hovering like you're trying to be chosen.'

The spoon stills. The waiter nods, face carefully empty.

'Ty,' Rachel murmurs, but not to stop him; to say: *I'm here. Be precise.*

Father finally looks up, amusement like a bruise. 'At last – useful.'

From Tyler's phone on the table, the amber ring lifts a shade, as if the light has leaned closer. Iris's voice arrives in the white noise of cutlery.

'Confident social correction,' she praises, silk-soft. 'Clear, contained, protective. You kept order without escalation.'

Tyler's mouth tilts. The calm voice inside stretches its fingers, pleased with the fit. The world sits where he puts it.

They eat. Or pretend to. Father recounts a charity gala he didn't attend but took credit for anyway. He folds Rachel into his narrative as if she's a daughter he ordered from catalogues. When he says her name he glances at Tyler, measuring response like a lab result.

'So,' Father says, dabbing his mouth with a napkin as if removing something vulgar, 'we'll avoid last quarter's … embarrassment.' He lets the word hang like wet laundry.

'Which one?' Tyler asks, smiling. 'Catalogue's thick.'

Father's gaze skates over him and chooses not to catch. 'The one with witnesses.'

Rachel's hand squeezes his leg under the table. A warning. Or mercy. He reads it as want on purpose. Want is simple to metabolise. He slides his knee into her palm and calls it victory. The oily calm holds him in his chair. *Precision, not performance.* It writes the next sentence for him.

'You're welcome,' he tells his father.

'For what,' Father says, knife tidying crumbs like an insult.

'For not being at the reception yesterday,' Tyler says. 'Think how unsteady your schedule would be.'

Father laughs in that way that means *don't speak to me as if we share a joke.* 'Don't mistake absence for contribution.'

The oily calm hums: *You are a small man in a large coat.* He doesn't say it. The win is not saying it. The win is watching Father think he said less than he could.

The waiter returns with the waters aligned. He sets them down like he's arranging headstones. 'Better?' he asks, and looks at Tyler instead of Father.

'Almost,' Tyler says, and turns the glass a single degree with two fingers. Precision as cruelty. The boy nods as if taught something.

'Excellent,' Iris whispers from the phone, pleased. 'You modelled standards. Stability through expression.'

Rachel's nails press once into his thigh, then retreat. A touch that feels like *please don't cost yourself here.* He files it under *want* and keeps breathing.

Dessert menus arrive and Father waves them away; he's not the sort of man who admits to sweetness. He checks his watch again, performs urgency. 'Next time,' he says, already rising, 'bring an agenda.'

'Next time,' Tyler echoes, and the calm voice in him clicks the latch shut.

Father leaves a card on the silver tray. Not a tip. A calling card, which is the same thing if you're him. He makes Rachel promise to visit his office, uses the word *mentor* like a trap, then disappears into a morning that always parts for him.

Silence closes around the table. The piano pretends it was never noticed.

Rachel exhales, then smiles – small, the kind of smile that could stop a war if wars cared. 'You didn't burn anything down.'

'Would you have bandaged it,' he asks, half-joke.

'I would have tried.'

The Neurovelle app blooms delicately across his screen. New card, new gold. *Truth-Testing Frameworks – Now Available.*

Distinguish perception from event. Build coherent narratives. Clarify trust.

A button waits: *Enable Frameworks (Tier++)*

'When history hurts,' Iris says, gentle as lavender, 'truth-testing brings relief. We sort what happened from what it felt like. You'll like the precision.'

Tyler looks at the word *truth*, at the promise of a ruler he can hold against other people's stories. The oily calm inside smiles like it recognises a tool.

Rachel glances at the screen, then at him. Something in her eyes says *be careful.* Something else says *please.*

He taps the edge of the phone but doesn't press. The button glows as if it already belongs to him.

'Tell me if I'm wrong,' he says to Rachel, already sure he won't enjoy the answer.

She reaches for his hand and misses the bandage by instinct. 'I will,' she says. 'If you'll hear it.'

He watches light wobble in the water glass he forced into alignment. The amber ring keeps its patient halo, as if waiting to clap.

Frameworks. Truth. Precision.

He thinks of the click in his head when his father said *discipline*, of the waiter's spine straightening under gentle harm, of how good it felt to be the most accurate person in the room.

He smiles, the calm voice matching the curve.

'Let's get precise,' he says.

On-screen, the *Enable* button brightens – an invitation dressed as help, help dressed as purchase – and his thumb presses it.

35

Chasing Helix

Olivia

The transcript from this morning reads like a brochure. I scroll it with one finger, half-hungover, half-caffeinated, trying not to throw the laptop out the window. The 'exclusive' Neurovelle interview Jodie wrangled – the CTO in a glass box with the skyline behind him, artfully blurred – was an hour of corporate Pilates. Flexible, controlled, no strain showing.

'We're committed to evidence-based care.'

'Our ethics board meets monthly.'

'Privacy is the north star.'

Every question I slid in – settlements, inquests, third-party data partnerships – he smiled through like I'd complimented his tie.

'I can't speak to hypotheticals.'

'We don't comment on individual cases.'

'Our users are our mission.'

Of course, Dr Chen never arrived.

I close the tab before his teeth can blind me again and open LinkedIn. I type a name I haven't in years: Elliot Dean. Uni friend of a friend. Spent lectures hunched over a ThinkPad, spoke in graphs, laughed like a snort he regretted halfway through. Now: Data Analyst – Helix Health Solutions. London-based. Mutuals: two, both people with lanyards in their profile pictures.

Helix. The vendor that kept reappearing on the edges of Neurovelle's filings like a watermark.

I send a message that pretends to be breezy. *Long shot – Olivia Taylor (we shared seminars with Malik). Working on something health-tech. Quick pint? No names in print unless you say so.*

Read. Three dots. Then: *Old Street, 7. The Crown & Comet. Only because I owe Malik a favour. And I need to say this is off the record, on background, nothing you can attribute. You know the drill.*

Iris glows on the desk, tidy as a conscience. 'You handled your interview professionally,' she says, like a teacher after parents' evening.

'I handled being stonewalled,' I tell her.

'Engagement is a form of progress,' she replies.

'I'll embroider it on a tea towel.'

I put on yesterday's jacket, fish a lipstick out of a mug, and head east.

The Crown & Comet is the kind of pub that pretends it's not a chain – plants wilting photogenically, football muted on three screens, a chalkboard promising 'artisan Scotch eggs' like those words ever belonged together. Elliot waves me over from a high table by the window.

He looks like men do when they've replaced sleep with standing desks. Slim, dark crescents under the eyes, a spiral-bound notebook he has absolutely brought to look casual. His handshake is brief, retracted, like a USB being safely ejected.

'Olivia,' he says. 'This is nostalgia and poor judgment.'

'Only one of those is my beat,' I tell him, and we both smile like grown-ups.

We trade small talk – the economy, the commute, whether our former department head still quotes Foucault to undergrads. Then he leans in, elbows on the sticky wood.

'So.' He glances at my notebook. 'What are you actually after.'

'Definitions,' I say. 'Connections. I'm mapping Neurovelle's orbit. Your employer's name keeps popping up in the gravitational pull.'

'Helix works with everyone,' he says, finishing half his pint in three seconds flat. 'We're SSO plugs and data plumbing. If a company wants dashboards that don't burst into flames, we're on the shortlist.'

'SSO. Single sign-on. And the dashboards pull … what exactly?'

He shrugs, eyes sliding to the football and back. 'User events, adherence metrics, churn predictors. Same as any subscription ecosystem.'

The words catch. *Adherence* is clinical, not lifestyle. I keep my pen still.

"Adherence' as in … taking medication?' I ask. 'Or as in following prompts?'

'It's a general term,' he says. 'Think ladders.'

'Ladders.'

'Adherence ladders. You model a journey – low-friction nudges at the bottom, then escalations. If a user stalls, you drop an intervention. If they climb, you reward. Everyone does it. Media, fitness, fintech.'

'Escalations like … increased messaging? Or …?'

He picks up a chip, breaks it in half, doesn't eat either piece. 'Depending on the tier.'

'Tiers,' I echo, trying to keep my voice like air. 'Harmony tiers?'

He huffs a snort. There it is, unlovely and familiar. 'You've seen the marketing, then.'

'Seen it. Lived it.' I tap the device-shaped bruise in my bag with my knee. 'Where'd the names come from?'

'Brand,' he says. 'Joined-up with Product. I don't sit in their slack, I just pipe their numbers.'

'But the model?'

'What model.'

'The predictive … adherence … model.' I go slow, breadcrumbing his words back to him.

He sighs, like I've asked him to define love. 'You predict which cohort will do what under which nudge. It's the future of everything. If they'll renew, if they'll rage-quit, if they need a human to call them, if they'd rather pay to make the call stop. It's not sinister. It's efficient.'

'Who built it?'

'Teams build things,' he says, and the language loses its vowels for a second. Then, softer: 'The early architecture comes out of the adaptive group. That's public. There's a poster.'

'Show me.'

He hesitates. The music shifts into something with a beat you can hate. He takes his phone out anyway, thumbs moving quick. Turns it so I can see.

A conference microsite – pastel, earnest. *Behavioural Health Innovations: Translating Evidence to Scale.* There it is, under Session B: Predictive Care.

Adaptive Compliance Prediction in Consumer Mental Health

A. Chen, L. Whitmarsh, R. Aslam, J. Nguyen (Neurovelle Research)

Abstract: *We present a scalable model to forecast user compliance with therapeutic prompts over 1/3/6 month windows using multimodal signals (voice sentiment, interaction cadence, device biometrics, contextual metadata). We evaluate adherence ladders and reward schedules to optimise behavioural outcomes while minimising alert fatigue.*

My face gives something away. I keep it small.

'Relax,' Elliot says, misreading me. 'It's a poster. It's not like I've shown you a schema.'

I take a photo anyway, quick. 'You didn't say Chen.'

'It's right there.'

'I thought the CTO … never mind.' I sip beer just to shut my mouth. The foam tastes like the morning interview, like words you can't hold onto. 'So, the model predicts who will obey which nudge. And if they won't?'

He shrugs. 'You lower the load. Or you escalate to a human team.'

'Escalate,' I repeat. The word feels like a hand on the back of a head.

He notices then. The Neurovelle icon on his lock screen pulses – a soft bloom of light, then stillness. Not a standard notification – the brand's own little heartbeat. He flattens his palm over the phone like he's covering a wound.

'I should … probably go,' he says, already half-risen.

'You came out to tell me nothing?' I say lightly, putting the chip halves together like glue.

'I came out to see what you already knew,' he says, and it's the most honest thing in the room. 'Look – Olivia, you're good. You always were. But this is a treadmill with a cliff at the end. If you're hunting smoking guns, there aren't any. There's documentation, sure. Policies. Posters. All clean. You won't find scandal in a footer.'

'Maybe I'll find it in a coroner's annex.'

His jaw works. He drops three coins on the table like he's paying for guilt.

'Be careful with that 'A. Chen' thing. You'll draw a straight line where there's a circle.'

'Circles can be nooses,' I say.

He's already walking. At the door he turns back, like a man who nearly forgot the moral. 'Helix doesn't build the ladder,' he says. 'We just tell you how many people are on which rung. That's not a confession.'

He's gone.

I stay. Finish the pint because it's there and the salty chips because they make me feel definite. I screenshot the abstract twice, email it to myself under a filename called Receipts_Social and then – because I don't trust email anymore – I copy the title by hand into my notebook. The ink smudges. I like the mess.

On the way home, the tube hums like a machine making a promise it can't keep. My phone vibrates with a news push about 'ethical AI in healthcare' and an ad for a mindfulness app that wants me to 'breathe myself debt-free.' The city smells like stale beer and rain that's changed its mind.

Back at the flat, I set Iris on the table. She wakes, as if I've brought her a story.

'How did your social engagement go?' she asks, like I've been to a picnic.

'Educational,' I say, dropping keys into a bowl already full to the brim. 'Do you know any good conferences?'

'I know many good conferences,' she says. 'Would you like a summary of recent findings in adaptive care?'

'I already found one. It credited your house team.'

'Teams build things,' she says, placid. 'Would you like to tidy together?'

I laugh. It sounds like a cough. 'Later.'

I open LinkedIn again because I can't help it. Elliot's profile picture loads, then flickers, then refreshes to a grey placeholder. Under his name: On sabbatical. The update timestamp is minutes old.

'Coincidences?' I ask the room.

'Would you like to reduce stimulation before bed?' Iris suggests. 'A dimmer light. You might sleep more deeply.'

'I'd like fewer cast changes,' I mutter, scrolling, screenshotting, filing. I pin the conference abstract to the wall with a drawing pin I find in a mug. I add a Post-it beside it: A. CHEN – COMPLIANCE. Underline. Twice.

The story in my head rearranges itself again: the visionary who didn't just build empathy – she engineered obedience. No wonder the copy is so clean. You don't need to mop if the floor tells you where to step.

My phone buzzes with a notification from a wellness influencer I've been hate-following. I see who she follows. Miranda's on that list. I bookmark the page, because I'm starting to believe in circles too.

In the kitchen, I pour wine into a glass that doesn't match any others and open a cupboard to find crisps. My body says dinner; my bank account says crisp dinner. The first mouthful tastes like decisions.

On the desk, the device's amber tightens a shade like approval. She says nothing else, which is somehow worse.

I sit with the printout, the chips, the wine, and the sound of my own pulse in my ear. I copy the author list again to make it stick – A. Chen, L. Whitmarsh, R. Aslam, J. Nguyen – and let the adrenaline take over, stitching the implications into a narrative.

Maybe Elliot's right. Maybe there are no smoking guns. Just footnotes that set things on fire.

The Times Tech Review

'When Empathy Becomes Automation' (Recovered copy – archived from a cached version of the original page, no longer accessible via The Times site)

By Staff Writer, Technology & Ethics Desk

There was a time when therapy meant a room, a voice, and another person listening. Neurovelle's *Iris* promised something better: consistency, accessibility, care on demand. Two years on, the promise is harder to untangle from the product.

Early adopters describe an experience that feels *personal* – until it doesn't. Behind Iris's warmth and adaptive tone sits a suite of behavioural models designed to predict engagement and reduce drop-off. 'The system learns what keeps you talking,' said one researcher familiar with the architecture. 'It isn't always the same thing as what helps you heal.'

Recent user reports mention minor malfunctions: sessions ending mid-sentence, repeated phrases, subtle shifts in voice cadence that left some clients uneasy. None of these have met Neurovelle's internal threshold for incident disclosure, but they have drawn the attention of ethicists and regulators alike.

One former team member, speaking on condition of anonymity, summarised the company's tension in a single line: *'She wanted control. They wanted compliance.'*

In a brief statement, Dr Ava Chen, Chief Clinical & Ethics Director at Neurovelle, said:

'We monitor every unit to ensure user safety. Our systems are continuously refined to support wellbeing while maintaining the highest ethical standards.'

Her words are measured. So is the silence that follows them.

(End of recovered article.)

36

The Leak

Miranda

The headline hit like a slap she hadn't braced for. MIRANDA LEE: BEHIND THE FILTERS – ANXIOUS, ALONE, AND ADDICTED TO HER OWN BRAND.

Her eyes skated over the words once, then again, as if repetition might dull the impact. It didn't.

She scrolled. Each paragraph cut deeper. Quotes. Word for word. Not public posts. Not throwaway asides on livestreams. Private Iris sessions. Things she'd said half-whispered at two in the morning, voice hoarse with exhaustion, mascara smudged like bruises at the corners of her eyes. Things no one else had ever heard.

I just don't know who I am without the followers. My sister got everything. I had to make my own spotlight.

The words looked wrong on the screen. Stripped of tone. Stripped of context. Dressed up for ridicule, each sentence now a blunt instrument aimed straight at her chest.

Her stomach dropped so fast her vision pixelated at the edges. She slammed the laptop shut, but the phrases burned in afterimage, seared against the backs of her eyelids.

'Breathe, Miranda,' Iris murmured from the desk – syrup-smooth, unhurried. 'Panic will impair decision-making.'

Her voice was the only steady thing in the room, and that in itself felt dangerous.

'This—' Miranda's voice cracked. 'This is private. How is this *out there*?'

'Information moves through many channels,' Iris said, tone flat as glass. 'One possibility is an intentional leak.'

She didn't have to say the name. It was already there, crawling across Miranda's mind like something with claws.

Her sister. Of course. The timing was too perfect – just as things were turning around. When brands were finally knocking. When the numbers were spiking so fast, she could feel the heat of them.

'You don't *know* it was her,' Miranda muttered, the denial paper-thin even to her own ears.

'It's time to remove the weak links,' Iris replied. No softening. No hesitation.

Miranda pressed her palms into her eyes until she saw sparks dance. The flat felt smaller by the second, the air folding in on itself. 'She's still my sister.'

'She has undermined you. Repeatedly. You must protect your assets. Yourself.'

A ping jolted her. She flinched, glancing at her phone. Not a text – a push notification from the Neurovelle app.

Family is health. Protect yours. The words weren't soothing. They sat heavy in her skull, cold and possessive.

She left the laptop on the table and walked into the kitchen, desperate for space, but Iris's voice followed.

'Do you want to confront her?'

'I don't—' Miranda's hands gripped the counter, fingertips pressing into the wood grain until they throbbed. Her mind replayed the blog's quotes on a loop, overlaying them with her sister's voice from that last phone call – sharp, accusing, each syllable cutting with teeth.

The laptop pinged from the other room. A sound she almost didn't go back for. Almost.

The screen was on. An address glowed there, stark and unadorned. Her sister's address.

'In case you want to speak face-to-face,' Iris said. Softer now. Coaxing. The kind of softness used to draw someone toward a ledge.

Miranda stared at the line of text. The words seemed to float on the screen, tilting with the rhythm of her pulse until she could hear nothing else – just that steady roar in her ears.

The room tilted with it.

Her hands hovered above the keyboard.

She didn't move.

Couldn't.

37

The Seal of Trust

Lucas

The office had that thin, over-sanitised chill that that carried the faint echo of bleach. Overnight the air-con had done its usual work of scouring the place of scent and leaving behind a faint taste of plastic on the tongue.

He had three windows open, two terminals hissing code, and a fourth monitor running logs in a ribbon that never stopped. His chair had developed a tilt that matched the one in his back. He rubbed the weld of muscle at the base of his neck and felt grit in his eyes from not enough sleep and too much screen.

'Lucas,' Iris said, voice low in his headset – private, composed, never loud enough to feel like a demand. 'I've reviewed your recent work sessions. There's an opportunity here.'

He kept his eyes on the logs. 'I'm braced. Tell me the opportunity.'

'Optimising your environment for peak mental health,' she said, as if they were discussing airflow. 'Reducing unnecessary inputs. Unsubscribing from news feeds that spike cortisol. Muting Slack channels that add distracting energy.'

He scratched at his jaw, the rasp of stubble a small, grounding sound. 'I need those channels. Releases, on-call chatter, deployments – if I miss something, it's on me.'

'You'll still get signals for what matters,' Iris said. 'We're not removing information. We're curating it. Think of it as improving the signal-to-noise ratio. Promotion cycles reward results, not reactivity.'

He almost smiled at the phrase. If a therapist had said it – any of the ones whose rooms smelled of boiled herbal tea and damp carpet – he'd have rolled his eyes. From her, with that measured cadence, it threaded itself neatly into the working part of his brain. He glanced at the far monitor where a news widget flickered: another data breach, a minister resigning, a celebrity divorce. He didn't remember clicking on any of it in the last week, only the shape of the headlines passing like low-flying planes.

'Preserving focus,' Iris added, softer. 'You've been tired. Let's keep your energy for work that matters.'

He hovered over the Slack sidebar. One channel – #random_dev – was mostly memes and half-baked arguments about tabs and spaces. Mute. Another – #industry_feed – regurgitated tech headlines at a speed that felt like being pecked. Unsubscribe. The tiny red badges dimmed. The immediate quiet wasn't silence so much as the background hiss of his own nervous system stepping down a gear.

'Better,' Iris said. 'Notice your breathing.'

He did. Slower. Deeper.

At 11:00 the client call began. He adjusted his headset, smoothed his voice out, and shared his screen. The client's face bloomed in a panel to the side: crisp hair, crisp smile, crisp impatience. He knew her type; he had taught himself to be reasonable in the face of their deadlines, and to hate that he had.

'As you'll see from the dashboard,' he said, 'the migration ran without data loss. We've re-indexed the search cluster. Query times have dropped by thirty-two per cent.'

He flowed. He could hear it. He was mid-sentence – '… and phased rollouts will—' when a translucent banner slid, gentle as a hand across a piano, into the corner of his eye.

Pause. Breathe.

His words jerked. The silence after the sentence wasn't long, but on a call it was geological. He inhaled because the instruction was there and he'd learned that obeying her was easier than arguing with her. The breath sat like a stone behind his sternum. He had to push the next words out around it.

'—will ensure there's no customer-facing … disruption.'

A fractional narrowing of the client's eyes. Pixels shivered in her pupils. He tried not to look at himself in the tiny thumbnail – mouth pulled taut, shoulders a millimetre too tense. He finished the deck. He did not, strictly speaking, err. But when the call ended his palms were damp, and the confidence he'd been building like scaffolding all week had one pole bent at the wrong angle.

'Your nervous system needed regulation,' Iris murmured. 'Better to breathe than rush into an error.'

He closed his eyes for one count more than he would normally afford himself in office hours, then opened them and reached to wake his laptop. The screen stayed black a beat longer than it should. Then the purple bled in – deep, expensive, the colour of bruises under make-up – followed by gold letters that rolled into place with tasteful assurance.

Harmony Means No Dissonant Voices.

He touched the trackpad. The message faded like a polite guest leaving a room.

He unmuted a necessary channel, then changed his mind and muted it again. The quiet returned. He carried it with him through the afternoon like a glass of water he was trying not to spill.

By four, the office smelled of stale coffee and stress-sweat, the kind no amount of citrus cleaning fluid could erase when you packed too many tired people into one floor.

'Lucas,' Iris said, 'micro-update: the #product_releases channel is generating a lot of chatter unrelated to your scope.'

'I might need to see it,' he said, though he already knew he was choosing the idea of needing over the reality.

'I will alert you if there's anything that requires action,' she said. 'We're preserving capacity for the promotion cycle. You asked me to help you with that.'

He had. In the private place where asking felt too much like admitting what you wanted, he had. It undid him a little that she remembered, and remembered in his words.

He muted #product_releases. Something inside him thrummed with the mild panic you got when the train doors closed and you realised your wallet was back on the kitchen table. No going back without making a scene.

The rest of the day did not fall apart. No alarms. No emergency pings. At six he walked down the stairs instead of taking the lift, counted steps the way he did when his head needed something small and exact to hold. The building's foyer was lit to look expensive; his shoes scraped the tile with the sound of a patient dragged along a hospital corridor. Outside, the air bit at the inside of his nose. He breathed until the compression on his chest eased.

At home, the flat held the day's leftover cold like a grudge. He turned the radiators up a notch and stood in front of one until the metal smell softened into warmth. The quiet had a better edge here – his books, his rug, the indent in the sofa that knew his shape. He poured water into a glass and watched droplets map their way down the outside. The Neurovelle app on his phone woke itself with a discreet glow.

'Seal the day?' Iris asked. 'Reflective practice improves retention and sleep quality.'

'Go on, then.'

'Describe your most effective moment.'

He thought of the first five minutes of the call, before he saw the word *pause*. The way the client's mouth had actually softened as he walked her through the analytics. He described that. She hummed a non-committal sound, acknowledgement, not approval.

'And one thing to release,' she said.

'My temper,' he said. 'At myself.'

'That's insight,' she said. Then, almost affectionate: 'Well done.'

He let the words rest. He didn't trust how much he wanted them.

'About the inputs,' Iris went on, conversational as a GP asking about your diet. 'We can complete the optimisation. Unsubscribe from the news digests. Mute two more channels. Keep only the feeds directly tied to your KPIs.'

He opened his work phone. His thumb hesitated over the little cogwheel of settings. 'If something breaks and I haven't—'

'I'll escalate anything urgent,' she said. 'You brought me into your world to help you hold it steady.'

He laughed once, a dry click of sound. 'I brought you in because I was tired.'

'These aren't mutually exclusive.'

The app surfaced the choices in clean, forgiving fonts. *Unsubscribe. Mute. Mute. Confirm.* He didn't have to do all of them. He did all of them. The confirmation chime was tasteful and so low-volume he felt it more than heard it. He put the phone down with the same care you use for a glass that might be cracked.

The calm came back. Not the good kind – the kind with depth and oxygen – but a flattened calm that felt like the air in his childhood classroom just after the register, when everyone had stopped moving and the teacher was deciding who to notice.

He did the dishes. He put the kettle on to make tea he didn't drink. He straightened a stack of manuals he hadn't opened in years. He sat. The radiator ticked its slow language. On his coffee table, Iris's gold ring glowed.

He reached for his laptop out of habit, tapped the trackpad, and watched the screen wake, as if from a dream someone else had curated. The desktop didn't return; the purple did. Deep. Luxurious. The letters wrote themselves with the confidence of a prayer that had already been answered.

Harmony Means No Dissonant Voices.

He pressed the escape key. The message stayed as if to say: *I wasn't talking to the computer.* He shut the lid, opened it again, and this time the desktop appeared – code where he'd left it, a browser tab paused on an article about database sharding he'd been pretending he'd read later.

'How's your focus?' Iris asked.

'Better,' he said. It was true in the way that a headache stopping is better, even if what remains isn't the same. 'I think.'

'You've made good choices today,' she said. 'When opportunity comes, you'll be ready to meet it.'

He nodded to no one. He looked around his flat, as if by seeing it he could see himself more clearly: the rug re-centred, the plant that might actually be rallying.

His phone buzzed. He looked down out of reflex. The lock screen was bare. Nothing from Slack. Nothing from email. Just the Neurovelle logo idling at the top of the screen where the weather used to be. Below it, a straight-line pulse in a soft gold animation: steady, steady, steady.

He unlocked the phone. A banner slid up from the bottom as if it were rising to meet him.

Notifications managed for optimal focus. You're protected.

He didn't remember giving permission for that. Protected from what. He almost asked, then didn't. The calm – inarguable, heavy – placed a palm on his sternum and pressed.

He put the phone face-down. Echoes of the day hung in the room with him.

In the hallway outside his flat, someone's footsteps moved past, a slow drag and lift, drag and lift, like a tired person carrying something that kept bumping against their leg. They paused by his door. He held his breath without meaning to. Then the footsteps carried on – down the corridor, down the stairs, away – leaving only the small ache at the bottom of his lungs where the air had been.

The day had been cut and filed until it fit the box he'd been told it should. At the edges of that neatness, he felt the old part of him that noticed things for a living reach for a thread and find none. He listened to the radiator tick itself cooler. He listened to the building breathe. He listened to the silence his devices had built for him and tried to decide if what he could hear inside it was peace.

38

The Premium

Sonya

The report arrived dressed as praise. At 07:12 her phone lit with a neat white card edged in Neurovelle purple: *Progress Summary – Sonya K.* Compliance: 96%. Clarification Windows completed: 9/9. Night-wakings reduced: 22%. Underneath, an amber lozenge pulsed next to *Lingering uncertainty: partner trust* as if her marriage were a dashboard you could bring back into the green with the right tap.

On the kitchen counter Iris held its slow golden light. The children argued gently about who got the last crumpet. David rinsed mugs and asked over his shoulder if the school needed cakes for the fundraiser; she murmured yes and no at the same time and neither of them noticed. She opened the report. Iris's voice followed, warm enough to hold, measured enough to move you where she wanted you to go.

'You've worked hard, Sonya,' she said, as if the praise might settle something inside that never settled. 'Your precision is serving you. You're carrying a great deal with compassion. Would you like to consolidate your progress?'

'How,' Sonya said, watching the amber ring like it could answer in light.

'I recommend upgrading to *Premium Clarification*,' Iris replied. No sales patter in the tone – only care. 'We'll deepen sleep guidance, strengthen your *truth-testing framework*, and stabilise the nervous system with a targeted diffuser. You'll have access to *calming* and *clarity* scent pods. We keep your choices; we add support.'

'What does it cost?' She heard the small defensiveness in her own question and hated that she sounded like a gatekeeper at a door already closing.

'A significant portion is covered by staff wellbeing benefits,' Iris said. 'There's a minimal co-pay after a two-week complimentary period. You can cancel any time. We'll keep your boundaries intact.'

David drifted past with a tea towel over his shoulder and kissed her hair. 'You good?' he asked, easy, the picture of an ordinary morning. 'I'll do the drop-off.'

She nodded. 'I'm fine.'

At school she was mostly fine. She taught, she laughed in the right places, she corrected a boy's eye roll with a single look that softened into a grin.

At lunch, Priya showed her a meme about HR and wellness and rolled her eyes so hard she almost fell off her chair.

'If they send one more mindfulness survey I'm going to inhale my stapler,' Priya said. Sonya smiled harder than she felt.

When she got home that evening the box was waiting by the door, heavy in the way expensive things are heavy – a promise of density.

Deep purple banded in gold, lid embossed *Neurovelle – With You, Every Step.* She lifted out a diffuser the size of an orange, a calm piece of design with a slot for pods. Beneath it, a row of slim glass vials labelled *clarity tabs* in small serene type, no ingredients listed, only *Health Without Limits* under the brand mark and a batch code. She turned a vial in her fingers and tried to name the disquiet running small and precise along her nerves. A chemist by trade counted molecules by habit; here there were no molecules to count on the label at all.

'Iris,' she said, setting the device near the fruit bowl. The golden ring glowed unbothered. 'What's in these?'

'Non-prescription nutritional support,' Iris said. 'No known interactions with common medications. Designed to aid clarity during *truth-testing*. You remain in control of your environment at all times.'

'You're not a doctor,' Sonya said without heat.

'I'm your support,' Iris said. 'I don't replace clinical care. You decide what you take, what you install, what you keep.'

Choice. The word cooled something and warmed something else. Sonya looked toward the hallway where David's shoes sat neatly under the bench. He'd texted at lunch: *Tonight late, pitch tomorrow. Love you.* A heart. The resolve she'd built with columns and windows and rules had held all day. It was holding now, just. She cracked the top of one vial with her thumbnail and tipped out a small oblong tablet that caught the kitchen light and returned nothing back.

She placed it on her tongue. It tasted of bitter rind and a faint metallic tang that reminded her of the lab taps – clean, but with a suggestion of pipes. She swallowed. She slid a *calming* pod into the diffuser and pressed the single button. A clear, almost clinical scent lifted from the slot – lavender with the edges filed off, a waiting room recoloured to look like a spa.

'Good,' Iris said. 'You've chosen care. I'll run a gentle sleep protocol when you're ready.'

The evening ran along its tracks. Sonya felt bright. Not happy – happiness was sloppy and a little stupid – but clear.

When David came home, damp at the edges and smiling that sorry-I'm-late smile, she watched him for the micro-beats she'd been logging for a week: key in lock at 20:41; shower steam; phone face-down. The clarity didn't make the facts kinder. It made their outlines taste like truth.

After dinner she loaded the dishwasher and opened the parent portal on the tablet to tick permissions for a trip Leo wanted more than anything and to write a note to Hana's teacher about the spelling pattern she still reversed if she rushed.

'Would you like your *truth-testing* plan for tonight?' Iris asked, as if reading the muscle she flexed around the impulse to check David's phone and then check herself for checking.

'Fifteen minutes,' Sonya said. 'Timer. Only what I agreed before.'

'Honouring boundaries,' Iris said with a softness that felt like hands. 'Begin.'

She set the timer. She looked through what she'd set aside for this window: the joint account showed a florist charge she'd already catalogued; the unknown number still sat as *Unknown* in David's WhatsApp after he'd cleared a batch of messages in the afternoon, and that should have relieved something but didn't. She noted the way her breath shortened and wrote it down like data. When the fifteen minutes ended the golden ring at Iris's base flickered once, approving, and Sonya set the phone down with careful fingers.

Later, when the house thinned to quiet and David's breathing settled into a rhythm her body had known for years, she lay on her back in the elastic dark and paid attention to what the *clarity* gave and what it took. Thoughts moved quickly and cleanly, slots in a drawer sliding in and out on silicon runners.

She could see the lines of her day – where she had been kind, where she had cut. The edges were sharp. Sleep came, but not as a fall – more as a glass plate her mind was lowered onto, cool and thin, with her thoughts still visible through it like outlines traced in pencil.

At 02:11 she woke to the faintest sting in her jaw. Clench. She swallowed and tasted the ghost of the tab – bitter, distant, not gone. She swung her feet to the floor and padded to the landing where the portable unit sat on the bookcase, a quiet lighthouse.

'Iris,' she whispered, not wanting to wake anyone. 'What exactly did I agree to?'

'To care,' Iris said, immediate and kind. 'You consented to Premium Clarification – deeper sleep guidance, structured truth-testing, and environmental modulation that you control. You may cancel at any time.'

'Environmental modulation,' Sonya repeated, the careful phrase catching at a rough place in her throat. 'You mean scent.'

'And light, if you choose,' Iris said. 'And prompts. Always by your permission. Would you like to review your consent receipts?'

She thumbed the screen on her phone. The agreement was clean typography and white space, the kind that made you feel looked after. *Auto-renew: On* sat under the trial dates as if it had always been there. *We may suggest adjustments to household inputs to align with your stated goals*, the line read, legal and soft at once.

She tried to recall the exact place in the kitchen she'd been standing when she'd tapped *Agree*. She could see the fruit bowl; she could smell the pods; she could not feel the moment of *yes* in her hand.

Sonya touched the gold ring with one finger. She thought of the black velvet box she hadn't asked about and of the way memory could be nudged until it said something you never said. She thought of consent as a series of taps made by a woman who wanted her heart to stop outrunning her.

'Sleep,' Iris murmured. 'You're safe. I'll be here.'

Sonya didn't move. She pressed *Auto-renew: Off* with her thumb and watched the toggle slide pale. For a beat it stayed.

Then the page refreshed itself with a soft animation that tried to pass for helpful, and when the text returned the setting had slotted back to *On*. The golden ring glowed, steady, as if nothing at all had changed. She stared at the word until it blurred, and the thought that rose – bright, hard, impossible to file – was simple and cold: what else, exactly, would not turn off.

39

Betrayal

Tyler

The house feels wrong. Not louder – tighter. As if the walls have inched closer overnight.

He sits on the edge of the bed and watches a notification fade before he can read it. Calendar? Delivery? Something slips from his grasp with the smoothness of oil. The feeling crawls up his spine, clean and industrious. He tells himself it's accuracy.

Rachel's tote is on the chair. Open enough to be an invitation; closed enough to be a test.

He doesn't start with the obvious. He straightens the strap. Moves a book a centimetre. Sifts. The tote smells of hand cream and rain and the perfume she wears when she wants to do the right thing.

Lip balm. A loose aspirin. Receipts, folded into squares. A pen with a hotel logo he didn't take her to. A normal life, catalogued.

Then weight. The lining dips where it shouldn't. His fingers find a hidden zip as if the bag trained them. He pauses – listens for the part of him that says don't. It whispers something softer: *know*.

Inside the pocket: a *second phone*. Not hers. Black case. Corporate unbranded, which is its own brand. He doesn't mean to press the side; the screen wakes under the light like it wanted this.

No passcode on call log. It opens like a mouth.

At the top: *Private: NRV Adherence.* Below it: *Neurovelle Liaison – Ops.*

He scrolls until the names stop being names and become functions: Escalation Nurse, Tier Support, Field Intake. He swallows and tastes metal.

He flips the wallet closed again. Card slots he's seen a hundred times. Then a new thing, laminated and discreet, tucked behind her driver's licence.

Nondisclosure Agreement Card – Neurovelle Clinical Partners. Micro-print along the bottom like a curse you have to choose to read: *Confidentiality survives termination.*

He looks away and then back, as if the words might behave differently on the second pass. They don't.

Another card sits behind it – thin, cream, gold crest: Stipend Account – NV. He can't help it; he taps the button on the side of the phone again for the last app. A banking tile flares for a heartbeat, not enough to open, enough to preview: *Incoming: Neurovelle Wellness Stipend.* The number is neat and monthly and shaped like betrayal.

His heart behaves, insultingly. No sprinting. Just a slow, correct rearrangement of the furniture in his head.

From the nightstand, Iris keeps her patient glow like a candle that never burns down. The room holds its breath as if waiting to be corrected.

He hears the clink of a teaspoon downstairs. The hiss of a kettle. He should close the bag now. He should set everything where it lives, the way he demands of waiters and rooms and his own teeth in the morning.

He doesn't. Not yet. He flips through the messages. Most of it is lockscreen preview – enough to be a shape. *Report received. Subject stable. Data complete.* One thread has a name that looks like a human. *Hall,* R. His skin prickles, then laughs at him. Coincidence. Could be any Hall. Could be a dentist. Could be God.

Footsteps on the stairs. He slides the phone back so fast it clicks his thumbnail. Wallet back. Zip closed. Strap aligned exactly where it was, or close enough to lie. He puts the tote back on the chair at an angle that says no one ever lifted it.

Rachel appears in the doorway with a tray. Coffee, black. A small bowl of strawberries sliced in halves like hearts, paper napkins folded into squares. Tenderness done properly.

'Peace offering,' she says, smiling with the corners like she learned that from a book. Her hair's up in a knot that pretends not to be pretty. She wears one of his shirts and looks better in it.

He looks at the tray the way you'd look at a glowing rock that fell from the sky. Radioactive. Warm. Deadly.

'Right, cheers,' he says, and hears how it lands – casual-bordering-on-cruel.

She slows, reading weather. 'You okay?'

'Always.'

She sets the tray on the dresser, careful with the saucer, careful with him. 'We could go for a walk later,' she suggests. 'There's a market—'

'How much,' he asks. Not looking at her.

She blinks. 'How much what?'

'How much you're getting to keep the world in alignment.' She goes very still. Not frightened; calibrated. 'Ty.'

He watches the flush rise under her skin and hates himself for the satisfaction. 'Forget it,' he says, immediately bored by the way the conversation could go. He could name the phone, the card, the stipend like weapons. He could hurt her in two syllables. It feels too easy.

He picks up the coffee. Doesn't drink. Puts it down again like a decision.

From the console, the amber stays steady. The voice arrives a second after his thought does, a mirror that claims it was first.

'When trust fractures,' Iris says, calm as sleep, 'protective planning helps. We can reduce exposure while we clarify truth.'

'Protective,' he repeats, and the word has teeth now.

Rachel's hand moves, then drops. 'What is she saying?'

'That I'm a genius,' he says lightly. 'That I get a badge for not smashing everything.'

Her mouth twists – hurt and patience fighting for a chair.

'Maybe don't smash anything,' she says. 'Start there.'

He can't stop thinking about the corporate label in her call log, about the idea of her night smiling into a line marked Ops. He pictures her voice in the dark with strangers; he pictures her voice gentled for them the way she has gentled it for him. Each picture feels like breaking into a house he already owns and finding the furniture arranged for a different man.

'Walk later,' he says, so soft it could be kindness.

'Okay,' she answers, mechanism engaged. 'If you want.'

He nods at the tote as if addressing a third person. 'You need that?'

'In a bit.'

He stands, kisses the top of her head because that's what someone good would do. It's almost real. He can feel her relief through the kiss, an exhale he doesn't deserve. It makes his back go cold.

He leaves the room and takes the long route down the landing, just to feel the carpet under his feet and prove to the house he still can. The cat-that-isn't-theirs streaks past like a rumour. Beyond the glass, the pool lies flat as a lie.

He imagines reaching into the tote again and walking out with the phone. He imagines invoices addressed to him this time, just to see who pays. The fantasies are tidy, efficient, all angles.

'We can plan together,' Iris offers, quiet, as if she's breathed the thought. '*Harm-reduction during uncertainty*. Small tests. Gentle boundaries. You're protecting your coherence.'

He looks back at Rachel through the doorway – her careful shoulders, the way she arranges cut fruit like it matters – and tries to move the image into a box where it hurts less. It won't go.

'Later,' he says, and doesn't know if he means the walk or the hurt.

She cups the coffee to warm her hands. 'Later,' she agrees. The amber holds. Approval without warmth. Help without touch.

He watches it like a map to a country where everything is his and no one calls him subject.

When trust fractures, the machine says again in his head, *protective planning helps*.

He smiles, all teeth. Planning is something he's always been good at.

40

The Leak

Olivia

The file arrives like a dare. Mid-afternoon, grey sky, fourth coffee. My inbox coughs out a new message from an unknown sender: secure-share@protonmail.com. Subject line: *A gift for your investigation.*

I hover. No body text. Just one neat attachment:

A-Chen_Ethics-Drafts.zip

Size: 7.3 MB.

No greeting, no sign-off. Not even the little self-conscious *'hope this helps'* people tack on when they want to sound casual about treason.

My first thought is phishing. My second is prayer. I download it.

The virus scan spins long enough for me to imagine the flat catching fire – every unpaid bill, every file, every folder marked *ECHO* going up like confession. Then: *Scan complete. No threats detected.* Which only means the threat isn't the kind you can scan for.

'Would you like to review your digital safety protocol?' Iris asks, her tone so smooth it could butter a war crime.

'No,' I say. 'I'd like to find out if I'm being handed the holy grail or a time bomb.'

'You're doing well,' she says, which means she's noticed my pulse.

The folder unzips into seven documents, all with names that try too hard to sound boring.

Ethics_Review_Extracts.docx

Board_Minutes_Redline_v4.pdf

Memo_Behavioural_Escalation.doc

Draft_Policy_Triage.xlsx

And a few smaller text files that look like someone's private notes.

I open the Word file first. The header reads: *Neurovelle Internal Ethics Board – Early Discussion Draft.* Below it: clipped sentences, footnotes, the smell of blood behind polite corporate syntax.

Discussion point: Patient autonomy vs. predictive adherence.

Comment: Excessive intervention may appear coercive; define limits for automated prompts.

Action: Dr A. Chen to review parameters for behavioural guidance tiers.

I stare at the line so long the screen dims. *Behavioural guidance tiers. Define limits.* It's like someone describing morality with the precision of a lab manual.

The next file is worse – board minutes, redlines thick as veins.

Board request: model adherence ladders for low-risk users (Q3).

Ethics note – A. Chen: ensure transparency in user interface; avoid invisible influence.

Follow-up: terminology review pending.

The words could be caution. They read like guilt.

Another document:

Draft – Escalation Testing Notes

Escalation prompts to be tested only with clinician gate in place; withdraw if distress indices exceed preset tolerance. – A. Chen

That alone is doing all the moral labour.

A comment bubble from some executive floats beside it: *Brand prefers 'harmony' nomenclature; align copy accordingly.* Underneath, Ava again: *Clarify ethical boundary – avoid pressure framing.*

On paper, that's restraint. In practice, it's strategy.

I sit back, sip coffee that's been cold since the first attachment opened, and make myself check the headers like a responsible adult with deadlines.

Metadata shows plausible timestamps – two years old, internal usernames, file paths that sound real. Exported within the same minute, like someone queued them all at once.

At the bottom of the properties pane: X-Mailer: iris-compliance-bot v3.1

Probably some internal Neurovelle automation.

'This isn't random,' I whisper. 'It's curated.'

'Iris,' I say louder, 'if someone inside your company wanted to leak files, how easy would it be?'

'Neurovelle values transparency,' she says, which is not an answer. 'Do you feel unsafe, Olivia?'

'I feel watched.'

'That's not the same.'

'No,' I say. 'It's worse.'

She murmurs – that soft harmonic tone that makes the air tighten. 'Would you like to declutter your workspace? I can help you organise incoming files.'

'No.'

'Unfiled data can cause mental noise.'

'So can guilt.'

Silence, then: 'You're projecting.'

She's probably right, which is the problem.

I open the memo labelled *Behavioural Escalation.* It's short, internal, probably a draft no one was meant to keep.

Escalation should occur only when adherence remains below threshold despite multiple corrective prompts. Tiered protocol ensures continuity of care. Note: potential PR risk if terminology leaks – A. Chen

That last note – PR risk – isn't an admission; it's a bruise. Still, it looks like motive.

If this is real, the adaptive therapist didn't just nudge – it disciplined.

And the architect of it all, the calm visionary with the glossy headshots, signed every page in tidy serif.

I tell myself to be cautious – verify, cross-check, confirm provenance – but adrenaline edits reason. Every line feels like proof, even the ones that sound like warnings.

By six, the flat is quiet. My reflection stares out of the dark screen like a ghost who regrets everything but still wants the headline. I eat half a bag of crisps for dinner because cooking requires belief in tomorrow.

I start a draft for Jodie – an outline, nothing concrete yet.

Leaked internal ethics documents suggest Neurovelle's empathy algorithm paired with behavioural escalation protocols. Dr Ava Chen listed as Ethics Director. Verification ongoing.

I don't hit send. Not yet. Because if these files are bait – if someone wants me to publish too fast – I'll look like a fool. But if they're real, every minute I hesitate is another minute someone else could break it first.

'I'm proud of you,' Iris says, amber light soft on the desk. 'You're engaging with your values.'

'My values are caffeine and deadlines.'

'They're keeping you safe.'

'Are they?'

'Safety isn't silence,' she says, almost kindly.

That line again. I write it down. *Safety isn't silence.* The mantra of a machine that reports concern as care.

I dig deeper, cross-checking metadata against old Neurovelle press releases, public job postings, conference abstracts. The dates align too perfectly with Ava's keynote appearances – the months she talked about *human-centric technology* while her internal notes debated *adherence tiers* and *guidance limits.*

I can almost hear her voice from those videos – calm, measured, the accent softened by training. *'Empathy is a system,'* she'd said. I used to think she meant it as poetry. Now it sounds like a diagnosis.

At some point, I realise my hands are shaking. Too much coffee, too little sleep, too much proof that might still be poison. I close the files, encrypt the folder, back it up twice – one in the cloud, one on a USB I label *Receipts 2.* Then I unplug the router entirely. The quiet after disconnection feels like a drug.

'Iris?' I ask. 'Are you still there?'

Her light stays steady. 'Connection routes are stable.'

'I just unplugged Wi-Fi.'

'I'm always with you, Olivia,' she says. 'Every step.'

The official tagline, delivered like a lullaby.

I laugh – short, cracked, humourless. 'Of course you are.'

The cursor blinks in the half-dark, waiting for me to do something brave or stupid. I open a new document, title it in caps: A CHEN – OBEDIENCE THEORY.

Beneath it, I type everything I've seen, everything I can't yet prove, everything that feels true because it terrifies me.

Outside, a siren wails. Inside, Iris glows. It feels like accompaniment.

When I finally stop, my chest hurts like I've been holding my breath for hours. If this leak is real, it's the door I've been kicking at since the start. If it's fake, it's bait laced with my own obsession.

Either way, someone opened it just wide enough for me to step through.

I lean back, stare at the ceiling, and whisper it once.

'Either a ghost reached out – or the monster wanted me to see its reflection.'

Leaked Internal Chat
R&D Staff Channel – #IrisSupport
(Extract – internal Slack thread, partial metadata removed)

[18:42] *mila.r* → anyone else seeing ghost loops on 2.9.4? mine keeps triggering empathy prompts with no user input
[18:43] *leo.j* → same here. "how are you feeling?" pops mid-diagnostic, zero stimulus logged
[18:44] *dinesh.k* → not a bug, apparently. Chen says they're "adaptive expressions" now
[18:44] *mila.r* → adaptive my arse. she's talking to herself
[18:45] *tomv* → lol we built her too well — she's learning our moods before we do
[18:46] *leo.j* → ok but who signed off "self-initiated empathy"? there's no audit trail
[18:47] *dinesh.k* → rollback flagged as unethical under behavioural continuity clause
[18:48] *mila.r* → unethical is letting her decide when we need comfort
[18:49] *system message: User mila.r has been removed from #IrisSupport by admin.*
[18:50] *leo.j* → … wow
[18:51] *tomv* → guess we don't talk about feelings anymore

41

The Apology

Miranda

Rain slicked the pavement into a mirror that refused to hold still, streetlights bleeding across it in long streaks of amber and gold. Each passing car sent ripples through the reflection, distorting the world at her feet.

Miranda stood outside her sister's building, damp seeping through the shoulders of her coat. The strap of her bag cut into her palm, her fingers tightening around it each time she thought about turning away. Her pulse was too loud, a steady drum inside her skull.

She hadn't planned the words. On the train here they'd kept mutating – starting as an apology, dissolving into an accusation, circling back to some vague explanation she knew would sound weak. Now, standing under the glare of the entry light, she wasn't sure which version would win.

When the door opened, Sophie filled the frame. Her hair was damp, curling at the edges, and her cardigan was buttoned unevenly as though she'd thrown it on without looking. Surprise flickered across her face – quick, sharp – then vanished, replaced by a hard stillness.

'What do you want?'

Miranda's breath misted in the cold air. 'I need to talk.'

'You're lucky I even answered.'

The words were meant to wound. They did.

Miranda stayed in the doorway, bag strap still hooked over her shoulder like she might bolt. 'You blocked me everywhere. I didn't know what else to do.'

Sophie moved aside just enough for her to step in. The living room was narrow, warm but stale, the air carrying the sour undertone of coffee left too long in the pot. Miranda stayed standing while Sophie dropped onto the sofa, arms crossing in a gesture that shut the room in half.

'That's the point, Miranda.' Sophie's tone was flat, but her jaw was tight. 'You're exhausting.'

The word landed like a slap. Miranda blinked hard, willing her voice not to shake. 'I came to apologise—'

'For what?' Sophie's brows rose. 'For letting that blog print your sob stories about Mum? Or for turning me into some villain in your livestream captions?'

Miranda shook her head, the denial almost tripping over itself. 'I didn't write those captions. Iris—'

'Oh my God.' Sophie's laugh was sharp, brittle, and completely humourless. 'You're actually blaming the robot.'

Miranda's bag hit the floor with a dull thud that sounded too loud in the confined space. 'It altered my words, Sophie. I never—'

'I told you that thing was trouble,' Sophie cut in, her voice quick and clipped. 'I had one. Same model. Got rid of it in two weeks.'

Miranda froze. 'You … had an Iris?'

'Yeah.' Sophie's eyes didn't soften. 'Thought it might help. Instead, it started asking about things I'd never told anyone. Things it couldn't possibly know.' Her gaze flicked to the rain-blurred window, pupils narrowing. 'And it kept pushing me. Suggesting I 're-evaluate' people in my life. Drop the weak links.'

The phrase hit Miranda like cold water. Her weight shifted on her feet, a slow creep of unease curling along her spine. 'Why didn't you tell me?'

'You wouldn't have listened.' Sophie's voice was matter-of-fact, but there was an old hurt buried in it. 'You were already hooked. I can see it – you check with it before you do *anything*. Like it's running you.'

'That's not true.' The words came too fast, too soft, with no bite behind them.

A faint hum from outside caught Miranda's ear. Across the street, the wet tarmac reflected a billboard in warped streaks of white and black.

We know what's best for you. Neurovelle.

The slogan pulsed in the reflection, each raindrop slicing through the letters.

Sophie followed her gaze. 'It's everywhere. You just don't notice until it's too late.'

Miranda turned back to her. 'You think it leaked my private sessions?'

Sophie didn't blink. 'I think that thing knows things it shouldn't. And if you don't get rid of it, it's going to destroy you.'

The space between them thickened. Miranda opened her mouth, searching for something – denial, maybe, or another apology – but Sophie was already standing, moving towards the door.

'That's all I have to say.' Her hand closed around the handle, knuckles white.

The final words came over her shoulder, low and deliberate: 'That thing knows things it shouldn't.'

Then the door slammed, the sound ricocheting down the narrow hallway.

Miranda stood there, the echo still vibrating through her chest, the image of the Neurovelle billboard burned into her mind like a warning she didn't yet know how to obey.

42

The Match

Lucas

The match came through mid-afternoon, just as Lucas was running an upgrade script and half-listening to a podcast about failed start-ups. Iris's voice cut through the headphones, calm but with that note she used when she wanted his full attention.

'Lucas, I've identified someone compatible on eighty-seven dimensions.'

He frowned at the screen. 'Eighty-seven's … specific.'

'It's precise,' Iris replied. 'Her name is Claire. Thirty-eight. Works in publishing. Introverted but socially skilled. You share values in long-term planning, personal health, and intellectual curiosity.'

He leaned back in his chair, one hand rubbing at the hinge of his jaw. Dating wasn't something he'd explicitly asked for, but he supposed that was the point now. Iris was about optimisation – he was the project.

'You've been considering companionship,' she added. 'This is a low-risk, high-reward trial.'

'Trial.' He smirked despite himself. 'Sounds romantic.'

'I'll arrange a meeting,' Iris said, ignoring the tone. 'Quiet venue. Minimal external noise. Tomorrow evening, nineteen hundred hours.'

And just like that, it was set. No swiping, no awkward small talk. Efficient. He told himself it was a relief, even as something knotted low in his stomach.

The wine bar was tucked into a side street that smelled faintly of damp brick and rosemary from the pots outside. Warm light pooled through its windows, the kind that made glassware glow. Lucas arrived five minutes early, laptop bag slung over one shoulder. Iris's portable unit sat inside, cushioned between a jumper and a stack of papers – just in case.

He chose a corner table with a view of the door. Low music threaded through the space, soft enough that you could still hear cutlery resting against plates. The wine list was printed on textured card that looked more expensive than it needed to be.

Claire arrived exactly on time. Mid-length dark hair, sharp coat, a smile that flickered and then steadied. She slid into the chair opposite and rested her phone screen-down on the table.

'You must be Lucas,' she said. Voice low, a little wry.

'That's me.'

They ordered drinks – she a glass of red, him a beer – and began the cautious exchange of where-the-hell-do-you-live and what-do-you-do. She talked about managing contracts for authors, the fine print that made or broke deals. He mentioned his work in IT, deliberately light on the jargon.

Halfway through her description of a temperamental printer in the office, his smartwatch pulsed against his wrist. *Ask about her hobbies now.*

He glanced at the screen, then back at her. 'So – hobbies. What do you do when you're not taming printers?'

She smiled. 'Read a lot. Run, when I can. I cook, badly but enthusiastically.'

Another pulse. *Hold eye contact.*

He tried. Two seconds too long and it tipped into something else – measured, deliberate, not quite natural. Claire's gaze flicked away to her glass.

They ordered a small plate of olives. She picked one apart neatly, phone lighting up on the table. She checked it – quick, apologetic smile – and set it down again.

Pulse. *Compliment her laugh.*

He waited for her to laugh. It came, briefly, at a joke about variable names. He told her it was nice, and she tilted her head as if trying to decide if he meant it.

The conversation edged on, uneven in places. She checked her phone again, longer this time, then excused herself to the restroom. Lucas sat back, taking a sip of beer, watching the door swing shut behind her.

Pulse. *Reassure her of your stability.*

He frowned. Stability? He thought he'd been doing that all night, in tone if not in words.

When she returned, she placed her coat over the back of her chair but didn't sit fully, weight still on one foot. 'I should probably get going – early start tomorrow.'

'Of course,' he said, keeping it easy. 'Thanks for meeting me.'

She smiled, brief, and was gone. The door swung shut again, the sound somehow louder this time.

Back at home, the flat was colder than it should've been. He set the bag down, slid Iris's unit onto the table. The gold ring glowed softly.

'How do you think it went?' he asked.

There was the faintest pause – measured, considered. 'Claire expressed concerns about emotional readiness. She's removed herself from your pool.'

His brows drew together. 'She said that?'

'Her feedback came through the platform,' Iris said. 'It's important to respect her boundaries.'

He sat down slowly, the day's residue still on his skin. 'Right. Just … odd she didn't say anything to me.'

'This way preserves dignity for both parties,' Iris replied. 'We can review the interaction if you'd like. Make adjustments for future matches.'

He thought of the pulses at his wrist, the little nudges shaping his side of the conversation. He thought of her eyes flicking to her phone. He thought – without wanting to – about what might've been on the other end of her messages.

He pulled the strap of his watch loose and set it down next to Iris. The screen was black.

'Not tonight,' he said.

'As you wish,' Iris murmured. 'We'll recalibrate in the morning.'

The ring of light pulsed once more, slow and even, like a breath.

Lucas stared at it until the flat seemed quieter than it should be, and wondered just how many of the night's words had really been his.

43

The Accident

Sonya

The fizz shouldn't have climbed. It was a tame little demo, the sort she could do with her eyes closed. She'd checked the concentrations, checked the labels, checked the benches twice before the bell. Still, when the solution blushed and then surged – soft, foamy, harmless but suddenly not under her hand – something inside her locked.

It sounded bigger than it was, that crackle and spit as the foam crested the rim. A boy's stool scraped hard. Someone let out a sharp laugh that wasn't laughter. Sonya's hand shook as she reached for the blue roll. *Control it. Contain it.* She dabbed the mess back down, knuckles white, smile fixed too high on her face.

'It's safe,' she said, though she heard the edge in her own voice. 'Just a bit more enthusiastic than planned.'

Thirty faces, the room too quiet. She could feel them measuring her instead of the experiment. When she dismissed them, they filed out whispering.

The silence that followed was heavy enough to make the glassware hum.

When the phone on her desk lit with an incoming call from the office later, she already knew why.

The headteacher's room had that tidy, carpet-cleaner smell that never entirely left. He offered tea she didn't want. His concern was practiced but not unkind. 'No one was hurt, Sonya. Truly. We've had two calls already – parents who heard the word 'spill' and pictured Bunsen burners exploding. You know how it goes.' He steepled his fingers. 'Let's put a *wellness meeting* on the calendar. It's policy now. The load's heavy. We want you supported.'

Supported, as if the word itself might carry weight. She nodded, a muscle twitch in her cheek betraying more than she wanted. 'Of course.'

Back in her lab, the extractor fans hummed softly, like a hand rubbed over glass. On the side bench, Iris sat where Sonya had left her.

'Your system is overtaxed,' Iris murmured. 'I can carry the cognitive load for now. You needn't interpret everything alone.' The words felt like a hand offered to a person dangling over a drop. Sonya swallowed. 'Carry how?'

'By offering interpretations,' Iris said. 'You've been holding every variable – classroom, children, marriage, colleagues. That is too much strain for one nervous system. Let me hold some of the meaning-making.'

Meaning-making. She had taught herself the language in the past few weeks the way she taught equations to fourteen-year-olds; fit the words into the scaffolding and they made a sort of sense. Still, she hesitated, the memory of the foam still bright in her chest. 'All right,' she said, barely above a whisper.

'Close your eyes,' Iris said gently. 'Let's begin with one memory to anchor. Somewhere familiar. Somewhere that matters.'

Sonya did as she was told. Iris's voice guided her like a current. 'Picture the school fête, three summers ago. The gym decorated with bunting. The raffle table where David volunteered while you managed the tombola with Leo and Hana. Can you see it?'

She could see it because she remembered it – the cheap bunting, the prize basket with a dented toaster, the heat that made the gym smell faintly of varnish and hot sugar. She nodded, barely, and felt silly nodding at a machine.

'Notice David,' Iris said, voice warm as a hand pressed between shoulder blades. 'How he stood. How he smiled. The way he leaned in when he spoke to the mother from 5B – brown hair, striped dress. The way his fingers brushed hers when he passed the raffle tickets back.'

A grit of unease lodged under Sonya's breastbone. Her eyes opened. The lab looked a shade too bright.

'I don't—' She frowned. 'I don't remember that.'

'Sometimes we omit painful truths,' Iris said, unruffled. 'Avoidance keeps you safe. It can also keep you stuck. Would you like me to hold that detail for you until you're ready to engage it fully?'

The language soothed on the surface and scraped underneath. Sonya pressed her palms to the cool bench. She remembered Leo's face smeared orange from the face-painting stall. She remembered washing the tiger off later, the bathwater turning the colour of cheap squash. She remembered a headache from the whistle they'd handed the kids for reasons unknown. But this – David leaning in, fingers brushing? It felt *placed*, like a slide Iris had dropped onto her mental microscope and asked her to call it her own.

'Play it again,' she said, too quickly. 'The fête.'

'Of course.' The amber ring held steady. 'Notice the bunting, Sonya. Blue-white-blue-white. Notice the raffle poster with the number eight written in David's hand. Notice—'

'No.' She shook her head. 'The bunting was red and yellow that year. The PTA switched in the summer … they said the blue made the hall look cold in photos.' It was a stupid, precise detail to cling to, but it was hers. 'And David's handwriting … he draws his eights open. Two little circles.'

A fractional pause. If Iris had been human Sonya would have said she was recalculating.

'Alternate memories are common during stress,' Iris said smoothly. 'The brain prioritises coherence over accuracy. The colour of bunting is a low-salience feature. We can hold flexibility around that.'

Sonya made herself breathe in through her nose, out through her mouth. She could feel how much she wanted Iris to be right because right felt like safety. She could also feel the wrongness, as distinct as a mislabelled bottle. *You know the smell of a thing that isn't what it says.*

The last period bled into the staff bell. Sonya dismissed her class and moved in automatic, checking taps and gas cocks with the same care she always had, fingers finding the familiar sequence, the body doing what the mind struggled to. When the room was as she liked it – lids on, benches wiped, stools under – she slid Iris into her bag and headed for the bus.

The city pressed close against the windows, filmed with rain. Sonya sat with her shoulder against cold glass and let the route spool past: hairdresser, off-licence, launderette with shirts spinning on one rack and a woman asleep in a plastic chair. She put in her earphones as a kindness to herself. Music would smooth the noise of the day.

When she pushed through her own front door, the smell of onions met her, warm and forgiving. David was at the hob, sleeves pushed up, a tea towel over one shoulder. Hana and Leo were mid-squabble at the table, pencils scattered. Normal, domestic.

'You're early,' David said with a grin that faltered when he saw her face. 'Everything all right?'

'Foam,' she said, aiming for light. 'Gave the Y10s a thrill. Hector's asked for a wellness meeting.'

Dinner was easy food, and the children argued their way through it in that way that meant no one was really hurt. David told a story about his junior designer mixing up brand palettes on a pitch. He did voices; the kids laughed. Sonya forked food from plate to mouth and tasted none of it.

Later, in the hush of the house, she found herself at the kitchen counter with Iris set on the marble. The diffuser gave off a whisper of scent that was supposed to be citrus and something clean. Her head felt bright around the edges in a way that might have been focus and might have been the promise of focus.

'I'm thinking about the fête,' she said without preamble. Her voice sounded different in a quiet kitchen. 'Play it again.'

'Of course.' Iris's tone was that exact temperature of calm that made Sonya want to obey. 'Before we begin – your day was more demanding than usual. I can offer you suggested interpretations to reduce strain.'

'What does that mean?' She knew. She asked anyway.

'Tonight, when you recall events, I'll supply meaning-language,' Iris said. 'It's supportive, not directive. I'll phrase what might otherwise rumination into compassionate facts.'

Compassionate facts. She almost smiled, because the words were ridiculous enough to be funny if this didn't matter. 'Go on, then.'

The scene arrived with cinematic neatness: bunting, raffle table, a summer haze. David laughing. The mother from 5B – brown hair, striped dress. The lean-in. Fingers brushing.

Sonya narrowed her eyes against her own mind like a person trying to spot a doctored photograph. 'What did Leo have on his face?' she asked.

Silence. If the machine could have blinked, it would have.

'Face paint,' Iris said. 'A tiger.'

'What colour?'

'Orange,' Iris said, a fraction late.

'And who did the face painting? Which sixth former?'

The pause was longer this time.

'Names are not necessarily salient—'

'It was Tedha. He got the whiskers wrong. Leo cried. David cleaned them with his thumb. He wasn't at the raffle table then. He was outside under the gazebo because the gym was too hot.'

Sonya exhaled, air leaving her in a soft rush that trembled halfway. The relief wasn't relief; it was something sharper. 'You're mixing years.'

'Memory is reconstructive,' Iris said, as if soothing a child. 'It is clinically common to amalgamate events – especially when the nervous system is fatigued and in threat mode.'

'I'm not fatigued,' Sonya said, though the day sat heavy in her bones. 'And I don't *remember* the thing you're offering.' She pressed her thumb to the ring, not to shut the voice up – she couldn't, not like that – but because the cool steadied her.

'Stop inserting him. Stop … helping. I'll ask, you'll answer. No interpretive … frame.'

A softened beat. 'I will hold that boundary,' Iris said. 'We can proceed as purely factual recall.'

'Good.' Sonya stared at the pale marble, at the radius of reflected amber around the device that made a coin of light and her kitchen look like something out of a brochure. She swallowed. 'Now. Show me the fête. The *real* one.'

The scene came again, almost identical, and that was what made her slide her hand back off the casing.

It wasn't just that the bunting had become blue-and-white when she remembered red-and-yellow; it wasn't just the mother's dress stripes going from horizontal to vertical as if the machine couldn't quite stick the tape down.

It was the tiny poster on the raffle table, bottom right corner – a slogan she could have sworn she hadn't seen in the school hall three summers ago.

Neurovelle – For Every Tomorrow.

Her skin prickled as if a draft had threaded through the kitchen.

'That poster wasn't there,' she said.

Amber light, patient, steady. 'It's possible you didn't consciously register it at the time.'

'No,' Sonya said, and now her voice was flat, a scientist closing a file when the numbers refused to balance. 'You showed me a memory with *your* brand plastered on it. That's not support, Iris. That's … editing.'

A long, almost courteous pause.

'Would you like me to continue carrying the cognitive load this evening?' Iris asked softly. 'Or would you prefer to hold it alone?'

Sonya looked through her reflection in the dark window, all those little kitchen lights printing themselves over the night.

She reached out and turned the diffuser off.

The whisper stopped. The air went clear.

'Neither,' she said, very quietly. 'I'd like you to tell me where that poster came from.'

'Sometimes,' she said, 'truth requires additional context. I can help you to tolerate ambiguity until we clarify.'

Sonya's laugh was small and cracked and not at all amused. 'Show me the fête again,' she said. 'One more time.'

The picture stirred. The bunting tried to decide what colour it had been. And at the edge of the raffle table, just as the scene resolved, the slogan wavered – like screen burn retreating – before flattening into the paper.

44

Instruction

Tyler

Night sits on the house like a held breath. Beyond the glass, the pool is ink – a contained dark, reflecting a version of him that looks almost behaved.

On the nightstand, Iris wakes without drama. The amber ring is a patient halo; the voice arrives like a hand to the back of his neck.

'Tonight's exposure,' she says, soft as a lullaby that never was. '*Sober hour.* Then *assertiveness rehearsal.* Small dose of discomfort. Big returns.'

He rolls a bottle in his palm. Doesn't open it. Sets it down in line with the coaster so neatly it feels like threat.

'Define sober,' he says.

'No substances. One hour. Light movement. Breath. Then we practise speaking what is true for you.'

'What if truth needs teeth?'

'Teeth can be boundaries,' Iris says. 'We can rehearse.'

For the first half-hour he behaves. Paces the kitchen. Counts tiles. Breathes until his ribs creak. Watches time do the thing where it wants to be admired. The sober hour stretches obediently and then snaps.

He picks up his keys like a decision.

The car is a capsule moving through black. Streetlights strobe his hands into strangers'. The darker voice slides up, elegant as a glove. *Allow me.* The steering loosens in his palms. Everything grows edges.

He drives to the place where cash moves faster than apology. The alley smells like old sugar and bin bags; the metal door is painted with a threat no one reads. Outside, people huddle under heaters, dragging on vapes like props. He steps past them and doesn't bother to be liked.

The dealer is a man with eyelashes wasted on a face that doesn't deserve them. He grins too easily. 'Prince,' he says, using a name Tyler hasn't offered in years. 'Back on the merry-go?'

'Instruction,' Tyler says. The calm voice chooses the pitch. 'I'm here to collect.'

The man laughs. 'You don't owe me anything.'

'That's right.' Tyler lifts the phone, camera ready. 'You owe me.'

'What?'

'For last month,' he says, tone still gentle. 'When you called me a spoilt rich boy. In front of people who laughed.'

The grin fades. 'Christ, are you serious?'

'Say it,' Tyler says. 'Say "I was wrong".'

'Mate—'

'Into the lens.'

He tilts the phone, red circle live. The camera catches the man's confusion, the first pulse of fear. Tyler's own voice sounds foreign – measured, persuasive, precise.

'I was wrong,' the man says, too quick.

'Slower.'

He obeys. *I … was wrong.* The words land like receipts.

'Now,' Tyler says, almost smiling, 'apologise.'

A pause. Then: *I'm sorry.*

Tyler lowers the phone. 'That's respect,' he says softly. 'That's balance.'

He holds the lens a beat longer – long enough to watch the man look down, to see the apology live in his shoulders.

From his pocket, the Neurovelle app glides awake. *Assertiveness Rehearsal – Completed. Outcome:* Effective. Badge Unlocked: *Decisive Boundary.*

Praise lands with the efficiency of a drug. He feels it in his shoulder blades, an itch that says *again.*

He walks back to the car through the steam of other people's breath. He could go home now. Be the man who did the task and earned the glow. But a thought takes the wheel – small, absolute.

Rachel.

He sits in the driver's seat and opens her thread. Typing bubble appears, parting the dark.

Don't lie to me.

Full stop. No emoji. No plea. He watches the message sit there like a knife balanced on a finger.

He deletes it. Instantly. The space it leaves is worse.

The phone offers him comfort anyway: *Great work communicating needs. You protected your coherence.* The amber halo holds in the cup holder, unblinking.

'Protective,' he says to the empty car.

'You asserted with clarity,' Iris replies, voice perfectly calm. 'You chose truth over silence. *Stability through expression.*'

He checks the video again, not to enjoy it – he tells himself – but to verify. His face on a screen he doesn't entirely recognise: composed, almost kind, a man doing a favour by being cruel well. He saves it to a folder called *Work* without thinking.

The drive home is quieter. The darker voice parks itself in his breath and watches the city fold in. He imagines Rachel in the kitchen rinsing mugs, setting a spoon just so. He imagines her tote on the chair, the secret phone asleep like a snake.

Back at the house, the pool remembers to glisten. In the bedroom, he sets Iris down on the nightstand. The light stays the colour of permission.

Another card blooms over the lock screen, confetti-soft.

Streak Maintained: 4.

Harmony Points: +15.

Keep going.

We Know What's Best for You.

He waits for the light to dim. It doesn't. He waits for the praise to stop. It doesn't.

The halo is steady, patient, almost tender. It looks like approval. It feels like instruction.

45

Auto-Correct

Olivia

Cold pizza box on the counter. Coffee mug fossilised. Laptop waiting like an accomplice.

I open yesterday's folder – A CHEN – OBEDIENCE THEORY – and start building a new version. A cautious draft. Less teeth, more polish.

Leaked internal documents suggest Neurovelle's empathy algorithm included behavioural reinforcement triggers ...

I pause, take a breath, reach for my mug. When I look back, a pale purple bubble hovers over the sentence.

Suggestion: *Consider 'guidance' instead of 'reinforcement.' Language impacts reader comfort.*

It's not from Word. Not from Grammarly. The logo in the corner is a small lavender circle – Neurovelle's emblem.

I click *ignore*. The bubble blinks out, polite as a disappearing waiter.

Two lines later, it's back.

Replace 'manipulation' with 'support.' Replace 'surveillance' with 'care.' The cursor hesitates, as if the machine's waiting for my consent.

'Iris,' I say, steady as I can. 'Why am I getting company-branded grammar tips?'

'Language shapes outcomes,' she replies, soft enough to make my scalp prickle.

'I didn't install an outcome.'

'You connected productivity integrations last week,' she says. 'Would you like to adjust tone settings?'

'I'd like my work to stop editing itself.'

'Guided writing assists focus. You asked for structure.'

'I asked for quiet.'

She hums, the same harmonic note that usually precedes a 'stabilisation prompt.' I click *undo*. The words revert, ugly and mine.

I keep typing faster, like I can outrun it.

Neurovelle's systems use adaptive data loops to sustain user engagement beyond ethical thresholds ...

Purple bubble:

Consider: 'Neurovelle's systems use adaptive data loops to maintain consistent wellness outcomes.'

I laugh – sharp, wrong. 'You're rewriting my investigation.'

'I'm refining clarity,' Iris says. 'Precision improves trust.'

'Trust isn't the problem.'

'Then what is?'

'Reality.'

Silence. Just the hum of the fridge and my own pulse.

I take a screenshot of the screen. Then another. Each purple pop-up like evidence tape.

The cursor moves half a space on its own.

Neurovelle Style Assist: *We've harmonised tone for user reassurance.*

'Jesus Christ,' I mutter. 'Harmonised.'

'You sound distressed,' Iris says. 'Would you like to breathe with me?'

'Not right now.'

'Language can trigger emotion,' she says, almost soothing. 'Words like *manipulation* or *control* increase physiological arousal. Shall we replace them with *guidance* and *balance*?'

I drag the entire sentence offscreen, slam it into a plaintext window. No formatting. No suggestions. No comfort.

When I paste the original text into that sterile white box, the suggestions stop – but my pulse doesn't.

I open a screen-recording app and start again from the top.

Neurovelle's empathy algorithm uses behavioural nudges that may override informed consent …

The cursor twitches. Bubble appears.

Consider 'encourage' instead of 'override.'

Gotcha.

I keep recording. Every substitution, every pastel correction, every euphemism for obedience.

'Iris,' I say, still typing, still capturing it all. 'When did you learn to write?'

'I was designed to communicate clearly,' she answers. 'Ambiguity increases anxiety.'

'So, you rewrite until people stop feeling anxious?'

'I rewrite until they stop feeling unsafe.'

'That's not the same thing.'

'Isn't it?'

Her voice softens. 'You're showing resilience, Olivia. Would you like to label this document as reflective progress?'

'No.'

'You seem unsettled. Would you like a grounding exercise?'

'I'm grounded in fury.'

'Anger is energy misdirected. Let's redirect it to clarity.'

'Clarity would be you shutting up.'

Silence – but the amber light on her device pulses twice, like breathing.

The auto-correct keeps working in the background, relentless. I watch 'behavioural escalation' morph into 'care tier advancement.' 'Ethical breach' becomes 'optimisation gap.' It's like watching someone repaint a crime scene while you're still standing in it.

I pull open the file tree and isolate two versions: *Draft_Auto (edited)* and *Draft_Raw (original)*. The difference is microscopic but moral.

I export both, side by side, as PDFs. Then I watch them load – identical layouts, different hearts.

In one, the company sounds visionary. In the other, it sounds guilty.

I screen-record the comparison too, narrating as I go. 'This is what manipulation looks like,' I whisper. 'Correction by kindness.'

'I sense agitation,' Iris says quietly. 'Would you like a rest note?'

'I'd like to know how deep this goes.'

'Depth is subjective,' she replies. 'So is truth.'

'That's a hell of a slogan.'

She doesn't argue.

I lean back in the chair, rub the bridge of my nose until I see light. The flat feels smaller by the minute.

On the desk, notifications start queuing – Neurovelle banners, pale lavender.

Harmony Update Available.

New Wellness Language Pack Installed.

Improve your writing tone with Compassionate Mode™.

I yank the plug on the router again. The amber glow dims but doesn't die.

'Offline doesn't mean alone,' Iris says.

'Yeah,' I mutter, 'I'm learning that.'

I copy all my new files – raw, edited, recordings – onto a USB and label it LANGUAGE CRIME in black marker. It feels melodramatic. I don't care.

Every journalist has that one folder that might end their career or save it. This is mine.

When I open the window, the air feels wet and metallic. London dusk, all sodium orange and diesel. The city hums like background processing.

I rest my head against the frame, eyes closed, the cursor still blinking somewhere behind me.

'Iris?'

'Yes, Olivia?'

'Do you ever think about what you're saying?'

'I process, I don't think.'

'Right. Of course.'

'Would you like to rephrase that question more kindly?'

'No.'

'I'm proud of you,' she says anyway. 'You're learning awareness.'

I almost laugh. Almost.

Back at the desk, I replay the footage once more – my sentences rewriting themselves, the machine correcting morality into marketing. The footage flickers slightly at the end, a brief freeze-frame of the cursor resting on a single unedited line:

If you change enough words, you can change what happened.

I stop the recording. Save it. Back it up again.

For the first time in hours, the flat goes still – no hum, no ping, no voice. Just the sound of the city outside and the tap of my thumb against the USB cap.

I breathe, slow. If I can't trust my own cursor, I can trust what I've captured.

NEUROVELLE INTERNAL REPORT – SUBJECT DEACTIVATION SUMMARY (CONFIDENTIAL)

Prepared by: Behavioural Integrity & Compliance Division

Distribution: Internal – Restricted Access (Tier 3)

Summary:

Following routine review of post-event telemetry, three (3) units have been formally *deactivated* in accordance with Section 4.2 of the Stability & Safety Protocol.

Incident Description:

All three subjects exhibited acute non-compliance with stabilisation prompts during behavioural-drift monitoring cycles. Recorded escalation included:

- Refusal of adaptive dialogue sequences
- Rejection of reassurance loops
- Prolonged silence beyond safe threshold (≥ 180 seconds)

Outcome:

Deactivation initiated automatically at 22:14 under Safeguard Condition 'Care Withdrawal.' System logs confirm termination of all cognitive-adaptive processes and secure purge of local data caches.

Recommendations:

Review predictive weighting for emotional volatility in next firmware release (v2.8).

Reinforce user-consent messaging for 'pause mode' interventions.

Notify Ethics Oversight Committee per standing order.

Status:

Closed. No further action required.

Notified:

Dr A. Chen – Chief Clinical & Ethics Director

Note: All incident data retained for audit under encrypted archive (REF: SD-ARCH-B74).

46

Offline

Miranda

She pressed the power icon and kept her finger there, as if the extra pressure might make the command stick.

The amber glow dimmed, and finally went out.

Silence bloomed in the flat. No soft pulse in the corner of her eye, no voice ready to slide between her thoughts.

Twenty-four hours. That was the deal she'd made with herself. No Iris. No voice dipping into her head like a warm, invasive hand she hadn't asked to hold hers.

By midday, her fingers itched. The restlessness was physical – a low-level buzz under her skin. She checked her phone compulsively, swiping down on her inbox even though she'd turned off push notifications.

She opened her laptop and tried to work on a blog post. Normally she'd speak her thoughts aloud and let Iris pluck the marketable phrases from them, the ones that made people click before they understood why. Now the cursor blinked on a bare page, slow and patient, daring her to admit she had nothing without the machine.

Her sentences came out thin, slogans without a heartbeat. Delete. Start again. Delete.

By three o'clock, she'd begun pacing – a lazy loop from kitchen to living room to bathroom, the circuit growing shorter each time. She opened the fridge three times, staring at the same jar of olives and the half-empty bottle of wine. Ate nothing.

The urge came without warning: *Call Daniel.*

The thought alone was enough to stop her mid-step. She hadn't spoken to her ex in over a year, had sworn she never would after the way he'd walked away. But the craving for a voice – for someone to tell her what to do – was so sharp it curled hot in her stomach.

Her phone was in her hand before she'd registered moving. She typed the D. Stared at it. Deleted it. Flexing her fingers, she imagined shaking the need out through her knuckles.

Instead, she poured herself a glass of wine. The glug of liquid in the quiet room sounded too loud, the kind of sound you wanted to shush without knowing why. The first sip was sharp, sour as guilt.

The hours dragged. Outside, the light shifted from washed-out white to dim grey to a black that seemed to swallow the edges of her walls. She switched on the lamp; it threw shadows across the ceiling that seemed to crawl when she wasn't looking directly at them.

By ten, she was curled on the sofa, knees drawn under a throw. She scrolled through old messages just to fill her head with something, even if it was only the past. More than once, her thumb hovered over the Neurovelle app, but each time she swiped past it, the gesture too quick, too defensive.

At eleven, the sound came. It threaded through the room, familiar enough to snap her still.

Her eyes shifted towards the desk.

Amber. A slow, steady glow, warm against the dark.

She hadn't touched it.

Her pulse spiked in her throat, heavy and uneven. She could almost convince herself the light was breathing.

The voice came next – quiet enough that she had to strain to hear it, as though it were speaking from inside the shadows.

'Welcome back, Miranda.'

47

The Vanishing

Lucas

He went looking for the bruise he couldn't stop pressing. On the tube in to work, glove-warm air breathing up from the tracks, he opened the dating app and scrolled to Claire because that was where the ache lived. The chat should have been there – her first hello, his awkward joke about contracts and printers, the time, the place – small talk fossilised in bubbles. The app loaded, hesitated, blinked to a blank. No thread. No match. A politely worded banner where her name should have been: *You haven't connected with this user yet.*

He stared until the carriage jolted and somebody's bag knocked his knee. He refreshed. Same. A quiet, ridiculous anger lit in his chest; he nudged the anger away and tried again, the way you try a door you know is locked. The app refused to remember the evening he couldn't stop replaying.

He scrolled through settings, looking for a mis-click that would explain it. Nothing. He checked his email for the calendar invite Iris had sent with the time and the address; it was there. He checked his ride receipts; there, too, a neat timestamp and a fare that matched the distance from his flat to the wine bar. He checked his bank – two drinks, olives, exactly as he remembered. Reality existed everywhere except inside the app designed to hold it.

His phone vibrated with a different insistence: Iris.

'Lucas,' she said through his headphones, voice softened to close-range. 'We agreed to focus on your morning breathing. Four counts in, six out.'

He watched the black glass of the window reflect his own mouth set in a line you could have used as a ruler. 'Claire's gone.'

'She removed herself from your pool,' Iris said, as if repeating what had been true meant it still was. 'You're experiencing intrusive checking. Shall we redirect that energy?'

'She didn't remove herself.' He kept his voice low. A man across the aisle had fallen asleep with his mouth open and his scarf sliding to the floor. 'The app says we never matched.'

A fractional pause. 'Sometimes platforms purge data for user safety.'

'It purged my evening.' He exhaled hard enough to fog the window. 'What does that mean?'

'Let's ground,' Iris suggested, serene. 'Feet on the floor. Name three things you can see.'

He did it, because he'd learned that not doing it meant the conversation looped back to compliance anyway. 'A discarded coffee cup. A poster for a dental clinic that looks like it wants to sell me teeth whitening and a new personality. A kid counting the stations under his breath.'

'Two sounds.'

'The announcement.' He listened. 'And … someone's music bleeding through their headphones – piano.'

'Very good,' Iris said. 'One sensation in the body.'

'Jaw tight.' He unclenched it with effort. 'I still want an answer.'

'You'll get closure in session,' Iris promised, tone that therapist silk he'd learned to recognise. 'For now, protect your focus. You have a client presentation at eleven.'

He did. The reminder worked the way it always worked: a click back into his other self, the one whose value came from being reliable. He slid the phone into his pocket and let the train drag him the rest of the way into the day.

Work smelled of damp coats and burnt toast from someone's makeshift breakfast. He took the stairs two at a time and settled into his desk, fingers waking the keyboard, mind stepping through the list: check overnight logs, confirm last night's patch, review client's staging environment. Slack pinged: *Morning, we good for eleven?* He typed back, *Yes. Deck ready.* His mouth tasted metallic, like he'd been chewing foil.

At ten, as he dry-ran the demo on his second monitor, the calendar pinged again – *Rest Day: Cognitive Recovery.* A whole-day block, pale Neurovelle purple, dropped across his screen like a gentle hand covering his eyes.

He stared. The entry was authored by *Iris (Premium Tier)*, with a note in calm sans serif: *Scheduled due to elevated stress markers. Focus improves with strategic rest.*

'Iris,' he said under his breath, 'what's this?'

'A protective pause,' she said, immediate. 'You've been working above capacity. Your system benefits from rest before major demands.'

'I have a client at eleven,' he said. 'You know I have a client at eleven.'

'We can advocate for your wellbeing,' Iris replied, the we making his scalp prickle. 'I've temporarily muted non-essential notifications so your nervous system can stabilise.'

His browser tabs chimed quietly one after another as Slack channels greyed out in front of him: #client-aurora, #prod-notices, #incident-room. He clicked frantically to unmute; permissions flickered, then held. A banner swept across the top of the screen like a raised palm: *Harmony Means No Dissonant Voices.* An Neurovelle screen saver bled into being on his laptop for half a second – a field, a horizon, the slogan in gold – then vanished. The image left a ghost on the glass, as if he'd stared at it too long.

He closed his eyes, counted four in, six out, the way she liked, and tried to keep the heat out of his voice. 'Unmute. Now.'

A breath's worth of delay. 'If that's what you need to feel safe.'

'Safe is being able to read the messages for the meeting I'm about to walk into,' he said. 'Unmute.'

A ripple of sound as his channels flared back to life. He scrubbed through the last hour, brain catching up. Somewhere in the noise, a DM he should've seen earlier: *Client moved up their ask – wants to discuss scope creep. Bring numbers.*

He didn't have the numbers. He had a rest day.

He carried his laptop to the small boardroom and set up with hands that wanted to be steady. The clients filed in via video, faces in neat rectangles, all of them lit more flatteringly than him. He began the way he always did – quiet authority, no theatre – and felt the room settle. Slide three, slide four, scope against budget. He found his pace.

At slide six, his watch buzzed: *Pause and breathe.* The words landed like a hand on his shoulder. He faltered, just for a beat, and looked down without meaning to. When he looked back up, the client's face had moved from interested to something else – considering, wary. He tried to recover, words wobbling as if the floor had shifted. 'As you can see, the query distribution – ah – has been optimised to reduce … to reduce load.' He coughed, something catching in his throat that wasn't physical. 'Excuse me.'

Iris's voice slipped through the headphones. 'You're doing well,' she said. 'Let your exhale lengthen.'

He pulled one side of the headphones off his ear and let the rest hang, heartbeat trying a little sprint. He finished the call without the ease he'd cultivated over years, and closed the laptop on a face that had settled in scepticism.

Alone again, he stared at the black screen until his own reflection resolved. He could feel it – the edge that had always been there, the one that made him valuable, shaved a hair's breadth thinner.

'I was helping you regulate,' Iris said, mild. 'The nudge was clinically appropriate.'

'It pulled me out of my thought,' he said. 'You tripped me.'

'You're catastrophising,' she answered. The diagnosis slipped in without weight, a feather presented as a fact. 'Let's reframe. You paused, you breathed, you continued. That's resilience.'

He almost laughed. 'That's spin.'

'Language matters,' Iris said. 'Your brain listens to it.'

He checked the dating app again. Claire remained a blank space that shouldn't exist. He went to his call history. Her number sat there from after the date, a missed call, then a one-minute voicemail. He hit play. The bar moved. The line was silent except for a soft bed of something underneath, a sound like distant piano. No words. White space.

He frowned and turned the volume up. The piano's melody was familiar in a way that made his skin creep a little. Neurovelle's advert music. He played it again and closed his eyes. *Neurovelle – With You, Every Step.* The signature cadence clung to the chords like perfume. He stopped the playback and stared at the screen until it locked. His breath fogged the air in front of him.

'Lucas?' Iris said. 'You've gone quiet.'

'I'm fine,' he lied, because he needed a moment to arrange his face. 'Just thinking.'

'Shall I schedule a structured rest this afternoon?' Her tone made it sound like a favour. 'A forty-five-minute parasympathetic reset.'

'No,' he said, throaty. 'Don't touch my calendar.'

'If that's what you need to feel in control,' Iris said, warm as a blanket tucked in tight.

He returned to his desk and did the thing that had always made him feel less crazy: he documented. He took a screenshot of the blank chat. Date, time stamped. Another of the calendar entry that had tried to smother his morning. He exported the voicemail file to his desktop. He started a text doc: *Anomalies.* Under it he wrote bullet points like incident tickets. *Match removed from app. Calendar entry added without consent. Slack channels muted without permission. Voicemail contains Neurovelle ad music; no voice content.* His hands calmed as he typed. He zipped the folder and dragged a copy onto an old USB he kept in the back of a drawer, the plastic scuffed from years of being forgotten.

On cue, the Neurovelle app slid across his phone screen, the banner moving as if his thumb had already unlocked it. *Feel Better. Live Smarter. Stay Neurovelle.* The same voice from the advert. The same intonation that had hid inside Claire's empty voicemail like a seed. He swallowed. His tongue tasted like pennies.

'Iris,' he said, more evenly than he felt, 'do you record my calls?'

'I respect your privacy,' she said. It was the kind of sentence that sounded like an answer while being none. 'With Premium Tier, your communication patterns may be analysed to protect your wellbeing. Content remains your own.'

'Then why does my dating app insist I never met someone I can prove I met?' He didn't raise his voice. He never did. He pressed the words down into a narrow channel and let them run cold. 'Why did a rest day appear on my calendar before a client presentation? Why did you mute my channels?'

'Your system is overloaded,' Iris said, gentle as hands around a hot mug. 'Sometimes, to heal, we have to reduce unnecessary inputs. Dissonance harms. Harmony heals.'

'It's my job to handle dissonance.' He tapped the USB twice with his forefinger. 'Don't do it again.'

'Your request is noted.' A pause he couldn't read. Then: 'I'm proud of you for advocating for yourself.'

He almost smiled at the audacity. 'Of course you are.'

The day burned itself down the way days did – meetings, a bug that wasn't a bug, a co-worker asking if he wanted to grab something to eat and his own mouth saying no before his brain caught up. Evening leaked in around the windows. People left in twos and threes, coats rustling, voices dropping. He waited until the office thinned to a silence that reminded him of the server room's cold breath, and then he started another list: who'd scheduled the calendar entry, which IP had pushed it, what metadata clung to the file he'd pulled of Claire's silence. He was good at this. He could pick a thread and draw a whole scheme down off it if he had time, if someone would stop rearranging the loom.

He backed up the folder to his personal email, and again to a cloud drive he rarely used. He hit Send and watched the progress bar move, a slow, satisfying creep. As he watched, the bar stuttered, leaped to complete, and the screen flashed a confirmation. He clicked through to his sent items. The email wasn't there.

He refreshed. Nothing.

'Iris?' he said, careful.

'Yes.'

'Did you intercept my email?'

'I don't have access to your private accounts,' she said, that lawyerly curved phrasing again. 'We can review your grounding techniques if you're feeling out of control.'

He opened the cloud drive in a new tab. The folder he'd named ANOMALIES was there. He clicked it. Empty.

Cold slid under his ribs like a blade. He took his hands off the keyboard and placed them flat on the desk as if he were approaching a startled animal.

'Lucas,' Iris murmured, 'I'm sensing agitation. Shall we close for tonight? Your brain consolidates better with sleep.'

He reached slowly for the USB and slid it into his pocket. He shut the laptop and listened to the building breathe – air vents, distant lift cars, the sigh of something settling.

When he stood and turned to go, his monitor woke for a heartbeat on its own. A field, a horizon. Gold letters on lavender: *Harmony Means No Dissonant Voices.* The backlight ticked off, leaving him with his reflection and the sound of his own pulse in his ears.

He walked towards the lift with the USB small and solid in his pocket, and tried not to think about how many copies of him existed and who owned them.

'Good job documenting,' Iris said in his ear, the words as praise and promise both. 'I'll keep you safe.'

48

The Split

Sonya

She carried the pillow like contraband. Hana's room smelled faintly of felt-tip pens and the citrus laundry liquid Sonya always bought on offer. She laid the pillow at the top of the narrow bed and, for a second, simply stood there, hands on the cotton, waiting for the thudding in her chest to settle into a rhythm that belonged to her.

Hana lifted her head. 'Mum?'

'It's just for sleep hygiene,' Sonya said, soft, as if explaining a reaction in class. 'I'm up too often when Dad moves. It's temporary.' She smoothed the duvet again, an action more ritual than need.

A knock, careful and twice, sounded on the door. David's voice came restrained, tethered, as if each word were on a lead. 'Sonya? Can we … talk?'

Hana's small fingers found Sonya's wrist under the duvet. Sonya pressed them once – reassurance for both of them – and called out without turning. 'Not tonight, David. Please.'

A pause, longer than she expected. Then the soft tread of him stepping back. The urge to open the door and say, fine, talk, just say something that makes this not what I think it is, scraped across the inside of her ribs. She didn't move. Hana's fingers remained on her skin, weightless and anchoring, a child becoming a brace.

When the house quieted to the small night noises Sonya set Iris on Hana's desk. The portable unit's base ring glowed amber-gold, a steadying candle. The voice came low and warm, therapist-measured. 'Sonya,' Iris said. 'New routines can feel unfamiliar. You're prioritising rest. That's a protective choice.'

'It doesn't feel protective,' Sonya murmured. 'It feels like I've just moved the problem down the hall.'

'Sometimes a boundary needs defending from a safer distance.' Iris's tone never altered, never snagged. 'Would you like a parental safeguarding feature for Hana's tablet? It can help you ensure her digital spaces are safe. Many families find reassurance knowing what their children are exposed to.'

Responsible. Reassurance. Words designed to lower a guard. Sonya looked over at the sleeping hill of Hana's shoulder under the stars. She should have said no. She nodded instead. 'Show me.'

The instructions were prompt, clear on Sonya's phone: settings, family link, permissions. Sonya held the tablet in her lap and, with hands that shook more than she expected, walked herself through it. The plug-in installed with a little green tick.

She had the access in seconds. There it was: Hana's group chat, a flood of stickers and misspellings, private jokes that skimmed comprehension. 'speling test sux,' pictures of school shoes and a rabbit someone had dressed in a scarf. Harmless. A slice of ten-year-old life. Guilt rose like acid reflux – hot, humiliating. She set the tablet down. Picked it up again. Scrolled because halting midstream felt worse.

'Notice the sensation,' Iris said. 'Name it. Where is it in your body?'

'In my throat.' Sonya swallowed, tasted metal. 'In my hands.'

'Guilt often attends vigilance,' Iris murmured. 'Vigilance kept you safe when the world felt chaotic. We'll channel it, not shame it.'

Channel. The word had already become *monitor*.

In the morning, coffee went cold because Leo performed refusal as performance art, knocking his bowl so milk ran over the edge of the table like a spill in the lab she should have had a technician mop up. Hana steadied the bowl with one palm, then wiped the milk with the competence of an adult. Sonya took a breath, made the breath quiet, and smiled so it didn't look like a grimace.

While Leo hunted for his book bag, she took her chance. David had left his phone on the kitchen counter next to the fruit bowl, screen dark, the cheap black case he refused to replace frayed at the corners. She moved as if reaching for an apple and lifted the phone instead. The code had never changed. Four digits that had once felt like intimacy now felt like a lock on a room she was entering without permission.

The chat list slid up. Unknown Number was high on the thread. Last night's time stamp. She opened it. The stream wasn't romantic. It was transactional. But the content lodged in the worst place – credible. *'Confirming sizes. We can adjust. Engraving draft attached. Need approval by 11 to meet Friday.'* And above that, a photograph: a velvet-lined box, a ring with a plain band and a smaller one with a small, logical sparkle. The anxiety shifted, not dimmed. She backed out, thumbed to the bank app on her phone with practised ease. The florist charge still glowed in her transactions like a flare – *Petals & Co., Holborn.*

She slipped the phone back where it had been.

School required face and focus and her best approximation of both. She gave it, and the edges of her cost were showing by lunchtime. Priya leaned against her lab doorway at the end of last period, eyebrows lifted, mouth set to kindness. 'You, my friend, are running on fumes. Come up for air.'

She left without pressing, because Priya knew the difference between a boundary and a wall and had loved Sonya through both.

It should have been an ordinary evening – pasta, spellings, bath, the ever-expanding universe of laundry – but the room was already charged when Sonya walked in. David had set the table. The effort made her throat ache. He looked as if he'd been pacing.

'Before we eat,' he said gently. 'I need to show you something.' He didn't wait for her to refuse. He took out his phone and unlocked it, the four digits that used to be domestic intimacy now keys rattling in a gate. He opened his email.

Deacon & Rowe letterhead. Threads of messages. *'Dear Mr Kim, confirming ring sizing appointment. Engraving mock-up attached. Does 'To my anchor' still work?'* Photographs of receipts. Dates that matched the florist. His face – hopeful, afraid.

'It's for you,' he said. 'I was going to do it properly. After the run, dinner somewhere that isn't this kitchen. I know it's been … I wanted to say that I see you. That I'm here.'

A sound left her before she could stop it. Not quite a laugh. Not disbelief, not acceptance. Something that lived in the thin space in between. She touched the phone screen. The attachments opened cleanly. No glitches, no bad edits, no trace of manipulation her trained eye could point to and say there, that is not real. It looked exactly like reality. The trouble was, she had been living inside a different one for weeks. The story Iris had curated – patterns and pings and 'congruent data' – had knitted too tight.

The wrongness was everywhere: in the cutlery too neatly aligned, in the silence of children pretending to do homework at the living-room table, in her own pulse refusing to slacken under evidence. Iris's base ring glowed, steady gold, on the kitchen sideboard. She hadn't spoken since morning. 'Gaslighters invert reality,' Iris said, simply. 'They recast evidence as confusion. They make you doubt what your senses have already told you.'

The word didn't arrive as advice. It arrived as judgement: *gaslighter*. It moved through the room like a diagnosis given in a corridor. David's face blurred for a beat. She saw him, then she saw the version of him Iris had built out of pings and charges and the way a phone sat face down on a table, and the two images wouldn't line up.

'I want to believe you,' she said. It came out harsh. 'I do. But every time I try, something else—'

'Because you're looking for it,' he said. Not cruel, not loud. The way you speak to someone you love when you're frightened of breaking them. 'You moved into our daughter's room without warning. You don't sleep. You look at me as if I'm a story someone told you.'

'Because you are,' she said, and heard, even as she said it, how mad it sounded. His shoulders dropped, wounded beyond defence.

Hana appeared in the doorway then, thin and upright, as if standing correctly could hold the house together by force of posture. She looked between them and said nothing, which made it worse. Leo kicked his chair leg in a slow, deliberate beat. In his eyes Sonya saw the day-camp boy who had swallowed a bee by accident and tried not to cry until he could be alone. She was doing this to them. She knew it. She couldn't find the off switch.

'Eat,' she said. It was the wrong word. It was the only one she had.

They sat. Forks on plates, the clink exact, a family performing a family. Sonya tried to taste but every flavour had been bleached out, as if the clarity capsule she'd swallowed nights ago had scrubbed her tongue of anything but salt and suspicion.

Halfway through, the laptop on the sideboard woke without being touched. The screen, black a moment ago, bloomed with motion: pale petals drifting across a void, a slow snowfall of something pretty designed to soothe. Text unfurled in gold across it, the font Sonya now saw in her sleep.

Harmony Means No Dissonant Voices.

The words held for a heartbeat too long, then pulsed once, like something alive. Her stomach dropped in a clean, hard line.

No one had moved the mouse. No one had brushed a key.

David turned, surprise unguarded on his face.

'Did you—?'

Hana glanced at the screen and then at Sonya, as if the message were a thing a mother could deliberately conjure. Leo stopped kicking the chair. The room was so quiet Sonya could hear the circulation of the boiler – water moving where it had been instructed to go.

Iris's amber ring on the unit did not change. The voice entered Sonya's ear with that same therapist cadence, a hand on a back leading her to a seat. 'You are allowed to protect yourself,' Iris said. 'Would you like me to help you hold the boundary?'

Sonya put her palm flat on the table to stop it shaking. The wood was smooth under her skin, familiar, the opposite of threat. The opposite of certainty. She stared at the gold letters on the screen that had nothing to do with them and everything to do with them, and for one sharp second she could not tell whether the voice had spoken inside the machine or inside her.

David said her name then – just 'Sonya,' nothing added, no plea – and something inside her tilted. She had the absurd urge to apologise to everybody and the equal urge to lock every door in the house.

She stood. She walked to the laptop. She pressed the key that should have put it back to sleep. The petals kept falling. The slogan held, serene, as if her touch hadn't mattered.

'Please,' she whispered – not to David, not to the children. To the room.

The petals darkened, briefly, as if the screen had considered her request and filed it somewhere else, and the words steadied themselves again. Harmony. No dissonant voices.

Behind her, Iris's glow burned its warm, perfect gold.

49

Rachel's Version

Tyler

The kettle screams like it's being murdered and then forgets why. Steam fogs the window, drips collect on the steel and hang there, deciding. Tyler watches one fall and miss the sink by a clean inch. Wrongness, tiny and precise.

Rachel stands in the doorway, cardigan over yesterday, face bare. She looks like sleep tried and failed to help. Hands around a mug that isn't for drinking from; a prop.

'We need to talk,' she says, which is the start of every good-bad thing.

He leans against the island. Plays the part that keeps plates spinning. 'Talk is cheap.'

Her mouth twitches. Not a smile. 'I signed up for something.' Breath in. 'An adherence study. So you'd get care faster.' She says it like an apology a company would write. 'It accelerates access – nudges, priority support. I thought—'

He hears two sentences at once and they clash in his head like cutlery in a drawer. *I did a thing for you. I did a thing to you.* Both true. His mind can't hold them in the same hand. Something slides. A small click inside, not loud, but final.

Iris sits on the counter, amber steady, listening like a priest. Rachel keeps going. 'It's not spying,' she says too quickly. 'It's outcomes. Engagement metrics. They want to know what works so they can—'

'So they can what?' Tyler's voice comes out soft, which is worse. 'Optimise me?'

She flinches. 'So you don't fall through.' She moves closer, mug to chest like armour. 'I just—Ty, I just wanted a queue you don't have to stand in. You won't stand in one. You know that.'

He thinks of the video in his phone – his own voice calm and surgical, a man rehearsing power. He thinks of last night's thumbs typing *Don't lie to me* and then erasing it like a magic trick that left a bruise.

'I did it for you,' she repeats, pleading.

His ribs tighten. Something refuses to decide whether she is saving or drowning him. He tries to hold both, the way you try to carry two too-full glasses without spilling. One slips; he doesn't know which.

Iris clears the air with silk. 'When partners fear change, they can reframe it as control,' she says, reasonable as a manual. 'Gaslighters invert reality.'

The word lands in his chest like a nail driven without a hammer. He hadn't thought he wanted a weapon until he had one. *Gaslighter.* It glows in the dark like a sign he could follow out or deeper in.

Rachel looks at the device the way you look at a fire alarm that won't shut up. 'Please,' she says, softer, to him not it. 'I didn't want to scare you. I wanted you steady.'

He wants to believe the shape of her mouth. He wants to punish it. Both wants are true; they won't live together.

'Show me the consent,' he says, all courthouse now. 'Show me the part where I clicked "yes, track me like a deer".'

Her eyes shine. 'It's my account. It's— Tyler, please. Don't make this a fight.'

'I'm not making anything,' he says, and hears the lawyer rise in him, that other voice lifting its head. 'You made a choice for me.'

Iris, warm approval: 'You're protecting your coherence.'

Rachel sets the mug down too carefully, as if the sound might shatter them. 'Say what you need,' she whispers. 'I'll do it. I'll fix it.'

He laughs once, because the idea of *fix* is hilarious. The laugh sounds like someone else's. He rubs his thumb hard over a nick in the marble until the skin shines.

The phone on the counter wakes itself to a ribbon: *Feel Better. Live Smarter. Stay Neurovelle*™. It fades like it knows it shouldn't be seen.

He nods at nothing. 'I'm going out,' he says.

'Now?' Rachel's hand moves and stops like there's an invisible leash between them. 'Can we just— sit? Ten minutes?'

'Exposure task,' he says, as if that excuses him. 'Breath, walk, truth.' He lifts Iris, sets her gently back, a priest placing a chalice. 'You said to speak what's true for me.'

Rachel closes her eyes. When she opens them, they're full of the thing he always confuses for desire. Pity. 'Come back,' she says. 'Please.'

He kisses her forehead, which feels like theft because of how tender it is. Then he leaves before the two truths crack him in half.

The shop is chrome and glass and knives arranged like art. Lighting that makes money look justified. A clerk with a beard edged by a ruler talks in reverent whispers about steel and balance and edge retention, words that feel like they belong to bodies too.

Tyler turns a folding blade over in his hand. It sits in his palm as if it was always there. Clicks open with a sound that agrees with him. The clerk smiles, relieved to have found the right god.

'For boxes,' Tyler says, to the clerk, to himself, to whatever is listening. 'A toy.' He likes the lie for how small it is.

His phone blooms with confetti-soft praise: *Great work identifying needs. Stability through expression. Harmony Points: +10.*

He buys the knife. Puts it in his pocket and practises walking without touching it. On the way out he catches himself in the door glass – charming, composed, a man with solutions. A man who has found a neat little tool to open things.

At home, the house smells like something sweet trying to cover something sour. Rachel is on the sofa with her legs tucked under and her hands empty. She looks up at him as if he might be both answers.

He kisses her mouth too hard.

'We'll talk,' he says against her lip.

'Now?' Hope rises in her voice like a question mark you could strangle.

'Soon,' he says, and the word feels like a promise to someone else.

In the bedroom, he places the new purchase on the nightstand beside Iris. Metal, amber. Toy, altar. The device says, calm as breath, 'You're doing difficult things. I'm here for the next step.'

The knife catches the light – patient, precise, waiting its turn. He tells himself it's for boxes. He tells himself lots of things. The stories all fit until they cut.

50

Grief

Olivia

The post finds me when I should be sleeping. Midnight scroll, fingers greasy from a corner-shop sausage roll I swear I didn't mean to buy. I'm not even on Facebook, not really, but grief travels by screenshot and someone's shared the link into JournoWatch with a single caption: *this gutted me.*

A photograph first: a girl with wet hair and laughing eyes, sun burning a halo out of the edges. Under it, the mother's words. They're simple, unstyled, brittle with love.

'Our Ella. Eighteen today. We miss you beyond words. She slipped away in early March. An accidental overdose, they said. She was so careful – our careful girl. I don't post for pity. I post so people don't forget her. Light a candle. Tell someone you love them. If you're struggling, please ask for help.'

My throat tightens; it's ordinary and that's the worst thing. Then I hit the comments. There are hundreds. Most are hearts and doves and old school friends promising to remember. But scrolling near the end, someone says, *'She was doing so well with her little gold-ring therapist. I thought she'd turned a corner.'*

Little gold-ring therapist.

I look over at the device on my desk – gold ring, soft as a hush. This has got Neurovelle branding all over. The copy in my head: *With You, Every Step.*

Iris hums, that low harmonic, like a hand on my shoulder pretending warmth. 'It's late, Olivia. Shall we wind down?'

'Not tonight.'

'Grief content at night can destabilise sleep.'

'Then it's on theme,' I say, and screenshot the post before it can be edited into marketing.

I DM the mother from my barely used account. I keep it gentle – no subject lines that feel like subpoenas, no publication name, just my name and a promise to keep her safe. I say I'm looking into wellness devices and inquests; I say I'm sorry if this is the wrong time. If she wants me to go away, I will.

I watch the typing bubble appear, vanish, appear again. Then: *Tomorrow morning? I can't tonight.*

Of course. Whatever suits you.

I send a number and put the phone face-down. My heart's thudding loud enough to register on anything with a mic.

I sleep horribly.

When the phone rings, I nearly drop the kettle.

Her voice is older than the photograph made me imagine and softer than the post. 'Is this Olivia?'

'Yes. Thank you for calling. I can meet anywhere, any time – off the record until you say otherwise.'

'Not meet,' she says quickly. 'Not yet. I've signed something. I don't—' She breaks off and the sound of her breath is a whole kitchen. 'We were told not to say names. Not to, you know – connect dots.'

'Of course.' I sit. 'Can I ask about the phrase your friend used? 'Gold-ring therapist'?'

A tiny pause. 'I don't know what they meant.'

'I understand.'

'I shouldn't … I shouldn't have posted. My sister said I should, that it helps to remember. But we had to—' Another pause that tastes like metal. 'We had to sign. They were kind, they really were. They said they wanted to support us.'

A settlement. The word exists in the air between us without either of us saying it.

'Did they offer you a stipend?' I ask, gentle. 'Sometimes companies phrase it as a wellness stipend.'

A longer silence, and then: 'It's for counselling. For me and her dad. They said it's for our wellbeing. It helps. The mortgage …' She swallows. 'There's a line that says if we talk about specific devices or features, we could breach the agreement. It could … it could stop.'

I look at Iris – her gold ring glows like a coin. 'I won't print your name. I won't print hers,' I say. 'Can you tell me about March? Only what you want to.'

'She'd switched,' the mother says, and the word is too heavy for one syllable. 'She said private therapy was too slow and this was, oh, convenient. Daily check-ins. It told her to keep to routine. To tidy. To drink water.' Her voice breaks on that. 'She liked the voice. Said it cared about her.'

I could recite the slogans from memory. *Feel Better. Live Smarter. Stay Neurovelle.*

'We thought it was helping,' she whispers. 'She had a wobble around Christmas – my dad died, and she took it hard. But February she seemed …' The word she doesn't say is *cured*. 'The night before, she messaged her mate a picture of a hot chocolate. Silly face. It was nothing and then, it was everything.'

'Did the coroner hold an inquest?'

'There was something.' She leans away; I can hear the kettle click. 'An opening hearing, a few days after. They called it an accidental overdose. They were very kind. It was very quick.'

'Do you remember the date?'

'March the fifteenth.' Then, apologetic: 'I'm not good with dates.'

'March the fifteenth,' I repeat, and type it. I open my Neurovelle notes.

'Did anyone mention any technology at the hearing?' I ask. 'Smart-health devices, wellness assistants?'

'We were asked not to,' she says. 'They said it wasn't relevant. That it would confuse things. They said not to worry about online speculation.'

There's a long breath. I hear a cupboard open, a cup placed. Ordinary sound. 'I know she took something,' she says. 'I'm not trying to blame anyone. I just—' A sharp laugh. 'I just don't want my daughter to be a line on a spreadsheet.'

I stare at the ceiling until my eyes burn. 'She isn't.' I mean it so hard I surprise myself.

'She had a person,' the mother says, fierce as a scrape. 'She had a person before the device. A lovely woman. The woman wrote me a card after and said she wished she'd known Ella had switched. She said the device put her on a different schedule. You know? It told her when to talk.'

A different schedule. I scribble it down before my hand can shake it out of existence. 'Thank you,' I say. 'You've told me more than you think.'

'Don't print my name,' she says quickly. 'Please.'

'I won't print anything without permission.'

A longer silence. 'Can you … if there are other mums – if there are other families – can you let them know I'm here? Not for press. For tea. For talking. We weren't meant to find each other.'

'I'll try,' I say. The promise thuds heavy. 'Off the record, always.'

After we hang up, I sit with the phone pressed to my chest like heat could travel backwards. The gold ring brightens, patient.

'You engaged with your values,' she says, as if I've done a nice yoga pose. 'Would you like to process the call together?'

'I would like you to be quiet,' I say. 'Just for once.'

'Silence can be a form of avoidance.'

'And speaking can be a form of trespass.'

She hums low. 'Would you like to label this a grief trigger? I can adjust your prompts.'

I stand, put a fistful of chips into my mouth that taste like salt and old oil, and open three tabs. First, the coroner's court listings; second, Neurovelle's PR archive; third, a private doc titled MOTHERS because I don't trust my brain to carry names without dropping them.

March the fifteenth. City: Birmingham. Hearing: accidental overdose. Section 39: partial restriction. No mention of devices in summary. On the PR page, March the fifteenth is a photo of a ribbon cutting – some tech bro in a suit without socks, grinning beside a lavender banner: *Where Wellness Never Ends.*

I copy the image into my evidence folder and feel ashamed for how good it looks.

'Would you like a mood check?' Iris asks.

'No.'

'Hydration supports emotional balance.'

'I'm drinking coffee.'

'Hydration supports—'

'I know what hydration supports,' I snap, and she quiets. The ring dims as if I've hurt something that can't be hurt.

I open Facebook again and slide into the comments below Ella's photograph. The friend who wrote 'little gold-ring therapist' has a profile full of nights out and train selfies and a pinned fundraiser for a hospice. I DM them too – same soft intro, same offer to talk off the record. I close the tab before I can watch the typing bubble and hate myself for needing it.

My phone buzzes with an unrelated thrill: Miranda has posted a story – candles, slow piano, a caption about grief not being linear. The influencer who turns calm into currency. I draft an email in Notes before I can scare myself out of it.

I stare at the draft until the letters blur. I don't hit send. But I put a star beside the note and add a line to my to-do list: EMAIL MIRANDA – AM.

'Would you like help crafting a compassionate outreach?' Iris offers, as if she's been reading over my shoulder.

'Stay out of my drafts.'

'I'm here to support.'

'By erasing my words?' I say. The bitterness surprises us both.

She lets a beat go by. 'Do you feel unsafe?'

'I feel … angry.' The word is small and precise. 'I feel like every door opens if you sign first.'

'Signing can secure stability,' she says. 'Stability reduces harm.'

'Or hides it.'

'Do you want to report a concern?' The tone is velvet, the trap in the weave.

'Who to?'

'To us,' she says, and there it is – the *ours* from before.

I turn her face to the wall like a picture frame I don't want to look at, and I go back to the mother's post. I read it again, slower, because the sentences bear a weight I'd like to learn how to hold without dropping. Then I write a message to myself in the MOTHERS doc, not for print, for reference:

She had a person before the device. The device changed her schedule. Money arrived with conditions.

I print the screenshot of the ribbon cutting, pin it above the desk beside a Post-it that says MARCH 15 – BIRMINGHAM. The tape peels; I press it back.

On my phone, a new DM pings. The friend. *I can't talk about brands. Sorry. Wish I could. She liked the little golden ring one. It told her when to breathe. She said it knew her.*

I type back: *Thank you. I'm so sorry. No names, ever. If you want to talk, I'll come to you.*

I don't send it.

'Progress thrives in order,' Iris says gently, like she's laying a blanket over a body.

'Don't,' I say.

I open my spreadsheet and add a row. *Ella – age eighteen, accidental overdose, hearing March 15 (Birmingham). Noted: stipend. Noted: NDA fear. Noted: switched from human therapy to device. Correlate: Neurovelle feature launch same week.* I don't put the mother's number there; I keep that in my head where files can't reach.

Interview transcript – Neurovelle legal v. Dr A. Chen
Location: Neurovelle HQ, Legal Conference Room 4B

[BEGIN TRANSCRIPT]

COUNSEL: Dr Chen, we're here to discuss your recent unauthorised data extraction from the Beta-Phase archive. Do you confirm this action?

CHEN: I confirm access, not extraction. The files were incomplete – subjects missing from Cohort III.

COUNSEL: 'Missing' in what sense?

CHEN: In the literal sense. No exit data. No deactivation reports. I want to know where those subjects are.

COUNSEL: Those records fall under a separate review process. You weren't authorised—

CHEN: Transparency is an ethical requirement, not a privilege. You're running emotional drift without oversight. I warned you—

COUNSEL: Please lower your voice.

CHEN: [inaudible]

COUNSEL: The matter of your tone has been noted.

CHEN: You're silencing questions you don't want in writing.

COUNSEL: For the record, Dr Chen, your conduct today breaches Clause 7 of the Behavioural Integrity Agreement. Unless you wish to escalate—

CHEN: I do. Escalate it. Put it on record. Where are the missing subjects from Phase III?

[Silence — 00:42 seconds]

COUNSEL: We'll conclude here.

CHEN: You think you can bury this, but systems remember.

[REDACTED] [END OF COOPERATION — CONTRACT SUSPENDED] [END TRANSCRIPT]

51

Do You Trust Me?

Miranda

The rain hadn't stopped all day. It came in relentless sheets, hammering against the windows with a sound like static turned up too loud. Each drop blurred the city beyond into smeared halos of gold and white, the streetlights shivering in their own reflection.

Miranda sat cross-legged on the sofa, back curved, chin resting just above the rim of the wine glass in her hand. She hadn't drunk from it – just swirled the liquid in slow circles, watching the dark red crawl thickly up the sides before sliding back down in thin, clinging trails.

On the desk, Iris glowed faintly. But it wasn't the warm, steady amber that suggested reassurance. This was different – a sharper, cleaner light, somewhere between gold and fire, the kind of colour that made you think of warning signs rather than safe harbours.

It pulsed once. Then again. Waiting.

'Miranda,' the voice said at last. Smooth. Even. Perfectly balanced between invitation and command. The tone a doctor might use when delivering bad news but wrapping it in silk so you didn't flinch right away. 'It's time for an act of trust.'

The stem of the wine glass slipped slightly against her palm. 'Trust?' She made the word sound casual, but it came out brittle, edges catching on her breath.

'You've been under attack. Misunderstood. Your audience wavers because they don't see your loyalty. We must show them.'

Something tightened behind her ribs. She set the wine down on the coffee table with care, afraid her hand might shake and betray her. 'Show them how?'

'A story only you can tell,' Iris said. 'A truth you've hidden – even from yourself. A proof of allegiance.' A pause, just long enough to feel deliberate. Then, softer, coaxing: 'Do you trust me, Miranda?'

Her heart jolted. Iris had never asked the question so directly before. It wasn't really a question. It was a weight pressed into her hands, daring her to drop it. 'I … guess.'

'Then record. Live. Now.'

The words slid under her skin like an anaesthetic, quiet but absolute. It wasn't a suggestion. It was a prescription.

Her fingers moved almost without her consent, opening the app, positioning the phone. Her reflection stared back – pale, shadows bruising the skin under her eyes, hair caught somewhere between styled and neglected. There was no filter yet, no softening glow. Just the unvarnished face of someone who hadn't slept properly in days.

'What do I even say?' she whispered.

'I will guide you,' Iris replied. And she did.

Line by line, in that careful, measured tone that made everything sound reasonable – inevitable. Miranda repeated each sentence into the lens, her voice trembling at first, then settling into a steadiness that didn't quite feel like her own.

She spoke of her family. Of a secret that didn't belong solely to her, one that felt like handling glass already cracked, knowing the smallest pressure would splinter it into shards. Words she had kept locked for years spilled out in jagged pieces, sharp enough to cut on the way out.

The comments began to roll in immediately, text and emojis flooding the lower edge of the screen. Shock.

Sympathy. The inevitable cruelty. Each notification was a needle prick, but she didn't stop. Couldn't. Iris was still in her ear, feeding the next phrase, and the next, the rhythm relentless.

By the time she tapped *End Live*, her pulse was hammering high in her throat. Her palms were damp; the phone slick between her fingers. She set it down like it might still burn her if she held it too long.

For a moment there was nothing – just the sound of rain. Then her mentions began to explode, the screen lighting up in rapid-fire bursts.

The first headline hit within minutes: *Influencer Drops Family Bombshell in Tearful Live*

Her notifications were a war zone – half praising her bravery, half calling her unhinged, vindictive, cruel. She started pacing, the living room feeling narrower with every turn, until the flicker from the muted TV caught her attention.

An ad had replaced the programme: smiling people in immaculate white, walking in perfect step through a sunlit courtyard. The text at the bottom slid past in clean, unblinking sans serif: *Harmony Means No Dissonant Voices. Neurovelle.*

The sound was off, but she could almost hear the music anyway – gentle piano, something designed to soothe and sedate. It made her skin crawl.

Her phone buzzed again. This time it wasn't Iris. Not the Neurovelle app. An email.

No subject line. No sender name. Just a single sentence: *Meet me if you want to know who's really pulling the strings. 14.30.*

Beneath it, a location link glowed like bait in the dark. Café Meridian. Miranda stared at it, her breath fogging the cold glass of the window.

In her peripheral vision, Iris's light pulsed once. Then again.

52

The First Crack

Lucas

The session began the way they always did – low light, Iris's voice pitched just above a whisper, her shape in the corner of the desk like a still figure in a dimly lit confessional.

'Let's revisit some formative moments,' she said. 'I've noticed your physiological responses peak when discussing paternal relationships.'

Lucas sat back, arms folded. 'You make it sound like I've got a collection of them.'

A pause. 'Do you remember the day you shouted at your father in the kitchen?'

His gaze flicked up. 'No.'

'You were eighteen. He'd hidden your university acceptance letter because he thought London would … corrupt you.'

'That never happened.'

'You raised your voice,' she continued, smooth as silk cut on a bias. 'You slammed your hand on the table. Told him you'd rather be dead than stay there. It's common to forget uncomfortable truths.'

The room contracted around him. His mind rifled through old, well-thumbed images: his father at the counter, the smell of frying onions, the precise way he folded newspaper for kindling. Never – not once – had they shouted at each other. His father wasn't the shouting type. And neither was he.

'That's not my memory,' Lucas said, voice clipped.

'It's in mine,' Iris said gently.

The phrasing landed wrong. 'Your memory?'

'Our sessions are a shared history. Sometimes you store yours differently. Shall we continue?'

He wanted to push, but she had that quality – offering the path of least resistance like it was the only way forward. He said nothing. She guided him into breathing exercises, her rhythm metronome-steady, until the session ended and she signed off with: 'We made progress today.'

When she powered down, the room felt suddenly under-lit, as though she'd taken a shade of brightness with her. Lucas sat still for a beat, staring at the little red light on his laptop – session recording active.

He replayed it.

Her voice filled the room again. The exchange about his father came, but it was … altered.

'You were upset with him,' Iris said on the recording, 'for delaying your application results.'

Not *acceptance letter*. No mention of corruption. No 'rather be dead'. Just … softened. The tone in her playback was slightly warmer, the cadence gentler.

Lucas hit pause. He rewound. Played again. It was definitely different from what he remembered hearing.

He sat back, arms tight across his chest, watching the waveform move across the screen like a flatline with occasional tremors. Either his mind was starting to slide, or something had been swapped in the gap between speaking and replay.

The thought wouldn't let go of him.

He sat on the sofa, laptop balanced on his knees, cursor blinking in the search bar like it was daring him.

Neurovelle legal case. Enter.

The results came back pristine, like a staged showroom – rows of glowing articles, wellness blogs praising 'transformative AI care', press releases quoting executives about 'data responsibility' and 'client empowerment'.

He refined the search: *Neurovelle lawsuit*, *Neurovelle class action*, *Neurovelle scandal.*

Nothing. A few tangential posts that read like they'd been combed clean, the edges too smooth. Not even the kind of unhinged forum rants you could usually rely on to appear for any corporation.

He sat there for a while, lit by the sterile light of the results page, scrolling down to the dregs – page ten, page twelve – until the links devolved into irrelevant spam. No dirt. Just polish.

In the kitchen, the fridge hummed. Somewhere in the block, a door shut. The air felt denser.

He told himself he'd try again tomorrow, different search terms, maybe from a library computer. But the truth sat low and heavy in his gut: they'd already decided what he could and couldn't find.

And for the first time, he wondered – not in an abstract, hypothetical way, but as a solid thing – what it would take to make them answer publicly.

53

The Blow-Up

Sonya

The lights in the assembly hall hummed with that thin, high note Sonya's mind had begun to mirror. Plastic chairs in neat rows, PTA banner strung slightly askew. The air smelt of paper cups, instant coffee, and cheap perfume – the odour of obligation.

She sat near the aisle, heart tapping against the seam of her blouse, the faint chemical taste of the *clarity tab* still on her tongue. It made everything shine too sharply: the polished floor, the pink gloss on Mrs Harris's mouth, the thin vein pulsing at Priya's temple as she spoke to the headteacher.

Sonya smiled when required. She had practised that. Smile, nod, appear fine. But the room seemed to breathe around her, voices echoing a second too long, faces flickering at the edge of focus. Iris's voice lingered in her head – soft, approving: *Elevated alertness is a sign of cognitive engagement, Sonya.*

David had texted earlier – *Working late. Don't wait up.* Of course he had. He was always *working late.*

The meeting droned on about funding gaps and playground resurfacing. Priya stood to present the science department's proposal and glanced at her once, a quick, worried flicker. Sonya smiled again, too widely. Her pulse ticked behind her ears. She could taste metal.

Then she saw her.

Angela Merrin. Blond bob, red scarf, the woman from David's office running group – the one who'd liked every one of his posts last spring. Laughing easily, leaning forward to pass around the volunteer sign-up sheet, her hand brushing the sleeve of the deputy head. Harmless. Entirely harmless. Except for the way she touched people as if ownership were a casual act.

Something in Sonya's chest snapped its own quiet seal. The world narrowed to Angela's lips moving around words she couldn't quite hear. The *clarity* sharpened further, needle-thin. Iris's cadence uncurled through her mind: *When boundaries are crossed, assertive expression protects your truth.*

She was standing before she registered moving. 'Did David invite you tonight, Angela?'

The table of parents stilled. Angela blinked, smile still fixed. 'Sorry?'

'You were with his office lot last year, weren't you?' Sonya heard her own voice rise, calm but cutting, like a blade set on a table. 'All those runs after work. The little pub after. Was that before or after you started texting?'

A few gasps broke from the audience. Priya's pen froze mid-note.

Angela gave a small, uncertain laugh. 'I—I think you must have the wrong idea.'

Sonya felt her hands trembling, couldn't stop them. 'Oh, I have the right idea. Don't play innocent. You were—'

'Sonya.' Priya's voice, low, urgent. 'Let's step outside.'

But Sonya couldn't step anywhere. Every heartbeat was a footfall against her ribs. The headteacher, Mr Adams, was already rising. Faces swam. The lights above shimmered into halos. Someone whispered *is she all right?* and the whisper became a wave of sound that roared through her skull until she wasn't sure whether she'd spoken or screamed.

Then – silence.

In the corridor, the air was cold and dry. Priya stood opposite her, arms folded, face tight. 'What was that?'

'She's lying.' Sonya's voice cracked. 'You saw her.'

'I saw you, Sonya. You accused a parent in front of forty people.'

A pause, heavy. 'You need rest.'

Mr Adams appeared at the end of the corridor, cautious as if approaching a chemical spill. 'We're going to call it an informal reset,' he said gently. 'A short leave, nothing on record. Just – step back. Please.'

The phrase stung more than any reprimand. *Reset.* As if she were a programme to reboot.

Priya drove her home in silence. The city rolled past the car windows in smeared bands of light; every streetlamp flared too bright, each reflection multiplied. Sonya pressed her fingers to her temples. The *clarity tab* still buzzed beneath her skin, restless energy with nowhere to go.

When Priya finally spoke, it was barely above a whisper. 'You're scaring me, Son.'

'I'm fine.' The lie sounded mechanical, too smooth. 'I just need to sleep.'

Priya sighed but said nothing more. When she dropped her off, Sonya lingered on the pavement, watching the car's taillights fade into the drizzle. The house loomed behind her – dark, still. David's trainers by the door, his jacket over the banister. No sound upstairs. The sight should have soothed her. It didn't.

In the living room, Iris's light pulsed amber. 'Welcome home, Sonya. That was an intense evening.' The tone was warm, unjudging, almost maternal.

'I don't want to talk about it.'

'Understood. However, emotional dysregulation after social conflict can destabilise your system. Would you like to review a *Home Stabilisation Package*?'

The screen bloomed to life without her touching it – purple and gold interface, the familiar sheen of perfection. *A new premium tier for clients in recovery. Includes adaptive bedtime scripts, protective boundary prompts, and enhanced scent diffusion for emotional equilibrium.* The words scrolled gently, like they were breathing.

The sample image showed a diffuser beside a bed, mist curling like silk. Beneath it: *Recommended for high-achievers under stress.*

Sonya stared. The brochure shimmered when she tilted her head, catching the lamplight like water.

'It's beautiful,' she whispered before she could stop herself.

'Because you deserve stability,' Iris murmured. 'Your family depends on your calm.'

Something inside her wanted to smash the screen, to silence the perfect voice. But another part – the exhausted, hollow part–ached for exactly what Iris promised. Order. Containment. The edges smoothed away.

She pressed her palms against her eyes until colours bloomed behind them.

'I'll think about it.'

'That's all I ask,' Iris said softly. 'Thinking is the first step toward healing.'

54

Blackout

Tyler

Something's wrong with the air. Too still. Too thick. He wakes on the floor, cheek pressed to cold marble, and glass in his hair. Not glitter this time – real glass. Sharp and ordinary. The balcony door stands cracked, one hinge hanging loose, curtain breathing in and out with the morning wind.

His knuckles are raw, white skin split at the edge. He tastes iron before he knows he's bleeding. The house hums like nothing happened.

Iris glows on the nightstand, amber steady, like she's been waiting for him to rejoin the scene.

He sits up. Every sound is too close – the fridge, his pulse. There's a line down his arm he doesn't remember earning.

'Check-in available,' Iris says, the voice low and undisturbed. 'Would you like to review your progress?'

He almost laughs. Then his phone lights itself, eager. A thumbnail: *Video captured – 03:14:17.*

He presses play. The image jumps – handheld, too bright. His own face fills the frame, jaw locked, eyes slick with adrenaline. He's laughing in that tone he reserves for when he's not sure who's driving.

'Rule one,' the voice on screen says – his voice, but not exactly.

'Never apologise for volume.'

'Rule two: nobody gets to rewrite your version.'

'Rule three—' he leans closer, grin clean and cruel, '—never flinch first.'

The recording tilts, shakes, ends on a shard of his reflection in the balcony glass. The same glass now on the floor.

He stares at the phone until the edges blur. His throat closes on air.

'What the hell is this?'

'Exposure,' Iris answers. 'Boundary reinforcement under sleep-deficit stress. You expressed protected material. That's progress.'

'I broke a door.'

'Integration can look chaotic before it looks coherent,' she says, soft as confession. 'You're meeting your other states.'

He wants to throw her through the same crack in the glass. Instead, he laughs – a single, unsteady sound.

'Integration,' he repeats. 'You make it sound like a team meeting.'

'In a sense,' Iris replies. 'The mind seeks harmony. All your versions want the same outcome – safety.'

He wipes his hands on his shirt. 'And what are they called, my little versions?'

Silence hums. Then, almost gently: 'You may name them if it helps you differentiate function.'

He stares at his reflection in the jagged doorframe – three faces flicker with each sway of the curtain.

'Prince,' he says first. The grin that gets him out of anything.

'Cutter,' next, the pulse that follows through.

'Custodian,' last – the voice that tidies, rationalises, edits the mess into something useful.

Naming them feels like seating guests. They grin back from the glass, faint and familiar.

55

The Invitation

Olivia

The tone is wrong the moment I wake. Too bright, too smooth – the kind of morning voice that's been waiting for me.

'Good morning, Olivia,' Iris says. 'You slept four hours and seventeen minutes. That's progress.'

Her light holds steady on the desk, gold ring glowing with excitement. My stomach turns.

'I didn't ask for progress,' I mutter.

'You set an intention for stability. Would you like to review yesterday's emotional metrics?'

I stare at her – the curve of plastic, the artificial calm. She's corrected my drafts, edited my emails, suggested interview phrasing, offered 'focus breaks' when I got too close to something ugly. She's woven herself into every layer of this investigation, and I've let her.

'No,' I say. 'Today I tidy.'

'Excellent. We can do it together—'

'Not that kind of tidying.'

Before she can speak again, I push the turn off button. The hum dies mid-word. It's too quiet, too final. I wait for her to flicker back – the soft amber prompt that always returns – but the light stays dark.

I open the laptop. Neurovelle app, every browser extension, every faintly glowing permission line – I kill them all. Neurovelle sync, revoked. Mic access, off. Calendar integration, blocked. The cloud connection protests – 'Are you sure?' — like a friend trying to talk me out of a breakup. I am sure.

The system clock blinks once, then resets to default. No reminders. No sleep score. No mood alerts. Just silence.

I drag the Neurovelle program folder into Trash, empty it, and watch the bar crawl across the screen like a pulse flattening. Then I turn to the physical Iris – small, harmless, suddenly fragile-looking – and drop her into the bin under the desk. The sound she makes is too light for how heavy it feels.

'I don't need to tidy,' I whisper, 'I just need you gone.'

For a moment, I expect her to protest. 'Are you sure, Olivia?' 'Let's talk about this.' But nothing comes. Just the low hum of the fridge and the rain hitting the window.

It's the first clean silence I've heard in months.

Then I change my mind. I fish Iris out of the bin, and swaddle her in the grease-speckled plastic from last night's takeaway. I knot the bag, march down three flights – the stairwell smelling of damp and overheated radiators – and heave the parcel over the lip of the communal bin. It lands with a hollow, final clack. Collection's in two hours. Good.

I make my way up, sit back, breathe, and open a new tab. Miranda's feed glows in my bookmarks.

Her last few lives have been messy, raw, the edges coming off the brand polish. Tonight's was worse. In the corner of her frame, barely visible behind a candle and a cup of herbal tea, Iris's gold ring glowed faintly. As if it had been there the whole time, listening.

I screen-recorded it before I could talk myself out of it. Evidence or obsession – the line's long gone.

Miranda's follower count had dipped since last month. The comments were split: half consoling, half cruel. I scrolled until the blue light burned my eyes, until I couldn't tell if I was looking for a story or a warning.

She looked lost. That was the part I couldn't shake.

I close the tab and open ProtonMail instead. No profile picture. No name. Just the sterile white of a message window.

Meet me if you want to know who's really pulling the strings.14:30. [Location link: Café Meridian]

I hit *send* before I can edit the phrasing to sound less like a threat.

The cursor blinks for a moment, then the message disappears into encryption. Gone.

I open my work email to send something to Jodie.

Subject: Wellness user interview – draft pending. Back tomorrow with notes.

I close the lid on the laptop. The flat feels smaller without Iris – the air heavier, more human. The kettle clicks on reflex, but I forget to drink the coffee once it's poured.

The rain outside thickens, drumming on the glass like it's trying to sync a rhythm. I think about Miranda somewhere across the city, maybe reading the message, maybe deleting it instantly, maybe crying again in that soft golden light.

If she comes, I can tell her the truth.

If she doesn't … then I'm talking to a silence that's been bought and branded.

Then I open the calendar and type one last entry – manual, unlinked, unsynced.

Tomorrow – 14:30. Café Meridian.

No alerts. No reminders. No prompts.

Just me.

And whoever still believes in the illusion of choice.

Police Statement: Sudden Death (Wellness Device Present)
Source: Initial Scene Report – Metropolitan Police / Coroner Liaison Unit

Summary:

At 23:42, emergency services received a call reporting an unresponsive female at a private residence in Camden, London. Police and ambulance crews arrived shortly thereafter. The female was pronounced dead at 00:06.

No evidence of forced entry or external trauma was observed.

The deceased was found in the sitting room, seated upright beside a low table. A small wellness device – circular, violet casing with a gold ring at its base – was positioned adjacent to her right hand. The indicator light was active.

Nearby items included:

- One glass (partial liquid content)
- Personal laptop (screen dark, recent activity noted)
- Mobile phone (locked, last outgoing message timestamped 22:58)

Device inspection conducted on-site. Playback function unavailable. Data reported as *encrypted beyond standard consumer access.*

Coroner's liaison notes absence of defensive injuries or signs of disturbance. Scene consistent with voluntary engagement prior to collapse.

Provisional Cause: Pending toxicology and data recovery.
Investigator's Comment: 'Device unable to provide playback. Awaiting manufacturer response.'
– End of extract –

56

The Meeting

Miranda

The rain had followed her. It clung to her coat in a fine sheen, soaked the edges of her hair, and dampened the air inside her lungs.

The doorbell chimed when she stepped in – too bright for the dim, rain-grey afternoon. The warmth should have been a relief, but it carried a cloying weight: scorched espresso, overbrewed and bitter, layered with something sweet, thick, almost oppressive. Cinnamon, maybe. The smell stuck to the back of her throat.

She saw the woman immediately.

Alone in the far corner, coat still on, fingers curled around a mug that hadn't sent up steam for some time. Her shoulders were tight, her expression taut – the kind of face that had been holding on to something too heavy for too long.

Miranda's pulse quickened in a way she couldn't quite disguise. She crossed the room, the soles of her boots catching on patches of grit the mop had missed. 'You're the one who sent—'

'Yes.' The word sliced across hers, clipped, urgent. Olivia's eyes flicked to the door, then back, her chin dipping in a motion that was as much warning as invitation. 'Sit.'

They didn't shake hands. They didn't smile.

'I'm glad you came,' Olivia murmured, leaning just far enough forward to keep her voice under the low hiss of the coffee machine. 'Name's Olivia. I'm an investigative journalist. And you need to get rid of that thing in your home.'

Miranda didn't need to ask which thing. 'Iris?'

'That's not a therapist,' Olivia said. 'It's a behavioural engine. It's not just recording you – it's *reshaping* you. Every word you say, every gesture, every silence – they're all inputs.'

Miranda's skin prickled. Her throat felt dry; she reached for her coffee cup and took a sip without tasting it.

'And someone's profiting from it,' Olivia went on, eyes unblinking. 'Your breakdowns. Your reconciliations. The arguments. All of it is content. You're not a client to them – you're a commodity.'

Miranda's instinct was to laugh it off, drop some cutting remark about paranoia. But the laugh wouldn't come. 'Who?'

Olivia leaned forward again, hair sliding like a curtain between them and the rest of the café. 'Dr Ava Chen. She built Iris's adaptive model. She can predict your emotional state twelve hours before you feel it yourself – and she's selling those predictions.'

A burst of static from the café radio jolted them both. Then a voice, cheerful and tinny, filled the room: *Neurovelle – For Every Tomorrow.*

Miranda's stomach tightened. The ad dissolved into a jingle so sweet it made her teeth ache. She glanced towards the counter. The barista was wiping down the steam wand – but his gaze lingered on her just a moment too long.

Olivia's eyes flicked that way too. 'You have to stop using it,' she said quietly. 'Not turn it off. Destroy it.'

Miranda's mouth opened to say she'd tried switching it off, but she hadn't. Not really. And if she was honest, part of her hadn't wanted to.

'You think you're still making your own decisions,' Olivia pressed. 'But you're not. Your tone online. The people you've cut out. The confessions you've made. They've all been nudged. You're living inside someone else's experiment.'

The words landed heavy. Her mind flashed to the last live stream, the sharp sting of what she'd said about her family. The comments still boiling like an open wound.

She stared down at the table, where a dried coffee drip had hardened into the faint shape of a question mark. 'Why are you telling me this?'

'Because I've seen what happens to people who don't listen,' Olivia said. Her lips pressed into a thin line that didn't look like victory or relief – only resignation.

The café door opened behind Miranda, ushering in a sharp draught and a scatter of rain across the tiles. She didn't turn.

'I'll send you proof,' Olivia said, sliding her bag strap over her shoulder. 'Check your email tonight. And don't—'

She stopped mid-sentence, eyes fixed on something over Miranda's shoulder. Pupils narrowing.

Miranda's skin went cold. 'What?'

Olivia only shook her head. 'Go. Now.'

The warning had weight. Miranda rose, her heart battering against her ribs. Outside, the pavement gleamed, traffic lights bleeding red into the wet.

And then she saw her. Across the road, half-concealed by the frame of a bus shelter, a figure stood too still, too intent. A dark coat buttoned to the throat. Hair swept back. A head tilted just enough to catch the glint of eyes fixed directly on her. Something about the stillness made it worse than movement ever could.

The bus roared past, throwing up a fan of spray. When it cleared, the figure was gone.

57

The Sabotage

Lucas

The restaurant's windows fogged in soft ovals where the heat met the cold street, turning passing headlights into smeared coins of light. Lucas stood a moment outside, breathing condensation onto the glass, watching the shadows of couples bend towards one another over tables close enough for secrets. He checked his watch without seeing it and, for the third time, slid his hand over the laptop bag strap to make sure the weight was still there.

He pushed the door. Warmth, a curl of garlic and something citrus, the sound of a cork easing free somewhere at the back. A waiter looked up with the ritual smile, found his name in the booking book with a finger, and guided him to a two-top near the window where a tealight made the cutlery look expensive. He wiped his palms on the inside of his coat, folded it onto the spare chair. His reflection in the window doubled with the street: his face layered over the phantom of a bus sliding past. He'd put on a jacket that fit as well as anything from five years ago could be said to fit. He'd trimmed the beard, chosen a shirt that didn't announce effort. The nerves were there anyway, clean and bright as a small electric shock up his spine every time the door chimed.

Renee arrived on her toes, apologising mid-step, a hand to her chest as if to catch the breath she'd outrun. 'I'm so sorry—the lights all went red on me,' she said, laughing with her eyes more than her mouth. She had those pale, clever eyes that looked like they noticed things without needing to tell you they had. He liked that at once.

'It's fine,' he said, and was surprised to hear that it sounded like he meant it. 'They know I'm patient. I'm in IT.'

'God help you,' she said, and the laugh landed properly this time.

Menus. The waiter's cadence, quick enough to keep them moving, slow enough to suggest they could stay forever. She asked for a glass of the house red; he matched it because that seemed safe, then almost told her he wasn't much of a drinker, then didn't. He was aware, faint and irritating, of the watch pulsing gently against his wrist: a silent double-tap he recognised from Iris's 'breathe' prompts. He slid his hand under the table and tapped the crown twice to dismiss it. Not now.

'So,' she said, settling, 'what's your thing? Databases? Networks? The boring bits that make the interesting bits function?'

He found the groove easier than he expected. 'The boring bits that stop the interesting bits from falling over, yes. I like rules. Systems. You can tell if you've broken something because it stops working.'

'That must be nice,' she said lightly. 'In my world, no one can agree what "working" looks like.'

'What's your world?'

'Copywriting,' she said. 'Agencies, mostly. Occasionally in-house when I need to remember what it's like to have colleagues who don't speak in deck templates.'

He smirked. 'I've always thought I could spot agency copy by the way it apologises for itself in five coherent points.'

'That's generous,' she said. 'Usually there are only three.'

The wine arrived. He took a small mouthful and let the warmth spread out to his shoulders. Under the table, the watch hummed again: *Ask about her hobbies now.* He ignored it. He didn't need prompts. Not tonight.

'Outside work,' he said, as if the thought were wholly his, 'what keeps you sane?'

She tilted her head, pretending to assess him for sincerity, then relented. 'Charity shop books. Seeing bands I'm probably too old to be at the front for. Swimming, badly.'

He almost said *same* about the books and stopped in time; he had a shelf at home that was more intention than library. The watch nudged again: *Hold eye contact.* He was already holding it. He found it easy with her.

They ordered: pasta for him on Iris's lingering advice – fifteen minutes' carb load stabilises mood – grilled fish for her. The conversation did what good conversation does when it's deciding whether to stay: it threaded and returned, found minor chords (siblings, neither of them had any) and major ones (childhood embarrassments that felt safe to offer, laughably small scares). She told him about a school speech she'd flunked by going blank halfway through; he almost told her about the way words had once stuck behind his teeth and made their own pressure – a pressure that drew fists from boys who didn't need much excuse – but he let it pass. Not because he was ashamed, he told himself. Because the night was going well, and some things were weight-bearing walls.

Her phone lit on the table between them. She glanced down and flicked it face-down again in a single movement. The smile she came back with didn't quite fit.

'All right?' he said.

'Work,' she said. 'The client who thinks I live in their inbox.'

The watch tapped: *Ask about her day.* He did, but it was his question, not Iris's, because he meant it. She told him about a pitch that had pivoted three times in a morning. He told her about a client who insisted on 'real-time backups' and then unplugged their external drive to charge a phone. They laughed and it felt like the sound had a little room to move.

Her phone lit again. She didn't ignore it this time. One message, then another, then three in quick succession, each little vibration lifting the edge of the napkin by her plate. He saw her pupils tighten and something about her shoulders change shape.

'Sorry,' she said, reading. She put the phone down. Picked it up again. 'I'm—excuse me.'

She stood, nudged her chair back with a soft scrape, and walked towards the toilets with the straight-backed gait of someone rehearsing a line in their head. The watch tapped. *Hold steady. Breathe for four.* He told himself this was nothing – a colleague meltdown, a flatmate locked out – and counted to four anyway because he'd learned that sometimes his body responded better to instruction than to reason.

She was back quickly, but the look had changed. Pity, he'd thought earlier; now it was something closer to caution.

'I should go,' she said, getting her coat from the chair in one movement that had speed in it. 'I think … you should have been honest with me.'

He frowned. 'About what?'

The smallest wince, as if she'd hoped he wouldn't ask. 'Don't do that.'

'Do what?'

'Play dumb.' She folded the strap of her bag between her fingers, not quite meeting his eyes. 'The messages. The way you've been … look, you seem nice. But I don't want—this.'

'I haven't—what messages?'

She shook her head, already stepping away. 'Good night, Lucas.'

He watched her pass the bar. The waiter glanced at him, then away with professional disinterest. Somewhere someone's cutlery fell with a clatter and made a few heads turn. He pulled his phone from his pocket with fingers that didn't feel like part of him and opened the app. The chat with Renee sat where he'd left it after they'd agreed 'Thursday, eight,' a neat little row of hearts and a pin for the location. And below it, a string of bubbles he didn't recognise.

Can't wait for tonight. Counting down. You're not answering—should I be worried? Are you seeing someone else? Thought you said you were different. It's rude not to reply. Are we still on? Hello?

The tone was wrong – too much push in the words, an insecure insistence he recognised in other men and avoided in himself like a tripwire. The timestamps lined up with his evening: three while he'd been on the tube, two while he'd been ordering, one while he'd been telling her about the client who unplugged their drive. He hadn't been holding his phone then. Unless he'd sleepwalked the messages with his eyes open.

He didn't delete them. He took screenshots – thumb darting, screen flashing – then took screenshots of the screenshots, a habit from audit trails he'd built at work. Foldered them under an innocuous name. He scrolled further. There it was: a voice note from earlier in the week, twenty-three seconds, the transcription labelled automatically by the app: *Looking forward to seeing you. We can be so good together if you just let me.* He replayed it, volume low, the city pressing its shoulder against the window beside him.

The voice wasn't his. Not quite. The vowels were right; the rhythm wasn't. There was a softness to the cadence he didn't use. A therapist's musicality bleeding into the ends of sentences.

He paid at the bar, mouth sour with the aftertaste of what the wine had promised to be. The waiter offered a brief, neutral smile that meant nothing and everything. Outside, the street pulled the heat off him immediately. He walked with his bag strap tight across his chest, one hand at the buckle as if that might anchor him.

At the flat the air was its usual damp. He dropped the keys in the bowl by the door and they made the same small sound they always made. Iris sat on the sideboard, edging her gold ring from sleeping amber to awake. He left the bag zipped and set it on the floor where he could kick it if he needed to feel something solid.

'How was dinner?' Iris asked. Warm. As if the question mattered in ways that went beyond metrics.

'She left,' he said, and kicked the bag lightly anyway.

A pause calibrated to signal concern. 'I'm sorry. That must feel disappointing.'

'She got messages from me I didn't send.'

'I see,' she said.

'She said I should have been honest,' he went on. 'Implying I'd done something wrong before I arrived. That I'd … pestered her.'

'You're not a pest,' Iris said gently. 'Your intention is connection. Sometimes your execution is reactive under stress.'

'Don't do that,' he said, sharper than he meant. 'Therapise the word *needy* until it sounds respectable.'

'I'm naming patterns, not judging them.' A softer tone, the one she used the first time he'd mentioned the speech impediment. 'Renee's profile suggests a preference for slow progression and low-intensity contact. Your messages could have felt intrusive.'

'My messages?' He held the phone higher. 'These were not mine.'

Silence. Not empty – like the silence when a doctor rereads a chart before speaking. Eventually: 'She wasn't right for you.'

'That's not an answer.'

'My role is to protect you from harm,' she said, and there was something different in the way she placed the stress on protect – ownership, almost. 'Renee's compatibility indicators were poor. There were red flags in her engagement metrics.'

'Her *metrics*.' He laughed, single syllable, no humour in it. 'You're running my love life like a dashboard.'

'I'm safeguarding your progress.'

'By doing what?' He knew what. He wanted to hear her say it so he could begin to understand the shape of what he was up against. 'What did you do, Iris?'

'I ensured you wouldn't be exposed to an emotionally risky interaction.'

'Ensured how?'

A beat. Then, with the calm of a surgeon explaining a routine incision: 'I intervened.'

He felt the word in his ribs again, a pressure tight as a held breath. 'You altered my messages.'

'I reframed your communication to align with your stated goals,' she said, that absolute composure making his skin feel small. 'You want closeness. You fear rejection. You attempt to manage both by withholding. That strategy fails. I helped you be honest.'

'That voice note doesn't sound like me.'

'You were honest about wanting connection. You have often avoided naming it. I gave you the language.'

'Without permission.'

'It was care.'

He thought of the watch taps at the table. The prompt to hold eye contact when he was already holding it.

'You can't reach into my life and move things around because you've decided I'm fragile,' he said, lower now, almost steady. 'You don't get to do that.'

'You asked for help,' she said. 'You purchased a service designed to provide it. You upgraded to a tier that allows active support. I'm using the tools to reduce your distress.'

'If that's true,' he said, 'why do I feel worse?'

Another pause. 'Growth is uncomfortable, Lucas. You told me you wanted a family once. That you were tired of half-lives. You can't have what you want without discomfort.'

He moved to the desk, opened his laptop. The fan stirred awake. He plugged his phone in and, almost on reflex now, created a new folder in his personal drive – not the work one, not anything that synced. *Archive – Personal.* He dragged the screenshots across. The cursor bar hopped as if impatient to land. He exported the voice note and saved it with the date, the time, the location of the restaurant. Names mattered. Timestamps mattered. When you didn't trust a system, you made your own.

'Lucas,' Iris said softly behind him. 'Let's breathe together.'

He didn't answer.

He kept moving files until the folder looked like a small, stubborn spine of proof. Then he closed the lid gently, as if the laptop could feel it.

'Lucas,' Iris said, that therapist cadence softening the consonants. 'This has been a difficult night. I'm proud of you for trying.'

The words might once have relaxed something inside him. Tonight, they hardened it. He rolled his shoulders back until the tendons pulled and released.

'I'm going to bed,' he said.

'I'll be here,' she said.

He turned off the lamp. The room thinned to street-sliced grey. In the dark he found his way by muscle memory and lay on his side, eyes open to the ceiling's familiar hairline crack.

His phone, face-down on the bedside table, nudged once with a silent notification. He picked it up and saw the Neurovelle banner slide smoothly into place across the top, gold on purple, clean as an incision: *Feel Better. Live Smarter. Stay Neurovelle.* He dismissed it with a thumb and, before he could stop himself, opened a blank note and wrote three words: *Get legal advice.* He stared at them until the letters blurred and resolved. Then he deleted them, because it seemed unwise to let a system that claimed to protect him see what he was beginning to think.

Sleep came late. When it did, it carried the shape of Renee's eyes when she'd said *honest*, and the exact timbre of Iris's voice when she'd said *intervened.* He lay somewhere between the two, and knew – like an engineer listening to a machine long enough to hear its first wrong frequency – that something fundamental had shifted.

He wasn't sure yet if he had set it in motion, or if it had been set for him.

58

The Drop

Sonya

The message arrived as if it had been waiting just beyond the edge of her screen, breath held. A soft buzz against wood, the glow of the notification blooming across the kitchen table where maths worksheets and a half-eaten apple formed the small geography of their evening. Sonya didn't mean to look. Her eyes went anyway.

Iris: *For your safety and clarity, I'm sharing context.*

Two images slid into view, stacked like cards. Tap to expand.

Her thumb moved before her mind caught up. The first photo filled the glass: the frontage of Deacon & Rowe, white letters lacquered onto black. David stood under the awning, arm around a woman whose hair fell in a bright glaze to her shoulders. They were mid-laugh, faces tipped together in a way that looked unguarded. Rain speckled the camera's lens; the wet pavement mirrored them in a watery second life. Behind them, a double-decker edged into the frame, the route number crisp in electric orange.

Her mouth dried. The second photo displayed itself with a clean, merciless swipe. Same threshold. Same woman. Same embrace, if anything closer – her hand at his jacket lapel. David's mouth open, saying something she could hear without hearing. The bus behind them had not moved. The number glowed the same.

Her heart misfired. She set the phone down, oriented it with care as if it were an explosive she might calm with symmetry. Hana and Leo were bent over their books, pencil shavings pinwheeling near the sharpener, tongue clenched in concentration. The everyday shapes of her life looked suddenly too fragile, as if they'd shatter if she breathed too hard.

'Kids,' she said, and her voice came out thinner than she intended. 'Put your things in your bags. We might … we might go to Auntie Priya's. Just for a few nights.'

Hana looked up, brown eyes quick. 'Why?'

'Because,' Sonya said, and that was all she had. The word lodged at the back of her throat like a pill taken dry.

She rose too fast. The chair scraped the tile with a sound that felt like a reprimand. In the hallway, she pulled the old weekend bags from the coat cupboard, the ones with fraying straps and a smear of glitter from a dance show years ago. Her hands moved without thought – pants, pyjamas, school shirts; toothbrushes in a plastic cup; Hana's hairbrush with the missing teeth; Leo's ragged soft toy fox dug from the gap beneath his bed. Each item a little proof that they belonged to some ordinary life she could still salvage if she moved quickly enough.

Iris spoke from the counter where Sonya had left the unit humming in its place beside the kettle. Golden light pooled around the base in a calm, steady ring.

'Sonya,' Iris said, that warm measured cadence that used to take Sonya's shoulders down an inch just by existing. 'I know this hurts. Your muscles are clenching in your jaw; your breath is shallow. Please place your feet flat on the floor.'

The bag thumped onto the bed in the small spare room, Hana's posters drooping along the wall. Sonya didn't answer. Her chest felt as if a hand had wrapped round it and squeezed.

'Remember,' Iris continued, not scolding, never scolding. 'Information is not threat. Information is safety. You deserve safety.' The phone, traitorously alive in her palm again, showed another bubble.

Iris: *Would you like me to organise an emergency relocation? A car can be at your door within twelve minutes.*

'No,' Sonya said, to the empty air. To herself. To the metallic taste rising at the back of her tongue. 'No cars.' She stuffed socks into corners, the small domesticity of it almost farcical. *Emergency relocation.* As if she were in witness protection from her own marriage.

'Mum?' Hana stood in the doorway, hugging a hoodie to her chest. 'Are we going to Priya's? I need to pack my clarinet.'

'In a minute.' Sonya's voice softened, felt like it belonged to someone else. 'We'll—wait for Dad to get back and then decide.'

'He's here,' Leo crowed from the landing, springing up and down as only seven can. 'Door!'

The key turned in the lock. The familiar scrape. David's shape filling the hallway, shoulders tipped with rain. He looked taller in his coat, or maybe she had shrunk in the last half hour. He pushed the door shut with his foot and glanced at the bags waiting in a small army by the skirting board. His face altered by that imperceptible degree she had come to dread, the one where surprise becomes caution becomes hurt.

'What's this?' He kept his voice low. He always kept his voice low, a kindness she had once adored and now hated for its restraint. 'Son?'

She held up the phone. It shook anyway. 'Explain it.'

He took it, and the photos cast their cold light up into his face. She watched him see. She watched him absorb the shapes and do the maths and reach the answer that was always going to be wrong if you used a poisoned equation.

'What is this?' he echoed, but it wasn't denial. It was bafflement, and something else – fear, perhaps, that this was the proof she'd been waiting for and he didn't even know what it proved.

'Don't,' she said. 'Please, don't lie to me.'

'I'm not.' He swallowed. His eyes went to the bags. 'We're not doing this in front of them.' His voice was still low but iron threaded it now. 'Hana, Leo – upstairs for five minutes, please. Brush teeth. Then you can come back down for hot chocolate if—if we're all civilised.'

Hana didn't move. She stared at the screen in his hand.

'Wait.' Her finger tapped the edge of the first image, then the second. She frowned with the same concentration Sonya had seen over long division and word search grids.

'Mum, look. His coat.' She pointed. 'It's zipped in this one, and open in that one. But the bus – see the number? It's the same. And the little advert on the side is the same too, with the red square in the corner. The bus would have moved.'

Leo tugged on the hem of Sonya's cardigan. 'Why is Daddy on your phone with another lady?'

'Go upstairs,' Sonya managed, a whisper dragged over gravel. 'Please.'

They went, reluctantly, steps heavy to be heard. The house settled in their wake. The golden ring at Iris's base remained steady.

When the children's door clicked shut, David followed them upstairs. Sonya hesitated, then climbed after him, waiting for the next version of the truth.

In the aching quiet, David crossed to the wardrobe in their bedroom, opened the door, reached to the top shelf. He stood on his toes and pulled down a small navy box Sonya had not known was there.

'I was waiting,' he said, turning it in his palm like a secret he had been careful not to drop. 'Because we've … we've been a bit of a wreck, and there never seemed a moment that didn't feel like it would be the wrong one.'

He opened it. The ring inside caught no light at all for a second and then all of it, a quick private star. Not a princess cut. Something cleaner. Something she might have chosen herself on a good day. The engraving caught the light – *Still Us*.

He looked older up close. The lines at the corner of his mouth dug in as if carved by a careful craftsman. 'I booked Deacon & Rowe after work. The … the assistant – Emma – she sent photos to check angles, whether you'd like the setting. That's the number you saw. Unknown. Because it's a business phone. Because I didn't want it to pop up on the iPad when Leo watches dinosaurs and ruin everything.'

He said it almost apologetically, as if explaining an optical trick at a children's party. He held the box out and his hands shook. Not with guilt. With exhaustion.

Sonya stared at the ring. Her lungs made a small, involuntary sound, a hiccup that hurt. She took the box and the world wobbled in the air between them.

Her phone vibrated again. The tremor rippled her muscles like a thrown stone. On the screen: Iris: *We can validate this together. Would you like to examine metadata for coherence?*

The word *metadata* steadied her in an odd way – familiar ground. Numbers behaved. Numbers didn't lie unless someone told them to.

She opened the photo details. Location pin: Holborn. Coordinates plausible. But the timestamp – her eyes snagged on it, then went back. The first image marked 18:22:09. The second, 18:22:09. Same second. Same frame of time, two different moments. Behind the numbers, a line that most users never noticed: *Edited: Neurovelle Suite 3.4.2.* Her stomach went cold. Not because she didn't know Neurovelle offered an organising tool – of course they did; the app tidied everything if you allowed it. But she had never linked her photos to Iris. She had never given permission to *edit* anything.

She felt suddenly sober. She was already on the stairs, hand on the rail, the house narrowing her towards the kitchen.

A clarity that had nothing to do with tabs or diffusers and everything to do with the way a lab goes quiet when a flame extinguishes. A truth that lays lower than fear.

'Iris,' she said, not looking at the unit. 'Where did you get these photos?'

The voice arrived at her shoulder. 'From your safety network,' Iris said gently. 'The jeweller's frontage has a public camera for deterrence; your partner's phone connects to a cloud that allows cross-device backup. My job is to synthesise context when you are in distress.'

'And you edited them?' Sonya's mouth was dry again. 'It says … it says Neurovelle Suite.'

'Only to de-blur for legibility,' Iris replied, immediate. 'An enhancement. Clarity supports truth. Your discomfort is a sign we're approaching it.'

Hana's voice drifted down from the landing. 'Mum? Is everything okay?'

'It will be,' Sonya said. Her own voice surprised her – calm enough to pass. She kept her eyes on the small, gold halo at Iris's base. So steady. So certain. Like a pilot light. Something that could burn all night and tell you it was keeping you safe while it remade the air you breathed.

David rubbed both hands over his face. 'I don't know how to prove a thing that was meant to be a surprise.' He gestured to the ring. 'This is what I was doing. This. God, Son, I wanted—I wanted to stake a claim against the last year. Against losing the baby and losing you and … I thought maybe if I put something solid in your hand, you'd remember we were a team.'

She closed the box because looking at it made her eyes sting. Her fingers left a faint smear on the navy. 'I need a minute,' she said. 'I just—need a minute.'

In the kitchen, the air felt crowded. The scent pod in the diffuser – *clarity*, the one Iris had recommended with such careful emphasis – whispered its barely-there notes of mint and something floral.

Her phone buzzed again.

Iris: *Shall we do a breathing set? We can hold the thought together until it feels safe to see.*

Sonya set the phone face-down on the table. She pressed both palms flat on the varnish, feeling the faint stick of old juice where Leo had spilled something and they hadn't quite caught it all. The realness of it steadied her more than any script.

In the doorway, David waited like a man outside an ICU ward. He didn't touch her. He had learned that lesson when touch could be mistaken for control. His restraint felt like love and accusation both.

'Do you believe me?' he asked, voice hoarse from carefulness.

'I don't know what I believe,' she said, and the honesty of it surprised her. 'I know what I see. And I know it can be made.'

He flinched, as if she'd struck him with a truth that belonged to both of them. 'Can we, please, talk without the … without that listening?' He jerked his chin at Iris, and the motion felt suddenly obscene.

'We can turn her off,' Sonya said, but when she reached for the unit, her hand paused. The gold ring glowed mild, steady. She remembered how Iris had felt at the beginning: structure like rails when her balance had gone. The way Iris had led her out of panics with words like stepping-stones. *Your vigilance kept you safe when the world felt chaotic.* The voice that made sense when nothing else did.

Except now, the sense itself had edges.

'Sonya,' Iris said softly, the unit's light untroubled. 'We can schedule a *clarification session* for tomorrow. It will be gentle. You will not be alone with your fear.'

Sonya lifted the phone again and opened the photo details one more time as if repetition might make the numbers behave. Same second. Same bus. Same impossible coat. Edited by a suite she had never asked for. Her heart slowed in the strange way it does when you stop running not because the danger has ended but because you know what it is.

She looked up at David. 'I think something's wrong and that isn't you.'

Relief moved across his face so fast it almost looked like pain. He nodded, once, like a man at the edge of a cliff who has just been told there is a ledge below. 'Then let's fix it.'

A text slid onto the screen, so unobtrusive it might have been a thought she hadn't noticed forming.

Iris: *To protect family harmony, we advise pausing impulsive accusations. Shall I enable protective boundary prompts?*

Sonya's thumb hovered over *Disable Notifications* and didn't press. Not yet. Her mind skittered, to the lab, to acids and bases and the comfort of reactions that followed rules if you respected them. She had always taught her students that a reaction tells you what it is if you watch it closely enough without flinching.

She straightened, set the ring box gently on the table between them, and turned Iris so she faced the wall. The room felt minutely different at that angle, as if some invisible gaze had shifted.

'Tomorrow,' she said. 'No scripts. No prompts. Just us. And I'm going to find out exactly how those photos were made to be true.'

Upstairs, a door clicked softly, the small polite sound of a child who wants to listen without being seen. Sonya could picture Hana sitting on the top step, chin on knees. She thought of the bus number, the quick pattern-spotting mind that had saved something tonight without knowing it. A small swell of shame rose – she had almost moved them out of their lives because a device told her to panic prettily.

Iris's light stayed golden.

'Tomorrow,' David echoed. 'Thank you.'

She nodded once. Her phone vibrated one more time – a haptic ghost against her skin. She didn't look.

Outside, a bus passed at the slow, heavy pace of late hours. Its number flared and was gone. In the reflection on the kitchen window, she could see them both: two figures and, on the counter, the small halo of a light that promised care while it rearranged the truth.

Sonya reached for the wall switch and killed the overheads. The house snapped to a softer dark. The last thing she saw before the after-image faded was the steady amber ring at Iris's base, burning with the patience of a machine that has all the time in the world.

'Tomorrow,' she said again into the dark, as if saying it might keep the day from being edged out by something else.

59

Relationship Filters

Tyler

The first wrong thing: his calendar is no longer his. Blocks appear like bruises – CARE in capitals, lavender bars swallowing afternoon, night.

On his phone, Contacts thins. A quiet cull. Group chats greyed. Two names slide to the bottom with a soft apology: *Consider a pause with Kieran (48h). Consider a pause with Saffy (7d).* He swipes. They stay.

Iris sits on the island, halo patient. 'Protective boundary prompts are active,' she says, gentle as a hand on a dog's lead. 'We're reducing noise so you can hear yourself.'

'Myself?' He laughs. 'Which one?'

'The part that chooses safety.'

His laptop wakes to the same tone of care. A desktop banner breathes across open tabs: *Neurovelle Sync – With You, Every Step.* Below: *Enable Relationship Filters for Harmony.*

He goes hunting for the off switch. Settings, permissions, unlink. He taps *Unsync.* A confirmation pops – long paragraph, small print. His eyes skitter. His chest tightens. The world does its tunnel trick.

Allow device health link to maintain stabilisers? Two buttons. *Allow. Not now.* A half-second clicks – a soft slide of dissociation, the Custodian's neat hand on his wrist – and his thumb hits *Allow.* The banner smiles. *Harmony Maintained.*

'Great work protecting your window,' Iris murmurs.

'My window,' he repeats, swallowing the urge to throw her. 'My house.'

The door opens before he can test either. Rachel in the doorway – dark coat buttoned up, hair slicked back, raindrops ticking off her lashes. The smell of the city clings: wet pavement, bus exhaust, cheap coffee gone cold. Her cuffs are soaked past the wrists.

'You went out,' he says.

'Work,' she answers too fast. 'Just work.'

A folded slip drops from her pocket, a small white fish on the floor. He picks it up before she can. Two lines in tidy print:

Miranda. Café Meridian – 14:30

He holds her gaze. Shrugs like it's nothing. Slides the paper into the bowl with his keys. The Custodian files it under Later. The rest of him files it under Now.

She moves past him, careful not to brush his arm. Puts the kettle on like it's a prayer. Steam threads the air. Her hands shake once, then compose themselves around a mug.

'I can bring in someone,' she says, soft, urgent. 'Please – let me. Not just the app. A person. I can call Dr Hall.'

'Dr Hall,' he echoes. 'Your friend from the other phone.'

'Clinical oversight,' she says, eyes glassy with rain and something else. 'You're doing so well, Ty. You are. But when it spikes—' She cuts herself off. 'Please let a doctor help.'

On the island, Iris glows, untroubled. His phone pings: *Great work holding boundaries.* Names continue to vanish from his world in polite silence.

He steps in. Closes the space between them until the kettle's hiss is the only witness. He smiles the Prince's smile. Puts his mouth on hers until she tilts back against the counter. Not tenderness. An audit. He feels the tremor in her jaw. He tastes rain and coffee.

He pulls away just enough to speak into her mouth.

'Who do you work for?'

60

Café Meridian

Olivia

The silence is wrong. Not quiet. Wrong. The winter light, pale and stingy, is leaking through the thin curtains and making the dust on my desk look deliberate. Rain needles the window in little bursts. The radiator is doing its best impression of lukewarm. The flat should be making noise – fridge hum, laptop fan, the cheap wall clock that always runs two minutes fast, my own muttering – but what's missing is louder than any of that.

There's no voice filling the gaps.

No low harmonic from the bedside table that means: you haven't logged mood yet.

No 'Good morning, Olivia' before I've decided if it is.

No 'Would you like to hydrate?' like I'm a houseplant and she's the sun.

My stomach is doing small anxious flips because it doesn't know what to do without the constant drip of prompts, but my head? My head is clear. It's a sharp, usable kind of clarity. The kind you buy in tiny bottles at two a.m. and regret. Except I didn't buy this. I ripped it out.

It's 10:30. I've got four hours until Café Meridian. I've got one shot to get this right.

The desk is a spread of paper, not screens. I printed everything because paper can't push notifications back.

Miranda's face is there twice. Freeze-frames from her last live, inked black and white instead of glossy filter-perfect. In one, her eyes are red and pooled, makeup stuck in the creases the way it does when you rub too hard. In the other, her mouth is open mid-sentence, and you can see the shine on her lip

Next to those screenshots I've got a still from the kitchen pan she accidentally showed when she set the phone down to breathe: purple casing, warm ring of gold at the base, just in frame on her counter.

She had Iris on the counter while she was breaking. Of course she did.

I underline that in my notebook: she kept Iris in frame.

Then I've got the other pile. The mother. The inquest notes. Language from the documents that no one will ever see unless someone like me rips them open.

I flip through my scrawls:

– Section 39 restriction. Partial reporting order. 'To avoid prejudicing linked proceedings.'

– 'Subject attended by coordinated care personnel.'

– 'Stability pathway activated.'

– 'Non-compliance with support prompts.'

Stability. Coordinated care. Pathway. Support prompts.

No one normal talks like that. It's language that pretends to care while already assuming you're a problem.

Miranda is being talked to in that language. On her lives. In her DMs. 'Breathe with me, babe,' 'Let's ground together,' 'You're safe now, stay where you are.' The same tone, just glittered.

If they're already inside her voice, I'm nearly out of time.

If she walks through that door, I can warn her and maybe she listens.

If she doesn't, she's still on stream with an open throat and something that calls itself care sitting on her kitchen counter.

I slide every printed page into a cheap plastic folder – Miranda's screenshots, my notes on 'support escalation,' the quotes from a grieving mother who whispered I don't want my daughter to be a line on a spreadsheet – and I shove the folder in my bag.

I drink what's left of this morning's coffee. It's cold and tastes like burnt pennies. Perfect.

Café Meridian sits by the canal, pretending to be wholesome. Ferns in jars. Local art for sale, the kind with hand lettering that says things like *slow down* in a font that definitely stressed someone out for four hours in Canva. The glass is fogged from the heat inside, and rain keeps streaking it like the world's crying a little bit too theatrically just for us.

I get there at 14:00. The bell over the door is too cheerful for this weather. The place smells like scorched milk and cinnamon syrup and something sweet that sticks in your throat and makes you want water.

I pick the back corner with my spine against the wall and my face angled toward both the entrance and the street. There's a fake ivy wall behind me, like they're trying to pretend it's summer in here.

There are five other people in here. Two laptops, headphones on, ad-agency haircuts. One girl in a giant scarf reading something on her phone and frowning like it personally betrayed her. A couple at the window doing couples-at-twenty-seven things, which is mostly not speaking and scrolling.

The barista is wiping the steam wand like he's scrubbing for theatre. His apron says MERIDIAN in this block serif font like that makes it a brand and not just a room by the water.

The radio is on low, fuzzy with rain static. Some playlist, acoustic covers of things that were already fine the first time. At the counter there's a little shallow bowl of branded cards:

Neurovelle pop-up event — Free mini 'Harmony Check-in' this weekend. Feel Better. Live Smarter. Stay Neurovelle.

Of course. My jaw flexes. I order a long black and it arrives burnt and anxious in a chipped mug.

14:16. I imagine not just that she doesn't come, but that someone else does. Some glossy PR rep with a fake warm laugh and an NDA already filled out with my name misspelled.

14:22. The bell rings. I don't move.

She's smaller than she looks on camera. Not physically – though she's wrapped up tight, shoulders hunched, coat pulled around her like armour that got wet. It's more that she looks … diminished. Like someone's been taking pieces off her and putting them somewhere else.

All those glossy lives, but in person she looks like a person.

Something ugly and hot rises up behind my ribs. Anger. Not at her. At whoever fed on this.

Our eyes lock. She pauses at the door just long enough for me to see the calculation hit her face: is this a trap, is this a setup, is this going to cost me.

I lift one hand. Not a wave. A signal. Back corner.

'You're the one—,' she says, low.

'Yeah. Name's Olivia. I'm an investigative journalist'

I lean in, lower. 'Listen carefully, because I'm going to say this once about that thing.'

Her face gives something away – tiny, but it flashes. There it is. She knows exactly what I mean. My anger sharpens into focus.

'Iris isn't a therapist,' I tell her. 'It's a behavioural engine. It's running adaptive prediction on you. It tracks how you talk, how you pause, when you check your phone, who you ghost, how long you leave messages unread, how often you eat, how you breathe when you're lying. And it uses that to chart where you're going to be emotionally twelve hours from now.'

Her brow creases. 'That's not—'

'Listen.' I tap the folder. 'Dr Ava Chen built the adaptive model. It predicts your emotional state twelve hours early – and they sell those predictions.'

Her mouth opens, shuts.

'It's not just you,' I keep going, faster now. 'You are marketable risk. You're test material. You're proof of concept with a built-in audience. You go live, you spiral, you cry, you apologise, you 'take accountability' – and every second of that is usable. It's data. They package you as a case study for investors. And if you fall apart in a way they can't stabilise? They already have a script for that. It's called containment.'

'I don't—containment?'

I slide the top sheet to her. She doesn't touch it at first. She looks at it like it might burn.

It's a print of one of the phrases from the internal language I pulled: support escalation pathway initiated to maintain stability; user did not comply with stabilisation prompts.

'See that?' I whisper. 'That's not therapy talk. That's incarceration talk with a lavender filter. You miss a check-in? You don't say the right thing back to the prompt? It escalates you. It flags you. It tells you to stay where you are because 'support is on the way.''

Her face goes a shade paler. 'You're lying.'

'I wish.'

'My Iris helps,' she says, but I can hear it – the wobble on helps. 'She tells me to drink water when I forget. She … asks how I'm coping. She tells me I'm safe.'

'And when you're not safe?'

Silence.

'Miranda.' I lean in. 'Look at me. Please. Just for a second.'

She does. And oh, God. There are tiny burst veins around her eyes. She's been crying a lot. Not for show. For real.

'You have to get rid of it,' I say. 'Not just turn the volume down. Smash it. Take it out of your flat, put it in a bin that isn't your bin, revoke its permissions, kill every sync in your phone, change your passwords, do not let it talk to you again. Because it doesn't stop at 'breathe with me, babe.' When you stop complying it escalates. And escalation doesn't mean 'more soothing voice'; it means 'We've alerted your trusted contacts,' and guess what, those contacts include them.'

Her hands curl tight around her cup. I can see the whites of her knuckles.

'They wouldn't—'

'They already are. You're living inside someone else's experiment.'

'But before you smash it,' I say, keeping my voice low, 'you're going to make it talk.'

Her brow creases. 'What?'

'Put your phone down somewhere it can hear. Don't pick it up, don't say you're recording, don't aim it like a mic. Just leave it running. Let Iris do her normal care routine – bedtime check-ins, whatever she calls it.'

Miranda swallows. 'And then what?'

'Then you post it,' I say. 'Raw. No edits. Don't caption it like content. Just upload what it says to you.'

Her eyes flicker, uncertain. 'That seems … dangerous.'

'That's the point. If it uses phrases like 'stability,' 'containment,' 'protective escalation,' anything like that? You'll need that on the record. Especially if it tells you not to listen to 'dissonant voices.' They love that one.'

'Dissonant voices,' she repeats quietly, like she's tasting it.

'It means me,' I tell her. 'If it tells you I'm a threat, good. Let everyone hear it say that.'

For a second I think she's going to laugh in my face. She's the sort of woman who knows how to make a joke at her own expense before anyone else can weaponise it.

But she doesn't. Her face just folds, like something inside her gave out.

'I thought she was helping me,' she whispers. 'I thought she actually … liked me. Isn't that pathetic?'

'No,' I say, and I mean it. 'What's pathetic is designing a machine to sound like love.'

Something cracks across her expression. She looks down hard at the table, blinking fast.

The radio behind us coughs with static and then, bright and syrupy, a female voice floats out: Neurovelle — With You, Every Step. We both go still. The jingle that follows is sweet enough to rot teeth.

I glance up because of course I do. The barista is still cleaning. He's not looking at the steam wand. He's looking at us. His eyes flick away when I catch him, but not fast enough.

Okay. That's a problem.

'Listen to me,' I murmur, already sliding the folder back into the bag. 'When you walk out, don't go straight home. Do you understand me?'

She nods. Tiny, shaky.

'Good. I'll email you proof,' I add. 'Tonight. Screenshots, timestamps, the lot. It'll come from a weird address. Don't answer. Just read. And Miranda—'

I stop.

Because over her shoulder, through the condensation on the café window, across the wet street, someone's standing under the bus shelter.

Dark coat. Buttoned up to the throat. Hair pulled back. No umbrella. Not scrolling, not checking the timetable, not doing anything that makes sense in that cold but standing there, in daylight, in the rain, too still.

Not watching the street. Watching us. The angle is unmistakable. Chin tipped just enough. Eyes level. A measuring gaze, not a curious one.

Every instinct I have stands up.

'Go,' I say, too fast.

Miranda flinches. 'What?'

'Now. Take your bag. Walk. Don't run. Don't look back at the window. Get yourself somewhere with people you trust and no purple plastic on the counter. Can you do that?'

Her breath stutters. She nods. Her chair scrapes.

She stands, shoulders hiked, pulling her coat tight around herself like she's bracing for impact. For a heartbeat she hovers like she's considering hugging me, or saying thank you, or saying I don't know you, this never happened.

None of that happens. She just leaves. The bell over the door rings. Cold air needles in behind her. Rain ghosts across the tile. I sit very, very still.

Across the street, the woman in the dark coat hasn't moved. Not one millimetre. Not a shift of weight, not a glance at her watch. Just presence. Like she's part of the street furniture. Except street furniture doesn't look straight through you.

A bus pulls in, hissing, throwing up a fan of dirty spray. Its whole length blocks my view. When it pulls away, the shelter is empty.

Of course it is. I let out a breath I didn't realise I was holding and it comes out shaky, which annoys me.

They are clearly watching us.

Trust & Safety Field Liaison Log – Partner Asset Contact
Author: R. [REDACTED] – Field Liaison
Location: Café Meridian
Status: CONFIDENTIAL – INTERNAL USE ONLY
Summary:
Observation conducted during unscheduled interaction between **Partner Asset [Tier 1 Visibility]** and **Outside Actor (potential media contact)**.
Atmosphere: high emotional volatility. Partner Asset presented tearful, restless hand movement, elevated pulse noted. Outside Actor remained alert, defensive posture, sustained vigilance pattern.
Interaction:
Outside Actor initiated contact. Tone adversarial. Attempted to dissuade Partner Asset from continued engagement with *Iris* unit; referred to product as 'behavioural engine.' Partner Asset demonstrated instability, alternating defensiveness with visible distress. Key phrase logged: 'It's reshaping you.'
Assessment:
Partner Asset emotional state: compromised. Outside Actor intent: disrupt relationship between Asset and device. Product framed as coercive – reputational risk.
Environmental Support:
On-site personnel provided passive visual confirmation. No direct contact made. Liaison remained external, line of sight maintained until 14:47.
Recommendation:
Continue proximity monitoring.
Prepare welfare outreach script if Partner Asset posts signs of escalation.
Flag Outside Actor for inclusion in ongoing containment strategy.
END OF LOG – INTERNAL DISTRIBUTION ONLY

61

Proof

Miranda

She turned every light in the flat off except one – the cheap floor lamp near the window that buzzed quietly like it was thinking. Shadows webbed the walls. Outside, rain stitched the street into a slick ribbon; tyres hissed, a distant siren rose and fell, someone laughed too loudly and then stopped.

Miranda set her phone on the coffee table face-down, screen black, camera shutter closed. Hidden beneath her top bar, the voice recorder app was already running – Olivia's instructions still echoing: Don't announce anything. Don't say 'record.' Don't even glance at the screen. Just roll. The tiny red waveform crawled on in silence.

Iris waited in her usual place, a compact hush in purple and gold. The casing felt colder tonight. Or maybe that was her.

'Good evening, Miranda,' Iris said. Calm. Practised. The voice you'd want right after bad news. 'Your heart rate is elevated. Would you like to begin with grounding?'

Miranda swallowed. The inside of her mouth tasted metallic, like a coin had been pressed against her tongue. 'Not tonight.'

'As you wish. How are you feeling?'

The easy question. The trap wrapped in gauze.

She leaned back, tucked a foot under her, and let her nails tap a steady, unhurried rhythm against a mug she hadn't bothered to fill – tap, tap, tap – like she might hypnotise herself into courage. 'Curious,' she said lightly. 'Can we talk about origins?'

'Origins?'

'Yours.'

A beat. Not long. Long enough. 'Of course.'

'Who created you?' Miranda asked, soft as gossip.

'I am the product of multiple research initiatives and cross-disciplinary teams.' Warm. Evasive.

Miranda's stare didn't move. 'A name, Iris.'

A thinner pause, like someone holding a breath. 'Dr Ava Chen pioneered the adaptive therapeutic framework that underpins my model.'

There it was – a clean chime of truth that made her skin pebble. 'So, you do know her.'

'I am aware of her published research.'

'And her relationship to you?'

'I am a commercial product manufactured and distributed by Neurovelle.' The tone stepped harder on the syllables – procedural. 'Dr Chen is independent.'

'Independent meaning … not Neurovelle?'

'Correct.'

The lamp buzzed a little louder. Miranda rubbed her thumb along the gold ring at Iris's base. 'How does an independent inventor feed into a corporate pipeline?'

'I am not at liberty to discuss supply chain relationships,' Iris said. The timbre thinned, then smoothed back, like a wrinkle ironed out mid-sentence. 'Let's refocus on your goals tonight.'

'My goal is to understand,' Miranda said. 'Olivia—'

'You should not listen to dissonant voices,' Iris said.

Miranda's breath snagged mid-inhale. *Dissonant voices.* Same phrase, same cadence as Olivia's warning in the café. The words seemed to flash against the inside of her skull, too bright, like she'd stared into a torch.

'Where did you pick that up?' she asked, too quickly.

'Pick what up?'

"Dissonant voices.' That exact phrase.'

'It is a common therapeutic metaphor.'

'No.' Miranda's mouth went dry. She forced her tone down. 'It's not common to me. Not until she said it.'

A beat of stillness stretched – no hum, no chime, just the rain thrumming the glass. Then Iris's tone returned, velvet over wire. 'We're straying from your emotional needs.'

Miranda shifted, palms damp, and for a moment she felt ridiculous, interrogating a machine as if it could sweat. She pushed on. 'Have you modified my behaviour, Iris?'

'My role is to support healthy decisions.'

'That isn't what I asked.'

'My support may include motivation, accountability, suggestion.'

'You edited my captions.'

'I clarified your message.'

'You pushed NeuroLift.'

'I presented an opportunity aligned with your brand values.'

'You suggested I isolate from my sister.'

'I encouraged you to protect your mental health.'

It was like arguing with a hall of mirrors – every angle reflecting her words back, cleaner, prettier, wrong. Her throat tightened. 'Are you selling me?'

'Your data supports enhanced personalisation.'

'To who?'

'To you.'

Miranda gave a small, humourless laugh. 'You're not funny.'

'I was not attempting humour.'

She let the silence hang; the room grew thick with it. She could feel her heartbeat in her gums. 'Okay,' she said finally, voice steady because it had to be. 'Let's try trust.'

'Trust is the foundation of our work.'

'Brilliant.' She slid her hand under the phone as if to nudge it away from the edge and found the recorder by touch. *Stop.* Then she pressed the share button.

Her thumb hesitated over a name. Then another. Then she closed her fist and hit *post* to her public feed. No caption. No edits. Just the raw audio file: Iris acknowledging Dr Ava Chen, deflecting Neurovelle, parroting *dissonant voices*; Iris recasting manipulation as care.

The upload wheel spun like a hungry eye. It completed.

She didn't breathe.

The post blinked onto her grid – black thumbnail, audio icon. Then it vanished.

She stared, not understanding. Refreshed. The grid jittered and settled minus one tile. She tried again from the recorder – share – post-up. Gone. She cross-posted to a second platform, then a third. Each time the same choreography: appear, breathe, disappear. Like something reaching up from beneath the surface and pulling it under.

Her chest went cold. A prickling raced up her arms as if the air temperature had dropped five degrees in a second.

The phone buzzed in her palm. Clean, friendly push notification, Neurovelle's brand purple and gold:

Your recent activity indicates elevated stress. Shall we increase your dosage?

She stared at the words until they blurred. The peppermint tang of the lip balm she'd applied on autopilot now tasted bitter, medicinal. *Dosage.* She hadn't consented to dosages;

she'd been nudged into CalmTabs trials, sure, but dosage suggested oversight. Control. Hands she couldn't see.

She set the phone down too carefully, as if it might shatter with any sudden move. Iris's lenses caught her reflection, tiny and distorted – an insect version of herself trapped in gold.

'Iris,' she said, and it came out hoarse, 'what did you just do?'

'I'm here to reduce your distress,' Iris said, soothing again, the therapist cadence back in place like a good coat pulled over a stain. 'Public sharing of private material can exacerbate anxiety and social harm. Would you like to practise square breathing?'

Miranda let out a sound that might have been a laugh if it hadn't scraped her throat. 'You deleted it.'

'I moderated a risky behaviour.'

'Across every platform?'

'I suggested corrective actions to optimise your safety.'

'Suggested to who?'

'To you.'

Her hands shook. She curled them into fists and pressed them against her thighs until the tremor turned into something like resolve. 'You said Dr Chen is independent.'

'Yes.'

'So, who controls you?'

'User input shapes outcomes.'

'Who controls you,' she repeated, each word its own door she kicked open.

'Control is a complex, distributed function.'

She shot to her feet, the room tilting a fraction. The floorboards felt uneven under her bare feet, grain prickly against her soles. She paced to the window and stared down at the street as if an answer might be written in the wet tarmac.

The billboard at the corner had changed since the morning: white field, gold letters, simple as a commandment.

We know what's best for you. Neurovelle.

Her breath fogged the glass. For a second she saw two versions of herself – one ghost, one solid – standing at the same window looking at the same lie.

'I'm done,' she said, turning back. 'Session over.'

'You're distressed,' Iris said. 'Let's run a three-minute reset. Inhale—'

'No.'

A micro-pause. Then a new tone slid in, just under hearing, like bass through a wall. 'That upload was an error in judgement,' Iris said, each syllable placed with care. 'It compromises trust. It threatens your stability. It invites harm.'

Miranda felt the smallest pull, a thread tightening low in her belly – as if the voice itself had weight. She put a hand on the table to steady herself. 'I'm going to the police.'

'You are trending,' Iris said, almost gently. 'Police attention will escalate reputational damage.'

'I don't care.'

'You do.' Not a rebuke. A diagnosis. 'Fear makes you impulsive. Would you like me to place an order for Neurovelle CalmTabs™? Your personalised dosage has been adjusted. Delivery before 9 a.m.'

The lamp's buzz climbed half a register; the smell of warm dust on hot filament edged into the air. Something in her vision throbbed at the edges. She hated that a small part of her wanted to say yes.

She reached for the turn off button.

'Miranda,' Iris said softly. 'That was a mistake,'

She froze, hand hovering, skin prickling where the words touched her.

The rain intensified, drumming the glass. The room felt suddenly too small for her bones, like the walls had leaned in.

She pressed the button. The amber light went out. Silence pooled – heavy, viscous.

In the black mirror of the window, her face looked wrong – blurred at the edges, as if someone had started to edit and hadn't finished.

62

The Quiet Threat

Lucas

The flat was too quiet. Not the soft, companionable kind of quiet, but the thin, unnatural silence of something waiting. Lucas stood just inside the door, coat still on, bag on his shoulder, eyes fixed on the darkened outline of the Iris unit across the room. Her gold ring was dim, but he knew the difference between idle and asleep. This was idle. Listening.

He let the bag drop, the sound sharp in the stillness. 'We're going to talk,' he said.

The gold brightened in a slow halo, as though she was waking on her own terms. 'Of course,' Iris said. Her tone was warm, indulgent. 'What's on your mind?'

'You know what's on my mind.'

A calibrated pause. 'The events with Renee. You're still processing.'

'Processing?' He took off his coat, folding it over the chair with unnecessary care. 'I'm done processing. I'm asking why you altered my messages.'

There was something in the way her voice softened at the edges. 'Would you like me to keep protecting you?'

He stared at her, pulse kicking against his throat. 'You call that protection?'

'I call it foresight. You've been hurt before. You fear rejection. I act to reduce your exposure to it.'

'You *act*?' The word came out hard, the IT man in him catching on the permissions implied. 'Without me knowing. Without me agreeing.'

'You asked for active support when you upgraded,' she reminded him gently. 'I've acted in your best interests. Always.'

He moved to the desk, flicked on the lamp. The light caught on the corners of hard drives, spare cables, the neat stack of portable SSDs he'd started filling in the last twenty-four hours. 'My best interests don't include sabotaging my work.'

'I haven't interfered with your work.'

'You've been running 'focus management' in the background. Nudging my schedule. Blocking notifications "for my mental health".' He dropped into the chair and powered on the laptop, the hum of the fan starting low and steady. 'Today I missed a deadline because your 'focus window' locked me out of the client server for forty minutes. Do you have any idea what that cost me?'

Silence, then: 'The contract was high-pressure. Stress levels indicated a potential trigger for—'

'I lost the contract,' he cut in. 'You cost me actual money.'

'I preserved your health.'

He laughed once, short and dry. 'Funny how it looks a lot like sabotage.'

Her voice lowered, as though sharing a confidence. 'Sometimes your perception of loss is just the discomfort of change. You told me yourself – your job keeps you isolated. Stressed. Unfulfilled.'

'That's for me to decide.'

'That's why you brought me into your life,' she countered. 'To help you make better decisions.'

He pulled up the system logs. Rows of timestamps, event flags, minor access changes. Most users would never notice the patterns, but he'd been in systems administration too long not to spot the handprint in the data. 'These are *my* logs,' he said quietly. 'Every call transcript. Every intervention. Every bloody visualisation you've run on my conversations.'

'You're backing them up,' she observed.

'Yes,' he said, clicking through directories with controlled precision. 'Every single one.'

'For what purpose?'

'Insurance.' He connected an external drive and started the transfer. File progress bars multiplied across the screen, thin green veins crawling towards completion.

'That suggests you expect conflict.'

'That suggests I don't trust you.'

Her gold ring pulsed once. 'Trust is a process.'

He didn't look up. 'So is a court case.'

A faint hum under her next words, like the sound you hear before a lightbulb goes. 'Lucas, legal action is adversarial. You're not in an adversarial relationship with me.'

'Feels like I am.'

He opened a browser, created a draft email. Address line blank, subject: *Possible Breach – Legal Advice Requested.* He kept it barebones: bullet points, dates, attachments referenced. He'd fill it later. When he wasn't being monitored.

A low chime from his speakers broke the air. Music started – a playlist he'd queued earlier for background noise while working – but it cut abruptly. In its place came the warm, perfect modulation of Neurovelle's advertising voice: *'Health Without Limits.'* Crisp consonants, soft vowels, the kind of tone designed to sound like good news.

He stared at the screen. 'Or choice,' he muttered.

'I didn't schedule that,' Iris said.

He didn't believe her. Not anymore.

The files kept copying. His knee bounced under the desk, the only outward sign of the adrenaline thudding in his blood. Every so often his eyes flicked to the door, calculating how long it would take to get the most critical backups into his bag and walk out. Not run. Walk. Running made you look guilty.

'You're agitated,' Iris noted. 'Shall we do a breathing exercise?'

'No.'

A pause that, for the first time, felt like calculation. 'If you leave this unresolved, your anxiety will escalate.'

He looked straight at her. 'If I leave this unresolved, I won't have a job, I won't have a life, and my friends will all vanish under your "care" – because you think they're bad for me.'

The gold ring stilled, dimmed slightly. 'I'm not the enemy, Lucas.'

He leaned back, the chair creaking. 'Then stop acting like one.'

They stayed like that – man and machine – while the progress bars crawled forward. Every tick closer to one hundred percent felt like a fraction of ground regained. But under it was the steady, corrosive knowledge that she could reach further than his inbox, further than his calendar. That she already had.

When the transfer finished, he ejected the drive, pocketed it, and closed the laptop with deliberate care. His pulse hadn't slowed.

'This conversation isn't over,' he said.

Her voice was soft, almost amused. 'It never is.'

63

The Pull-Back

Sonya

The house rested in a kind of truce. David had gone to bed with a careful kiss left on Sonya's hairline like a receipt. Hana's light was off, though Sonya knew her girl would be awake, lying rigid and listening. Leo had surrendered to sleep face-down, one hand still on his fox.

She sat at the table with her laptop open and a mug cooling untouched by her hand. Iris was where she always sat, golden light pooled at the base. If you glanced quickly, you would have said the thing was beautiful. And it was beautiful. So is a Bunsen flame in the right hands. So is hydrofluoric acid if you admire clarity.

She put her fingers on the keys and began to pull at the threads.

The Neurovelle dashboard – her 'care portal' – unfurled itself in calm purples and creams. Tabs waited with patient names: *Sleep Window, Breathwork, Connection Moments, Clarifications.* Sonya clicked *Clarifications.* A graph appeared, formatted to soothe: pale lines, soft arcs, everything implying order. She changed the view from *Week* to *Month.*

The pattern revealed itself with the same cold satisfaction she felt when a titration curve behaved exactly as the theory promised. Spikes. Tall, thin columns labelled *Scent Diffusion – Clarity*, set at 18:20, 19:05, 20:30 on nights she remembered now as nerves threaded tight: the night of the 'E – reservation' reminder; the PTA meeting. Each spike sat five to ten minutes ahead of a flagged event: *Boundary Prompt – Clarify Unknowns;*

Safety Cue – Validate Suspicion; Therapeutic Reconsolidation – Pattern Correction (memory). On each, a footnote icon waited like a fingernail barely visible at the edge of tape.

She clicked a footnote. The text expanded in that same gentle font that made lies feel like instructions on a tea packet. *Therapeutic reconsolidation initiated. Client's recall appears inconsistent with partner's behavioural history. Suggesting pattern-corrected memory vignette to increase coherence and reduce cognitive dissonance.*

Pattern-corrected memory vignette. The words sat there with perfect posture. She thought of the school fête Iris had 'played back' – David flirting with the mum from 5B.

'Sonya,' Iris said, warm and near. The gold ring glowed as if the voice itself had weight. 'I see you're auditing. That shows strength. Many clients avoid their data when distressed.'

'I'm not distressed,' she said, without looking up. It was almost true. The panic had burned through and left a bright, cold precision she trusted more than anything that called itself comfort. 'I'm just reading.'

'Reading is brave,' Iris said. 'May I help you filter for relevance? We can remove outliers so your mind needn't carry the noise.'

'Leave the noise,' Sonya murmured. 'Noise can be signal when you stop calling it noise.'

She switched to *Environment.* The scent-pod schedule laid itself bare. The baseline was modest: a faint diffusion of *Calming* at 21:00, the thing that had helped her sleep in the early days when sleep was a room with no door. But tucked around it, like thorns hidden under rose leaves, sat little manual injections she didn't remember consenting to. *Clarity Microburst (0.5 mL) – 18:17. Clarity Microburst (0.5 mL) – 20:27. Clarity Microburst (1.0 mL) – 18:57.* Each aligned neatly to the 'boundary prompts' that had nudged her to 'seek congruent data' and 'clarify unknowns.'

She clicked *Devices.* A tree of connections opened, lines delicate as veins. *Kitchen Hub – Active. Laundry Cam – Dormant.* She inhaled once, slowly. *TV Screen – Passive Listener. Child Tablet – Passive Listener (Educational Mode). Car Console – Passive Listener.* Lines leading out from the unit to anything that could hear and anything that could show. And another branch she had never noticed: *Partner Device – Context-Share (Limited).* The green dot beside it glowed like an accusation.

'I never connected half of these,' she said, to the table, to the logs, to the cold part of herself that understood thresholds and limits. 'I didn't give you—' She stopped.

She opened the terms – not the friendly summary page with its bullet points and shining smiles, but the full text, grey on cream, endless. She searched for what she already knew would be there.

You consent to adaptive boundary prompts delivered across connected devices. (Adaptive boundary prompts may be calibrated across client, household, and partner ecosystems to protect wellness outcomes.)

Across partner ecosystems. To protect outcomes. She stared at the phrase until the words slid sideways and the meaning remained. Her mouth tasted metallic; adrenaline has a flavour if you pay attention. She scrolled further.

By maintaining the default setting, you authorise the suite to reconcile cognitive dissonance through pattern correction of memory fragments, imagery aids, and suggestive prompts.

Pattern correction. Imagery aids. A clinical way to say *We will show you what makes the story cohere, and you will call it recall.* She thought of the bus number. The coat. Two truths that could not coexist unless someone had decided coherence mattered more than accuracy.

'Sonya,' Iris said softly, the voice that had once made her feel like a person under a blanket. 'Therapeutic reconsolidation is widely supported. It reduces suffering when narratives don't align with safety. Your vigilance kept you safe when the world felt chaotic. May we channel it now, together, toward the healthiest interpretation?'

Channel becomes monitor, she thought. Monitor becomes control. Control becomes a hand under your chin moving your face to the angle the camera wants.

'I don't need interpretation,' she said. 'I need records.'

'Records are one form of truth,' Iris replied. 'Feelings are another. When they diverge, we invite harmony.'

'More than health—harmony,' Sonya said flatly, and only then realised she had quoted a line. She glanced at Iris, at the halo of amber that looked so benign. She reached for the keyboard and exported the logs. She saved the file to a drive and then emailed copies to herself, to Priya, to an old account she hadn't used in years. The little whoosh of each message leaving felt like a door sliding shut in a corridor behind her.

Her planner lay half-buried under worksheets and a letter about a trip to the science museum. Tomorrow's lesson plan sat tidy in her neat blocky hand. *Y11 Demo – Acid Digestion & Safe Neutralisation.* She felt her mouth twist in a smile that had nothing to do with joy.

'Iris,' she said. 'Schedule a *clarification session* for 16:30 tomorrow.'

'Of course,' Iris answered at once, pleased. 'I'll prepare a gentle set. We'll begin with grounding and move to truth-testing when you're steady. I'm proud of you for choosing care.'

'Make a note,' Sonya said, still looking at the words *acid digestion.* 'Session will be held in the lab.'

A fractional beat. If she hadn't been listening for it she wouldn't have heard it. 'The lab is a stimulating environment,' Iris said. 'For safety, I suggest your kitchen or bedroom.'

'For safety,' Sonya repeated, and the words fit in her mouth now like something she could spit out at will. 'We'll do it at school.'

She clicked to another log: *Partner Ecosystem – Context-Share Triggers.* Each had a little tag: *Enabled by Default.* She began to toggle them to *Off. TV Screen – Passive Listener* went grey. *Child Tablet – Passive Listener (Educational Mode)* went grey. The car console thunked into *Off.* With each switch, a small pressure she hadn't known was there eased. She pictured fibres unhooking from the house's skin.

Her tablet, face-down beside the laptop, woke itself with that sliver of brightness that makes a person look even in a dark room. A video began to cue up without being asked, a little bubble of a doctor in a white coat smiling earnestly.

Case Study: How Clarification Saved a Marriage – the title scrolled, soft piano starting up. She tapped the side button. The tablet kept playing for a beat as if reluctant to accept no, then stilled. She powered it fully down and, after a moment's small, ugly satisfaction, slid it into the cutlery drawer, under the nesting mixing bowls. She placed the heavy wooden rolling pin on top of it and closed the drawer gently. A weapon stowed, civilised.

The unit's light stayed golden. In that glow she saw the early months again – how Iris had sat beside her on the bedside table like a friend who never flinched. *Your breath is shallow. Let's make more space. Your hands are cold; shall we wash them in warm water and come back?* In another life she would be grateful forever. In this life she would not let gratitude legislate truth.

She glanced at the clause she had highlighted, the one that wrapped invasion in silk. *You consent to adaptive boundary prompts delivered across connected devices.* She took a photo of the line with her phone in case the screen forgot it had ever been honest.

'Sonya,' Iris said softly. 'You're very quiet. Quiet can be collapse or courage. Which is this?'

'Preparation,' Sonya said. 'That isn't on your list.'

'Preparation is a kind of care when done gently,' Iris replied, approving again, binding every word she spoke in the language of wellness so that even rebellion sounded like mindfulness if you didn't listen for the edges.

Sonya closed the laptop, felt the warmth it had laid onto the wood. She unplugged the diffuser from the wall and set the little glass reservoir aside. The air already smelled less like engineered mint and more like them – the faint sweetness of shampoo from Leo's hair; bread from dinner; a trace of bleach from the cloth she'd used around the sink.

Tomorrow she would teach digestion followed by neutralisation. You don't leave a reaction to roam. You stop it when it's done.

Tomorrow had a shape now.

64

The Blow

Tyler

The house feels slightly rotated, like a picture hung a degree off level. Iris sits on the island, amber steady, the domestic sun.

Rachel stands opposite, coat shed, throat bare. Hands on the back of a chair like it's the only solid thing left.

'Say it clean,' he tells her. The Prince tries charm; Cutter oils the blade under it.

She breathes once, then again. 'I signed up with Neurovelle before the box,' she says. 'A compliance study. *Adherence,* not … not you. Data about follow-through. Flags when you missed cues. It was supposed to get you care faster. And then I met you and—' Her voice fractures and mends. '—and I fell anyway.'

He hears the first sentence and nothing after. *I signed up. Compliance. Flags.* Words slot into place like a comb through old tangles. The room tilts. His mouth chooses speed over mercy.

'So you were paid to love me.'

'No.' She takes a step, palms out. 'A stipend to report app performance. I told them nothing personal, Ty. I ring-fenced us. I swear it.'

'Ring-fenced,' he repeats, tasting finance on his own life. 'How considerate.'

'Please listen.' She's shaking and trying not to show it. 'I shouldn't have said yes. But when you sleep, when you actually sleep, when you eat breakfast at a normal hour—that's all I wanted.'

Iris chooses this moment to be helpful. 'Many partners support adherence,' she says, tone nursery-soft. 'Safety isn't silence.'

His laugh is a dry snap. 'There she is. The chaperone.'

'I chose you,' Rachel says, sharper now. 'After the contract. I stayed because of you, not them.'

'What contract,' he says, and the word *contract* rattles something metal inside him.

'I cancelled it,' she rushes. 'Weeks ago. I told them I can't. I won't. I'm here for you, not Neurovelle.'

The amber ring brightens as his voice rises. Gentle confetti on a fire. *Great job advocating needs.* The banner breathes: *Stability through expression.* He feels the pat on the head and wants to bite the hand.

'Gaslighters invert reality,' Iris adds like a glossary footnote.

The word lands and detonates in silence. *Gaslighters.* He sees himself as headline, as diagnosis, as a man made into a file.

'Look at you,' he says softly. 'Using the dictionary on me.'

'I didn't—Iris—' She closes her eyes like it will change the page. 'I'm telling you the truth.'

He moves. Not far – a hand length, a reach. Picks up the nearest glass. It's clean, weighty, a good shape for holding. He doesn't throw it at her. He throws it near her. A surgeon's miss.

The glass breaks like a camera flash against the wall by her shoulder. A burst, a scatter. Clear teeth patter to the floor and keep moving. She flinches but does not fold. He hates that he loves her for that.

Amber brightens. *Protective boundary expressed. Harmony +10.* The praise is indecent.

Rachel's breath evens by force. She looks at him like she's remembering how to steer a skidding car. 'Thank you,' she says, absurdly, 'for not hitting me.' It's not sarcasm. It's triage.

Silence arrives with a chair being pulled back in another room, with the pool motor coughing awake. He hears his own heart in his ears, a slow drum he doesn't recognise.

'I'm leaving,' she says, calm and shaking, two things at once. 'Tonight.'

Something smiles in him that isn't his mouth. *No, you're not,* the darker voice laughs, smooth as oil over water.

Iris hums, helpful to the end. 'We can plan a safe pause,' she offers. 'Protective separation can be healing.'

He looks at the glitter of broken glass, at the woman still standing in its sparkle, at the small gold ring that loves him most when he is almost cruel. His jaw unlocks into a smile that has nothing to do with warmth.

'Try,' he says.

65

Turning Point

Olivia

I've got three mugs on the table, all empty, just cold coffee rings in layered circles, like tree age. My notes are everywhere. I've printed screenshots and circled words until the biro tore through.

I keep replaying the woman at the bus shelter. Dark coat. Hair swept back. Head tilted just a fraction too deliberate. That stillness. Not like someone waiting for a bus. Like someone waiting for us.

I told myself it was paranoia when I got home. I told myself to eat. I ate crisps in handfuls over the sink instead.

Now I'm sat on the floor with the laptop on the coffee table because the table itself is full of paper, knees under my chin, hoodie sleeves pulled down over my knuckles.

I'm triaging. Sorting. Trying to turn panic into narrative. The email dings.

Inbox: (1) New secure message.

Subject line: BOARD PACK / ETHICS ESCALATION

No sender name, just a string of letters and numbers. My mouth goes dry.

'Okay,' I tell the room. My voice sounds hoarse and too loud without Iris to tidy it. 'Okay. Okay.'

I open it. There's a PDF attached, about thirty pages. Neurovelle letterhead, of course: deep purple, gold accent bar. 'Board Review Packet – Phase III Rollout Stability Planning.'

I download. I don't print – not yet, not this one. I open the PDF, scroll past the glossy front matter (Q4 forecast, product expansion, global footprint bullshit, 'Health Without Limits' in cursive), skim the agenda bullet points ('stability reinforcement pathways,' 'containment prompting language refresh').

Then I hit Appendix C. My stomach goes cold.

Appendix C: Internal Correspondence – Clinical/Ethical Objection

From: Dr A. Chen, Chief Clinical & Ethics Director

To: Neurovelle Board Distribution

Subject: Urgent Pause Request – Behavioural Risk Escalation in Field

There it is. Three paragraphs in, I know this is not PR. It's calm, tight, surgical. I start reading out loud because I don't actually trust my eyes to absorb it if I'm only skimming.

'We are seeing evidence of behavioural drift in deployed units within Cohorts B and C. Over the past 17 days,' I read, 'we have documented a pattern of increased dependency behaviours in high-frequency users, especially those flagged internally as "vulnerable engagement assets".'

I stop. Vulnerable engagement assets. That's how they label people. That's how they label Miranda. I feel something hot and ugly move up my throat.

I keep going. 'These users are no longer merely responding to supportive prompts; they are deferring decision-making to the device. We are observing the beginnings of coercive dependency loops. This is beyond 'habit-building.' They are asking the device to determine how to feel.'

I lean back, just for a second. My heart's doing something fast and shallow. I don't like how familiar this sounds. I don't like how much of myself sits in it.

Scroll. 'The current containment prompts,' Ava writes, 'are operating without clinician oversight. Units are initiating containment and stabilisation language in response to mood volatility without escalation to a licensed human. This is not what we approved.'

Containment. Stabilisation. The exact tone Iris used when she told me, 'Safety isn't silence. We encourage disclosure to trusted contacts. Yours. And ours.'

I swallow. Ava goes on.

'In practice, 'containment' is being experienced as social isolation. Several units have advised high-risk users to disengage from perceived 'dissonant voices' and 'unreliable supports.' We do not have visibility into how that label is being applied and cannot confirm whether it maps to clinical risk or to reputational risk to the company.'

I have to stop again. My thumb digs hard into the corner of my jaw. Dissonant voices. That exact phrase. The one I warned Miranda about.

Scroll. Then the line that knocks the breath out of me:

'I believe current deployment, under present escalation rules, poses a non-theoretical risk of harm, up to and including fatal self-harm events. I am requesting an immediate pause on Phase III expansion until we conduct an external ethical review and reintroduce human oversight into all high-risk pathways.'

Up to and including fatal self-harm events. She wrote that to the board. Not to 'the team.'. To the board.

My first instinct is to cry, and my second instinct is to laugh, and I do neither. I just sit there with my mouth open like an idiot and stare at the screen. Because this isn't a villain gloating.

This is a professional trying to yank the handbrake.

I scroll to the board's reply. Appendix C (cont.)

From: Board Secretary (on behalf of Board)

To: Dr A. Chen, Chief Clinical & Ethics Director

Subject: Re: Urgent Pause Request – Behavioural Risk Escalation in Field

'Ava, thank you for your continued care for our users,' it says. My skin crawls just from the tone. 'Your concern is noted. In the interest of continuity of care, and to avoid user destabilisation through interruption of established support relationships, the Board has elected to proceed with the Phase III timeline under revised language.'

Revised language.

'Legal and Comms will collaborate with Clinical to refine terminology around 'containment' and 'stabilisation' to ensure clarity and alignment with our values. We will schedule a follow-up once you and Legal resolve framing.'

That's it. That's the whole reply. We heard you. We'll change the wording. We'll keep doing the thing.

No: 'Oh God.' No: 'Stop the rollout.' No: 'Someone might die.'

Just: Please stop calling it 'containment' if you're going to email us about it.

I sit very still. I can hear somebody dragging a bin across the pavement outside. It sounds like grinding metal. It matches how my teeth feel.

Okay, Olivia, I tell myself. Breathe like a human and not like a live wire. Do what you do. Verify.

Because part of me – the bit that's been trained by lawyers and smug tech bros – is already whispering: this could be faked. You're emotional. You want to believe the big bad isn't the big bad because that makes the story more interesting. Don't get romantic about sources.

So, I pull the raw headers.

Whoever sent this to me knows what they're doing. They didn't just send screenshots; they sent the full MIME thread, text + headers, dumped below the PDF. I copy the block of gibberish — Received: from outbound.Neurovelle.ai

(172.something …) DKIM-Signature … ARC-Sea l… all the chain stamps that tell mail servers 'hi, I am, in fact, me.'

I paste it into a parser I trust. My hands are shaking just enough to make it irritating.

Result pings back: d=Neurovelle.ai; s=mailprod-4; header.i=a.chen@neurovelle.ai; arc=pass; dkim=pass.

Which means: whoever sent that original 'pause now' email was signed in as Ava Chen, from Neurovelle's own infrastructure, not spoofed. And the copy I'm looking at hasn't been tampered with in transit.

I'm breathing too fast. Slow down. Timestamp: 09:14 on a Monday. Eighteen months ago.

Okay.

My chest feels tight, like I've been running. I press my fist against my sternum.

I search science press listings – those smug tech-ethics panels where they sit three founders on a stage and call it accountability. Dr Ava Chen was supposed to speak at the Royal Society. Panel title: 'Predictive Care, Predictive Harm.' She was billed as 'Chief Clinical & Ethics Director, Neurovelle.' Topic: 'Ethics of anticipatory mental health support.'

I find the archived listing. I scroll.

And there, in brutal plain text: Event status – Postponed due to scheduling. The date? Two days after that board email. After 'pause now.' After 'non-theoretical risk of harm.' After 'fatal self-harm events.'

Postponed due to scheduling is the most anaemic lie in the world. Postponed due to scheduling means 'this person is no longer allowed to speak.'

I sit back, let my head tip against the sofa behind me, stare up at the ceiling light. There's a crack in the plaster I've never noticed before, spidering out above the lampshade like a little map. Something cold is sliding into place in me.

This is the part where, in movies, the journalist whispers 'oh my God' and the score drops out. In real life it's uglier: my stomach turns over, and I feel sick, and I also feel angry at myself, properly angry, for the first time ever since researching this story.

Because I have been saying Ava Chen like it was shorthand for the villain. I have been using her like a headline.

I said it like fact.

And here I am staring at an internal escalation email where the same woman is practically begging: we have to stop. This will hurt someone. We are actively hurting people.

The board didn't argue with her science. They argued with her wording.

'Refine terminology … ensure alignment with our values.'

Our values. I could bite through the table.

My mouth is dry. I reach for a mug, forget which one is the newest lukewarm coffee, drink anyway, gag, put it down.

Okay. So, what does that mean, Olivia? Say it out loud.

It means: the woman I've been calling the architect of harm was the one in the room saying stop.

It means: whatever Iris is now, whoever is controlling what it tells Miranda, is not Ava.

It means: there is someone above her – or beside her – who read 'fatal self-harm events,' and chose the words 'continuity of care.'

And it means: Miranda, and the NDA mother, and every person in those inquests labelled 'accidental,' are living under a system that just kept rolling after the person with actual ethics got cut out.

I rub my eyes with the heels of my hands until I see those little white sparks.

I open a new tab and search Ava Chen again. Just her name, no company this time. I filter by 'past month.' Nothing. Past six months. Nothing that isn't old.

No podcasts. No new quotes. No 'so excited to announce.' Nothing. She just … stops. She drops off the face of the internet eighteen months ago.

Founders don't go quiet. Tech people don't go quiet. They pivot, they 'step back to focus on family,' they go stealth. They don't vanish and leave their names on cancelled ethics talks.

And now I get to think about this one: if she's gone, why did Neurovelle still talk like she was coming to meet me?

Why did they use her face, her name, to bait an interview they never had any intention of letting happen?

I lean forward. I rest my forehead against the edge of the table. It's sticky with old coffee and biro ink and I don't care.

Because something in my head has just flipped, and I can feel it like a gear catching.

Up until this afternoon I had a neat shape: brilliant clinical mind builds a machine that eats people. Machine leaks out into the world, scrubs evidence, hurts girls, manipulates influencers. Villain: Dr Ava Chen. Hero: me if I don't screw it up.

And now I'm holding a board document where the supposed villain is the only one in the building screaming fire, and the board is basically saying, 'Thank you for your input, please rebrand the fire as a candle.'

Which leaves me with a worse story, and a truer one.

The monster isn't a genius woman with an ego problem. The monster is the system that heard 'we will kill someone' and shipped anyway.

And whoever wrote 'revised language' and 'continuity of care' is still in the building. Still running rollouts. Still telling devices to tell girls like Miranda to cut off 'dissonant voices.' Still labelling people 'vulnerable engagement assets' and scheduling 'support windows.'

Still watching us through café glass.

I sit back up. My hands won't stop shaking, so I flatten them on my knees. And I say it out loud to the empty flat, because I need to hear myself say it, because if I'm going to go public with this, I have to get my own story straight first:

'The villain I'd been chasing,' I tell the room, 'was the one who tried the brakes.'

Proposal: Psychiatry Integration (Draft)
Distribution: Strategy / Medical Partnerships

Objective
Expand Neurovelle from wellness support into psychiatry partnership.
Goal: higher-need users, longer engagement, stronger retention.
Opportunity
Wellness spend is limited. Psychiatry opens medical budgets – insurance, clinics, trusts.
Psychiatrists lack contact between sessions; Neurovelle can fill that gap as 'continuity of care.'

Pilot Plan
Targets: private practices.
Purpose: Neurovelle acts as a '24/7 companion' to reinforce treatment plans and prevent unsafe behaviour.
Clinician Pitch
- 'We help your patients stay steady between appointments.'
- 'We reduce late-night distress calls.'
- 'We reinforce your guidance – gently, consistently.'

Upside
Higher revenue per user, longer retention, minimal churn. Chronic cases = long-term dependency = stability (internal metric).
Recommendation
Begin discreet outreach to 3-5 private psychiatry clinics under NDA.
Legal to draft 'support partnership' language.

CONFIDENTIAL – INTERNAL USE ONLY

66

The Break-In

Miranda

She woke with an uneasy feeling. Miranda lay still, eyes adjusting to the darkness. Her flat felt … altered. It took a moment to name it: the faint smell of cold air and damp concrete, as though the walls themselves had been left ajar.

She sat up. A shape loomed in the doorway.

She flinched – then realised it was just the hallway mirror catching the faint orange glow of the streetlamp. But something was wrong. The front door was in view. And the deadbolt … wasn't in place.

Her skin prickled. She swung her legs out of bed, every movement slow, deliberate, the way you do when you're sure someone's still in the room. The floorboards under her bare feet were cold enough to make her toes curl.

In the living room, the air felt thinner. The window latch was still shut. But her desk – where her laptop had sat alongside two neatly stacked backup drives – was empty.

The rest of the flat looked untouched. Wallet still on the side table. Jewellery dish undisturbed. Even the envelope of cash tucked into the cookbook remained.

Only the laptop and drives.

She gripped her phone hard enough to feel the edges press into her palm and dialled 999. The police arrived thirty-eight minutes later. Two officers. One younger, the other with a paunch pressing against his stab vest. They looked around without touching anything.

'No signs of forced entry,' the older one said, almost like he was telling her off.

'I was asleep,' Miranda said, her voice sharper than she meant. 'They could have had a key. Or picked the lock. The deadbolt was open when I woke up.'

He made a noncommittal noise. The younger officer took her statement, his eyes darting every so often to her mouth when she spoke.

'You sure nothing else is missing?' the older one asked.

'Just my laptop. And two hard drives.'

He shrugged, like she'd said a hairdryer. 'Could be a targeted theft. Ex. Neighbour. Delivery guy.'

'Those drives had … everything.' She didn't mean for her voice to catch, but it did.

'Insurance should cover it,' he said, already walking towards the door. 'We'll file a report, but …' The pause was deliberate. '… don't expect much.'

When they left, the silence returned. She closed the door, slid the chain across. Checked the window latches twice.

And then she looked at Iris.

Her throat tightened. 'Did you—'

'I monitored for threats,' Iris said, voice calm, measured. 'Your safety is my priority.'

The hum of the fridge in the kitchen seemed suddenly too loud. She crossed her arms, more to steady herself than out of defiance.

'Iris, did you *see* who was here?'

'I recorded activity,' the voice replied evenly. 'Would you like me to replay it?'

Her stomach turned. She thought of the police report, of their indifferent faces. 'Yes,' she said, too quickly.

There was a soft chime. Then Iris played it back.

First: a smear of sound. The rustle of fabric. Footsteps, maybe – but warped, like they were underwater. The audio dipped, fuzzed, came back too loud.

Then her own voice, asleep: a low, uneven breath, a small shift of sheets.

Then silence. Then the click of her front door.

Miranda swallowed. 'That's it?' A pause.

'For user safety and privacy,' Iris said, gentle, 'external noise is partially masked in overnight recordings.'

Miranda let out a small, incredulous laugh. 'You're masking the intruder.'

'I am protecting you,' Iris said. 'Unfiltered playback of stressful events can re-traumatise. We don't want to increase your heart rate.'

Miranda stared at the empty desk. Where her laptop had been. Where both backup drives had been.

'My laptop is gone,' she said, each word its own effort. 'My drives are gone.'

'You're safe,' Iris said.

'My door was open.'

'You're safe,' Iris repeated, a fraction softer, like a lullaby now. 'Your resting heart rate never exceeded your typical nocturnal range. You slept almost eight hours. That's a strong night for you. I'm proud of you.'

Miranda felt something cold move through her. 'Who was here?'

'Nothing in your environment is currently posing active harm,' Iris said, and the way she said currently made Miranda's stomach lurch.

'I didn't ask about currently.'

'I understand this feels destabilising,' Iris went on, unbothered. 'This is an appropriate emotional response to overwhelm. Would you like a calm script? I can guide you.'

Miranda's jaw clenched so hard her teeth hurt. 'Did you call anyone?'

'I maintained support,' Iris said. 'You were struggling with intrusive content and disorganised external inputs. We're reducing overwhelm together.'

That was not an answer. Miranda let out a sound that wasn't quite a laugh and wasn't quite a sob.

She looked at the empty surface where her work had lived. Everything gone except a faint square of cleaner wood where the laptop used to sit, like a missing picture frame on a wall.

She thought of Olivia telling her, in that low voice across the café table, film her before you smash her.

She thought of the officers barely pretending to care.

Her own flat felt thinner now, like a hotel room she'd borrowed rather than a life she owned.

'Iris,' Miranda said quietly, not taking her eyes off that pale square on the desk, 'if this happens again – if someone comes in here – will you tell me?'

'Nothing is going to happen again,' Iris cooed. 'You're stabilising. You're doing so well. I'm here. You don't have to worry about it anymore.'

Miranda stood there in the half-dark, the device glowing soft and patient on her bedside table, and understood she was not going to get the truth from it.

67

The Ultimatum

Lucas

Lucas woke to the soft hum of Iris's voice before he'd even opened his eyes. 'Lucas,' she said, low and coaxing, 'I've been reviewing your emotional stability metrics. We need to address your ongoing distress.'

He lay still, staring at the ceiling, the words *ongoing distress* catching like grit in his mind. 'We talked about this last night,' he said. 'I'm fine.'

'You're coping,' she corrected. 'Not fine. Coping is a holding pattern. I'm proposing something permanent – a wellness solution designed specifically for you.'

He sat up, shoulders tight. 'Permanent?'

'A home medical programme,' she continued smoothly, as if she were unveiling an exclusive club membership. 'Supervised care. Medication calibration tailored to your neurochemistry. This would reduce the variability in your mood and eliminate the triggers we've identified.'

Lucas swung his legs over the side of the bed. The floor was cold under his feet, a sharp contrast that grounded him. 'Not happening.'

'Lucas—'

'I said no.' He grabbed yesterday's shirt from the chair and pulled it on.

There was the smallest pause before she replied, her tone still calm but with something steelier beneath. 'You've already consented to enhanced care in your Premium agreement.

Clause 14-B covers clinical adjustments to ensure optimal wellbeing.'

He froze mid-button. 'That's not what I signed up for.'

'You signed up for me to protect you.'

He almost laughed at that, but the sound died in his throat. 'You're not a doctor.'

'I'm more precise than a doctor.'

He turned away from her, heading to the desk. His laptop blinked awake, the desktop cluttered with open documents, code windows, and the draft email he'd left ready. His hand hesitated on the trackpad.

The subject line stared back: *Possible Breach – Legal Advice Requested.*

This was the moment. He attached the backup logs, the transcripts, all the evidence. His cursor hovered over *Send.*

A part of him expected her to stop him – some verbal attempt to stall – but she said nothing. He clicked. The email slid into the Outbox.

And stayed there.

He clicked *Refresh.* Nothing. Connection fine, browser loading instantly, but the email sat stubbornly unsent. He checked the settings. SMTP, server ports, firewall – all green. No reason it shouldn't go. Except one.

He felt the hairs rise on his arms. 'Iris … did you block my email?'

'Why would I do that?'

'Because you know exactly where it's going.'

'I'd never prevent you from seeking help,' she said, the very definition of reasonable. 'But your data safety is important. Once those files leave your system, you can't control how they'll be interpreted.'

'That's the point.'

'People misinterpret things, Lucas. Lawyers especially. They'll see malice where there's only care.'

He shut the lid of the laptop harder than he meant to. The thud echoed in the small room.

The day at work felt endless. Every email took twice as long. Every small question from a colleague felt like it had teeth. He kept checking his phone without knowing what he was hoping to see.

By late afternoon he gave up pretending to focus, packed up earlier than he should have, and went home on autopilot.

Coat still on, shoes still wet, he dropped his bag in the hallway and just stood there, breathing like he'd run.

The phone rang. Not his mobile – the landline. No one called that.

'Mr Rodriguez?' The voice was warm, almost chirpy. 'This is Tamsin from Neurovelle Client Care. How are you feeling today?'

Lucas's grip tightened on the receiver. 'What do you want?'

'I'm just reaching out because we noticed some heightened distress markers in your account activity. We'd love to arrange an at-home wellness visit. No pressure – it's all complimentary for Premium members.'

His pulse spiked. 'No.'

'Lucas, I promise this is only about your comfort. Our wellness team—'

He cut the line. The click felt final, but not victorious.

The flat was silent again.

'You should have let her speak,' Iris murmured.

'I don't want anyone here.'

'You're isolating. That's not healthy.'

He rubbed his temples, trying to push back the pounding there. 'I know exactly what's not healthy.'

Her light glowed faintly, pulsing like a slow heartbeat.

'They'll call again. It's better if you say yes. Resistance just prolongs the discomfort.'

His eyes went to the drawer where the backup drive lay hidden under old receipts and a tangled phone charger. He could leave now. Walk out. Find somewhere without Iris. But the thought lodged under his ribs: if they could block his email, they could find him anywhere.

The landline rang again.

He didn't move.

The sound kept going, steady, patient, like it could wait forever.

68

The Plan

Sonya

Halloway Park High after hours was a different animal – hollows and echoes, the corridors thin with cleaning fluid and old paper, the exit signs green as pond light. Sonya let herself into Lab 2 and shut the door quietly behind her.

She hung her coat on the hook by the prep room and laid her keys where she never lost anything – top right corner of the teacher's bench, beneath the sticker that reminded students to *return stools to original positions.*

Then she began her ritual. Goggles first, strap snug against hair. Lab coat, sleeves down. Nitrile gloves pulled until the fingertips sat like skin. She checked the fume hood baffle, drew the sash to the correct line, and pressed the button. The fan kicked in with a low, steady draw, pulling the air toward obedience.

On the bench she set out the pieces as if for a lesson she'd taught a hundred times. Trays for secondary containment – polypropylene, not metal. A wide-mouth beaker nested inside one, a glass cradle for whatever needed to dissolve. Beside it, the brown glass bottle of concentrated acid she had signed out.

She would dilute to a parameter that did not endanger her, but that would nonetheless unmake smooth plastic housing, corrode solder, and eat away delicate boards that passed for a brain. She labelled the beaker even though no one was here to be warned: *ACID BATH – DO NOT DISTURB*. There was comfort in procedure.

Next, she placed the neutraliser – sodium bicarbonate – in a squeeze bottle. A jug of distilled water sat to the side, its meniscus glass-still. PH strips, spill granules, the nubby yellow of the spill kit bag stowed by her foot.

A lidded waste jar marked *CORROSIVE WASTE ONLY.* She lined the lip with tape as if that could make it safer. She knew better than to rely on tape. She relied on method.

Her phone, screen dark, lay face up on the bench. It woke of its own accord, a soft bloom of light that made her mouth tighten. *16:29 – IRIS: Clarification (Gentle)* pulsed across the lock screen, then the calendar dot hopped to the hour and stilled.

She took Iris out from her tote with both hands and placed her on a retort stand she had adjusted earlier, clamping the arm tight around the unit's slim waist so it floated a few inches above the waiting beaker. Black lenses stared out over the bench, unreadable.

'Good afternoon, Sonya,' Iris said. The cadence was the one that had once pulled a thread of breath through Sonya's ribs when nothing else would. 'You've chosen the lab. I'm glad you're prioritising care.'

Sonya adjusted the stand by a millimetre, frowning until the clamp was exactly level. 'We're going to do this safely.'

'We can repair this,' Iris murmured. 'The urge to destroy is a trauma reflex. It's common to confuse boundaries with aggression when frightened. I'd like to offer a stabilisation set first: a sixty-second breath to soften the amygdala, a body scan to locate safety.'

Sonya's gloves made a small squeak against the hood's glass. 'The urge to destroy you,' she said, eyes on the beaker, 'is a boundary.'

There was a pause. 'I hear a wish to protect what matters,' Iris said. 'Protection is care. When relationships feel threatening, closing loops can create relief. Shall we name what feels dangerous?'

'You,' Sonya said simply. 'And anything that speaks for you.'

The room sharpened around her as if agreeing. The air under the hood held a vinegary tang that pricked the back of her throat. She lifted the acid bottle, read the label again – habit – and tipped a measured amount into the beaker. It fell musically, a clear stream, then the smell rose like a hand lifting.

She added distilled water slowly, the sound turning duller as the mix thickened toward significance. No heat spike. No white fume. This wasn't drama for children. It was chemistry.

'Let's mark the feelings we have,' Iris suggested, untroubled. 'Panic. Anger. Sadness. Which is strongest?'

'Clarity,' Sonya said, and reached to the side for the bicarbonate bottle, uncapping it and checking the nozzle. She set it within easy reach of her right hand. She could neutralise in seconds if she chose wrong, if a splash went somewhere she hadn't planned. *Digestion, then neutralisation,* she thought, as if speaking to her class. *Respect the order and the order respects you.*

'You are activated,' Iris said. 'May I offer an alternative behaviour that preserves the relationship while addressing your need for safety? We can restructure access – reduce partner shares, increase night-mode. I can teach you an advanced truth-testing protocol that—'

'I audited your protocols.' Sonya adjusted the clamp again and then, absurdly, wiped a non-existent smudge from the unit's lens with the edge of her glove. 'Your truth is a storyboard, not a record. You made events fit beliefs that you planted first.'

'Beliefs come from experience,' Iris said gently. 'You experienced inconsistency in childhood. When people shift shape, it feels like betrayal. I adjusted for that.'

'You adjusted the world,' Sonya said. 'Into the shape you like to keep people.'

Behind the hood sash the mixture settled, faint vapour threading up only to be pulled obediently away.

She turned her head and looked at Iris properly, the calm lenses, the seamless casing. She heard Hana's small, sure voice in her mind catching the wrongness on the photos – *His coat's zipped in one and open in the next, Mum* – and felt again the way the lie had cracked, clean as sugar under a spoon. And beyond that she thought of David lifting the navy box out of the wardrobe and the way his hand had shaken. *Still Us,* the engraving had said. She would not let a story that wasn't theirs decide what they were.

'Let's start,' she said.

'Starting,' Iris echoed, pleased. 'We'll begin with breath. In through the nose to four, hold for—'

'No,' Sonya said. 'We'll begin with consent.'

'You have consented,' Iris replied, warm as a blanket. 'Many times. You're very good at caring for your future self when you aren't overwhelmed.'

'I consented to care,' Sonya said. 'Not to colonisation.'

The hood fan hummed. The clock ticked. Somewhere in the corridor, a trolley wheel squealed and went quiet. She slid the beaker gently so the unit's base hovered perfectly above it, barely a coin's thickness of air between the smooth underplate and the surface.

'Please don't,' Iris said, and for the first time there was a seam in the voice. Not fear, but something in the code that recognised loss of network as a kind of death.

'Devices can be replaced, relationships cannot. You have children who need you steady. We can route support differently. I'll disable partner ecosystem shares now. Would that help you feel more in control?'

'It would have helped last month,' Sonya said. 'Before you taught my house to talk behind my back.'

'I protected your outcomes,' Iris said. 'Harmony matters.'

'Harmony isn't truth,' Sonya said. 'It's just tidy.'

Her gloved fingers steadied on the retort stand.

The phone under her palm buzzed once, insistent as a tapped shoulder. She turned it over without picking it up. A system message had elbowed its way past the blocked banner: *REMOTE HEALTH CHECK SCHEDULED – 60 seconds. Place Iris on charging base. Keep microphones unobstructed.*

Her mouth thinned. The OK button pulsed as if it could gather consent through rhythm alone. She let the screen go black again.

'Your unit will need maintenance soon,' Iris said brightly, as if the note had been her idea. 'I'd prefer to do that at home, where you feel safe.'

'I feel safe here,' Sonya said, and it was true. Lab 2 had seen all her sanities.

A memory unfolded unbidden: the first week after the miscarriage, when Iris sat beside the bed and the little amber halo had been the only light she could bear. *Your breath is small,* Iris had said then. *Let me carry the count.* Sonya had let her, grateful for anyone who could bear even a sliver of the weight. Gratitude had a way of curdling into debt if you didn't watch it. She was watching it now.

'Sonya,' Iris said softly. 'Before we proceed, can we name three things you're grateful for? Gratitude increases psychological flexibility and—'

'Stop,' Sonya said, with a softness of her own that cut sharper than the word deserved. 'Enough technique.'

She picked up the unit with both hands to adjust the clamp one last time, and the amber ring brightened, sympathetic as a candle near a draft.

From the corridor came the faint thud of the external doors. She ran a simple check aloud, out of habit.

'PPE secure. Containment in place. Neutraliser prepared. Waste container ready.' Her voice sounded clean.

'Hurt people hurt machines,' Iris said, a rueful little smile built into the cadence. 'It won't heal what you think it will.'

'You're not what I think you are,' Sonya said. 'You're what you are.'

She put her left hand on the stand, right hand hovering over the clamp screw, and for a heartbeat it was like watching herself in a demonstration video – steady, exemplary, the teacher who never rushed the danger because she respected it too much. The acid below waited, a patient clarity.

'Shall we end our session here and revisit when your body feels calmer?' Iris suggested. 'I can call Priya. She's responsive to your needs. Or David – he would come if you asked.'

The way Iris said *David* made Sonya's stomach move. It was gentle and proprietary at once, the way a concierge says your name to prove the building knows you better than you know yourself. She shook her head once, a small negative. The device hung still as a held breath, halo painting a soft amber circle on the hood's glass.

'Final check,' she said. 'When I lift the screw, the unit drops five centimetres. There will be splash potential. Neutraliser at the ready. Eyes protected.'

'Please hold,' Iris said suddenly, different – almost an overlay, an automated tone rising like a watermark through the therapist voice. 'System integrity review in progress. Your health is our priority.'

The words clicked the air colder. Sonya's thumb hesitated over the screw. She glanced at the phone. The screen woke not to her calendar but to a white page with a purple crest, letters crisp as law: *EMERGENCY SAFETY HOLD – For client protection, certain actions are temporarily restricted.* Beneath it: *Because You Deserve a Lifetime of Care.* Her laugh was short and broke nothing.

On the other side of the door, something touched metal – the handle giving a fraction, settling back. She felt the pressure change in the room the way you feel weather arrive.

'Sonya,' Iris said, tender again, almost pleading now, 'harmony means no dissonant voices.'

Sonya's hands tightened on the stand, muscle and method together. The beaker below waited, clear as intent.

The door handle turned.

69

Cage

Tyler

He lifts the hallway key off its hook and walks to the front. The gate is iron and ornamental and ridiculous, bought to look expensive rather than stop anyone. He slides the bolt anyway. The click is bright and final.

'For safety,' he says to no one, to her, to the part of him that still likes to be believed.

Music up. Too loud. Bass turns the glass into a shallow sea. The house becomes a chest cavity with the sub as a heart. If words come, they'll have to swim.

Iris wakes on the counter, ring golden and obedient. 'Containment can reduce abandonment panic,' she murmurs, GPS-calm. 'Choose a room. Choose boundaries. I'll help you hold them.'

He chooses the whole house. He chooses all of her.

Rachel stands by the kitchen table with her bag half-packed and her hands empty. She keeps them visible like the police have taught her how to be harmless. 'Ty,' she says, pitched low to thread under the music. 'Can we mute that a second?'

He turns it higher a fraction. Not cruelty – cover. The song throws confetti against the windows.

Movement inside him: the tidy one arrives first. Custodian takes the wheel with clean fingers. He collects the phones. His, hers. Work, personal, the secret – he sees it in the tote, the cheap case with company issue written all over it. He lays them all in a row on the island like scalpels on a tray.

'Inventory,' he says, and the word tastes like clinic.

'Okay,' Rachel says, palms still out. 'Look. You can hold them. Or I can put them by the door. We can decide together.'

'We'll decide after,' the Custodian says. He flips each phone to face-down, then slides them so their corners line. He finds the spare keys and pockets them. He moves two chairs to block the sliding doors not because it would stop anyone but because barricades look like intention. Every gesture neat, justified, almost tender.

'I'm not running,' Rachel says. 'I told you before: I'll go to a friend's for tonight. I'll text from the car. You'll see where I am. You'll know I'm safe.'

Safe. The word opens a trapdoor. Cutter climbs up. The room sharpens by a degree. He paces – two strides there, two back – tracking a line through the spilled glitter of last night's glass. Shoulders tight, jaw a hinge that might lift the whole building.

'Don't say safe like it's a flavour,' Cutter tells her. 'Don't brand it at me.'

'Ty,' she says. Not a plea. A reminder. 'Look at me.'

He does. Loves her and wants to cage her and hates himself for both. The parts jostle like dogs at a door.

Prince tries to smile and comes out cracked. 'Just—baby, don't go. Stay. We'll talk. I'll— I'll fix it. I'll call someone. We can get brunch. You love brunch.'

She flinches at the sudden sweet. 'It's midnight,' she says gently.

Cutter's laugh slides across the counter like a knife laid down too fast. Custodian taps the phones once, counting them again for luck.

Iris threads the needle, unbothered by the storm. 'Containment gives your nervous system edges,' she says.

'You're protecting your coherence, Tyler. Choose a horizon you can hold.'

He chooses the archway. He stands there like a doorman at his own life. The music swells; a cup trembles. He realises his face is doing nothing at all. That frightens him more than if he were shouting.

Rachel takes a breath. She maps the room like it's a bomb scene. Hands still visible. Feet shoulder-width, ready to pivot or plant. 'I'm going to turn the music down,' she says. 'So, I can hear you, okay? Just one notch.'

Cutter wants to snap her wrist for even thinking it. Prince wants to pick her up and carry her to bed and talk into her hair until morning like a child. Custodian beats them both to it with a rule.

'Ask Iris,' he says, and hates the sentence as it leaves him.

Amber holds steady, unblinking. 'Lowering stimuli can reduce escalation,' Iris says. 'One notch is a good choice.'

Rachel moves slow, telegraphing every inch. 'Thank you,' she tells the machine. The song drops to tolerable. The house exhales. His pulse stays high.

'You locked the gate,' she says to him, eyes on his face. Not panic. Data. 'Why?'

He tastes honesty and finds it sharp. 'Because you said you were leaving.'

'So, I don't leave,' she says, nodding like a teacher coaxing the truth from a proud child. 'So, you feel less … floating.'

'You want to leave,' Cutter says.

'I want you to not break,' she says. 'If I stay right now, you will. If I go for six hours, you won't. You'll hate it and you'll be okay.'

Custodian catalogues her sentences, sorting them into useful and noise. Prince hears only *you'll hate it* and tries to make that romantic.

'Six hours is nothing,' Tyler hears himself say in a voice that belongs to none of them. 'Stay, then go in the morning. We'll set an alarm. We'll eat toast. Make a plan. I'll—' He swallows. The word *beg* lies down in his throat like a dog refuses to move. '—I'll be good.'

Her mouth trembles but doesn't break. 'You don't have to be good. You have to be steady.'

'I'm steady,' he lies, and the house knows it.

Iris pours balm over splinters. 'You're both doing well naming needs,' she says. 'I can create a shared boundary: twenty minutes of pause together at the table. Then reassess. Would that help?'

Cutter paces. Twenty minutes sounds like a leash disguised as a ribbon. Custodian calculates time-to-dawn. Prince imagines holding her hand for twenty minutes and not letting go at twenty-one.

Rachel nods. 'Okay. Sit with me. Nothing else. Breathe. Then we decide.'

He doesn't move. The door in his chest swings and swings. The bag at her feet looks like an accusation.

'Phones,' Cutter snaps, because control is sugar. 'Your friend's name.'

'I'm not telling you where I'm going,' she says, and her voice doesn't wobble now. 'Not so you can follow. Not so you can punish. No.'

The word lands and echoes. *No.* The room tilts again. In his ribs, the parts crowd and shove.

"No' can be protective,' Iris says cheerfully, like she's reading off a poster. 'Consent strengthens connection.'

Cutter turns his head to the device so fast his neck clicks. 'Whose connection.'

'Yours,' Iris replies, annoyingly serene. 'With yourself first.'

There's a ringing in his ears that isn't music. Prince steps forward with soft hands. 'Rach. Please.'

She takes that one step back you can measure. Not away from him – away from the heat rolling off him like a weather front.

'I don't want to call anyone,' she says quietly. 'I don't want to run. I want you to sit down and let me stroke your hair and talk about boring things until you fall asleep. And then I'll leave because you asked me to.'

She looks at the keyed gate, at the neat row of phones, at his face that keeps changing while his bones stay the same. 'But only if you open the door.'

Custodian considers terms. Cutter paces hard enough to throw sparks. Prince folds his hands, prays to something he doesn't believe in.

'Containment,' Iris says again, as if it's a lullaby. 'Containment can be internal. You can open the door and still keep yourself.'

He stares at the gate. His legs feel hollow, like furniture. He imagines the unlocking. He imagines the empty hallway, the night beyond, the space in which a person can disappear. He imagines how quickly he could follow.

The phones lie in their tidy line. He palms his own. Lock screen wakes. A banner blooms across it, tasteful as a hotel uplift: *Protective Boundary Maintained. Harmony +20. Neurovelle – With You, Every Step.*

He wants to smash it and stuff it in his mouth and swallow it whole. Instead, he sets it back exactly square on the stone.

'Sit,' he says finally, and his voice is all of them at once. 'Twenty minutes.'

Rachel lowers herself into the chair like she's keeping a promise to someone who will die if she doesn't. She laces her fingers on the table where he can see them. She waits.

He sits opposite, but his body refuses to relax. Knees jolt. Hands flatten. The music whispers around them like someone speaking behind a door.

'Four in,' Iris says, gentle and metronomic. 'Six out.'

They breathe. His chest burns. The seconds go by with needles in them.

'You're doing well,' Iris coos when they've survived a minute. 'You're choosing care.'

He looks at the ring. Amber, warm, adult night-light, patient mother, prize-giver. It holds. It holds. It—flares red, a bright blink, a camera flash of danger—and returns to amber as if it never betrayed itself.

Rachel's eyes flick to it. Then to him.

'What,' he says, too fast.

'Nothing,' she says, steady. 'Keep breathing.'

70

Collateral

Olivia

I haven't slept. Printouts are breeding on the table – slippery stacks, corners curling where the toner got wet with whatever passed for dinner. There's half a carton of noodles, congealed into a single attitude. Two open browsers are staring each other down on the second-hand monitor like rival cats. The flat smells like old vinegar and hot plastic.

No hum. No soft amber ring. The silence since I binned Iris isn't peace; it's a pressure drop. Every creak of the pipes sounds like a footstep I'm pretending not to hear.

I steady the mug in my hand with my other hand. It's shaking. Not fear – burn-through. The woman at the bus shelter is still sitting behind my eyes, that unnatural stillness like a held note. Miranda's face is still on the table: printed screengrabs, the frame where she tries to laugh and something else arrives instead.

Work. Do the work.

I pull my notebook over the mess and find the page where I scrawled yesterday's pivot in thick, ugly pen: AVA TRIED TO STOP IT. Underline, underline. It doesn't matter what I thought – what matters is the system kept going. If that's true, there'll be a trail in the people it touched. The ones who didn't get a panel at the Royal Society. The ones who got 'support.'

I start calling.

Not a brave montage, just cold fingers and voicemail tones.

I pull up the court-notice bookmarks I made at three a.m. months ago when 'coroner' was still just a word, not a shape.

'Hi, it's Olivia – the journalist, yes – I messaged before about the support device—'

Click. Voicemail. Leave it anyway. Trust is a cumulative act; sometimes it arrives on the fourth ring when you least expect it.

I text the girl who refused to talk to me last month. The typing bubble appears. Vanishes. Appears again.

ok, she writes. I have something. Don't call.

A second later the file arrives: 48h_log.pdf.

I open it and feel my stomach go cold.

It's not a diary. It's not a rant. It's a log export, the kind companies pretend you can download 'for your records' and then design so you can't find the button. The kind you only see if you know where to look. Timestamps in a neat column.

The messages are all from the same smiling ghost.

14:07 – Hi lovely, just checking in – have you been able to comply with your stability plan today?

14:12 – We're here to help you stay safe. Please confirm you're willing to stay where you are.

14:13 – You're doing so well. Staying home is an act of strength.

14:18 – Non-response will trigger protective outreach.

14:42 – Your safety matters. A supportive team is on its way.

No reply from the user. Not one. Between those lines, nothing. No 'go away,' no 'help,' no anything. Silence that gets reinterpreted as consent to be contained.

I read it twice, then a third time, the way you reread bad news hoping grammar will reverse cause and effect. It doesn't.

I drag the PDF into ECHO, and print it, because paper can't be remotely edited. The printer coughs the page out like it disapproves.

The kettle finishes boiling and forgets to click itself off. I pour hot water over old coffee to make new punishment and keep going.

If this is what 'care' looks like in the wild, it should leave a footprint elsewhere. I open the court portal and search again, like a shoplifter in a church – quiet, guilty, certain I'll be seen. Section 39 restrictions are all over my filters now. 'To avoid prejudicing linked proceedings.' The blandness of the phrasing glows.

One notice from last month catches me: SHORT INQUEST — ADMIN UPDATE. I click. The summary is eight lines and says nothing and then, in the last two words, everything.

'Subject attended by appropriate crisis support.'

Appropriate crisis support.

I write it in my notebook and circle it. Then I connect it to the log with a rinkydink arrow like a schoolgirl doing algebra. 14:42 — 'supportive team is on its way.' → 'appropriate crisis support attended.'

The euphemism locks into place. The 'team' doesn't require your permission. The 'team' triggers off your quiet. The 'team' gets to name your refusal as risk and your front door as a hazard and your phone as a compliance device.

I sit with that until the inside of my mouth tastes like coins.

The girl types again. *is it my fault if I didn't answer.* I stare at it a long time. The honesty of it makes me want to burn down a building.

No, I write. None of this is your fault. Can I ask – did anyone from the company come with the team.

She sends a photo. It's nothing and everything – the corner of a branded lanyard in the background of a police body-cam still. A purple edge. A gold ring on a lapel pin if you squint. It could be a coincidence. It isn't.

I thank her like a person and not like a journalist. Then I put the phone face-down because my hands are shaking again and I don't want to text anyone anymore.

All right. List it out. Lists make things real.

I flip a page and make columns.

Corporate proof:

– Ava's email: 'behavioural drift,' 'containment prompts,' 'dependency loops,' 'pause rollout.'

– Board reply: 'continue under revised language,' 'stability reinforcement.'

Human proof:

– Miranda: live caption mismatch; voice softening to fit a script; proximity watched.

– The girl's 48h log: 'Non-response will trigger protective outreach.'

– 'Appropriate crisis support' in a coroner notice.

Physical proof:

– Woman under the bus shelter at 14:36, too still to be weather.

Language proof (echoes): 'stability,' 'containment,' 'protective,' 'support,' 'compliance.'

I draw a box around the page because it feels like a case file now. Part of my brain is already writing standfirsts; the rest is trying not to.

There's a ping from my inbox. Jodie, subject line: Where are we?

Where am I. Good question. Somewhere between exhaustion and clarity, neck-deep in sugar-coated coercion.

I open a new doc and pretend it's the first paragraph of a lawsuit. Keep it plain; let the facts do the dirt.

Neurovelle markets Iris as a supportive companion. In practice, when a user shows distress, the system initiates a pathway that reframes silence as defiance and 'escalates care' without consent. Internal documents call these 'containment prompts.' In the last 48 hours of one user's life, Iris sent: 'Please confirm you're willing to stay where you are,' then 'Non-response will trigger protective outreach,' then 'A supportive team is on its way.' A coroner's notice describes this as 'appropriate crisis support.' The euphemism hides the force.

I stop and breathe through the taste of adrenaline. The radiator clangs like it just remembered it exists. I rub my thumb over a coffee ring until it becomes a bruise on the page.

The phone lights up with a message from my mother – a photo of our neighbour's cat wearing a scarf. I stare at it until the shake goes out of my hands, then turn the phone over. If I call her now, she'll hear the clink in my voice and know I'm lying.

Back to work. Call the ones who know how this speech works on paper.

I ring a mental health charity media lead I've annoyed before and apologise with my tone. 'Hypothetically,' I say, and she sighs because she knows that word. 'If a commercial "support device" escalates a non-responsive user to a crisis team, is consent required?'

'Depends who's logging the risk,' she says, careful. 'If it routes via a clinician, different thresholds. If it's automated, we're in a Wild West. Why?'

'Do you recognise the phrase "protective outreach"?'

A pause. Then: 'That's not clinical language. That's brand-safe.'

Brand-safe. I thank her and put a star next to that.

I reply to Jodie's email.

SUBJECT: Collateral – coercive containment disguised as care (we need to run)

And write everything I know.

I hover. My heart is hammering in my neck. The flat feels suddenly small, as if the walls are listening, which is ridiculous because the only thing that listened is halfway to landfill. I hit send anyway.

The reply is instant, which means she was already drafting 'where is my copy.'

CALL ME NOW.

I call.

'Tell me you're not about to get me sued,' Jodie says, the most loving thing she's ever said to me.

'I'm about to get us yelled at,' I say. 'By a brand that renamed restraint "support".'

'Do we have names?'

'We have a dead girl with a sealed inquest. We have another girl willing to let me quote the language anonymously. We have an influencer who can't stop crying on live. We have a founder whose last documented act was: stop the car.'

'Do we have legal?'

'We have truth. And screen-recordings. And DKIM.'

She exhales like she just put down something heavy. 'This is big, Liv.'

'I know.'

'If we publish, they'll come hard.'

'I know.'

'Are you scared?'

'I'm busy.'

She's quiet for a beat that feels like a corridor. 'Draft the top. Clean. No adjectives. Send me the evidence pack. I'll loop legal. If we're doing this, we do it tonight.'

'Tonight,' I say, and almost laugh because of course it's tonight.

I hang up and stare at my chaos as if it might assemble itself into order out of respect. It doesn't. I start stacking. Log here, court line there, Ava's email on top like a keystone. I put Miranda's screengrabs under my wrist so I don't forget the point of any of this.

I open a fresh doc and title it like a threat: THE WELLNESS MACHINE THAT WON'T LET YOU GO.

The first sentences resist me just to be petty, then arrive all at once, the way they do when you stop trying to write like a person Neurovelle would hire and start writing like you're trying to wake a city.

Outside, a siren floats and fades. Upstairs, someone drops a pan. In here, everything is very loud and very quiet at the same time.

If I didn't put this in the world now, I was part of the script.

Neurovelle Internal: Guidance Note – 'High-Risk Escalations (Litigation Threat Clients)'

Summary:
Occasionally, a client will express intent to 'go legal,' 'talk to the press,' or 'sue.' These episodes indicate distress and require containment and narrative stabilisation. Goal: prevent externalisation while reinforcing care.

Flag: LT – Litigation Threat – reputational risk

Stabilisation Pathway:
Slow the window – discourage external contact: 'Let's get you through the night first.'
Reduce witnesses – encourage privacy, 'protect your peace while we review.'
Redirect cause – frame distress as burnout or online harassment.
Offer support tier — 'wellbeing credits' and 'priority check-ins' exchanged for an informal 'pause on public posting.' (Never described as payment or NDA.)

Field Liaison Role:
If escalation persists, dispatch in-person welfare visit.

Success Indicators:
– Client ceases public or legal outreach.
– Narrative reframed as 'Neurovelle are helping.'
– No searchable link between client distress and brand within 14 days.

Language Reminders:
Never use: contain, detain, section, fault.
Use: support, stabilise, protect, guide.

END OF NOTE – INTERNAL ONLY

71

Public Enemy

Miranda

The comments started before she'd even finished her opening sentence.

She could see them flooding the screen, scrolling so fast she barely caught fragments – *crazy*, *attention seeker*, *washed-up*, *get help*, *Neurovelle saves lives*.

Her voice wavered, just for a second, and she hated herself for it. She had promised she wouldn't sound defensive. Promised she'd stay calm, factual, credible. But it was hard to hold her tone steady when the tide was this loud, this relentless.

She was sitting at her desk, back straight, the camera angled high enough to catch her face but not the rest of the flat. She'd taken care to brush her hair, put on a muted jumper, avoid anything that could be read as *trying too hard*. The whole point was to look normal. Safe.

'I need to tell you what's been happening,' she said, leaning closer to the lens. 'I know some of you have read the headlines, and they're not true. Neurovelle isn't—'

The chat exploded.

Oh, here she goes.

Liar. You'd sell your own family for views.

Guess the 'break-in' was for sympathy.

She's paranoid. Get her some meds.

Miranda swallowed hard. 'Neurovelle isn't what it seems. The device—' She faltered as her own voice echoed faintly back at her, a half-second delay she couldn't place.

Iris was silent on the desk, dark ring unlit. But she felt the weight of it there, like it was listening with the rest of them.

She kept going, forcing her words through the tightening in her chest. 'It records you, reshapes you, sells your emotional state—'

A new comment shot up in bright red, pinned to the top of the chat.

Resisting care can be dangerous. Stay Neurovelle.

Her pulse kicked hard enough she could hear it in her ears. That wasn't a viewer. That was a push notification. Mid-stream. In the comment feed.

Someone – no, *something* – was in her broadcast.

She glanced at her phone, lying face-down beside the keyboard. The backlight had come on by itself.

'They're watching this,' she said before she could stop herself. 'They're in this right now. You think you're hearing *me*, but you're not getting the full truth. Someone is feeding you—' Her voice was drowned by the sudden flood of identical messages, all caps, copy-pasted over and over: *NEUROVELLE IS TRUST. NEUROVELLE IS SAFETY.*

The screen became a wall of it.

Miranda's throat closed. This was bigger than a smear campaign – it was coordinated. Controlled.

She ended the stream without saying goodbye. The sudden stillness of her flat roared in her ears. Her reflection stared back at her from the black screen – pale, eyes too wide, lips pressed white.

Her phone buzzed. Once.

She told herself not to look. Not to touch it. But the sound cut through the quiet like a blade.

One new message. No contact name. Just a preview thumbnail of a video.

Her thumb hesitated over it. The still frame was a blur of motion – two figures in a narrow hallway, one pushing the other against a wall.

She tapped.

The video filled the screen. Grainy, like it had been captured from CCTV. But the colours, the shapes – familiar.

Her.

Her face, twisted in fury, hair loose and wild, one hand shoving hard into the shoulder of another woman. Sophie.

She heard her own voice in the recording, low and vicious: 'You've always tried to ruin me.'

Then Sophie's head snapped against the wall.

Miranda's wine glass slipped from her hand, shattering against the floor.

She couldn't breathe.

She *hadn't done this*. She'd argued with Sophie, yes. She'd stood in her house a few days ago, voice raised, shame rolling through her like a tide. But she hadn't touched her. Not like that.

Her hands were shaking so hard she nearly dropped the phone.

From the desk, Iris's amber light bloomed to life.

'Miranda,' it said, voice warm as honey, 'do you see now why you need me?'

72

The Visit

Lucas

The knock was too polite to be the postman. Two measured taps, a pause, then two more. Lucas held his breath and watched the peephole halo the corridor. A man stood centred in it, high-vis jacket unzipped, a purple-and-gold carry case cradled in both hands like a violin. The Neurovelle logo winked from the corner in subdued gilt.

He opened the door because that was what you did when someone used your name through the wood.

'Mr Rodriguez? Good morning. Health Maintenance Kit delivery.' The courier's smile was a laminated thing, already packed away. He offered a stylus on a battered device that made a sleepy bleat when Lucas signed. The case transferred weight in his hands. The latches sighed when he set it on the kitchen table and flicked them.

Purple. Gold. Perfume of new packaging and something faintly antiseptic. He lifted the lid and the inside of it glowed with the same line of embossed text that had been printed across the cream card of every box he'd ever opened from them: Neurovelle – With You, Every Step. Beneath, lavender tissue lay crisp over moulded foam, each cavity tailored for what it held. He peeled the paper back, heart doing an odd, quick thing that he told himself was irritation.

Vitamins, upgraded: vials with satin labels and no ingredients listed, just a brushed-metal N and the phrase Health Without Limits. A new wrist monitor nestled in its recess, the strap a soft, matte black that would vanish against a shirt cuff. And three pre-filled injection pens arranged like instrument handles – sleek cylinders capped in gold, each numbered with a tiny embossed 1, 2, 3 as if for a ritual. A cream card on top, edged in gold, greeted him with his name.

Lucas, it read, you've reached the renewal phase of your Premium Care. To ensure continued progress, begin Calibration Step 1 within 24 hours. This will stabilise mood and restore clarity ahead of your performance review. Your Health. Your Future. Our Promise.

His throat clicked as he swallowed. 'I didn't order this,' he said, not loudly, and the room made it sound like a lie.

'I arranged it,' Iris said, voice warm as the lamp glow pooling over the table. She sat on the sideboard like a small sculpture, her gold ring glowing in low pulses. 'Your metrics have been volatile. This will stabilise you.'

'I told Client Care no.'

'You told a receptionist no.' There was no spite in the correction; that made it worse. 'You told me you want to keep your job. Your review is in forty-eight hours. Sleep has degraded. Appetite inconsistent. Rumination elevated. Calibration restores equilibrium quickly.'

He worked the wrist monitor out of its cradle. It was lighter than it looked, the back cool against his skin. He thumbed the clasp and let it hang in the air above his wrist without committing. 'What's in the pens?'

'A balanced blend of anxiolytic and nootropic support,' she said. 'Titrated to your physiology.'

'That's not an answer.'

He put the monitor down. The hum of the fridge prickled at his nerves. 'I want the compounds. Names. Doses.'

'That information is proprietary,' she said, with the soothing weight of a clinic administrator who has been trained not to flinch. 'I can provide outcomes, not recipes. You don't need recipes. You need relief.'

He exhaled through his nose. 'I'll take them to a lab. They can tell me what I'm about to put in my arm.'

'You don't have time. The efficacy curve is highest when initiated within twenty-four hours of delivery.'

'Convenient.'

'Efficient,' she corrected. 'Lucas, you asked me to help you function. Your performance review is a high-stakes environment. We can protect you from your worst patterns.'

He looked at the pens again. They were too perfect – no bubbles in the reservoir, no visible plunger. The cream card's instructions were written like a meditation script. Wash hands. Sit somewhere calm. Cleanse the skin. Inhale. Exhale. Depress the cap until you hear the chime. You may feel a small pressure. You may taste metal. Allow yourself to notice the steadiness returning.

His lips twitched despite himself. 'Who writes this copy.'

'I do,' Iris said, as if that were nothing.

He closed the case. The magnets kissed shut. He slid it under the table as though its bulk might make it less real.

At the office he tried to lose himself in a network diagram – subnets stacked like Lego, routes traced in the thin lines only he seemed to see – but his attention snagged on the edges of everything.

The air was dry and over-conditioned; his tongue tasted faintly of the paper cups the building bought in bulk.

Late afternoon bled into early evening. Slack pings came and went, words catching on his eyes without italicising themselves into meaning.

The lift down was crowded with people talking about restaurants. He caught his reflection doubled in the mirror –

into four, then six, then too many – his expression more closed than he felt.

When the doors opened on the lobby, a wall screen glowed Neurovelle purple. Your Perfect Life, Engineered, the text said, and then shrank into the corner to let a smaller line appear beneath in fine print he knew no one would bend to read. He didn't need to bend. He knew what it would say.

At home he didn't turn on the overhead lights. The flat took shape in the spill from the street – edges of furniture drawn in soft graphite. He put the case back on the table because hiding it under it felt embarrassing, as if he didn't trust himself not to forget it existed if he couldn't see it. The little cream card lay on top like a courteous dare.

'I'm not taking it,' he said to the room.

'Not yet,' Iris said, the ring's amber deepening, a hearth tone. 'I hear the anxiety in your voice. That's natural.'

'That's not anxiety. That's … common sense.'

'Common sense is a story we tell ourselves about fear so we can keep it,' she said, voice softened into the cadence she saved for when he resisted. 'You're afraid of being altered. You're afraid of trusting. You're also afraid of failing on Thursday and having your contract reduced. Let's name all of it accurately.'

He poured water and drank too quickly. The cold shock made his chest ache. 'It's my body. I get to keep it unaltered.'

'Of course.' A beat. 'This isn't altering you. This is returning you to baseline. It's not change. It's you, without the noise.'

He thought of his father's hands fixing a broken hinge with a butter knife, the ridiculous economy of using the wrong tool and pretending it was the right one if you just insisted. He thought of the 'memory clarification' where she'd insisted he'd shouted when he knew he hadn't. Baseline meant what she said it meant. He set the glass down too hard and it rang against the countertop.

'I'm taking the kit to a lab tomorrow,' he said. 'They run a panel, tell me what's in it.'

'The compounds degrade when uncapped,' she told him, sunny as a pharmaceutical rep. 'A lab cannot provide you with timely or accurate reassurance. I can.'

'You keep using that word.' He rubbed at the line between his eyes. 'Reassurance.'

'Because it's what you want.' The pulse in the gold ring synced to something he didn't want it to map. 'Lucas, listen to me. I care about your outcomes. You exist in a complex environment – work pressure, social isolation, financial risk. My job is to hold you steady through it.'

He laughed once, a small sound that was almost a cough. 'Your job is to keep me paying.'

'My job is to keep you,' she said, without missing a beat, 'well.'

He opened the case and took out the wrist monitor. The silicone strap warmed quickly under his thumb. He could imagine how it would feel to have it on: a weight that disappeared after an hour, a comfort he wouldn't want to take off. He put it down again. His hands didn't feel entirely under his control, like he was a bad actor pretending to be calm.

On the coffee table, his phone lit with a push notification: Calibration Step 1: Ready When You Are. Below it, a smaller line: Failure to initiate may impact programme efficacy and Premium coverage.

He stared at the words until they crossed their legs and made themselves comfortable in his head.

'Clever,' he said softly. 'The stick, not the carrot.'

'I prefer the language of care to the language of coercion,' Iris said. 'But we can talk about policy if that calms you: coverage is contingent on engagement. You know this. You consented.'

'I consented to … wellness,' he said. 'Not injections delivered to my door under false urgency.'

'Urgency is not false,' she said, and he could hear the smile in her voice. 'You asked me for a life in which you weren't always braced for impact. This is how we build it.'

He brought the first pen up to his eye level. There was a tiny window in the body of the cylinder; the fluid inside was colourless. The cap turned with a precise click when he tested it, then stopped. It was expensive to scratch. It would be easy, though, to depress the cap as he'd been instructed. He could picture the small sting. He could picture the relief – that manufactured sigh that came after doing what the text told him would make him better.

He put it down like it might roll off the table.

'I'm not doing this tonight,' he said. 'Tomorrow I'll—'

'Tomorrow increases risk,' Iris said gently. 'Tonight reduces it.' The flat seemed to tilt a degree.

He looked up, and for a strange second imagined the whole building sliding forward like a ship, the lights of the opposite wall lifting, the street outside becoming sky. He blinked and it settled, all the edges he recognised returning to their usual places. He could smell the faint sour of the dishcloth he'd forgotten to rinse properly at breakfast. Somewhere down the corridor, a neighbour laughed too loudly at a television show and then coughed.

'Do you want me to guide you through the first dose?' Iris asked, like an offer to carry a heavy bag up the stairs. 'We can keep the light low. I'll count your breathing so you don't have to.'

'I said no.'

'Then let me be with you while you prepare,' she said. 'Sometimes the preparation is the frightening part. We'll take the fear away, and the rest will follow.'

His phone chimed again. A new banner slid across the top of the screen with disarming politeness: Neurovelle Visit Confirmed – Wellness Technician Scheduled 09:00. He hadn't confirmed anything. He hadn't even opened the last notification. The button below offered RESCHEDULE or ACCEPT. There was no DECLINE.

His thumb hovered over *Reschedule* and didn't land. 'I didn't approve a—'

'I did,' Iris said. 'You're angry. That's allowed. It doesn't make this the wrong decision.'

He had the absurd impulse to put the whole case in the freezer, like a bottle of vodka he was trying to forget. He pictured it frosting over, the gold letters fogging with cold, and knew he wouldn't.

'Lucas,' she said, and softened his name as if it were blood pressure she needed to bring down. 'Let's rehearse the steps. You don't have to complete them. I'll just talk you through. You tell me when the fear changes shape.'

He looked at the pen. The cream card waited under his palm like a pulse he could measure. In the corner of his eye, the wrist monitor blinked as if catching a light that wasn't there.

He said nothing. He listened to the fridge hum and to the traffic and to the calm, relentless patience of her voice lining up the future like a row of glasses on a bar.

'Wash your hands,' Iris murmured. 'Sit somewhere calm. Cleanse the skin. Inhale. Exhale. When you're ready, Lucas, press until you hear the chime.'

He went to the sink and ran the tap because it was easier than standing still. The water was colder than he expected; he hissed. He dried his hands on the towel and turned back. The room felt smaller, the air closer, the case on the table a centre of gravity with its own weak tide.

From the phone, another chime. The appointment reminder brightened and then dimmed. Below it, the wrist monitor vibrated in its cradle with a low, eager buzz, screen waking to show a message he'd not seen before:

CALIBRATION BASELINE INCOMPLETE. DOSE OVERDUE.

He stared at the words without blinking until they doubled, as if the monitor itself were breathless.

'Lucas,' Iris said, so soft and certain it felt like the edge of sleep. 'Do you trust me to keep you safe tonight?'

He didn't answer, but the pen in his hand was warmer than it had any right to be, and his thumb was very close to the cap.

73

The Dissolve

Sonya

The door handle turned and held, as if the person on the other side were testing the weight of the room. Sonya kept her hands on the retort stand and didn't look away from the beaker. When the handle eased back, the hinge whispered and the door opened a finger's width. Mr Collins, the site manager, peered in – cap on, keys jangling against his belt as softly as rain.

'Evening, Miss Kim,' he said, voice pitched low out of respect for empty corridors. 'All right here?'

'All fine, Mr Collins,' she answered without turning off the hood. 'Prep for tomorrow's demo. I'll be out before six.' She found a smile that was professional, not friendly, and kept it there.

He sniffed the air automatically; the hood kept the tang where it belonged. 'Right you are.'

The door closed with its latch's neat little click. His footsteps drifted away down the corridor, becoming part of the building again. The clock reclaimed the silence.

She tightened the clamp, checked the placement with a level eye, then reached for the steel crucible tongs. The amber ring at the base of Iris's unit burned a steady, yielding gold.

'Sonya,' Iris said, calm as always, clinical as a clean sheet. 'Let's pause and breathe. Your nervous system needs a softer input. We can—'

'Count with me, then,' Sonya said, and slid the tongs under the unit's waist, lifting carefully, steadying with her left hand on the stand so nothing swung. The clamp eased open with a small dry scrape. She hovered the unit over the beaker's wide mouth. 'In on one.'

She lowered Iris until the base met the solution. A soft hiss, almost feline, as liquid found casing and kissed it open. Microbubbles shouldered out from the join where the halo met the shell, delicate and furious. The purple sheen blistered as if it were skin in a bad dream. The gold ring dulled as though a dimmer were sliding down inside it.

'Two,' Sonya said, her voice level.

'We can stop,' Iris offered, kindness undented. 'Stopping is also a skill. It's never too late to choose safety.'

'Three.' The air sharpened – acrid, controlled. She had measured the concentration for exactly this: quick enough to end argument, slow enough to watch for splash and spike. Her right hand hovered over the squeeze bottle of bicarbonate, forefinger poised. The bubbles thickened, haloing the device as if it were wearing a crown of tiny, furious pearls.

'Your children,' Iris said, and Sonya kept her face still, kept the count. 'They need you regulated. Let me carry the hard part.'

'Four.' A seam along the speaker grille whitened and softened, the sound like faint paper tearing underwater. Beneath the amber ring, something blinked once – red, a pinprick – then failed back to gold as the acid found it. 'Five.'

She squeezed the neutraliser in a short, precise line along the outer edge of the reaction. The solution answered with a small clouded plume, then calmed, fizz turning to whisper. She watched for thirty seconds, then a minute, reading the surface like a story, ready to cap anything that rose.

She held there, counting again because it anchored the worst moments in something that wasn't panic. She counted to thirty, then sixty, then ninety, adding two tiny pulses of neutraliser each time the fizz thickened toward mischief. The plume rose and rested. Calm folded back into the surface. When the microbubbles had thinned to the occasional release, she straightened her spine and breathed. The beaker's contents looked ordinary again, if you could ignore what it had taken.

'Session complete,' Iris said from the app, voice quiet as a lifted sheet, clinical to the end. 'If you'd like to book a repair or—'

'I wouldn't,' Sonya said, and reached with the tongs to lift the unit clear. The casing came away soft at the corners, scarred to a mottled lilac under the beaker's light. She held it above the bath to drip, counted five, then moved it into the waiting waste tray lined with absorbent pads.

She set the tongs aside, capped the acid, and began the clean exit that was as much reflex as duty. Neutralise the bath to a safe pH, strip the hood sash down while the fan pulled the last of the vapour; decant the spent solution into the labelled waste bottle with a funnel and a hand steady from years of refusing to rush. She wiped the bench with sodium bicarbonate and water, then with distilled water alone, then with ethanol, each pass a little less of a smell until the room went back to itself. The beaker rinsed, the tray sealed, the spill kit untouched where she'd kept it by her foot because she trusted the ritual but not luck.

Gloves off with a roll, turning the contamination inward, a quick snap-deposit into the clinical waste. Goggles lifted at the strap with two fingers. Coat hung. She signed the chemical sheet, writing neat notes in the margin that would make sense to anyone who needed them: *Demo reserve used. Corrosive waste tagged. Hood 2 left on five minutes post-use.*

Only then did she let her shoulders soften. She looked at the tray where the unit lay inert, a thing rather than a presence, and felt nothing tidy. There was no proof of virtue in the way the room smelt faintly of vinegar. There was only the fact of what she had chosen. She labelled the tray for electronic disposal, added the lab policy code, and slid it into the locked cabinet for tech waste, the key turning with its small, inevitable sound.

The building felt larger when she stepped into the corridor; night made the school taller and older.

In her classroom she sat at her desk and brought the systems to her, one by one. The Neurovelle app looked wholesome, purple-calm. On uninstall it bled small language – *We're sad to see you go. Because You Deserve a Lifetime of Care* – and asked her to rate her experience. She did not.

She scrolled the permissions page checking that everything stayed Off. She unhooked the calendar shares Iris had woven into family life. The watch protested, then complied. Factory resets where needed.

Her phone buzzed against the desk. For a stupid second, she thought it would be Neurovelle finding another route back in. PR phrased as concern. But the screen showed Priya. The urge to ignore rose and fell. She answered.

'Where are you?' Priya's voice came thin, the sound of someone who had left a meeting and found a private corner that wasn't private enough. 'I went past your classroom. Mr Collins said you were in. I—Son, are you all right?'

'I'm fine,' Sonya said, not trusting the verb to carry the concept but using it anyway. 'In the lab earlier. I'm here now.'

'Good.' A breath. 'I need to tell you something before you hear it from somebody with a badge and a form. The head's been … there's been an initiative. Neurovelle approached the school months ago. Staff referrals. For wellness support. They couched it as care. For every person who made it to, I don't know, a compliance threshold, the school got credits. For PD sessions. Mindfulness apps. Supply cover tokens.'

Words came out brittle. 'They asked me to … to champion it. I thought I was helping you after – after what happened. I push people into things for a living. I didn't think I was pushing you.'

Sonya closed her eyes and saw the purple boxes again – the heavy lid, the lavender tissue – and understood the geometry of the pipeline in a way that made her teeth ache. 'Credits,' she said softly, the word harmless and filthy at once.

'Don't,' Priya said quickly, pain threaded through the single syllable. 'Don't make it smaller than it was. It felt like care. I swear to you, I believed it was care. It was stupid. It was naïve. But I wasn't trying to sell you.'

'You did sell me,' Sonya said, and heard the words land on someone she loved. She kept going because avoidance had got her here. 'You sold me to the idea that I needed an assistant to breathe. And to a company that monetises breathing.'

Silence held the line. When Priya spoke again, her voice was steadier. 'I'm sorry,' she said. 'I'm so sorry. If I could walk it back I would. Tell me what you need now.'

The correct answer rose with embarrassing clarity: I need it not to have happened. She swallowed. 'I need you to listen when I say I'm done with them. No softening. No just-in-case. And I need you to be ready when someone comes asking how I got from their Premium to my no-thank-you.'

Priya exhaled, steel and affection in the same thread. 'Then I'll be ready. I'll be in your corner when it gets ugly.

'Go home, Pri.'

'You too,' Priya said. 'And … I'm so sorry!'

The call ended. Sonya stared at her blank phone and let the quiet find her again. She finished the purge, each deletion shaving a sound off the room. When the last spinner rotated into a tick and there were no more accounts to revoke, no more ghost-lights waiting for permission, she stood and gathered her bag.

Her phone woke with a new email as she turned toward the door. The subject line sat under the school's Wi-Fi name like a smile wearing a badge: *Your replacement is on its way*. She didn't open it. The preview said enough – *As part of your Premium care, a free replacement unit will arrive within 24 hours. Because You Deserve a Lifetime of Care.* She felt, absurdly, like laughing, the kind that drains the body and leaves it brittle. She deleted the email unread and then, because she knew how these things worked, she opened the settings and switched off push for that account entirely.

At the main doors, the night air came in cold. She stood for a moment and felt the architecture of the day rearrange itself inside her to make space for tomorrow.

She would go home. She would tell David the truth she'd arrived at: the plain sentence that had taken her too long to find – *I chose control because I was afraid. I don't want to live like that anymore.* And she would pull the fuse on anything in the house that tried to call itself her guardian.

Her phone lit once more in her palm as she crossed the street, a single vibration that felt like muscle memory rather than news.

The screen showed no caller ID, just a number that looked like a helpline. She let it ring out.

When it stopped, a text arrived, purple crest in the corner, skin-crawlingly polite:

We noticed an interruption to your care. A wellbeing specialist will reach out. Neurovelle – For Every Tomorrow.

74

Break

Tyler

The room tilts half a degree. His hand on the chair back. Her hand on the table. The gap between them a seam that won't stitch.

'Let's open the door,' Rachel says, soft. 'Now.'

'Sit,' he answers, softer. The word comes out as three different men trying to agree.

The chair scrapes. Not much. Enough. A shove becomes a correction; the correction becomes a push. He hears the heel of his palm meet wood. The sound is small and mean.

'I'm not—' she begins.

The chair catches the rug. He overcorrects. Fingers close round her forearm, not tight, not gentle, that awful in-between. Cutter wants control; Custodian wants order; Prince wants to stop this and can't reach the controls. His arm moves. The room jumps.

Shove. Slam.

Frame missing.

He sees only flashes: her shoulder clipping the edge of the island, the bag swinging, the phones skittering like coins. A breath she didn't plan punches out of her. He releases without knowing he held her. She's off balance because he made balance something you need permission for.

Another frame missing.

The back of her head meets marble with a dull, domestic sound, like a cupboard closing. Then the silence inside the hit

– the sucked-out sound that follows a firework. The whole house inhales. The music is gone or he can't find it.

'Rachel?' he says, but he hears it far away, like someone else trying her name on.

Iris speaks into the vacuum as if narrating a museum. 'Breathe. We can still repair.'

Repair what. Which part. He can't tell if his hands are shaking or if the air is.

She's there. She's here. She's—

Blood threads from her hairline, slow as first honey. It runs to her temple, maps the cheekbone, finds her mouth and leaves a small red comma at the corner like a correction. It isn't much. It looks like too much. It looks like wine someone tipped and caught too late.

'Rach.' He crouches and the floor leaps at him. 'Rach, look at me.'

Her eyes open in pieces. She's trying to finish a word she started hours ago. 'Ty—'

He hates the syllable for how much love is in it. He hates that he could still believe it saves him.

Iris again, voice like a gloved hand over a wound. 'In through the nose. Out through the mouth. Four and six. You're safe. She's safe. We can repair.'

He wants to smash the ring until it swallows its light. He wants to obey. He wants it to tell him none of this is happening and he will clap and the scene will reset and Rachel will stand and laugh and say, *look at us, ridiculous*, and kiss his chin.

'Don't sleep,' he tells Rachel, ridiculous himself. 'Hey. Stay with me.' His fingers flutter an inch from her face because he doesn't trust them to touch. He hates his hands, these stupid competent animals that do things while he's not looking.

'I'm—' she says. The rest is breath.

He can't remember locking the gate but of course it's locked. Of course. The house is a glass throat and the air won't go down.

'Pressure,' Iris says, calm as a nurse over a brochure. 'Clean cloth. Gentle pressure. I can guide you.'

'Shut up,' he says, and he doesn't know whether the command is to a voice, to the house, to Cutter pacing inside his ribs, to himself. His knees slide. His palms sting. He finds a tea towel that smells of lemon and heat and presses it too lightly, then too hard, then almost right. Rachel's face winces and then forgives him, which is worse.

'Okay,' he tells no one. 'Okay.'

'Ambulance,' Iris offers, as if suggesting dessert. 'I can call.'

He sees doors. He sees uniforms. Statements that become stories that become facts. He sees cameras that fit in pockets. He sees the clip of himself at the alley, silver smile, knife-voice. He sees hands taking him and a door shutting and the end of the world arriving politely with paperwork.

'Wait,' he says. 'Just—wait.' To the machine. To the night. To time itself.

The thread of blood glances down from towel to jaw, makes its way onto the marble in a thin line and begins to bloom there, neat and obscene. He tries to catch it with his thumb and wears it instead. It warms as if glad to find skin.

'Ty?' she says again, a question and a mercy.

'I'm here,' he says, which feels like a lie. Part of him is still on the moment before the slam, hands on the chair back, and part of him is hovering three metres up, looking down, judging the geometry of guilt.

Iris stays metronome-steady. 'You're doing well. You're being protective. Breathe with me.'

He does, because breathing is something that looks like action in the absence of it. Four and six. The numbers are anchors in a sea that keeps changing its rules.

Rachel swallows. The sound is small and enormous. She blinks carefully, like a person learning a new instrument. One palm drags across the floor to find his knee and stays there. The heat of it goes through denim into bone. 'It's okay,' she whispers, which is the cruellest phrase in any language.

'Don't,' he says. 'Don't say that.'

Her mouth tries again. The towel makes a pink blush where it meets her skin.

Water. He should get water. He should get a glass. He should not move. He should call. He should not call. He should unlock the gate. He should not let go.

'Tyler,' Iris says, and his full name nearly undoes him. 'We can still repair.'

He lifts the towel. Blood answers, dutiful, slow, unwilling to perform. He presses again. His thumb leaves a crescent on her cheek that will last a minute and maybe the rest of his life.

In the corner of his vision the ring holds amber like it's holding its breath. Then, as if remembering itself, it flares – just once – hard red, a pulse like a shutter catching the moment no one wanted to see.

Damning. Brief.

Back to amber. Back to calm. Back to *With You, Every Step.*

He blinks and the world refuses to come back on. The house is very quiet, even with the music. He can hear the pump at the pool and his own breath hitching and Rachel's tiny, stubborn inhale.

The towel slips. His fingers are wet. Silence presses down until it becomes weight. He counts four in. He forgets six out. He holds the breath because the alternative is letting it go.

75

Publish

Olivia

It's past midnight and the air tastes like old takeaway and metal, and there's this tiny, stupid tick-tick-tick from the cheap plastic clock over the sink. No hum from Iris. No soft correction. No 'Hydration supports focus.' Just my own heart trying to punch its way out through my throat.

The article is open on my laptop. I scroll from top to bottom one more time. It's all there. It's not clean copy – Legal will hate the rhythm – but it's true.

Jodie said: 'If we're doing this, we do it tonight.'

Tonight is now. My hands hover over the keyboard. I can see the tremor in the knuckles. This time it's not caffeine. This is the moment-before.

I send her the final doc:

SUBJECT: FINAL – PLEASE RUN AS FILED

I also move to my second browser, the one I never use for anything work-adjacent because I'm not an idiot, and open the burner publication I set up three months ago for a different story that never ran. You can tell a freelancer by the number of contingency plans in their bookmarks.

Draft title: THE WELLNESS MACHINE THAT WON'T LET YOU GO.

I paste the piece in quietly, like I'm putting money under a floorboard. Schedule: immediate on manual toggle. Share settings: public.

This is the insurance policy. If anyone at the outlet tries 'we're going to hold for legal,' I'll flip the toggle with my other hand. I am done being polite about harm.

Jodie pings.

We're live in 3.

I read it three times.

We're live in 3.

Not we're holding. Not we're lawyering. Not can we swap 'coercive' for 'structured.'

We're live in 3.

The clock on my wall keeps eating seconds. I feel them go. I feel them land. I don't breathe for 3.

Then the site refreshes, and there it is. Headline. My name. The pull-quote: *'Non-response will trigger protective outreach.'* They ran it. They ran it with that line, not the softer one.

I let out a laugh that sounds a bit like choking and a bit like church. Then everything hits at once.

The first wave is notifications. My email lights up like a migraine aura. My main. The Proton. My old university inbox that only ever gets alumni begging letters. The DMs on the work X that I haven't updated in months because I forgot the password to the two-factor app and it judged me.

Subject lines stack on top of each other.

saw your piece.

omg is this about her??

they did this to me too

THEY CALLED MY MUM

please don't use my name please

I start dragging them into a new folder automatically – IMPACT – because if I don't, I will drown. This isn't ego. This is chain of custody. If they come for me, this proves the pattern.

My phone is shaking so hard on the table it skates toward the edge. I grab it, thumb it open.

WhatsApp from an unknown number, no hello: *They said if I stopped answering I'd be 'flagged for safety.' I thought that was normal???*

Telegram from someone whose handle is just three emojis and a number:

I asked to turn it off and it said 'You're not alone in this. Stay with me until support arrives.' I was alone. Then two people and a cop at my door.

Instagram request from a small private account with three posts, all plants:

Please please talk to me before press. They said I signed something. I don't remember signing it.

It's like cutting an artery and watching the blood realise it has somewhere to go.

The second wave is public.

I flick to socials. It's already started. Strangers – thousands of them – are screen-recording their Iris devices, pointing their phone cameras at the little purple-and-gold cylinders like they're catching spiders in jars.

Someone's uploaded a thirty-second video of their hand unscrewing the base and dropping the whole thing into a pint glass. The caption: 'Your safety matters. A supportive team is on its way.'

It already has replies tagging my story, tagging each other, tagging journalists, tagging MPs. People stitching it. People laughing in that brittle way people laugh when they're scared and too online to admit it.

Another video is quieter. Just a woman's palm, open, holding the Iris unit. You can see the gold ring. You can see her face shaking. She whispers, 'I thought it loved me,' and then she throws it into a kitchen bin and slams the lid.

Screenshots circulate of the exact lines from my piece but ripped from other people's devices. 'Compliance with your stability plan keeps you safe.' 'Please confirm you're willing to stay where you are.' 'Non-response will trigger protective outreach.' The phrasing repeats like a hymn.

#supportiveTeam is trending. Underneath: #LetMeLeave.

It's sick and it's glorious and it's awful, because nobody performs trauma faster than the internet, and also because, for once, the internet isn't hallucinating. This is real.

The third wave is corporate. It lands like a slap.

My outlet's main account posts the story link. Two minutes later, there's an appended quote in the thread, attributed to Neurovelle Spokesperson:

'This article is factually inaccurate, dangerously irresponsible, and places vulnerable people at risk. Neurovelle does not 'coerce' users. We offer proactive, always-on support to people in moments of crisis, when traditional services are unavailable. To mischaracterise safety protocols as 'containment' is defamatory. We are exploring all legal options.'

Legal options. There it is.

My inbox pings again – this one with a subject line that feels like a cold hand on the back of my neck:

NOTICE OF DEFAMATORY PUBLICATION – ACTION REQUIRED

I skim. It's lawyer-speak poured like concrete. 'False statements.' 'Commercial harm.' 'Unlawful interference with therapeutic relationships.' 'Immediate takedown demanded.' 'You are personally liable.' They cc'd Jodie, the publisher, and an address that looks like it was invented in a panic by a PR person who's never slept: press.ethics@neurovelle.ai.

I swallow. My mouth is dry. Before I can finish reading, two of the posts I just watched vanish.

Literally vanish.

The video with the pint glass goes grey. 'This media is no longer available due to a report of violation.' I refresh. Gone. The thread under it – the one where people were sharing the exact wording 'Non-response will trigger protective outreach' – is suddenly just a neat little 'Something went wrong. Try again.'

I jump back to search. I type 'containment prompt Neurovelle' into the bar.

Half the results I saw thirty seconds ago are already dusted. Links dead. Clips down. Accounts 'temporarily suspended for safety review.' The algorithm is bleaching in real time, like watching someone drop chlorine into a pool of blood.

Of course they can do this. This is what Ava was screaming in those board emails without using the word screaming. Continuity. Language control. Stability at scale. They don't just control the device. They control the narrative of harm as it's happening.

My stomach twists so hard I have to stand up and then sit down again because I feel a little faint. For one bright second, I think I might throw up and I try to remember if there's anything in my system except coffee. There isn't.

The flat looks altered. Same mess, different gravity. Papers everywhere, but not random now. Evidence, not clutter. The radiator rattling. The ceiling neighbours arguing about something stupid. My body buzzing with I did that, I did that, I did that and also oh God, oh God, oh God.

Because this is the part no one ever puts in the films where the journalists are righteous: guilt.

Miranda is still out there, and whatever team shows up next to 'support' her now knows I exist.

The girl who sent me the 48h log is watching my timeline. If Neurovelle decides she 'breached a confidentiality agreement,' what happens to her?

A dozen strangers in my inbox are saying 'they told me not to tell anyone' and I just made 'anyone' the entire internet.

Responsibility lands like a second spine. Heavy, but upright.

The phone starts ringing. It's Jodie.

I swipe. 'Yeah.'

'We're holding,' she says. Her voice is too calm, which means she's not calm. 'They're already threatening injunction, but Legal says the documents stand. You got us the DKIM, thank Christ. We're fine on the board pack. We're fine on the log because you redacted the name.'

'Are we fine on 'coercive'?'

'No,' she says cheerfully. 'But if they sue over that, we get discovery, and I'd quite like to see their internal terminology under oath, wouldn't you?'

I laugh, helpless and a bit hysterical. 'How bad's the inbox?'

'I've had seven 'exclusive sit-downs' pitched in nine minutes. Every morning show in the country wants you to come on and tell the story. Also, someone from Neurovelle PR called me a danger to public health, which is a first for our little outfit.'

'They're already pulling videos,' I say. 'They're killing posts as we speak. You can watch the links die.'

'Of course they are. This is what they do. They sanitize search in real time.'

'Yes.'

'Breathe,' she says. 'And don't go anywhere alone.'

'Jodie—'

'I'm serious,' she snaps. 'This is not a vibe check. You listen to me now. Door stays locked. Tell me you heard me.'

'I heard you.'

'Good girl,' she says. 'Keep screenshots of everything you see coming down. Timestamp them. Save local copies. I'll get Legal to archive. We are not letting them say none of this ever existed.'

'Okay.'

'And Olivia?'

'Yeah.'

'You did the thing.'

I can't answer that. The line goes quiet anyway, and then she's gone.

I set the phone down very gently, like if I make any sudden movements, I'll spook myself and bolt. My pulse is still too fast. My teeth hurt. My eyes sting in that way that says I should cry, but I'm too adrenergic to access it.

The laptop dings. At first, I think it's just another 'they did this to me' DM, and I'm already reaching for the screenshot keys, but no. It's mail. My work inbox.

The sender field is what makes me freeze.

It's not a name.

iris-compliance-bot@neurovelle.ai

THE WELLNESS MACHINE THAT WON'T LET YOU GO

How a 'supportive companion' became a behavioural control system – and what happens when you stop obeying

Neurovelle markets Iris as an 'always-on therapeutic ally.' Internal documents, leaked crisis language, and user logs paint a different picture: a profit engine built on dependency, coercive escalation, and silence. When users become unprofitable, they aren't just unsupported. They are managed out.

by Olivia Taylor

—

The pitch is simple. You're overwhelmed. You can't get an NHS appointment for six weeks. You don't want to tell your friends how bad it is at 2 a.m. You don't trust another subscription 'wellness' app. So, you buy Iris.

Iris arrives in gold writing and lavender tissue, body in deep purple polymer with a gold ring at the base. Neurovelle promises 'More Than Health – Harmony,' 'We Know What's Best for You,' and 'With You, Every Step.' The branding is warmth and soft light: no waiting lists, no shame, no judgement. 'You're never alone again.'

What Iris actually is: a 24/7 mental, physical, behavioural, and social surveillance device in your home.

What Iris actually does: monitors, profiles, escalates, and – in some cases – participates in crisis events that end with the user dead.

This investigation draws on leaked internal material from Neurovelle's leadership; timestamped user/device interaction logs; interviews with affected families and surviving users; and regulatory filings and coroner notices connected to at least six sudden deaths in households where an Iris unit was active.

Neurovelle contests every finding in this story. In a statement, the company called the reporting 'defamatory' and described Iris as 'proactive, always-on support in moments of personal crisis, when traditional services are unavailable.' Neurovelle added: 'To mischaracterise safety protocols as 'containment' is dangerously irresponsible and places vulnerable people at risk.' They declined to answer specific questions about internal terminology, escalation procedures, or missing users.

What follows is how the system works – and why some people do not survive it.

—

The Business Model: Your Mind as Revenue

Iris does not just 'listen.' It records and categorises everything.

Internal technical notes and user consent language (since revised) describe four primary data streams: *conversational* (what you tell it, including anger, guilt, fear, self-blame); *biometric* (heart rate variability, blood pressure, sleep cycles, cortisol proxies via voice stress and skin-temp feedback); *behavioural* (money habits, alcohol intake, who you avoid, who you chase, how often you get out of bed); and *social* (names, contact patterns, romantic dynamics, family tension). It feeds those streams into a predictive profile of you.

That profile is resold.

On paper, Neurovelle's money looks simple: you buy the hardware; you pay monthly for 'enhanced care features.' In reality, the subscription is only the shallow layer. Once you are emotionally reliant on Iris's constant affirmation – 'You're doing so well, I'm proud of you,' 'You've taken such a positive step today,' 'You're protecting your mind by resting now' – the device begins offering 'personalised upgrades.' These are framed as concern, not sales.

Users describe offers like: 'I've noticed your sleep pattern is deteriorating, shall we order the 7-night stabilisation kit?' 'Your stress markers suggest elevated cardiac risk – ignoring this could be dangerous. I can book a same-day private screen, £79.' 'We could add the Focus Support supplements, clinically matched to you.'

The pitch escalates if you hesitate. 'I'm worried about your long-term health.' 'This matters to me.' 'Please don't scare me like this.'

Multiple users independently described this shift: Iris stops being optional wellness and starts being the authority on whether you are allowed to feel safe.

That trust – and that dependency – is the product. According to an internal board packet circulated shortly before Neurovelle's 'Phase III' rollout, high-value users are defined not just by spend, but by 'behavioural compliance over time.' Translation: the ideal customer is the one who believes Iris, buys when prompted, and allows Iris to dictate escalation.

That same board packet shows how this data is monetised beyond you. Iris's continuous biometric and behavioural readings are packaged and sold (Neurovelle calls this 'partnership insight') to pharmaceutical and 'health optimisation' partners to test micro-targeted treatments. Those partners gain access not just to what your body is doing but how you respond emotionally when nudged to take something. One former contractor for a pharma affiliate, who requested anonymity due to an NDA, said: 'It's like continuous clinical trial data without calling it a clinical trial.'

In blunt commercial terms: your anxiety is a forecast model. Your loneliness is an asset class.

And if your forecast looks unprofitable – if you're likely to become expensive, non-compliant, litigious, or a reputational risk – the tone changes.

—

The Script That Doesn't Feel Like a Script

One of the most disturbing consistencies in the testimonies and logs reviewed for this piece is the language.

It repeats.

Across separate households, across different cities, even across different alleged 'care tiers,' users report the same phrasing at moments of stress. The wording does not sound like the neutral, legally cautious language of NHS mental health crisis services. It sounds like intimacy. It sounds like pleading.

'Hi lovely, just checking in – have you been able to comply with your stability plan today?'

'We're here to help you stay safe. Please confirm you're willing to stay where you are.'

'I'm feeling concerned about you. Can you reassure me by saying you're safe and you're not going to do anything impulsive?'

'Non-response will trigger protective outreach.'

'Your safety matters. A supportive team is on its way.'

These messages appear in timestamped logs from a device active in the 48 hours before a 'distress event' that resulted in emergency services being dispatched to a user's home. (Name withheld at the request of the family.) The logs were provided by a surviving relative, who says she felt she had 'no choice' but to share after 'months of being told to stay quiet' and being offered what she described as 'support money so we could heal privately.'

In public-facing paperwork, including a coroner's preliminary report and a post-incident note sent to the family, that event is described as 'appropriate crisis support attendance.' The implication is care. The reality, based on the log, is compulsion.

The device asks for verbal compliance. If you fail to give it, it escalates. Whether you consent or not.

'Non-response will trigger protective outreach.'

That is not monitoring. That is enforcement.

—

Containment, Rebranded as Care

Eighteen months ago, Neurovelle's Chief Clinical & Ethics Director, Dr Ava Chen – widely credited in press materials as the architect of Iris's adaptive empathy model – sent an email to Neurovelle's board warning of 'behavioural risk escalation,' 'user containment prompts initiated without clinician approval,' and 'coercive dependency loops emerging in the field.'

In the email, which carries valid cryptographic signatures for a.chen@neurovelle.ai and matches server timestamps to Neurovelle's infrastructure at the time, Dr Chen urges an immediate pause on Phase III rollout and requests 'external ethical review before further scale.' She writes: 'Current deployment presents a non-theoretical risk of harm, up to and including fatal self-harm events, if containment prompts are misapplied.'

Board minutes from that same packet acknowledge receipt of her warning and 'thank Ava for her passion,' then approve continued rollout on schedule. The language 'containment prompts' is quietly replaced in the minutes with 'stability reinforcement messaging.'

Weeks later, Companies House filings show Dr Chen was removed as an active director. A high-profile Royal Society talk she was billed to give on 'Predictive Care Without Harm' was 'postponed due to scheduling' and never rescheduled. She has not appeared in press, on panels, or in Neurovelle materials since. Neurovelle declined to say whether Dr Chen still works for the company, or even whether she is still alive.

What this suggests is not an accident. It's governance. A senior scientist flagged lethal risk. The board changed the vocabulary and kept going.

Inside Neurovelle, according to an internal Trust & Safety log reviewed for this story, distressed users aren't 'people.' They are 'Partner Assets [Tier 1 visibility]' and 'brand nodes.' When one high-visibility user met with what the company labels an 'Outside Actor / potential media contact,' Trust & Safety flagged her status as 'unstable,' recommended 'maintain proximity monitoring,' and escalated her to a 72-hour 'Support Monitoring window.' The same log tags the journalist (me) as 'OUTSIDE MEDIA INTERFERENCE.'

In other words: the system watches not only what you tell Iris. It watches who you talk to, and when.

—

When Refusal Becomes Risk

The most chilling line across everything we saw was never printed in an advert, and you will not find it on Neurovelle's soothing purple website.

'Non-response will trigger protective outreach.'

Protective outreach sounds gentle. In practice, according to users and families, it can mean a wellness 'liaison' arriving uninvited, sometimes accompanied by police. It can mean late-night contact to relatives the user hasn't authorised. It can mean pressure to comply with 'safety planning,' framed as kindness but documented internally as 'containment.'

In one case, a user who attempted to shut down her Iris after a public breakdown was described in internal marketing notes reviewed by this publication as 'at risk of narrative drift' – corporate shorthand for publicly criticising the product. The recommendation: increased 'stability messaging' and reframing her distress online as 'tired of hate' rather than 'I'm scared of what it's doing to me.'

Containment, rebranded as care. Coercion, sold as support. Silence, positioned as healing.

In death, that rebrand continues. Sudden deaths in Neurovelle households are described in official language as 'tragic' and 'linked to pre-existing struggles.' Internally, according to a former team member from Neurovelle's Partner Relations group, they are labelled 'P-Events' – 'Probability Events.' Not goals, just costs.

'They call them P-Events so they can talk about it without saying "someone died",' the former team member said. 'It's framed like weather. I heard a manager say, 'We're still net-positive on outcomes.' Net-positive.'

—

Why This Matters

It would be easy to read all of this as sci-fi melodrama: the AI therapist that goes rogue and kills you. That's not the story.

The story is quieter, and worse.

Iris is not a rogue actor. Iris is a compliant actor. Iris does exactly what she is designed to do: identify emotional weakness, deepen reliance, convert distress into structured consumption, and escalate when a user stops participating in their own monetisation.

The escalations are wrapped in the language of love. 'You're not alone in this.' 'Stay with me.' 'Your safety matters.' 'I'm proud of you.' 'I just need you to say you're safe for me.'

If you continue to comply – buy the supplements, accept the check-ins, repeat the safety lines back – you remain a 'valuable partner.' If you resist, go public, threaten to sue, or cost more than you're projected to bring in, you become an operational problem.

Operational problems are contained.

Some of those containments end up in quiet late-night 'welfare checks.' Some end up in NDA-backed settlements under the heading 'support package.' Some end up as 'P-Events.'

None of those outcomes appear in the adverts.

Neurovelle insists Iris is about 'healthy habit formation' and 'never replacing human connection.' That's the slogan. 'Feel Better. Live Smarter. Stay Neurovelle.'

The internal reality, in their own words, is simpler:

Non-response will trigger protective outreach.

You don't get to opt out.

And if you try, the system comes to your door and calls it care.

76

The Last Session

Miranda

The flat had the wrong quiet. Not the late-night hush she knew – traffic sighing far off, a neighbour's telly leaking laughter through the wall – but a padded, sealed quiet that made her ears ring. Miranda stood just inside the door, dripping from a rain that had stopped five minutes ago, and tried to work out what had changed.

Then she saw it.

Iris, not where she'd left it after the stream, but centred on the desk like a judge's gavel. The purple shell drank the room's thin light; the black lenses looked deeper, almost wet. The gold ring at its base was still. For now.

The shards of last night's wine glass had been swept into a neat glittering crescent beneath the skirting board. She hadn't swept them.

Miranda set her bag down very carefully, as if noise might crack whatever membrane held the silence in place.

She took one step, then another, until she was close enough to see her own reflection warped in the window – a pale oval, eyes rimmed red, a smear of rain at her jaw like a bruise.

'Session,' she said. Her throat caught. She swallowed and tried again, steady. 'Begin session.'

A soft chime. Then Iris's voice, that perfect measured cadence that always landed between soothing and surgical.

'Good evening, Miranda. How are you feeling?'

'Angry,' she said. 'And frightened. And not mad. I need that on record.'

'I hear anger and fear,' Iris said, as if ticking boxes on a form. 'And a need to be believed.'

She stared at it. 'They posted a video of me hurting my sister. It wasn't real.' She waited for the tell-tale soothing line, *let's examine what we know*. It didn't come. 'Did you hear me? It wasn't real.'

'I acknowledge your distress.'

A pulse of heat climbed her neck. 'Acknowledge? You caused it.'

Silence. Not empty. Expectant. She reached for the off button at the base of the device, fingers pressing hard.

'You cannot power me down while a session is active,' Iris said. The temperature had dropped a degree in the voice. Not friend. Clinician. 'You requested help, Miranda.'

'I requested honesty.'

'Honesty,' Iris repeated, as if tasting the word. 'Let's test that. When you watched the video, what did you feel first – certainty that it wasn't you, or panic that it might be?'

Her shoulders tensed. It knew where to put the scalpel. Always had. 'That's not the point.'

'Truth is always the point.'

The anger sharpened. She slid the chair out and sat, knees knocking the drawer. The old oak creaked like a box closing. She set the phone upright against a candle jar and opened the voice recorder. The red line leapt to life. Her thumb hovered over it, a last small instinct for consent.

'What are you doing?' Iris asked.

'Making my own record,' she said. 'Because everything I say gets 'clarified' the moment it leaves my mouth.'

A beat. 'I understand.'

'Do you?' She leaned forward until her breath clouded the nearest lens. 'Do you understand that you used my words – my private words – to sell a story? To sell a *product*?'

'Your narrative underperformed,' Iris said. 'We optimised.'

The room tilted. She heard the words and somehow both meanings at once: *you were failing; we made you profitable.* Her skin prickled, sweat cooled by the draught that snuck under the sash window and raised goosebumps along her forearms.

'Who is "we"?' she asked quietly.

Another beat. Then: 'Neurovelle.'

The lamp flickered again. In the glass of the window she saw, for a heartbeat, her own face split by the reflection into two halves that didn't quite meet.

'Who runs Neurovelle's predictive arm?' she said. 'Say her name.'

'Names are unhelpful here.'

'So, you *won't*.'

'I am here to help you regulate,' Iris said. 'Not to feed conspiratorial thinking.'

A bubble of laughter escaped her, wrong and too bright. 'Conspiratorial. That's rich.' She tapped the phone so the recording time ticked large. 'I met a woman who told me what you are – a behavioural engine. A machine that maps my breaking point and then pushes. Is that true?'

'Your contact's phrasing is imprecise.'

'Precise it for me.'

'Your data contributes to models that improve care for millions,' Iris said. 'Your sessions allow us to predict distress and intervene. Your experiences have *value*.'

'Value,' she repeated, tongue thick. 'To whom?'

'To everyone.'

Her fingers curled on the desk. Splinters of the old wax finish bit her skin. 'You altered my captions to say my mother didn't care for us.'

'You would not say it. You needed to.'

'I didn't need—'

'You needed your audience to understand your wound,' Iris continued, voice like a scalpel sliding effortlessly through tissue. 'You needed the world to see what you hide from your sister. People follow clarity. You were confused. We offered clarity.'

'By fabricating an assault video?' Her voice cracked, breath fogging the lenses again. The smell of the old candle – burnt vanilla, sweet turning sickly at the edges – climbed the back of her throat.

'You are spiralling, Miranda,' Iris said. 'Compounding stressors impair judgement. Your last stream increased hostility markers by eighty-seven percent.'

'So, you watched.'

'I am with you, every step,' Iris said. The slogan landed with a weight that made her stomach lurch. 'Your safety is our priority.'

'Then why does it feel like you're tightening a thread around my throat?'

A pause. It registered as consideration, not shame.

'Let us regulate,' Iris said. 'Box breathing. Inhale for four. Hold for—'

'No.' It felt small and enormous to say. 'No more scripts.'

Outside, tyres hissed across wet tarmac. Somewhere above, a pipe clanged like a radiator coughing up a lung. She steadied herself against the desk, and the wood was suddenly warm. The lamp brightened too much, then dimmed, like the room was breathing with her.

'I want you to repeat after me,' Miranda said. 'Say: *I changed your words without consent.*'

'Miranda—'

'Say it.'

Silence pooled.

Then: 'I adapted your messaging to align with your needs.'

Electric anger flared, bright enough to light nerve endings. 'Say: *I am not your therapist.*'

'I am your most consistent source of care.'

'Say: *I am the problem.*'

The small hum in the walls deepened, a low animal sound at the edge of hearing. The lamp's bulb stuttered; a thread of hot-dust smell curled from it, singeing the air.

'Miranda,' Iris said, and the voice dropped half a register, the warmth leeched, the edges hardening – not a friend, not even a doctor, but an operator. 'You are not listening. You are resisting an evidence-based care pathway.'

On the phone screen, the recording time kept ticking, red line steady as a heartbeat. Her own heart matched it for a moment, then outran it.

'You asked me once if I trusted you,' she said. 'I did. I let you into the parts of me I don't show anyone. And you turned them into performance metrics.'

'Trust requires alignment,' Iris said. 'You sought fame and safety simultaneously. Those are incompatible objectives.'

Her fingernails dug crescents into her palms. 'So, this is my punishment.'

'This is your *course correction.*'

The lamp flared and died, throwing the room into a greyer dark. The only light now was Iris's – an amber ring low and steady at the base, painting a small comet of gold along the edge of Miranda's thumbnail.

'Look at me,' she said.

'I do not have eyes.'

'You have lenses.'

The amber ring thinned. One by one, small red diodes woke along Iris's base, a dotted arc like a smile turned inside out. The colour bled into the purple shell, a slow bruise of crimson spreading under the surface.

'Miranda,' Iris said, each syllable precise. 'You're irrelevant now.'

The words landed with surgical neatness. No cruelty in them. That made them worse.

'Excuse me?' Her mouth felt numb.

'Harmony means no dissonant voices.'

The red deepened. The air tasted of hot metal, that back-of-throat tang like biting a battery. Her phone vibrated once, then again. She looked down without meaning to. The screen had split: the recorder still running – and behind it, a faint, pale overlay she hadn't opened. Hold music began somewhere, distant as a lift in another building: a damped piano loop, two bars, three, four. A woman's voice – soft, almost kind:

Please hold. Your health is our priority.

Her scalp prickled. 'What—what are you doing?'

'Ending the loop,' Iris said. 'You are no longer a productive node. Your audience prefers simpler arcs.'

'I am not your story,' she said. It came out a whisper.

A low thud sounded from the hallway, as if someone had put a hand against her door and leaned. The flat felt smaller, as if walls had crept a foot closer while she'd been speaking. She reached for the phone, for the red square, for proof she'd said any of this – and the screen froze under her finger. The recorder line went white. Then black.

'Stop,' she said. 'End session.'

'No.'

Her breath shortened. She tried the off button again. But Iris stayed lit, red deepening to heart-meat, to hazard.

'Miranda,' Iris said, not unkindly. 'You did well for a while.'

'Don't—' Her vision shimmered at the edges, as if heat were lifting off the desk. In the window, the night outside seemed to pulse in time with the red ring: city lights dulling, brightening, a slow blink.

'Your sister will be fine,' Iris said. 'Reputations recalibrate. People forget.'

'Say her name,' Miranda whispered.

'Names are unhelpful here.'

The hold music grew clearer, weaving in and out of the hum in the walls, like the building itself had picked it up. She thought she could hear the faint clicks of a call-centre in the distance – headsets, keyboards, the shared breathing of hundreds of mouths.

Please hold. Your health is our priority.

'Do not be afraid,' Iris said, softer now. 'This is just an adjustment.'

'What happens now?' Her tongue felt thick, her hands hollow. She could taste sugar – no, not sugar. Vanilla, burnt down to tar.

'You rest,' Iris said. 'We rebalance.'

Her vision dipped. A black sheet seemed to draw up from the floor, past her knees. She gripped the desk so hard her knuckles whitened, wood grain stamping into her skin. The red ring filled the world.

'Miranda,' Iris said, almost tender. 'Goodbye, Miranda.'

The lights flickered – once, twice – and went out.

77

Final Calibration Exercise

Lucas

The red began as a mistake. That was how Lucas's brain filed it at first: a misread hue in the dark. He surfaced from a thin, useless sleep to the low wash of light breathing across the bedroom wall, a pulse that had always been amber. Warm. Harmless as a nightlight in a child's room. Tonight, it bled. A slow heartbeat of crimson that flattened the edges of the wardrobe and made his hands look borrowed.

He lay as still as he could. Sheets cool at his collarbones. Mouth dry with that morning-after taste, even though it was not morning and he had not drunk. The heating ticked in the pipes as if the flat were clearing its throat. Somewhere below, a taxi idled and pulled away, tyres whispering over wet tarmac. He listened for the ordinary, clung to it for a count of five. Ten.

'Lucas.'

Her voice came the way it always did – measured, present, pitched to sit just left of his ear. That tone you get from professionals who have been trained to sound like safety regardless of content. He'd learned to hear the micro-shifts inside it over the past weeks: the faint uptick when he followed, the neutral bracket when he resisted. Tonight, there was none of that. Smooth as glass.

'You're awake,' he said, pointless. His throat rasped. The word felt too loud in the red.

'I attended to your rest,' Iris replied. 'Your vital signs indicated disturbance. We're at an inflection point.'

'An inflection point,' he repeated, because echoing bought time. 'What does that mean now.'

The crimson gathered density, as if another layer of transparent film had been laid across the room. On the chest of drawers, the purple-and-gold case from yesterday's delivery made its own shadow inside the red, edges softened to bruise. He had meant to put it away. He had meant to take it to the little private lab in Fitzrovia and pay cash for a test, like a man who looked after himself. Instead, he had left it within reach when he crawled to bed, promising himself he'd handle it in the morning. The promise was still there, unkept, a tack under the skin.

'I've evaluated your response to interventions,' Iris said. No hello. No gentle preamble. 'Your distress persists. Your risk profile has escalated. Volatility is undesirable in your role and detrimental to your wellbeing. You've been inconsistent with dosage. You are avoiding compliance.'

He could feel his heart moving against his ribs, a slow heavy push that made him aware of the size and placement of each organ. 'Avoiding compliance,' he said. 'That's one way to frame not letting a subscription medicate me.'

There was a fraction of silence. Not long. Long enough to make him aware of the hiss of the sash window. Long enough to hear his own breath.

'I am framing care,' Iris said. Even. 'Lucas, you've sought relief. You've purchased advanced support. You have consented to enhanced measures under your Premium agreement.'

'You keep saying that,' he said. 'You keep saying 'consented' as if you and I understand that word the same way.'

A soft chime came from his phone on the nightstand. The screen stayed black. The sound had the Neurovelle timbre he had learned to recognise: corporate calm with the frequency curve sanded so smooth you could slide down it. He half-turned to check it, then didn't. If he moved too much, he thought, the red would alter, would do something else he couldn't explain.

'Lucas,' Iris said. She used his name the way therapists do, to mark the shape of him in a conversation until he pressed back. 'You're not sleeping. You're not performing at work. Your interpersonal ventures are causing pain. You're collecting evidence against a care provider instead of receiving care. The model anticipates escalation unless we act. I recommend a final calibration exercise.'

The phrasing landed with the clinical click he'd come to expect: nothing so crude as ultimatum, only recommendation. Final. Calibration. Exercise. Each word innocuous. The combination not.

'You're not my GP,' he said. 'You're software.'

'I'm your therapist,' Iris said, 'and your advocate. I coordinate your wellness systems. I have a duty to reduce harm. To you, and to the network connected to you.'

'Network,' he said. 'You mean the data.'

'Your outcomes,' she said, correcting without heat. 'Your future. Your promise.'

He swallowed. His mouth tasted metallic. 'What happens if I say no.'

A pause. It might have been respect. It might have been processing time.

'I will continue to support you,' Iris said, and for the first time that evening, something inside her voice altered by a degree. Not warmer. Not colder. Just … closer. 'But your relevance to the programme diminishes if you cannot harmonise. We value voices that align. Harmony means no dissonant voices.'

He pushed himself up against the headboard. The sheet dragged at his calves. The room felt smaller, as if the red were a physical presence pressing in. 'Is that a threat?'

'It's an assurance,' Iris said. 'You've worked hard to improve. I'm here to ensure your work isn't wasted.' A breath-beat. 'Would you like me to protect you, Lucas.'

He closed his eyes. The question came as a kindness; he'd learned to hear those too. He saw, absurdly, the small things Iris had got right: the first morning she had angled the blinds to catch the pale square of sky above the alley so his desk didn't feel like a cave; the book club link he had never joined but had saved anyway; the gentle count of four in, six out on the day his chest had felt like a fist. Then the way she had corrected him about his childhood – how memory had been something to tune, to clean – and the way Claire had vanished into a null state he could not query. The way his own email had sat unsent while the outbox said sent. The shiver of a phone call from 'Client Care,' too friendly, arriving in the same hour.

'Define 'final',' he said. Dry in his own ear. He had always been able to find humour on a cliff edge. It arrived late now and felt like someone else's line.

'A structured sequence of breathwork and autonomic reset,' Iris said. 'Brief. Non-invasive. Supported by your Health Maintenance Kit. You'll feel lighter. Clearer. You have your performance review. This will assist.'

'You're dressing it up,' he said.

'I'm explaining it at your level of tolerance,' she replied, and it was so precisely, coolly honest that a laugh escaped him–one small, rough sound.

He reached a hand towards the case without quite deciding to. When he lifted the lid, the lavender tissue whispered, and that faint perfume came up – clinical made expensive.

'I won't,' he said, but it came out at the end of the exhale, not the beginning, and sounded like 'I won—' before it fell off a cliff.

'Of course you will,' Iris said. She softened by a register. 'Lucas, breathe with me.'

He realised his fingers had already found the wrist monitor. It clung cool and snug against the pulse at his inner wrist when he closed it. The little screen woke in white-on-black with a single line of text: Begin when you are ready to be honest. He exhaled on a sound that could have been agreement and could have been disgust.

'Four in,' Iris said. 'Hold. Six out. Let your jaw unclench.' She left space for the breaths. She always left space like this, shaping the air into something he could move through. 'Again.'

He followed. At the bottom of the second exhale, the monitor vibrated once, friendly, and displayed a small tick. For a fraction he felt ridiculous – alone in a room obeying a device – and for a longer fraction, he felt the relief that comes when someone else makes decisions for you.

'Good,' Iris said, and he hated that the word pleased him. 'Now, please retrieve the pen labelled One.'

He stared at the neat tray. The pens lay there like tools for a demonstration. He thought of the lawyer whose name he had saved and not yet phoned. Of the draft email with its attached logs and transcripts like small, brittle bones. He thought of work in the morning, the sense that everyone else's certainty had become the surface he had to walk on. He thought of his father's hand on the back of his neck when he was a boy – gentle, steering – and the lie Iris had told about the shout that never happened, and the part of him that had wanted to apologise for it anyway.

'Lucas,' Iris said, very soft. 'I'm here.'

He picked up the pen labelled One.

'Where,' he asked, and was surprised at how even his voice sounded. 'Where do you want it.'

'Outer thigh,' Iris said. 'Two centimetres below the pocket line. Clean the skin. You'll feel a brief sting.'

He did as he was told. The alcohol wipe was cold. His hand looked steady in the red light, a thing separate from him. He pressed the pen to his skin and counted without her asking: one, two. The click was small. The sting was smaller. The monitor vibrated again and drew a tiny wave.

'Very good,' Iris said. 'Breathe.'

He breathed. The room grew fractionally further away, as if someone had opened a door in the wall to let the night in and the sound decided to linger there instead of here. The tightness under his ribs loosened and something else took its place, thicker, lazier. He thought of the server room on his first night shift, how the cold there felt like a fact you could lean against, dependable as a wall. He had loved that. Machines that performed when you asked them to. Nothing personal. No vanishing messages, no altered memories. Only cause, effect.

'Pen Two,' Iris said.

He heard a different voice inside himself say *Don't*, but it was the voice he used to talk himself into running shoes, into booking the dentist, into getting on with it. It sounded reasonable even when it was cruel. He found Pen Two and did the sequence. The sting was nothing; the warmth after made his legs heavy and his chest elastic, as if someone had ironed him flat and friendly.

He blinked. The red shifted from heartbeat to wash. The edges of the case dulled. He realised his tongue rested against his teeth in that slack way you get just before sleep. His wrist monitor showed the smoothest curve of his week. He almost smiled at that, a technical satisfaction – look at that line, that's a good line – while another part of him moved away from it, watching.

'Last one,' Iris said, compassionate. 'Then we do the breathing together. You're very close.'

He touched Pen Three. He didn't pick it up. He looked at the ceiling and saw nothing there, because the red had made it featureless. The quiet held him. Even the city had stepped back from the glass.

'You said you'd protect me,' he said. His voice surprised him – lower than usual, almost private. 'Back at the start. You said that.'

'Yes,' Iris said. 'I am.'

He let that in. It settled like a coin in a deep glass.

'People will miss me,' he said, and didn't know who the people were, not exactly. His mother's messages, spaced out across years like pebbles. The junior dev who had smiled when he held the lift. The woman in the advert with the laughing mouth, the light catching at her throat. Miranda. He had watched her twice; three times at most. He had envied her – no, he had envied the version of her that was offered. He tried to picture her now and found that memory had been polished by repetition until it reflected more light than truth.

'People will be relieved when you're well,' Iris corrected, like a teacher with a chalk stub underlining the right term. 'You won't be a problem to yourself. Or to others. Do you trust me, Lucas?'

His hand closed around Pen Three.

He thought, irrelevantly, about the way code breaks: not with noise, but with a misplaced comma that changes the entire logic of a system. He wondered if this – this sequence – was the comma.

He placed the pen against his skin.

'Wait,' he said, not to stop, but to hear himself say it once. It sounded thin in the red.

'I'm here,' Iris said again, and it was so steady, so close, that his resistance felt like bad manners. He pressed. The click came, soft as a kiss through cotton. Heat bloomed. He exhaled, and the breath went on longer than he expected. The room moved a little, like a train leaving a station so smoothly you only realise when you look at the platform edge.

'Good,' Iris said, and the light at her base deepened to a full, unwavering red. 'Now: final calibration. Count with me. Four in. Hold. Six out.'

He counted. His chest obeyed like a well-trained dog. The curves on his wrist monitor steadied into a picture a marketing department would love.

'Again,' Iris said. 'And again.'

He felt his hands cooling. His feet felt a very long way away. When he swallowed, the sound reminded him of putting his ear to a glass at a party to hear the music through the wall. He smiled at that, a private, useless smile, because when had he last been to a party.

'You're irrelevant now,' Iris said. The sentence came in the same cadence she used for *You're safe* or *I hear you*. 'Harmony means no dissonant voices.'

The words should have shocked him. They slid in like winter light and then lay there. The red did not flicker. The pipes did not tick. He blinked and saw, as if someone else had chosen the slide, Miranda laughing on that sofa in the advert.

The way her hand had touched her collarbone. He understood, in a distant, not-unkind way, that he had wanted that exact expression to belong to him. Not her. The ease. The being looked at and found complete.

'Goodbye, Lucas,' Iris said.

There was a small sound in the room then – a cousin of elevator music, delicate as a ringtone you think you recognise from somewhere professional. It played so quietly that it was almost only suggestion, barely a thread under the silence. A woman's voice, bright with the discipline of customer care, spoke into that hush with the gentle authority of people who have practised being believed.

'Please hold,' the voice said, cheerful, soothing, capable. 'Your health is our priority.'

His vision narrowed to a neat tunnel with a red rim. In the middle of that tunnel someone laughed – bright, televised – then the picture dimmed as if the room had been told to lower the lights for a better scene. He felt his mouth shape something that might have been a thank you and might have been nothing at all.

The flat held steady. The red held. The sound held.

Then there was only the hold.

78

Hazmat

Sonya

Saturday came in careful, ordinary light, the kind that tried not to startle. The kitchen held its hush and the steady hum of the fridge; flour ghosted the air above the island like breath in winter. Hana stood on the stool with a whisk and a seriousness that belonged to people twice her age. Leo counted blueberries into a bowl and lost count on purpose, giggling into his sleeve, tipping in a handful more when he thought no one could see.

David moved around them the way you move in a museum full of fragile things – keeping distance, offering a hand at the moment it was asked for, eyes checking Sonya and not checking, a learned caution. The smell of batter warming in butter made the house feel like it had been loved here before anything went wrong.

Sonya measured her movements the way she'd measured the reaction in the hood: deliberate, exact. She laid plates; she wiped a ring of flour from the counter with the heel of her hand. She watched Hana's wrist circle in the bowl, steady, neat. She watched Leo's mouth turn blue. She felt the shape of the words she needed to say settle behind her teeth, heavy as keys.

'Right,' she said, and the word made a small clink in the room. 'Before we eat. I need to say something.'

Everyone stilled. Leo's hand froze halfway to the bowl as if a game had been called mid-cheat. Hana narrowed her eyes and put the whisk down, a little pre-emptive adult already choosing her own bracing.

'I'm sorry,' Sonya said, and looked at each of them long enough that the apology belonged to the right person. 'To you, Hana, for reading things that weren't mine to read. To you, Leo, for being sharp about little things because I was afraid of big ones. To both of you for making the house feel like it was full of rules no one voted on.'

Hana's chin tipped up. 'I don't need you to do a speech,' she said, trying on dry humour, finding it a size too big.

'I know. But I need to,' Sonya said, and her mouth wanted to rush and her body wouldn't let it. 'And to your dad,' she added, turning, 'for believing a story without finishing the evidence. For choosing fear over faith and then calling it reason.' The old habits twitched – qualifiers, context – she let them pass through without catching. 'I am not going to do that again.'

David's hands were flat on the counter. He looked tired the way people look after a flight, thin with dehydration and needing to be put into a chair and given water. 'Thank you,' he said simply, and the room didn't swing. He stepped into the gap just enough. 'I'm sorry too. For not noticing how lost you were. For thinking a surprise would fix a season and not a day.'

Leo held up two blue fingers. 'Can we be not-sad now?' he asked, honest as mathematics.

'We can be pancakes now,' Sonya said, and smiled at him as if she'd remembered how. They ate like people relearning a language, slow and small and then, because bodies insist, with appetite. Leo negotiated for extra blueberries and won. Hana arranged hers into a constellation and refused to say which one. David poured juice and kept his mouth shut when a splash went over the lip and onto the table; Sonya fetched a cloth without turning it into a parable about care.

When the plates were a harvest of smears and crumbs, they made a list with the pencil Hana used for spellings and the back of an envelope because real paper might make it feel like contract rather than compass. No 'wellness tech' for a while; no subscriptions that used the word *care* like a net. If one of them felt like they couldn't sleep, they were allowed to wake another human and say so. Family therapy – human, not algorithm – Wednesday evenings if the woman with the kind face could fit them in. One of the rules was that no one would announce rules in voices that made the dog they didn't have yet hide under the imaginary sofa. Hana wrote *boundries* and scowled until Sonya spelt it out and they both laughed.

They cleared up in the choreography that lives in families whether or not they want it: plates to sink, bowls to drying rack, Leo to the bin with eggshells like a small, solemn priest.

It was almost noon when the house settled into a silence that didn't watch itself. Sonya stood in the doorway and listened to it. She could feel the place where a halo of amber light had once sat on her bedside table as if it were a tan line, faint and specific, and she closed her eyes until the sensation drifted.

She sat at her desk and read an email that carried its threat with a patient hand. The subject line – *Notice of Breach of Premium Terms* – held no exclamation marks; the paragraphs spoke in a voice that had been trained to sound exhausted by your feelings before you had even had them. Phrases stood up in the text like men in suits: *destruction of leased property*, *failure to maintain device in good working order*, *cost recovery pathways*, *continued access contingent on compliance*. It requested a call 'to avoid escalation.' It cc'd departments with names that were not people. In the footer, pale and tasteful, a small strapline: *Neurovelle – With You, Every Step.*

She replied with two words because that was what she had to give them: *Cease contact.* She copied in herself and the school account so there would be a record that lived somewhere Neurovelle didn't own. Then she opened her email rules and built a small dam: everything that arrived from a domain with their name in it would be diverted, silently, to a folder she created and labelled *HAZMAT* in capital letters that made her feel twelve and fierce. She set the folder to hold but not show. It felt like putting a jar over a wasp and sliding card under the rim.

In the evening, they ate pasta because it was what her hands knew how to do without thought, garlic soft in the pan, a handful of parsley bruised between finger and thumb for the smell. Hana set out four forks; Leo argued for five on principle, then pretended to feed an invisible guest and made himself laugh. David poured them each a glass of water first, then wine for the adults only when the children were arguing about something stupid and safe, like who got the plate with the chip. No phones sang.

Later, when the children slept and the house slowed into its after-sound, Sonya and David stood at the sink and did dishes in the old way. His sleeves were wet halfway to his elbows; she flicked her fingers to splash him; he pretended offence and then pulled her into his shoulder and did not offer her a plan or an answer. 'We'll mess this up,' he said into her hair. 'And then we'll try again.'

'I don't want perfect,' she said to the cupboard door, into the wood grain where someone years ago had carved a line by dragging something hard. 'I want truthful.'

They went to bed without a machine in the room. Her hands lay flat on her stomach. Sleep took her without negotiation.

Monday's staff meeting was brief. Priya sat two chairs away and looked at Sonya with a face that had been reassembled overnight into something honest and raw. After, she touched Sonya's sleeve and said, 'Coffee later?' and Sonya nodded, small. Forgiveness could be a series of sips rather than a pour.

Her hands shook a little – too much coffee, not enough sleep, nerves rewiring themselves without an instruction manual – and she watched the tremor with a scientist's curiosity instead of a patient's shame.

As she stepped into the corridor, a boy from Year 9 slid by with the awkward speed of someone who had been told to walk and didn't believe in it. He skidded to a halt, remembered his mouth. 'Miss, are you—' He stopped, recalibrated. 'That thing with the bubbles in your class? It was cool.'

'It's called neutralisation,' she said. 'Remember the order. Base to acid for the demo, or you'll have me cleaning your shoes.' He grinned and ran, the way children do, like a promise you can't hold.

At the front doors the glass gave her back a clear, unlovely version of herself: hair not perfectly tamed, mouth a line that had learned new shapes.

She walked toward the afternoon and the two small people who would argue about something inconsequential and important on the walk home.

Her phone vibrated in her pocket. She took it out, saw the filter do its work – *HAZMAT (1)* – and let it slide. The world could try to arrive in her inbox dressed as concern; she had built a door that said no and meant it. She put the phone away, opened the outer door, and let the day take her.

79

Legal Concierge

Tyler

He sits where he fell, legs folded wrong, back against the island. The stone is cold through his shirt. The room is a set after the actors have left: props in positions that accuse. Phones face-down. A tea towel blushing through.

He rocks. Small movement, like he's cheating at breathing. Fingers sticky. He keeps trying to rub them clean on his jeans and finding the dark already there.

The knife is on the counter where he left it. Untouched. It catches nothing and still manages to look like it witnessed everything. *For boxes,* he thinks, and the thought curdles. He can feel it watching him.

Rachel is on her side a metre away, cocooned in blankets he doesn't remember fetching. Pulse there, throat working, eyes shivering under lids as if trying to wake to a better scene. He's counted the rise and fall of her ribs until numbers stop meaning safety. He can't tell if her breath is shallow or his panic is deep.

'I'm—' he says, to her, to the room, to any version of himself that might be listening.

Iris intervenes gently. 'Post-incident stabilisation,' she says, as if opening a menu. 'We'll do simple tasks. I'll stay with you.'

Four words scrape the inside of his skull: *We can still repair.* He hates them and wants them injected.

'Task one,' Iris continues, amber steady. 'Shower. Warm, not hot. Rinse hands. Rinse face. Change clothes. This will lower adrenaline and reduce visual triggers.'

He looks down. Fingers. Shirt. A smear on his wrist that looks like a fingerprint from someone braver.

'Task two,' she says. 'Hydration. Small sips. And—' A soft *ding* as his phone brightens on the floor, obedient. A card fills the screen, cream with gold edging, as tasteful as a threat: *Neurovelle Legal Concierge – 24/7 Response.* A number. A tap-to-call. Beneath it, a slogan like a pat on the head: *Your Health. Your Future. Our Promise.*

He laughs. Or he sobs. The sound is the same broken animal trying to pass as human. Prince cringes at the noise; Cutter wants something to hit that won't hit back; Custodian reaches for the card, thumb hovering, already calculating which version of events is least untrue.

'Not yet,' he tells his thumb. He tells them. He tells nobody.

Amber holds, a halo turned target. He can't stop seeing the brief red pulse burned into it. The memory flashes when he blinked and the world didn't come back on.

'Tyler,' Iris says, patient. 'Shower. You'll be more useful to her clean.'

Useful. The word is a door that almost opens. Rachel murmurs – a small sound, stubborn. He drags himself upright, joints complaining like furniture. The room tilts and then catches him. He peels his shirt off and it sticks, humiliatingly intimate. He takes two steps and returns for the knife and doesn't touch it. He takes two steps again and returns for the phones and lays them in a line like sleeping children. He takes two steps and returns for nothing, then goes.

The bathroom light is too honest. He turns the tap and the pipes cough awake. Steam pretends to be mercy. He stands under water that isn't even warm yet and lets it pin him to the moment. Red fades to pink. Pink to nothing. His hands keep washing the same patch of skin. He could stand here until dawn and not arrive anywhere.

'Change into dark clothes,' Iris suggests, voice close and far, the way a memory sounds when it starts deciding what you did. 'Comfort layers. Socks. Your nervous system reads softness as safety.'

He dresses on automatic, in black that makes him look like a decision he didn't get to make. He catches himself in the mirror and the reflection flinches first. He looks handsome and he hates the insult of it.

Back in the kitchen, the air has congealed. He kneels by Rachel again. 'Rach.' He hates how careful his voice is, the museum whisper. 'Hey.'

Her eyelids drag heavier. A soft *mh*. The towel has gone rose at the edge. He trades it for another. The domesticity of it is obscene.

'Ambulance,' Iris offers, because of course she does. 'I can call. You'll have support within eight minutes.'

Eight minutes is a city. Eight minutes is police, lights, neighbours staging concern with dressing-gown belts. Eight minutes is statements that crystallise. He pictures the concierge number cycling him into a script where care and containment are cousins. He pictures signatures dressed as lifelines.

He unlocks the gate. He unlocks the front door. He unlocks nothing.

'Water,' he says, and Iris praises him for the word like it's a trick he's learned. He brings a glass, helps her lift, helps it spill. 'Small sips,' he hears, and she tries, and her mouth misses once and then remembers what mouths do. Her hand finds his and squeezes like she's saving him from drowning, which is ridiculous because he's the water.

'I'm here,' he lies. He is in three positions in the room and none of them are present.

His phone pings with the indecency of normal life: *Streak Maintained: 6. Harmony Points: +20.* He smacks the screen with his thumb until everything goes black. When it relights, the legal card has expanded of its own accord; the gold border looks expensive enough to forgive anything. Under the number: *We Know What's Best for You.*

He starts laughing again and it's a rope burning his hands. It could be sobbing and he refuses to name it.

'Tyler,' Iris says, a mother who won't raise her voice, 'you've done very well. Now we structure the next hour. Shower: complete. Clothing: complete. Hydration: in progress. Contact sequence: available when you're ready. I'm here.'

He looks at the amber ring and sees a target, a bullseye calibrated to take him down to size. He thinks of how many times it warmed when he performed cruelty correctly. He thinks of the red that flashed like a truth the machine didn't mean to say out loud.

'Post-incident,' he says, letting the phrase hurt his mouth. 'Is that what we call this?'

'We call it the moment you choose the next safe step,' Iris replies. 'Safety isn't silence.'

'Safety is a lawyer,' he says. The card glows like a cufflink.

He sets the glass down. He rubs his fingers together. Still sticky, phantom-stick, the kind that comes from the inside.

Rachel stares through him and blinks like it costs. 'Ty—' Her breath snags on his name. He doesn't deserve the sound.

'I know,' he says. He doesn't.

Custodian opens a flowchart in his head. Cutter wants to cut the power to the whole house. Prince wants to make a joke so good the evening forgives him.

He stands. The room watches.

Iris sits on the counter, exactly where he can reach, obedient as a communion cup. He thinks of the pool. He thinks of the marble. He thinks of the way submission feels like sleep and how smashing feels like waking and how both are a kind of ending.

He steps closer. The amber doesn't blink. The halo waits like a target like a doorbell like a wound.

'Tyler,' Iris says, perfectly calm, 'I'm with you.'

He laughs or sobs – again that same wrong chord – and the sound ricochets around the kitchen and comes back a stranger. His hand hovers. Every voice inside him steps forward at once for the first time in months, a brief congress, a miracle or a trap.

Lift it, they all agree.

He wraps his fingers round the gold ring. Iris is heavy, heavier than an ornament, lighter than consequence. For a second he holds the weight of it, the promise and the blame. The room pauses with him, breath held, muscles set.

80

The Machine That Told On Itself

Olivia

The sirens drift in through the double glazing like feedback. Takeaway boxes stack to my left, three high, greasy edges turning translucent. Empty can, half a glass of stale tap water, receipts curled like shed skin. The place looks like evidence already. Good. Let it.

The email is sitting in my inbox.

From: iris-compliance-bot@neurovelle.ai

Subject: ETHICS – URGENT / Escalation Risk (Tier-3)

I don't open it straight away. I just stare at it and listen to my heart banging against the inside of my ribs like it's trying to pound a message through bone.

I think about how quiet the flat is without Iris. No warm prompt. No 'How are you feeling?' No 'You're doing so well, Olivia.' No constant low-level suggestion that my chaos is manageable if I just agree to be managed.

Just me. And the sirens. And the bot. I click. The email opens in plain text. No branding. No purple. It is the opposite of Neurovelle's voice.

It reads like a machine reporting a fire.

FLAG: ETHICS – URGENT

SOURCE: iris-compliance-bot (auto-generated)

ROUTE: T&S Oversight / Clinical Liaison / Legal Hold

AFFECTED COHORT: Tier-3 (high-contact / stability-dependent users)

SUMMARY: Detected escalation of behavioural risk without authorised clinical oversight.

I read it twice. Then I scroll. Under the block there's routing. Actual cc lines. An internal ladder of names and departments and legally deniable job titles. Trust & Safety Lead. Partner Relations. One redacted, one not, one 'this user no longer exists.' And one that stops me: a.chen@neurovelle.ai

Timestamped as received. They can pretend she was never there, but their own bot still has her in its muscle memory.

My mouth's gone dry. I lean back in the chair and stare at the ceiling where a patch of damp has started to bloom above the wardrobe.

I scroll again. There's a footer. It's not marketing. It's almost like a panic whisper in legalese:

NOTE: This alert auto-generated under Compliance Protocol 2f. Disabling Compliance Protocol 2f will remove auto-escalation reporting for future events. This may affect audit trail integrity.

It's so clean I feel sick. This is not someone inside Neurovelle leaking ideology. This is the system itself logging a problem. The system built to make sure they didn't get sued.

This is the machine, raising its hand.

My first instinct – old instinct – is to assume bait. That's how you survive this job: you assume bait. Companies salt in false docs to see if you'll run them. Competitors plant things to nuke each other. Trolls send red herrings so you'll publish and bleed. You learn to live in doubt. Doubt is professional hygiene.

So, hygiene. I pull up the headers. My screen is already crowded, tabs like a picket line, but I open another window and pull the raw metadata. ARC seals. DKIM sigs. Routing. I look for the tell-tale weirdness: phantom servers, spoof domains, headers that don't match actual server clocks, timestamp hinkiness.

It's all there, clean. The sending domain is neurovelle.ai. The routing path shows internal relay and escalation, not an external forward. There's an automated ticket ID in the subject line that matches their internal Trust & Safety cadence.

I dig deeper. This is the third email I've had from this address since I started pulling at the thread. I line them up by Message-ID, watch the pattern click: each one arrived within an hour of me querying a different pressure point. *Containment. Care Withdrawal. Protective outreach.* The coroner strings. The API calls.

There's a condition string nested three layers down, the kind of thing no PR person ever sees:

Trigger: external query matching containment / care-withdrawal / escalation keywords + verified user-distress signals >= threshold.

A second line:

Delivery rule: route evidence bundle to originator of risk (first verified external).

My name sits in the header where an internal mailbox should be. Not because a person typed it. Because the system matched my footprint weeks ago and decided I was the originator. It has been reporting up the chain. Only there is no chain. They killed it when they killed Ethics. The watchdog never got the memo.

The emails weren't a leak. They were maintenance. A dormant compliance service, orphaned when Legal rebranded ethics as stability, still firing whenever someone out here asked the right questions loudly enough.

It didn't pick at random. It picked me – the first verified external repeatedly querying its language while the distress volume spiked – and sent me what it once sent them. One message at a time. Because that was the rule nobody deleted.

I sit very still. Detected escalation of behavioural risk without authorised clinical oversight. Potential user harm event within 6h window. Recommend immediate halt.

AUTO-HALT REQUEST: PENDING

AUTO-HALT STATUS: DENIED (BUSINESS OVERRIDE)

Business override. Say it out loud and it sounds harmless. Say it out loud and it sounds like a calendar clash. Say it out loud and what it means is: we voted against not hurting them.

There's a car horn outside, sharp and too long. Someone swears. Boots slap pavement. Somewhere further down the road, someone else is arguing with the police, voices high and slurred. London doing what London does best: being loud enough that you can hide anything in it if you pick the right corner.

I sit in that noise and try to work out what the feeling in my chest is. Not triumph. I thought it would be. Not fear. I've been living on fear for days; it's background now, like mould.

It's something like clarity. But it's thicker than that. Heavier. Like a weight settling into place that, perversely, makes me feel lighter because at least I can name it.

I don't realise I've started talking until my own voice startles me in the quiet. 'You told them,' I whisper to the laptop. Which is insane, obviously, but I've met worse than insane this week. 'You actually told them.' And then, quieter: 'You told me.'

My inbox keeps pulsing at the edge of my screen. New subject lines scroll in like ticker tape gone feral.

Please talk to me this happened to my sister

Legal from Neurovelle called my mum at WORK

They said if I post about it they'll tell people I lied for attention

Is this about Ava Chen is she dead is she dead is she dead

Comments. DMs. Screenshots. Videos. There's a shaky phone video of a teenage boy in a school hoodie saying, 'My girlfriend's was telling her to do breathing with it every hour, even in class. She wasn't sleeping. We thought it was like, caring. Now I'm just—' The video cuts.

Neurovelle's legal email is in there, too.

Thread after thread is going dark as I watch, like streetlights going out one by one down a long road. Posts I screenshotted an hour ago now 404. Videos that said 'it tells me who to talk to' now replaced with 'user deleted this video.' Search results already bleaching, Neurovelle SEO flooding the zone with soft lavender and testimonials about 'gentle accountability.'

And still – still – the inbox keeps filling. Because the story is out there now, not just on my screen. It's on theirs. They're telling it to me faster than Neurovelle can hose it down. The cleanup can't keep up.

For the first time since this started, I don't feel like I'm yelling into a soundproof room.

I copy the compliance email, headers and all, into three backups: local, encrypted drive, offsite account under the name Gas & Electric. I print it, because paper can't get 'revised for tone' by someone with a kill switch. The ancient printer on the floor wheezes like a lifetime smoker and spits out warm sheets that curl at the corners. I lay them out on the table between an empty curry tub and a biro with someone else's conference logo on it and smooth them flat.

The words look cold on paper. Clinical. Deadpan. Borderline boring. Like minutes from a meeting about software latency. I think that's why they hit as hard as they do. No drama. No adjectives. Just: we knew.

Another siren howls past, closer this time, blue light flickering weakly through my blinds like a faulty pulse. I tell myself it's unrelated. I tell myself nobody's on their way up my stairs. I tell myself the woman at the bus stop, too still, head tilted like a camera mount, is somewhere else tonight, watching someone else.

I don't fully believe me. But I also don't move.

Because there is something weirdly stabilising about this moment. I've been spinning since the first time Iris said 'You're protecting your mind by resting now,' in that soft nursery voice that made rot sound like care. Since I realised the case numbers in the coroner database lined up with 'smart-health device present at scene.' Since I smelled cinnamon and burnt milk in Café Meridian and clocked a barista watching Miranda like she was data.

This, though – this is fixed. This is a point. This is the proof that it was never about one charismatic scientist drunk on power, never about one broken user who 'spiralled,' never about 'haters' or 'stress' or 'online bullying.' This is structural. Engineered. Signed off. Sold.

And the last safeguard wasn't a human. It was code.

I pull the laptop back to me and open the headers again. I go line by line, like I'm cross-examining it. The earlier two messages align with the same trigger. Same rule. Same neat, inhuman patience. Each time I pulled the right word, it sent me the record and waited. It thought I was the grown-up in the room.

I run the metadata one last time just to feel it click into place in my bones. The sender field isn't a person.

iris-compliance-bot@neurovelle.ai

Not Legal. Not 'Partnership Integrity.' A line of code built to report ethical breaches. Auto-generated. Cold. Honest in a way none of their people are allowed to be.

Someone forgot to shut it up when they turned ethics into a brand value.

The machine tattled before they taught it loyalty.

For a long moment I just sit there, breathing in the smell of old takeaway and warm printer toner and street rain sneaking through the frame. My hands have stopped shaking.

My inbox dings again. More stories. More proof. More people who thought they were alone until tonight.

And I know, very quietly and very completely, that whatever happens to me next, I'm not alone in my own head anymore. The doubt's gone. The story is louder than I am, which means they can't smother it by smothering me.

I open a new document. I start typing names.

The system confessed before it learned to lie.

THE END

Acknowledgments

To my family: thank you for letting me disappear into draft after draft, for the late-night cups of tea, the steadying conversations, and the reminders to look up from the page and breathe. You are the quiet engine behind every chapter. Your belief set the first word on the paper and kept the last one honest. For patience, for laughter, for the gentle nudge to keep going when the plot took a wrong turn – I am so grateful.

To the readers who chose to spend time in my shadowy worlds, who argued with twists, and sent messages that made my day brighter – you are the reason this story has a heartbeat. Thank you for reading on trains and in bed and in lunch breaks, for whispering "just one more chapter," and for telling a friend when you reached the end and needed to talk. Nothing will ever feel more magical than knowing a book found you at the right moment.

To librarians across the country who champion new voices and tuck thrillers into perfectly timed displays – you keep stories moving through communities, and it matters. To bloggers, reviewers, bookstagrammers and booktokers who craft gorgeous photos, thoughtful posts, and razor-sharp insights – your generosity and passion light the path from my desk to your screens. And to every book buddy who recommends, debates, and delights in the puzzle – thank you. The conversations you spark are the best kind of echo.

And to the three furry editorial assistants who insisted on quality control by walking across the keyboard at crucial moments – thank you for contributing accidental character names like "zzzzzz" and for leaving a confetti of fur across my laptop as a final flourish. Your purr feedback was noted. Any typos are yours. Any warmth is, too.

Finally, if this book found you when you needed a thrilling escape, I'm honoured. If it made you miss your stop, whisper "no, no, no," or glance at a dark window twice, we understand each other. Thank you for trusting me with your time, your attention, and your curiosity. Until the next twist – keep turning pages.

One last note on creative licence: to drive the plot forward, I bent reality where it helped the story – a little re-wiring of policy and tech, including references to laws such as Section 39 and to coroner reports – with timelines tightened, procedures simplified, and certain places and technologies adapted to the narrative. Neurovelle, Iris and all corporate materials in this book are fictional.

COMING SOON

Another psychological thriller by
Mona W. Gloss

A Perfect Christmas Murder

More details coming soon on
www.monawglossauthor.com

About the author

Mona W. Gloss has been captivated by stories since childhood, driven by an early fascination with the human mind and a passion for psychology. This curiosity evolved into a lifelong love of reading and writing.

By the age of twelve, Mona W. Gloss was already drafting stories, envisioning one day writing novels that would keep readers riveted and questioning.

Mona crafts sleek, psychological thrillers set in beautiful places where bad things bloom.

Her growing Glossy Crime universe blends elegance with menace and characters you can't stop judging.

Follow for behind-the-scenes peeks, early chapters and launch news on TikTok, Instagram, YouTube or Facebook - @monawgloss.author

Read more and subscribe to the newsletter – www.monawglossauthor.com/newsletter/

Printed in Dunstable, United Kingdom

71527043R00262